MEN OF EARTH

Published in Australia by
Flying Chair Publications
PO Box 847 Crows Nest Sydney NSW 1585 Australia
www.ingridbanwell.com

First published in Australia 2022
Copyright © Ingrid Banwell 2022

National Library of Australia Cataloguing in Publication entry

 A catalogue record for this
book is available from the
National Library of Australia

ISBN 978-0-6454331-0-4 (paperback)
ISBN 978-0-6454331-2-8 (hardback)
ISBN 978-0-6454331-1-1 (epub)

Cover layout and design by 99Designs Michael Johnson www.skylightbookcovers.co.uk

Printed by Ingram Spark

MEN
of
EARTH

Say Goodbye
to the
Patriarchy

INGRID BANWELL

'Let me keep my distance,
always, from those who think
they have the answers.
Let me keep company always
with those who say "Look!"
and laugh in astonishment,
and bow their heads.'

MARY OLIVER

Long ago, before the history of man, woman ruled the world. Woman worshipped Mother Earth, who shared with her the secrets of creation.

Working closely with Mother Earth, woman created golems – giant, peaceful and strong creatures who helped build cities and empires and civilisations.

But man became jealous of the power of the golems and sought them out and persecuted and killed them.

Woman knew the only way to protect the golems and prevent their extinction was to make them more closely resemble human men.

Channelling powerful magic, woman endowed the golems with qualities that made them indistinguishable from human men. The golems grew hearts and lungs and livers, they wept and loved. They sired children. They grew old and died.

Gradually over the course of centuries, the golems and their part-golem children merged with ancient humans until they became an entirely new species.

Their purity muddied by humanity, some half-bred golems and their progeny turned treacherous and succumbed to their dark sides. They became unruly, betrayed their creators and shared some of the magic of creation with man. But it was incomplete magic – hungry magic, power untethered from Mother Earth and woman. Without the influence of woman, it was ugly magic. Dark magic. Man abused this magic to undermine the rule of woman and fight wars. Man used this power to wage war with Mother Earth.

Horrified at the way in which Mother Earth's power was being used against her, woman sought to bury her power and hide it from the eyes of man. But it was too late. Man had abused this magic to become the most powerful sex. Man rewrote the story of creation, supplanting Mother Earth's history with man-stories and a man-God.

Excerpt from *The Book of Creation* @2500BCE

CHAPTER ONE

My Disastrous Career

Early Autumn,
Well Over Four Thousand
Years Later

In hindsight, I realise I was the ideal candidate. Divorced, no dependents, an only child of deceased parents. Menopausal. Socially isolated. And most importantly – a mess.

Mess is, of course, relative. I wasn't a refugee escaping misery and political oppression. My particular mess was a middle-aged miscreant's mess. Blighted by personal and professional failures, a fermenting fruit on the tree of life's boughs, I was ready for anything that would pluck me from my apathy, heal my wounded soul and restore my crushed spirit.

Yindisha Retreat's website promised a transformative experience – healthy food, massage, meditation – the usual items offered to the soul hungry for healing and change.

Had I been a more superstitious type, I might have been unnerved by the timing of the siren screaming down a nearby street as I typed Yindisha Retreat's web address into my search bar, or by the way the site repeatedly crashed and glitched, as if some celestial hand was trying to shoo all those pixels from my gaze. But, as the daughter of a scientist, I didn't subscribe to such nonsense.

Instead, I swooned over the photos of sweeping green lawns, quaint white cottages and hills bathed in a blue eucalypt haze. The cool and leafy world of the New South Wales Southern Highlands beckoned. I believed Yindisha's spiel. We don't know the things we aren't told. We can't anticipate what we can't imagine.

Guest. Employee. Oblivious participant in a radical social experiment. Accessory to murder. Perhaps it's just as well we travel through our lives in manifest oblivion of our fates. If we knew what was coming, we would spend our brief time on earth frozen in terror.

Three months before my encounter with that alluring web site, my first art exhibition opened at a local Lower North Shore art gallery. I'd taken a year off paid work to paint and this was to be my art world debut, the fulfillment of a dream. My rich and famous moment. Not a single piece sold. It turned out my work was not cheap or vacuously decorative enough to match carpets and lounge suites for recently renovated homes or stylings for real estate sales. Nor was it deep or bold or edgy enough to attract collectors and impress art critics. I learned that a year in creative solitude can make you feel more important and cleverer that you really are.

'Painter? Artist?' A drunk patron at my opening said. 'Pah!' He leaned forward and blew a gust of breath tart with the smell of Riesling in my face. 'People spend lifetimes committed to their art. You think taking a year off is all you need to become a fully-fledged artist and dazzle the world with your brilliance?'

In a flagrantly dismissive gesture, he swept a hand holding an asparagus *vol-au-vent* around the gallery. 'All this slavish attention to detail – those flowers so intricately rendered one can almost see their molecular structures, those clouds so full and moist they seem to weep from the canvas – it's nothing more than *showing off.*' He sniffed. 'Anyone can, over time, master techniques and imitate reality. True art is something altogether different.'

He regarded me as if he were oh-so-tired of ordinary people like me thinking they were artists. He pointed to one of the stiff white human shapes that inhabited my paintings. 'Inhibited,' he added. 'You should loosen up.'

His insults were as brutal as the absence of red sold stickers under my paintings. It was clear that, as far as he was concerned, I hadn't suffered enough for my art. I wasn't an indigenous artist enriched by tens of thousands of years of cultural heritage and intimacy with the landscape. I wasn't a man so tormented by his inner demons, his ravenous sexuality and his creative genius that, in between painting masterpieces and mis-managing a tumultuous love-life, I had to do drugs and battle alcoholism. Instead, I was a lonely and directionless woman with too much spare time on my hands to do silly things like paint and think it meant something profound.

Fed up with being lectured to and criticised by men, and a tad tipsy, I told him he was a pompous, up-himself arsehole. A shame I didn't know he was Art Castle, the Upper North Shore's influential, self-important, self-appointed art critic. I found out a few minutes after I'd deployed my insult.

So, when the review arrived in the local newspaper, I knew I was in for a demolition job.

The men and women in amateur artist Alethea Braxton's paintings are blank negative spaces, anonymous beings, repressed creatures set against backdrops of intricate natural grandeur, stormy seas and island idylls. This exhibition manages to be all at once pretentious, derivative, mindlessly decorative and intellectually convoluted. The people that inhabit these inhibited and laboured works should be back where they belong – on the doors of public toilets.

Two weeks later, instead of those 'public toilet people' making me a small fortune, I got a bill for gallery rental, advertising and opening night catering. The message from the universe was clear – I was simply another middle-aged woman trying to make a mark on the world and failing to deliver even a single scratch.

And then, four weeks after my exhibiting failure, I met Matthias the Masseuse. My rejected paintings once more in my possession, when I ran out of wall space in my cramped post-divorce semi, I jammed the remaining canvases into the attic, pulling a muscle in my neck in the process.

As I explained the story behind the pain in my neck to Matthias at my local massage centre, he listened attentively. He was so good-looking my thoughts tripped over themselves and my tongue followed. With his flawless gold skin and curly brown hair, he looked more like a movie star or a male model than a therapeutic masseuse. His eyes were an extraordinary golden green set in whites as creamy-bright as fresh yogurt. He had a faintly Spanish accent, a charming lisp. Columbia? I wondered. Of course, I asked. I am innately curious.

'Ecuador,' Matthias replied. He explained how he was here on a temporary work visa. He'd always wanted to visit Australia. He had a cousin living in Northbridge and he was staying with her.

May I add, his massage was masterful. Delicious. Afterwards, I felt all soft and gloopy, as if he had turned me into elastic woman. I complimented him.

He was not only aesthetically pleasing and a gifted masseuse, he was nice. Modest. Humble. He made me feel special. Alive. Flirty. I had to remind myself that massage and making a woman feel good was his *job*.

He asked what I was planning to do following my exhibition. Of course, I realise now he had an agenda. But at the time, I was delighted someone so gorgeous was taking an interest in pathetic, shop-worn me.

I bluffed. I boasted. I still did this at forty-eight years, even though my chances with this beautiful much younger man were about as unlikely as being hit by a piece of rogue space junk. I can't help myself sometimes. I'm an aesthete. I appreciate beauty. My ex-husband called me an airhead. That was when he was being polite.

I told Matthias I was taking time out to reflect. His attentiveness was so genuine, his engagement with me so flawless, I shared with him a good chunk of my work history. He nodded, smiled, chuckled in all the right places and kept me prattling on. I told him how I had trained as a graphic artist but struggled to keep up with the shift into computer graphics. Plus, even the thought of sitting at a computer screen day after day, was enough to give me back-ache and instant repetition strain injury. Instead, I defected into part-time paid work I could balance with painting and later, motherhood. I was, in various incarnations, a real estate receptionist, a corporate librarian, an executive assistant and researcher for corporate tyrants, sociopaths and profit-focused misanthropes. Matthias chuckled at my description of corporate life.

I mentioned I'd also done a bit of casual part-time art tutoring for community colleges, night classes and a few private students.

As Matthias listened, I noticed his eyes glazed intermittently, as if he were listening to something I couldn't hear. Or perhaps he was trying to be polite but was becoming increasingly tired of the story of my life.

Enjoying my engagement with this handsome, attentive creature, I blithely carried on, explaining I was relatively good at picking things up. On the downside, I was easily bored. And when I was bored, I got sloppy. Intolerant of petty office politicking, I often voiced my objections. More than once, I was told I wasn't paid to have opinions or venture beyond my pay grades. But it was during a working holiday in the UK – that island so attached to its class systems – amid the hierarchical corporate world of suited men, corruptions and tyrannies – that I met my husband. Thoughts of my ex made my mouth screech to a stop. I didn't want to burden this stranger with the miserable details of my tumultuous marriage and acrimonious divorce.

I apologised to Matthias. 'Sorry. I talk too much. My ex-husband told me I have verbal incontinence.'

Matthias politely told me he had enjoyed my story.

The long and short of this encounter was that Matthias handed me a business card for Yindisha Retreat. 'My aunt owns the retreat,' he said. 'They're looking for an art tutor. You might be just what they're looking for.'

I doubt it, I thought. *I'm the last person they need.* I thanked him anyway and said I would contact the retreat immediately. I did not.

In storytelling, the inciting event is the moment when an ordinary life turns into a story. It's the explosion of Krypton, the moment when Darth Vader attacks Princess Leia's ship. It's that tornado in the Wizard of Oz. At this point, you might think that my encounter with Mathias was that inciting event. But Matthias was a masseuse, not an event. He may have been an enticement, but he was not inciting.

My inciting event was more mundane. It came in the form of my neighbour's leaf blower.

Although I should have been looking for work, six weeks after my exhibition, I wasn't feeling brave enough to face any more disappointment and rejection. Besides, I told myself, work prospects for a woman nearly fifty with a career history as fickle as mine were about as probable as a visit from a genie. Instead of picking up the phone and ringing Yindisha Retreat, I wallowed in the swamp of my misery. I nibbled into what was left of my savings and inheritance. I spent evenings binging on Netflix, drinking too much wine, devouring fruit-jubes or blocks of chocolate. Sometimes all in one sitting. I would wake up the next day feeling like crap.

And then came that morning with the leaf blower.

Is there any more annoying sound than the suburban leaf blower first thing in the morning (or any time, really)? I was sure at that point that machine was designed purely for irritation. I jumped out of bed, strode into my back garden and threw a terracotta pot at the fence. 'What the fuck is wrong with a broom?' I yelled.

My poor neighbour Verne. He was a nice man. Apart from his oblivion when it came to noise pollution. It was not a good morning. It was the second anniversary of my mother's death. My stomach was still processing last night's fruit-jube and chocolate binge. Yet in that moment, I caught sight of the creature I had become. I was the flaming madwoman my husband had back-burned out of the family home.

I realised something had to change.

So, after I'd apologised to Verne, I dug the Yindisha Retreat business card out from the bottom of my handbag, drooled over the website and made the call. I spoke with the current art teacher, who was moving to Melbourne. No, they hadn't found anyone suitable yet, she told me. She told me my experience at Yindisha Retreat would be unique. Transformative. Her salesmanship skills were exemplary. After we'd spoken, I wanted that job more than anything.

After frantically polishing up my resume, following an application process that was – to put it mildly – perfunctory – I was offered a job at Yindisha Retreat as a part-time art teacher. In exchange for a seventy percent reduction in the accommodation costs, four times a week I would teach painting and drawing to the residents. The rest of the time, I would enjoy the retreat's offerings free of charge.

I should have been suspicious. But like I said, I'd decided things had to change. I'd had enough of myself. I wanted to be someone different, somewhere different.

I found a young couple ready to rent out my modest semi for nine months while their own home was renovated in preparation for parenthood and blissful family life. I didn't mention my neighbour's leaf blower. Or that forty percent of marriages end in divorce. And that child custody negotiations are nightmares.

Four weeks after that offer, feeling like an oversized ball in a pinball machine, my skin flushed from the heat of Sydney's lingering summer, I dragged my wheeled suitcase through Sydney Central Train Station's sweating masses. I'd decided not to drive. I'm not good in traffic. I get impatient. I swear. I get tension cramps in my neck. Today, I remembered how much I also hated crowds. Head down and chin set, I forged onwards, reminding myself that in order to reach heaven, one sometimes has to navigate hell.

Finally, I found the platform, where the train sat waiting to ferry me to that perfectly presented digital paradise in the peaceful heart of the Southern Highlands. With a sigh of relief, I stepped on board in blissful ignorance.

One minute after midday, the train lurched to life. My suitcase nested in the empty seat beside me, I settled into scribbly patterned graffiti-proof fabric that smelt faintly of body sweat, vinegar and chips.

Fleetingly, I caught my reflection in the window and, as often happens these days, got a shock. I saw my mother's face gazing back at me with a wounded look. I was now the same age my mother was when she became a widow. Although I'd inherited my mother's brown hair and eyes, in that reflection, I saw my father as well – my unruly curls, heavy eyebrows and strong nose were all his. He had kind, lavender-blue eyes that would ignite with an inner radiance when he answered my endless questions about life and the universe. He told me how scientists struggled to understand the nature of human consciousness and time. He told me it was very possible, given the vastness of the universe, that there was life on other worlds. Life's mysteries enthralled him. Every day, I wish I had known him for longer.

My mother never remarried. My father was a hard act to follow.

Pained, I looked away from that face, down to the body that was all mine. Once considered voluptuous in all the right places, I had become bulbous in all the wrong places.

I thought of those empty men and women in my paintings – my public toilet people – those painful reflections of my hollow vanities and dashed hopes.

Outside the train, the landscape of apartment towers and industrial buildings punctuated by dusty eucalypts rippled and buckled in the midday heat. Suddenly, I started to feel hot and panicky. What the hell was I doing? Was this another of my reckless, financially irresponsible decisions?

I shook off those self-pitying thoughts. *Move on Alethea*, I told myself. *Move on.*

I thought about a future of sensible eating, weight loss and practicing yoga in pretty gardens. And, ensconced in my air-conditioned cocoon, safe from that whiskered furnace outside, I told myself at least there wouldn't be any art critics at Yindisha Retreat.

The train rocked and rolled towards that place that would change me forever. I dozed off. A few times, I drowsily opened my eyes to vistas of pasturelands punctuated with sheep and trees. I must have slept through the burnt parts because already, the landscape looked kinder and cooler. Those temperate highlands planted with English trees and English gardens by early settlers who missed the Motherland filled my insides with a warm, familial flush. My German-born mother, on a husband-hunting holiday, had met my Australian father in Manchester where he was doing a post doctorate at Jordrell Bank Centre for Astrophysics. I was conceived in the Motherland and born in Australia. It felt in a way as though I was returning to a facsimile of my pre-natal home. I thought of my daughter Sophia. A political science graduate, she worked as a policy writer for the Federal Department of Environment in Canberra and was flatting with fellow university graduates. Here on the train heading south, I was moving closer to her.

Lulled by thoughts of family, I slipped into a deeper sleep.

What seemed only moments later, I woke suddenly, gasping for breath. I opened my eyes to a passenger turning around and giving me a startled stare. It took a few seconds for me to remember I was in a train on the way to Bowral in the Southern Highlands. I was still half in my dream world, standing on Dee Why Beach, watching my father as he bobbed in the ocean, drifting further and further away. My mother and I screamed from the shallows as a life-saver swam to him, stopping short of the rip that a few moments later, took him from us. Eventually that tiny dot that was my father's head vanished under the waves. I never saw him again. I was eleven years old when he drowned and the wrench still comes back at unexpected times, erupting like volcanic magma, swamping me in grief when my guard is down.

I drew a breath and pulled myself together. Along the train line, buildings once more appeared. The train stopped at Mittagong. A girl disembarked along with another elderly male passenger. They gave me concerned looks. I knew why. Although the frequency of my outbursts had waned over the years, during those nightmares when he is drowning all over again, I still call out to my father in my sleep. 'Come back, Daddy! Come back!'

CHAPTER TWO

No Ordinary Retreat

Day One

The sun beat hard and hot against my face as I disembarked at Bowral, looking for the minivan the retreat had promised would meet me at the station. In this season of transition, in the middle of the week, I was one of only a few passengers. They vanished into cars and vans and left me standing alone on the footpath, feeling – in the midst of all this oh-so-British tamed nature and Victorian architecture – as though I'd stepped back in time. Pacing up and down, I peered down the street. Where the hell was the retreat's minivan? I began to wonder if this was a setup. The internet was full of scoundrels. They'd taken my deposit and now I was abandoned. *I told you so. You never listen. You are a fucking idiot.* That voice from another life arrived with its familiar rebukes.

Just as I felt the fluttery beginnings of a panic attack, a black electric car quietly slid up to the footpath and stopped in front of me.

An angular woman of indeterminate age leaned out the

passenger window. 'Alethea Braxton?' she asked, deploying an orthodontically perfect smile.

'Yes,' I replied my legs almost buckling in relief. I recognised her from the website. It was Galilea Nightingale – the owner of Yindisha Retreat.

'The retreat's minivan broke down,' she said as she stepped out, effortlessly lifted my suitcase and hurled it in the trunk before I had a chance to object. 'You're the only one today. Most of our guests don't arrive until late Thursday or Friday. I had a free morning, so I decided to come and meet you myself.' She had a voice at once hard and smooth – like liquid metal – and an accent I couldn't place. Her Antipodean vowels were neither sharp nor flat, nor were there any rolling American R's or distinctly British plums. Her accent sounded as though it came from nowhere and everywhere.

Feeling intimidated and simultaneously flattered by this elegant, slender woman, I slid into a passenger seat that smelt of brand-new car infused with a hint of lemon geranium. Taking in her slate-grey hair groomed back from a sharply featured face into a chignon, I tried to decipher her. My first impression was of a rigid, yet accomplished woman. A confident woman. Did she have children? Or was she divorced? I glanced at her long, liver-spotted hands. No wedding ring. Not that wedding rings or their absences say anything these days. I noticed, apart from the crow's feet around her eyes that, unlike her hands, her facial skin was smooth and glowing and her nose perfectly straight in a way that hinted at plastic surgery.

Despite the day's warmth, she wore a long-sleeved, crew necked sweater bearing Yindisha Retreat's logo – the 'S' of Yindisha breaching the text in an extravagant forest-green flourish, like a fern frond.

'You've picked a gorgeous time of year to arrive,' she said warmly. 'And I do hope you'll take advantage of everything

Yindisha Retreat has to offer.'

She mentioned the retreat's yoga and meditation sessions, the cooking classes, community gardens and orchards.

'We're trying to become entirely self- sufficient, but we're not quite there yet,' she added with a soft laugh. 'Some of our visitors still love a good tuna steak every now and then...'

She mentioned how she hoped if I had any questions or concerns, I would feel free to come and see her in her office.

'But I think you'll find the staff more than helpful,' she added. She paused, as if considering her next words carefully.

'You do know the retreat only has female clientele?' she said.

I noticed she glanced at me when she said this, as if testing my response.

'Yes.' Although there was nothing specific on the web site, I'd gathered that from my interview.

'I've yet to find anyone unhappy with the setup,' she added. 'A lot of our clients relish the break from family responsibilities.

'...and husbands,' she continued, the faintest hint of subversion in her tone.

I didn't immediately answer and instead hung my head, staring at my ringless marriage finger and bitten fingernails. Out of the corner of my eye, I noticed she once more glanced at me.

'Happy marriages are all alike, every unhappy marriage is unhappy in its own way,' she said.

I turned and smiled at her. 'Anna Karenina, I chortled. 'You've splendidly paraphrased that famous first line.'

A warmth – hardened by something I couldn't quite shape, rippled between us.

'If you like to read, we have a wonderfully stocked library,' Galilea said.

'I love reading,' I replied.

'Just as our bodies are nourished by the food we eat, our minds are nourished by our thoughts and the ideas of others,' Galilea replied. 'We are shaped by life's in-puts. And our lives aren't defined by our wounds, but by the ways we choose to heal...'

Her long fingers tapped the wheel, as if she wished to say something even more, but couldn't, or wouldn't.

My gaze jumping between the contradictions of that smooth face and those aged hands, I felt a sudden squirm of unease. I sensed something deeply hidden beneath her layer of smoothly applied charm.

I nodded and said nothing.

In the distance, the highway buckled and shone like a pool of water – a mirage of light and heat. I wondered if Galilea Nightingale was her real name or some kind of disguise. It carried a whiff of manufacture: Galilea – embracing science and reason. Nightingale – reflecting beauty and compassion.

A few minutes after we had joined the highway, we turned east. The winding road dipped into an area of dense bushland.

After I'd enquired about Yindisha's origins, Galilea told me how she had founded Yindisha Retreat after a long career working in corporate public relations. 'I got tired of varnishing lies with murky truths to appease those stakeholders and shareholders who were my clients. I decided covering up corporate breaches and embarrassments and keeping secrets under wraps wasn't my idea of a fulfilling career path.'

Having spent six months working as a public relations assistant in a crisis-riddled financial services organisation, I barked a laugh and wholeheartedly agreed.

'It was a no-brainer,' Galilea added. 'Here, I'm out in nature every day. Helping to heal the planet. Helping women. Making the world a kinder, more loving, more balanced place.'

After I emitted another grunt of agreement, we fell into another moment of silence. Despite her warm words, something about Galilea felt too slick, too forced.

We turned into a road with no sign. My inner compass began

to feel confused. Fleetingly, I wondered how I might find my way back to civilisation if everything went askew and I needed to escape. We drove past a ragged scar of burnt bush, the trees on either side of the road charred; new green growth pushing up through the ashen ground.

Where is this woman taking me? I suddenly wondered.

I'm not a good car passenger. Since my divorce, I've detested letting others having control of the steering wheel, dictating the direction of my fate, compromising my safety, controlling my destination. Yet here I was, stuck in a car with a stranger of hidden depths, heading for the unknown.

The panic, as it often did, came out of nowhere. A fluttering in my chest, a shivering in my belly and a shortness of breath. As if my fear held power, the bush darkened and the sun hid behind a cloud. Jagged mossy rocks flanked the road. Ahead, yawned the black mouth of a tunnel.

No matter how hard I tried, I felt as though I couldn't draw in enough air.

Desperately, I tried to make myself relax, take a deep breath.

Galilea must have sensed something amiss, because she glanced at me. 'Are you alright?'

'Yes,' I'm fine,' I gasped, gazing at that looming black arch.

Amorphous memories – dark and oily things – bubbled to the surface of my thoughts. Scrambling to contain them, struggling to breathe, my heart palpated wildly as we entered the tunnel. I was drowning. Fighting to resurface. Losing me. I gripped the strap of my handbag to steady myself. I struggled to take that deep breath that would restore my body's equilibrium. Even though I knew it was all in my mind, the air wouldn't come.

I thought how the last time I visited the Southern Highlands I was a married woman on a holiday which was more like purgatory.

I thought how the only way to get back home was with the help of Yindisha Retreat and this woman I had only just met. My imagination went into overdrive. *Perhaps Galilea is going to kill me,* I suddenly thought. *Perhaps she's a contract killer.*

When we came out of the tunnel, the light was so bright it hurt my eyes. Rhododendrons, oleanders and azaleas flowered under the canopy of eucalypts. Dancing pools of sunlight dappled the bush. A fog hung low to the ground, swirling and rising in curlicues off the road surface ahead.

Galilea asked me how I had found out about the retreat.

I relaxed a little. Air – fresh and deep – flew into my lungs. A contract killer probably wouldn't be interested in my back story.

'Your nephew, Mathias,' I said as we sped through that enchanting landscape. 'He gave me a massage.' Thinking of him made me feel all flushed and adolescent.

Galilea was silent for a moment, as though trying to work out who Mathias was. Which puzzled me, because Mathias wasn't exactly forgettable.

'Ah, Mathias,' she finally said. 'I'm so proud of him. He turned out very well.'

I noted this was an interesting response. Had she raised him? Had she married into a huge, close, South American family? And if so, why had she paused as if she couldn't immediately recall him?

'You raised him?' I asked.

She gave me a look that was a baffling combination of oblique and smug.

'In a manner of speaking.'

Well, what the hell did that mean?

'I hear you had a recent exhibition,' she said, smoothly changing the subject.

Before I could stop myself, I shared my disappointment nothing had sold. When Galilea didn't reply, I cursed my big mouth and regretted mentioning that wretched experience. 'I suppose that's the artist's lot,' I added trying to sound more accepting than I felt. *Stop sharing your personal shit with people. Nobody cares.* Oh, that voice again, that leech on my psyche, that disruptor of my fragile equilibrium! Sometimes unfortunately, that voice was right. This woman was my employer and I was opening up to her about my failures. It was something my ex would never have done. He never admitted failure. He knew how to play the game. He never overshared. He knew how to impress. He was a master of image. To the uninitiated and impressionable, he radiated success.

Willing my mouth shut, I gazed out the passenger window admiring the flowering hedges of camellias flanking the road.

'Perhaps the market simply wasn't ready for your message,' said Galilea. 'People can take a while to catch up with ideas that are ahead of their time...'

Well, that was a nice way of putting things. My ideas – if you could call them that – weren't ahead of their time. They were just wrongly pitched. I wanted to sell my work and had misread the market. I had indulged myself, created derivative, pretentious artwork and suffered the consequences.

I replied with a sceptical grunt. 'Perhaps...'

'Ideas and ideals can suffer on the stage of the market economy,' Galilea added. 'People must stop worshipping the gods of money and greed. We must stop putting our desire for endless economic growth ahead of the welfare of our planet.'

I regarded Galilea's firm profile, the stone-setting of her jaw. *Environmental Fundamentalist.* The phrase, recently used by a right-wing politician to slander an adversary popped into my head.

'Indeed,' I replied, thinking how this was all very well, but people still had mortgages and bills to pay.

We turned down another road. In the thickness of this bush, I had no idea any more if we were heading north or south or east or west. We passed under a stone arch dripping with mosses and ferns. 'Humanity resists truly progressive acts of creation,' Galilea continued. 'So instead, we need to practice patience, softly sow the seeds of change. That way, when transformation is complete, we will have changed the world without it even knowing.'

I wondered then if we were talking about the same thing. There was an intense, defended quality about Galilea, as if she were holding something tightly back. Her idealistic words and tightly calibrated demeanour grated against one another. It was like sitting next to an immaculate, German-designed pressure cooker, strategically releasing just the right volume of steam so its contents didn't over-cook.

No longer knowing how to continue our conversation, I said nothing. And Galilea didn't elaborate. I knew right then she was hiding something. My gut clenched. Even if she wasn't going to immediately kill me, I had an inkling then this fiercely armoured woman was going to mess with my head. Penetrate. Weaken. Destroy. That was the technique of the master strategist. As with my marriage this would not be instant death but – as punishment for my turpitudes – a long, slow torture.

Moments later the bush opened into a vista of grasslands, bush and distant purple mountains. Galilea told me we were south of the Kangaroo Valley and that most of this area was bush reserve. The landscape painter in me swooned. What a sublime place to take my art students for some open-air painting.

'There are glorious bush walks and lookouts around the retreat,' Galilea said. 'Just keep to the tracks.' Her voice darkened. 'It's easy to get lost.'

The road narrowed. We came to a fork and turned left.

Here, gravel driveways, neatly mowed lawns, letter boxes and Victorian cottages flanked the road. 'The village of Watson,' Galilea said. 'It's a twenty-five-minute walk from the retreat through public reserve.'

Galilea told me Watson had a small bed and breakfast, a kindergarten and primary school. There were only four hundred residents, mostly older people and a few tree changers and their offspring. An unreliable private bus service shuffled once a day between Bowral and Watson. There was no police station here. Criminal matters were dealt with back in Bowral.

As she explained how this area had once been famous for its silver and gold mines, I realised how nervous I'd been. I relaxed back into the seat. If things didn't work out at Yindisha Retreat, at least I could escape to Watson.

We drove into the heart of the village, passing a pub and a small art and craft gallery before pulling up outside the wide-fronted Watson General Store and Post Office.

'I hope you don't mind – I'm just going to pop in and pick up my mail,' said Galilea.

'Not at all,' I replied. I exited the car as well, breathing in the cool and moist Highlands air. Beyond the short strip of shops, I glimpsed a pretty sandstone church at the end of a leafy driveway flossed with blue hydrangeas still blooming in summer's last sigh.

A man in full religious regalia – long black robes and a white dog collar – stepped out of Watson General Store as Galilea approached. Somewhere in his forties, he was fresh-faced, square-jawed and pastor-handsome. A nimbus of holiness surrounded his person.

He stopped suddenly, looked from Galilea to me. He regarded me with an expression I couldn't quite fathom. Was it pity? Or derision?

'Another recruit?' He asked Galilea, his grin forced.

'Yes, Quentin,' Galilea replied coolly. 'Another woman who appreciates fresh air and fresh thinking.'

The atmosphere prickled. A mass of unsaid things swelled between them.

Galilea introduced us. 'Quentin from the local parish,' she said without enthusiasm.

'Reverend Quentin Nader,' he corrected Galilea as he shook my hand. 'And welcome to the village of Watson.'

I smiled respectfully. I could well imagine women swooning over this Bondi Vet of tormented souls.

After I had introduced myself and thanked him for his welcome, Galilea glanced at the package in his other hand. 'And what do you have there, Quentin? More Bibles? Or perhaps cartridges of silver bullets for vampires?'

Reverend Nader didn't flinch. 'Bamboo stakes for Mary's vegetable garden,' he said coldly.

'Ah, yes, your wife's garlic plantation,' said Galilea. She smiled lightly. 'Where would we all be without Mary's delicious aioli?'

I felt more invisible spikes fire between them.

Galilea explained to me that Mary ran a small business selling her aioli to local shops. 'Mary is a practical woman,' she added. 'A woman in touch with the real world.'

Beginning to look faintly irritated, the Reverend glanced back at me. 'I'll pray for you,' he said. He took a few steps back, clearly keen to leave.

'Oh please, don't bother. We have other ways of channelling the beneficence of the divine,' said Galilea.

We parted on that strange note and, as I waited for Galilea, I walked up and down the footpath, taking in hanging baskets dripping with fuchsias and the neatly painted facades of the shop fronts. This was a well-cared for, well-loved village. But why had Galilea dismissed that man of the cloth as if he were nothing more than a stone in her shoe? And why had the Reverend referred to me as a recruit?

'I suspect he thinks I'm running a coven,' Galilea said when we got back in the car.

I forced a laugh. 'Well, *are* you?' I said in an attempt to be playful.

'Oh, we're doing something far more shocking,' she replied with a proud smile. 'We're reclaiming women's stolen spirits.'

And there it was again, that feeling of more, much more, behind her words.

I decided to offer an equally enigmatic, but hopefully faintly subversive reply. I wasn't anyone's recruit. I could think for myself.

'No one should take anyone's spirit without their permission,' I said with a carefully calibrated measure of agreement and defiance.

'Absolutely,' Galilea replied, a smile of approval in her voice. 'I think you're going to fit in well with Yindisha's ideology.'

Again, she gave me that sharp, probing look. Yes, I thought. I was being evaluated. And this test had nothing to do with my ability to teach art.

As the car swept down a road flanked by soaring eucalypts, Galilea explained how Yindisha Retreat was once a Methodist girls' boarding school and sat on four hectares of land. Embracing a sustainable, nature-based philosophy, they used solar power and storage batteries and water recycling and composting systems. She told me Yindisha Retreat respected and paid homage to nature as the ultimate source of the divine.

Regarding those eucalypts with their orange trunks and twisted limbs, I told her I agreed – that nature was indeed, divine. And more than a little mysterious.

She replied with an attractive, melodic, and faintly satisfied laugh.

A few minutes later we pulled into a grand circular driveway with a central fountain surrounded by neatly clipped Japanese box and purple salvia fronting a majestic two-storied Italianate mansion. 'The school's main building is now the retreat's lifestyle centre. It includes a gymnasium, swimming pool, the dining area, classrooms and of course, the library,' said Galilea.

When we parked outside the mansion, a tall, slender man emerged from the double doors and sauntered down the steps.

Dark haired and eyed with smooth brown skin, he had the same build as Mathias, but his hair was pulled into a man bun. He had dreamy eyes the colour of melted Toblerone.

Galilea strode over, threw her arms around him and gave him a kiss right on his lips. 'This is Jock, my personal assistant,' she said to me, her eyes shining with subversions as she pulled away.

That was the moment I realised Yindisha was no ordinary retreat.

CHAPTER THREE

Emancipations

The sight of that kiss launched a thousand thoughts into this new guest's brain. Jock looked at least thirty years younger than Galilea. And she was his boss. Don't get me wrong here – I went to art school. I graduated with an Honours degree in not only appreciation for the mad, the quirky and the profoundly impractical, but also an acceptance of unconventional lifestyles.

But sex – or at least the sex that I had experienced – is about power. It's a dance between submission and domination. My failed marriage was proof and point – my ex often complaining I wasn't submissive enough. So, while on the one hand I was happy to see a woman in charge, in that kiss, I witnessed a power imbalance. After years temping in offices, I had learned that shagging the boss (invariably a man) never ends well. And usually, the parties involved are far more discreet.

Yet, as I stood there in a body singing its hormonal swan song, I also felt a stab of envy.

Another gorgeous man sat behind the reception desk inside

the main building. He welcomed me charmingly, handed me the key to my cottage and a map of the retreat. Behind me, Galilea and Jock waited with my suitcase. A sensuous smell of musk and citrus, like some expensive designer aftershave, filled the foyer. Full of tremulous anticipation and even more excitement, I inhaled deeply.

'I need your mobile phone,' Jock said after I'd finished all the paperwork.

I balked. 'You're on a digital detox here,' Galilea reminded me. 'We keep your phone secure and charged. If any of the numbers listed on your emergency contacts list appear on the screen, we will notify you immediately.'

Very unhappily, I handed my phone to Jock. I felt as though I was giving this stranger one of my arteries. 'I trust Jock implicitly,' Galilea said. 'He's been with me for fifteen years.'

I did a few mental calculations. That meant Jock was just a boy when Galilea first employed him. The phrase shot into my thoughts. *Cradle snatcher.* Not only that, but possible *lawbreaker.* I looked away. Down the hall, another comely man was vacuuming an adjacent room. My imagination flashed into overdrive. Kidnapping young boys and orphans? Moulding them into women's servants? Just as quickly I shut my thoughts down. I was being ridiculous. *Stupid,* as my ex would have said.

Somewhere, a bell tinkled and Galilea excused herself, instructing Jock to escort me to my cottage.

I sat beside Jock who drove the retreat's electric utility vehicle down a network of landscaped paths bordered by topiary hedges and native grasses. Picturesque and neatly maintained white cottages sat cheek by jowl, separated by small front lawns and flowerbeds with bamboos and shrubs planted for maximum privacy. 'There are seventy-five one and two-bedroom cottages housing employees and guests on the estate,' Jock explained. 'And each cottage is named after a woman of accomplishment.'

By that point, I had dozens of questions. But rather than interrogating this possible toy-boy whose words seemed faintly scripted, I decided I would investigate myself. I had a couple of hours before my appointment with the art tutor I would be replacing and would use that time to explore.

My cottage sat right at the back of the estate in front of an ivy-covered wall that separated the dwellings from the utility buildings, tennis courts and golf course beyond. It had a small kitchenette, a lounge area, and a bedroom with French doors that opened onto a garden courtyard. Framed, tastefully atmospheric historical prints of the old Methodist Girls' School hung on the walls. Everything looked modest and immaculately clean. That same fragrance of citrus and musk infused the air.

I had paid extra for my own residence. Twin shares have never been an option for me because my snores sound like the arrival of the apocalypse.

Feeling pleased with this new and private abode, and looking forward to investigating my surroundings, I unpacked.

My cottage was called 'Tahire'. A plaque under her picture in the main lounge/dining area explained how this nineteenth-century Persian poetess was a member of the radically progressive and persecuted Babi Faith, which eventually transitioned into the Bahá'i Faith. Innately curious and bright, Tahire attended university in a culture in which women were denied education. During lectures, she hid behind a curtain in the lecture hall, so the men wouldn't be upset. Eventually her husband, who considered her behaviour unbecoming, took over full custody of her children and married another woman. Famed for her poetry, the beautiful and spirited Tahire caught the attention of the King of Persia. After declining his marriage proposal and refusing to be part of his harem, on the day of her execution, she turned to her accusers and said: 'You can kill me but you cannot stop the emancipation of women.'

Her murderers strangled Tahire with her own veil. She was, according to the plaque, the world's first suffragette.

Once I'd unpacked, I took a leisurely stroll through the retreat, enjoying the peace. How fabulous it was to be away from the city and its constant noise. Here, there was not a petrol-fuelled car, leaf-blower or hedge-trimmer in sight. No sound of traffic, no horns or sirens. Instead, along with the sigh of wind through leaves and the twittering of birds, shirtless men with perfectly sculpted bodies quietly tended the lawns and gardens and paths with clippers and hand-mowers and brooms. Yindisha's sights and sounds were soothing. Hypnotic.

The men looked up at me and smiled respectfully as I passed. There was not a sour-looking, decrepit, or ugly individual among them. I noticed a similarity to their physiques and wondered if they might all be related. But their features and colouring were varied enough for me to appreciate they were all delectable representations of a multitude of different nationalities. I saw in quick succession, a man who looked Indian, another African American, a pale redhead who resembled a Viking and another who looked as though he'd stepped out of the story of Aladdin.

I imagined the recruitment ad for the male employees: *Race not important. Must be gorgeous, fit and not object to serving an exclusively female clientele.*

A few pairs of men and women strolled past – in every case the women – in early to late middle age – were older than the men. And oh, my goodness, those women looked happy. They smiled at me as if they had found the source of everlasting bliss. Their joy was infectious. I smiled back, gazed at the men and inwardly drooled. Perhaps, I fleetingly mused, all Yindisha's men were dealing with oedipal complexes.

Before returning to the main building to do my induction, I decided to take a look behind the ivy-covered wall that separated the dwellings from the rest of the estate.

There, I discovered a row of buildings that resembled army barracks. With their corrugated iron roofs and small windows, they were much more basic than the cottages in the main estate. Later, I learned these were the men's quarters. They slept in groups of four in small rooms with two sets of bunks and all shared the facilities at the adjacent shower and toilet block. Initially, I didn't find this strange. After all, my mother had found my father in Manchester, living in a garage in the front of his landlady's property. He was not a man who fussed over his surroundings. My mother once told me that, as long as he could get on with his science, he would have happily lived in a hole in the ground. I just assumed these men, like my father, weren't fussed about their domestic arrangements either.

Back then, early on, I rationalised. Everything made a kind of subversive sense. With such a smorgasbord of delectable men, why wouldn't the owner of the retreat take on a younger lover? Jock was probably just healthy and much older than he looked. And fit-looking men living together in army barracks? Why not? They were employees. This was, after all, a health retreat. A women's retreat. If the men looked good, and the women looked happy, it was clearly a sign the retreat was doing something right.

I recalled the words in the attractive brochure left on my dining table: *During your stay at Yindisha Retreat, your world-view will change. You will return home a new woman.* I told myself I was ready for this. I was ready to be transformed into a new woman. I was oh-so tired of the old and bitter Alethea Braxton. With a great deal of effort, battling deeply ingrained habits of resistance, I forced myself into the warm, rose-petalled bath of acceptance.

※

Reminding myself I had come to Yindisha to pull my tattered self together and heal, I made a supreme effort to be a cooperative guest and employee. When Camilla – the art teacher I was replacing – escorted me to the back of the main building past rooms converted into yoga, Pilates, Zumba and pole dancing studios, I praised the retreat's efficiencies and initiatives. When we passed a hall inhabited by neatly piled chairs, a stage and an upright piano, I made appropriate noises of approval as Camilla told me this was where the retreat held regular, Friday night events. At the rear of the main building, in an extension, were more small, airy classrooms with desks and chairs and blackboards. Everything was clean and orderly; it was easy to feel impressed.

As we walked, Camilla explained she was moving to Melbourne to work as an art therapist in a psychiatric hospital. I silently admired her courage and generosity. During my twelve years married to an undiagnosed mental patient, I'd experienced enough insanity to last a lifetime.

The art room where I would teach had floor-to-ceiling windows, practical linoleum flooring and a row of sinks at one end. My heart lifted. I was going to enjoy teaching in this space. The north-facing light was perfect. My schedule wasn't exactly taxing – four days on, three days off. My classes – one a day – lasted three hours with additional private sessions if requested. In between, I could relax, take courses, go on long walks and heal. When I asked Camilla about the surfeit of gorgeous men, she smiled warmly. 'The retreat has a meticulous recruitment policy,' she replied. I admit, I was a little puzzled. My recruitment process hadn't exactly been meticulous. A single video interview with Camilla. A patchy resume.

Shovelling my suspicions aside, I accepted her explanation. Aside from the disconcertingly intense and simultaneously charming Galilea with her evidently cougar-like tendencies, I had absolutely no complaints. I spent the rest of that first afternoon settling in, deciding which classes I wanted to attend and exploring the gardens and surrounding bushlands in familiar solitude. I put that faint niggle down to my usual problems with adjusting to new situations.

Dinner was rostered between six and seven-thirty in the evening. Although I had the option of ordering room service and dining alone, I decided it was probably good to be sociable on my first night and join the communal dinner.

I made my way to the main building just after six. In a spacious, high-ceilinged room, guests and employees sat together at a long wooden table in what was once the school's dining hall. Most guests, I learned, arrived on Thursday evenings or Friday afternoons for long weekends. There were fifteen of us at the table that evening – Galilea, myself, plus five extended stay guests (all women) and eight employees, of which five were men. All gorgeous, of course. None of the men looked older than forty, from what I could tell. I admired all that male beauty, feeling like a fox salivating over a pasture of spring lambs.

Galilea, minus Jock, and flanked by two beautiful men, sat at the far end of the table, introduced everyone and promised us that – no matter how long or short our stay– we would be replenished by what Yindisha had to offer.

'So please enjoy Mother Earth's gifts,' Galilea added before inviting us to begin our meal.

The buffet meal consisted of vegetarian and vegan dishes, leafy green salads all grown in the retreat's vegetable gardens and dishes with eggs supplied by resident hens. Cheeses were made from the milk of the retreat's sheep and goats. Fruits came from the surrounding orchards. There was no alcohol, only homemade lemonade and water. Inebriation no longer an option, I consoled myself by once more drinking in the sight of the intoxicatingly beautiful men.

'Good to know Mother Earth isn't a beer drinker,' I said

facetiously, addressing Tamati – a Polynesian man on my right. 'Who knows what she might get up to if she were permanently pissed?' He chuckled heartily at my feeble attempt at wit, revealing a splendid set of healthy white teeth. When I asked, in my best motherly tones, about his background, he told me he was born in Rotorua and, like many kiwis, had to come to Australia because there were more career opportunities. He was doing a hospitality course and Yindisha was giving him practical experience. Wreaths of evangelical flora blossomed in his eyes as he told me about his iwi, his tribe back in New Zealand, before flawlessly segueing into more esoteric matters. He spoke to me about his own personal philosophy; one that combined his Māori heritage with an understanding that all faiths are products of transcendent thinking as well as social laws and traditions.

'Underneath, religions are essentially trying to achieve the same objectives – peace on earth and love among humanity,' he said in his lovely, faintly raspy voice. 'And that includes – above all – respect for women – the creators and givers of life.'

Along with his perfect white teeth, I admired his simple sincerity, his diverse take on the delusions of religion, myth and creationism. It was hard to disagree with such idealism coming from the mouth of such a beautiful man.

The problem was, I mistrusted religion. And perfection. Perfection is strawberries pierced by needles, a real estate paintjob disguising water stains and subsidence cracks, a hedge of lavender hiding Chekov's gun. And religions are just fairy tales and social constructs created to oppress the masses into submission.

And idealism? Well, it's all just too simple.

Well, aren't you a well-raised boy? I was tempted to say. *Even if you are a bit sweetly naïve.* Had I been tipsy and feeling cocky, I might have let the words slip out. Instead, I smiled soberly, nodded approvingly, and glanced away.

Diagonally across from me, one particular man grabbed my

attention. Light-eyed, pale-skinned, dark-haired with heavy eyebrows, he reminded me of my father.

Tamati noticed me looking at the man. 'That's Kaden,' he said. 'He escaped from Iran with his family just after the 1979 revolution. They crossed into Pakistan by hiding among a flock of sheep. He's trained as a nurse,' he added. 'He works with the retreat's doctor.'

My heart squeezed as I stared at Kaden. I thought of my father vanishing into the waves. Lost forever. My call to him rose to my throat as a choke.

Intermittently, I glanced at Galilea smiling and chatting to the new guests and, every now and then, flirtatiously patting a male arm. I noticed how the men looked at her – with a kind of worshipful deference.

I tried to distract myself by once more taking in the beauty of those five gorgeous men. I watched them eat. There was not a pig among them. Not a single dribbler or gorger. They all had impeccable table manners, as if they had studied Debrett's *Guide to Etiquette and Modern Manners*. My mother, born in Germany and later enculturated by the world of British upper-class twittery, would have been impressed.

I suddenly felt lost, alienated and profoundly alone among these strangers. I didn't like myself right then. These people were so nice and I felt like a rapidly crumbling ball of unpolished shit in their midst.

I recalled Galilea's words: *We're reclaiming women's stolen spirits.* My spirit hadn't just been stolen, but shredded, trampled and dispatched to a distant landfill.

My mood plummeted. By dessert, I was feeling heavy and unwell. I'm not good in large, noisy groups. Following a severe flu when I probably should have been hospitalised but instead chose (translate: was pressured by an aggrieved husband who didn't like it when I got sick) to stay at home to care for husband and baby, I have tinnitus and a deaf ear, which makes listening challenging. I was tired. Overwhelmed. My head spun and a sense of unreality enveloped me.

Despite the warm and companionable atmosphere, I began to feel twisted all out of shape.

Skipping the after-dinner musical entertainment, I excused myself and made my way back to my cottage in the waning light. Sitting on the sofa, I furiously bit my nails. The men felt wrong. Maybe it was their confidence, instilled not by just by their good looks, but also by an awareness of something beyond my understanding.

I went to bed feeling as fragile as a piece of porcelain, as if I might, in a single moment of carelessness, shatter and break.

CHAPTER FOUR

Steam Cleaning and Artificial Stimulants

Day Two

I slept deeply, woke at first light to twittering birds and a fading dream. I frequently have strange and vivid dreams on first nights in new beds. And sometimes, those dreams include my ex-husband. Drifting in that realm betwixt illusion and reality, I felt his presence, his provocations still imprinted onto the soft tissue of my dream-memory.

In that dream, I ironed shirts, swept, mopped, and dusted in a huge empty house with floor-to-ceiling windows that looked out onto an endless landscape of dry tufts of grass and sandy dirt. Following me from room to cavernous room, my ex badgered me, criticised the way I dusted sloppily, mopped too infrequently, ironed in more creases that I removed.

I lingered in bed, recalling my dream as if it were the plot of an irksome movie. I understood its symbols. My marriage was an empty prison devoid of respect and love, but with plenty of enforced labour. Outside, however, without my husband, lay an unchartered wasteland of nothingness and unknown terrors called the life of the single woman.

Apart from that house I didn't recognise, my dream's plot bore an uncanny resemblance to reality. My ex waved a bill in my face. 'Why is this phone bill so high?' He asked. 'Who have you been calling?'

I placed some grocery bags on the kitchen counter. He began sifting through them. 'Why do we need all this stuff? I want to see the receipts!' he demanded.

When I submissively handed him the grocery receipt, he looked at it and said: 'I need to keep an eye on your spending. You're not good with finances. You don't understand money. You are useless.'

Of course, I realise now what he was saying reflected his personal blueprint of life. *Women* didn't understand money.

'You see what happens when you don't behave?' he added, gesturing at the young and pretty creature who had materialised by his side. 'I find someone better.'

I lingered in bed, squinting at a crack in the ceiling, which in the absence of my contact lenses, resembled a furry outline of the Great Australian Bight. For some reason, that crack annoyed the hell out of me, as if had been put there just to irritate. Further indulging my indignation, I recalled some of the other humiliations I had escaped in real life.

'Try and do something about your awful cooking,' my ex had once said, pointing to a post-it note he'd put on the fridge with instructions on how to make an acceptable hamburger – one he would eat. *No beetroot. No processed cheese. Only camembert or brie. No mass -produced supermarket buns. Gourmet bakery buns only. Go easy on the pickles and make sure the lettuce is fresh. No tomatoes. No garlic. Make sure the meat patties are GRILLED NOT FRIED.*

I remembered the dream's full trajectory now. Just before I woke, I'd answered back. I'd screamed at him. *Fuck you! Why the hell are you still here giving me nightmares?*

Galvanised by fury, I sat up. Of course, I'd shakily moved on since I left him. I'd taken back my power. I was responsible for my own life. And that man had no business inhabiting my subconscious.

Yindisha Retreat had given me an outfit to wear– cream linen pants and a sage-green tee shirt bearing the retreat's logo. It was my choice on my days off to wear either my ordinary clothes or the uniform of an employee.

Unable to decide, I plodded sleepily into the bathroom and put in my contact lenses. Short-sighted since my teens, I have the unique privilege of seeing the world in two ways – from blurry impressionist Monet to photo-realist David Hockney.

Lenses in, my hearing sharpened as well. Outside, birds chittered, shrieked and squawked. Lulled by those avian languages indecipherable to humans, I moved through my new residence in a floaty realm of thought.

You are here to relax, lose weight and become a new woman, I told myself as I pulled a pair of pants and shirt from my suitcase. *Enjoy Yindisha's offerings and stop beating yourself up,* I reminded myself after I winced at the sight my bulbous stomach. *Aim to be flexible and open and stop being suspicious of men who are just being nice.*

On my way out, I realised I had put my linen pants on inside out. I stopped at the front door, removed them and turned them outside out. I am often absent-minded. Early on in our courtship, my ex found my dithering quaint. That was before I was demoted to *dense bitch.*

Finally dressed like someone in full possession of her senses, I stepped outside, glimpsing between the shrubs, one of Yindisha's men striding down the path. Shirtless with a toned chest, that exquisitely sculpted man made my insides tremble.

What was it about Yindisha's men that both thrilled and disturbed me?

Thinking how my subconscious was in need of a good steam clean, I reminded myself I was here to heal both body and soul – wherever that took me.

I regarded the lawns where dewdrops captured prisms of morning light. I admired the beautiful flame-coloured liquidambar tree that flanked the path. The unknown landscape beckoned. Shaking away the last threads of my dream, I walked to breakfast, my gaze now firmly focused on the real world.

At breakfast (wholesome, grainy and seasonally fruity), I discovered there was no coffee. Used to at least two strong cups a day, I had a minor moment of panic. How was I going to survive Yindisha without coffee?

When the man refilling the jugs told me the retreat offered guests Ayurvedic, dandelion and assorted herbal concoctions, I gathered, by his response, that I looked irritated.

He looked as though he belonged on the cover of a men's health magazine. 'Coffee is an artificial stimulant.' he replied, bemused. 'Natural stimulants are better for your body.'

Did I see a faint waggle of his eyebrows when he said that?

'I like my stimulants strong and fake,' I replied.

'We can arrange that too,' a woman sitting at the table behind me replied in a breathy voice.

When I asked her what she meant, she said, 'One day when you're ready, dear, you'll see.' She regarded the man sitting next to her and released a delightfully unhinged giggle.

That was as much sense as I got out of her. Her name was Elise Cranston and she was one of the retreat's oldest residents. And a bit senile, I gathered. After that enigmatic comment she seemed to fade as if she had used up all her energy delivering her message.

The man by her side – Jerome – her caregiver – explained how she was a former teacher at the old Methodist school and an old friend of Galilea. She had lived here in her cottage for thirty years. He had been with her for nineteen of those years.

I tried to chat with her, but she was hard of hearing, an air of distraction in her milky-distant gaze. I'd seen that same far-away look in my mother's eyes in her last few months of life and knew Elise was slowly retreating to the realm beyond, gently closing life's door. But lucky Elise. With a gentle, patient carer by her side. She wouldn't die alone.

I left the breakfast room feeling melancholy. *What a lovely place to die*, I thought.

Attached once more to my inner gloom, I wandered down the mansion's dimly lit hall. Inhaling a faint scent of lavender, I gazed up at the ornate plaster ceiling populated with cherubs, lyres, bows and ivy borders and thought of my mother who spent her last year of life in a nursing home. Suffering from dementia, she needed full-time care and I was working long hours at a real estate agency to pay the bills. I wasn't there when she died. Nurses, who were busy with other residents, found her lying at the foot of her bed, a bloody lump on her head where she had knocked herself on the edge of the bedside table as she fell trying to get to the bathroom. She died alone and on the floor.

Whenever I had free time, I visited that rest home that smelt of boiled cabbage, lavender bleach and uric acid. Despite her age and exhaustion, that frail homunculus dwarfed by her hospital bed would come to life, rise from her pillows when I entered the room. 'Have you put on weight?' She would ask, her brown eyes – cocooned by wrinkles – brightly alive. 'You look like a clown in that dress! Is this today's fashion? Shocking! Don't you ever iron your clothes?'

By this point, I would have managed to take a seat at her bedside. Down the hall, the oriental short hair cat that belonged to one of the other residents would let out its banshee howl and someone – invariably a curmudgeonly old man – would yell at it to shut the fuck up. Oblivious to the surrounding dramas, this once elegant, stoic woman would, with great effort, heave forward and study me with her characteristic eagle gaze. Nothing escaped her eye – she could, in the speed of a breath, shift her focus from awe at nature's beauty to the defilement of a stray brown hair on a white shirt.

'When did you last pluck your eyebrows?' She would demand. 'They look like a pair of doormats. And what is going on with your hair? How can you possibly see anything with that messy fringe? Those earrings. Shocking! Too loud and tarty. Is that the message you want to send to men? Decent, respectable men will be scared off by such flagrant accessories. And are you still biting your nails? At your age?'

Weary of her criticisms (it took me a long time to understand criticism of others comes from a place of deep sorrow), I would change the subject and ask her what she had been doing. She might tell me how yesterday she went shopping with my father at Harrods. They had bought a new couch, which was going to be delivered tomorrow. Or that they'd been out to dinner last night at a lovely French place. Although she was in those last weeks, truly away with the fairies, I was glad my father was there keeping her company.

I howled when she died her lonely death. For all her flaws, her anxieties, her Teutonic bluntness, she loved me fiercely and was never afraid to show it. She was my best friend. My great love.

Stepping through the main door of the mansion, I stood on the veranda, my gaze drawn to a pot of bright lobelia and petunias, those blooms drawing their last autumnal gasp. I had tried my hardest and my mother was now at peace. I was here to heal and forgive myself. I was here to let go. *Move on, Alethea*, I told myself again. *Move on.*

After breakfast, I attended an early morning yoga session run by a woman around my age and a younger man (gorgeous) who appeared to be her student.

Later, as I strolled through the retreat's gardens, I studied the men more closely. I noticed how they all held themselves the same way, walked the same way – a kind of faintly self-conscious, measured strut. I noticed the way they engaged with the women – with great respect and civility. I watched a man with a tray of food knock on the door of a cottage named after Helen Keller and recalled how – even though we both worked full-time – I had once given my ex breakfast in bed every weekend morning until the birth of Sophia. When I finally said I couldn't manage his morning treats anymore, he was furious. It was the moment I realised he didn't want a wife; he wanted a servant.

Berating myself for staying so long with such an arse, I went back to the art room and checked the stocks of canvases, paints, cartridge and butcher's paper, charcoals and pencils.

Later that morning, I attended a class I'd seen advertised in the retreat's brochure on the history and philosophy of spirituality and religion. I listened to a handsome, seventy-ish woman speaking about Gnosticism, theosophy and the perennial wisdom underpinning the world's religions. No more than four minutes into her talk, she began to speak of the matriarchal religions of prehistory and Mother Goddesses channelling spiritual wisdom, fertility, and strength. In a voice with barely suppressed tones of triumph, she spoke of how archaic knowledge once dismissed as ignorance and superstition was now in the hands of those who understood its power. 'All this arcane wisdom has been suppressed by patriarchal religions,' she stated forcefully. 'The powerful feminine has been nullified since the dawn of history by cultural expectations, social obligations, doctrines and mandates written by men and perpetuated by submissive women.'

I glanced at the other women in the audience, quietly listening and nodding. No one challenged her. The delectable man sitting beside our lecturer never said a word either. Instead, he graciously smiled, nodded at the appropriate moments and filled her water glass when it was empty.

It was clear that when it came to Yindisha's version of the history of religion, woman was in charge and man was apprentice.

After the class, I strolled back to my cottage, nursing the beginning of a headache. I ordered a salad niçoise for lunch and dined alone. *What the hell am I doing here?* My inner voice grumbled. *This isn't the real world. This place is a feminist cult!* Trying to manage another domino-fall of despair, I sank my teeth into a chunk of perfectly grilled, sustainably fished, tuna steak. *Pull yourself together, Alethea,* I told myself. *You are behaving like a paranoid idiot.*

CHAPTER FIVE

Invisible Waves

By mid-afternoon on my second day at Yindisha I had a full-blown coffee withdrawal headache. I *needed* my artificial stimulants. Deciding the only way to get rid of it was to break the rules, I set out for Watson to find a good cup of strong coffee.

Thirty minutes later, despite a soothing scenic walk I should have noticed more, I arrived in Watson with a headache that had morphed into a nimbus of dull pounding that circled my skull.

A van – the magenta words 'Bowral Blinds and Awnings' printed on its chassis – was parked in front of the Watson General Store. On the footpath a few onlookers, including the Reverend Nader – regal and handsome in his black robes – gathered to watch a small man in a magenta tee shirt that matched the van, unfurl the blue and white striped awning he had just installed. Amid exhortations of how stylish it was, how visitors would now be able to sit outside for coffees when it rained or was too hot, Reverend Nader glanced at me, giving me the faintest nod of acknowledgement. Once he caught my eye, he looked swiftly away as if he didn't like what he saw. After our meeting yesterday, he'd clearly decided I was, along with Galilea, another *persona non grata*. He was also blocking the door to the café.

After giving him an equally indifferent greeting, I stepped towards a display of wooden crates filled with assorted potpourris, sniffing some of the samples, hoping they might help clear my headache. As I inhaled fragrances of desert heathers, lemon eucalypt and lavender, I heard Reverend Nader say, 'Care to join me for a cup of tea?'

Thinking that invitation was addressed to me, I turned. Reverend Nader slid me a quick, sly, look then smiled beneficently at the man from Bowral Blinds and Awnings. He'd wanted me to hear his invitation. To be confused by his words. It was a subtle manipulativeness I recognised from another life. A veiled insult. Along with annoyance, I felt the faint stirring of a premonition.

'Yes, please, thank you,' the man from Bowral Blinds and Awnings replied in a reedy voice.

As Reverend Nader and his guest entered the general store, I lingered outside, selecting some potpourri to give Sophia.

Once they were clear of the counter and seated, I walked into the general store, ordered a takeaway coffee and paid for it along with my packet of potpourri and a bar of fruit and nut milk chocolate.

Waiting for my coffee, I ate a piece of the fruit and nut chocolate and looked around. The general store smelt of gardenias, roasted nuts and autumn berries. Baroque music softly played in the background. West-facing picture windows flanked by colourful pots of fiddle-leafed fig trees and hanging pots of ferns infused the space with a faintly green and wholesome light. While one side of the store sold fruit, vegetables and grocery basics, the other side was devoted to the café which comprised a row of private booths and round metal coffee tables and chairs set in front of a wall of books. At three-thirty in the afternoon, Reverend Nader, the man from Bowral Blinds and Awnings and I were the last and only guests in the café. It was quiet. Sound carried.

I scanned the bookshelves and pulled out a book on Escher. Focusing on Escher's sublime detail and challenging perspectives, I tried to reign in my escalating annoyance as nearby, Reverend Nader spoke in the deep and assured tones of a seasoned preacher, telling his guest how he'd just been re-reading some passages from the Bible and how the messages of that book were powerful and profound.

'For instance, could it be any more obvious?' he announced. 'Leviticus says you shall not lie with a male as with a woman; it is an abomination.'

I watched that small, plain man with the wide-eyed look of a dog eager to please nod at Reverend Nader in agreement. Reverend Nader was making it clear he was not a homosexual. He was not hitting on the man from Bowral Blinds and Awnings.

I felt my brow grow dark and heavy, like a thunder loft. I bit off another piece of chocolate and chewed furiously. My head throbbed.

Reverend Nader obviously wanted me to hear his words. Every now and then, he glanced at me without looking, in that way that some men of religion do – afraid to catch your eye because you are an inferior creature so beyond salvation, a daughter of Eve so fallen into disgrace and spiritual darkness, so fully corrupted by the vices of the flesh that to look directly into your eyes might poison them or, glimpsing those Medusa-like snakes in your hair, turn them to stone.

My hand shook as I slid the book on Escher back into the shelf.

The little man from Bowral Blinds and Awnings moved onto the subject of sport. Briefly, the Reverend Nader chortled and listened to his comments about some recent win of his favourite rugby team. For a while they bonded over men chasing balls. I could hear the message beyond Reverend Nader's words. *I'm a great guy. One of the people.*

'I like to cheer for the winning team,' Reverend Nader said proudly as my takeaway coffee arrived. 'And that winning team is Jesus's team.'

My irritation ramped up another notch. To calm myself, I took a long sip of coffee.

Instead of departing now I had my coffee, I lingered, gripped by grim curiosity and a self-destructive compulsion. *What kind of shit is going to come out of Reverend Nader's holy chops next?* I wondered. I pulled another book from the shelf – this one by William Blake – an engraver. A poet. A mystic. A man who wrote of the evils and oppressions of institutionalised religions.

The man from Bowral Blinds and Awnings mentioned then that he'd been to high school and worked with a few Hindus and Sikhs. They seemed nice enough he said. Kind and respectful. Good values. Generous. Humble. What did Nader's God and Jesus make of those chaps and their prayers?

'Pointless!' Reverend Nader exhorted. 'God would find their prayers *pointless!*'

The evangelical fervour coming off Reverend Nader was hotter than the late afternoon sunlight fighting to breach that newly installed awning. His fervour felt like a physical force. It pulsed off him in waves, heating this pocket of the café, heating my skin and my blood.

I looked up from my book on Blake as the man from Bowral Blinds and Awnings glanced outside at his van, looking in that moment as if he wished for nothing more than to return to turning his screws and hammering his nails, delivering shade and protection to places where the sun was too bright.

'Sin. The world is full of it,' Reverend Nader continued. 'It's my job to help those who are corrupted.' Again, he glanced at me. 'I could have gone into investment banking. But I chose theology school. I wanted to make the world a better place. I wanted to study truth. Truth is eternal. The word of God is eternal. It is the law. The Bible is the one true book.'

Well, fuck you, I thought, once more looking away. In that moment, my gaze fell on a passage in that book on the work of William Blake.

> *That stony law I stamp to dust; and scatter religion abroad*
> *To the four winds as a torn book, & none shall gather the leaves.*

Reverend Nader continued. 'I love what God loves and hate what God hates. Evil and sin. The world is full of it. Evil is a heretic who turns from the true word of God. Only a fool shuns the Bible and indulges in vain and idle fancies. Satan's destructive forces are everywhere. Sin is a *seductress.*'

That was it. My insides ignited. Full of caffeinated energy and sinful fruit and nut chocolate, I stepped towards their table.

I slammed down the William Blake book. A little too hard. Reverend Nader's tea slopped onto the saucer, the cup tinkling in protest. The scone crumbs on the table jumped as if in fright.

'William Blake has more to say about truth than any passage in your so-called holy book,' I said. I tried to keep my tone calm, but I could hear the furious bite in my voice. 'The Bible was written millennia ago by a collection of tyrannical, misogynist fossils.'

Reverend Nader's eyes filled with fire and brimstone. His guest's jaw dropped in shock. I looked Reverend Nader hard in the eye. 'Perhaps you should have worked in investment banking after all,' I added. 'It would have been a more honest form of evil.'

I turned to leave. 'There's no empirical evidence of God,' I added for good measure.

And with that, I flounced towards the exit.

'God exists! I have evidence! I can prove it!' Reverend Nader shouted. My back heated as I imagined dragon fire shooting from his nostrils. I pushed open the door and scoffed.

It occurred to me in that moment that I had come to the Southern Highlands for a change of scenery, for a change of pace, for peace. And I had, on my second day, already made myself an enemy.

Still refusing to look back, I exited Watson General store in a blaze of triumphant indignation. Like everyone, I have triggers. Leaf blowers. Evangelical nut-bags. You can't argue with people like Reverend Nader. Their beliefs are as inflexible as a corpse with rigor mortis. I binned my empty coffee cup. *Sin is a seductress. What a load of shit.*

I thought how Reverend Nader might take that William Blake book home to burn.

As I walked past the church and carpark towards the road that led back to Yindisha Retreat, it occurred to me that – for maximum offense – I should have slammed down a book about a woman artist instead. Georgia O'Keefe's vaginal renderings of orchids, perhaps. Or the poems of Anne Sexton.

I looked up at a sky clear of thunderclouds and potential lightning bolts that might strike down this female apostate. The gravel crunched under my feet as I marched into the bright blaze of the late afternoon sun.

No doubt Reverend Nader was, at this moment, shaking his head in disbelief. Another Yindishan lunatic, he was probably saying to that little man. Another unstable, menopausal maniac.

Conceited bitch. Shrew. HAG.

That voice from my married life joined my imaginings. I was a woman who dared to answer back. I had challenged the holy word. Blame my crappy marriage for my explosive nature, I thought as I walked and fumed. Blame last night's dream. But mostly, blame my old Anglican high school for my aversion to all things evangelical. I recalled the headmistress's exhortations during assemblies about the virtues of virginity and how she was educating us to be good wives and mothers because that was what the Bible ordained. 'We are raising our girls to be *ladies*,' she once told the local press.

What utter fuckwittery, I muttered to myself.

Instead of heading back to Yindisha, I decided to calm myself down by taking a stroll through Watson's Botanical Gardens. Among the rose beds, a weariness fell over me. I thought of the way I wobbled through life, lurching between submission and flaming fury, like some badly tuned engine. I thought how, despite the lessons I'd learned, I was still reacting to obvious provocations.

And did you have to be quite so rude to a minister of religion? a prim, teacherly voice in my mind asked.

I flinched. Of course, I didn't believe Christianity was evil. Christianity had saved as many lives as it had damned. Christians fed the starving, housed the homeless, comforted the destitute. My school had encouraged us to give to charities, to be of service to our communities. And there was common sense in the Bible. Like the Good Samaritan's message about kindness to people in need and the meek inheriting the earth.

Back at the Café, I had been arrogant. Foolish. Impulsive. I knew nothing. I had offended a man of God. Not given him a chance to defend his views.

Do you know what you are? You are a horrible person pretending to be nice.

There he was again. My ex sliding back into my thoughts like some latent virus, still trying to find ways to bring me down.

My back hardened. *Fuck off, arsehole.*

Trying to cleanse my thoughts, I spent over an hour meandering among the Botanical Garden's native plantings, reading the neatly written signs, watching a pair of pink and grey cockatoos twittering companionably as they grazed on the lawns. Cockatoos, apparently, mate for life. Now *there* was a happy marriage.

On my way out of the gardens, I saw Reverend Nader striding towards the Watson Bed and Breakfast. I recalled his exhortation. *Satan's destructive forces are everywhere!*

My stomach lurched as I – a destructive force not wanting

to be seen by that warrior of righteousness – ducked behind a shrubbery before slinking onto the unpaved road that led back to Yindisha Retreat.

The sun dropped as I walked. The blue of the sky deepened. The world felt fragile, quaking under the behest of some unseen, all-powerful force. I shivered. Around me the bush blackened and chilled. It was cold in the shadows. I suddenly felt afraid.

Pull yourself together, Alethea. Taking a deep breath, telling myself my fear was irrational and superstitious, I noticed my headache had vanished. I squeezed the sachet of potpourri in my pocket, releasing a waft of lemon eucalypt. I thought of Sophia, my mother, my father and felt an explosive love well to the surface of my thoughts.

A gentle breeze carried the smell of honeysuckle and the song of some early roosting bird. Against the flame-coloured backdrop of the setting sun, birds sat on the powerlines like notes on a musical score.

I paused and listened to the shrill call of that bird, inhaling nature's beauty, feeling some inner loosening of strings.

The dead's presence often arrives unexpectedly – a whisper through our thoughts, an ethereal manifestation carried on invisible waves. *Well done, Alethea. Well done with that minister. You stood up for yourself and what you believe.*

My father's voice – warm and resonant – folded around me like a hug.

How I missed that beautiful man as wise as the sky and as fathomless as the ocean. An astrophysicist who studied radio waves from outer space he was, in his last years, a university lecturer. And I was student zero. As a child, I drank in his words in adulation. We adored each other. I was his little princess. He was my hero. My guide.

Sharing his knowledge was almost a hunger in him; he filled my young head with so many thoughts and ideas – it was as if he knew his time with me would be brief. Not only was he a scientist, but he was fascinated by mysticism and the world's religions.

'Everything begins with a thought, Alethea,' he once told me during a chat about the insights of Buddha. 'And with those thoughts we create the world.'

He took our thoughts to places others feared to go. In my mind, I travelled with my father – that scientist and lover of mysticism and the wisdom of the ancients – to the end of the universe and the beginning of time. Together we visited the alien worlds of Russian science fiction writers, pondered passages from scriptures in which descriptions of angels resembled alien visitations.

With our thoughts we create the world.

That ghost of my father and those messages from beyond the grave filled my insides with a warm glow.

As the sun fell towards night's nest of pink and orange clouds, the tree's shadows lengthened, casting long, warped black shapes across the road.

Show the world you are proud of who you are, my old high school's deportment teacher had once said. *Bosom out. Shoulders back. Walk with pride.*

Regarding my own long shadow, bent like a crone, I straightened my back and sped my pace, determined to get back before it got dark.

Eventually Yindisha came into view.

Show the world you are a lady. That was another piece of advice from our deportment teacher.

I paused for a moment at Yindisha's entrance, regarding that mansion with its groomed gardens and strategically lit shrubberies glowing in the waning light. Inside me, some inner moral compass quivered towards its true north. I was not a lady. I was not a good Christian. I was an artist. I believed in wonder. Beauty. Truth. I believed in the restorative power of art. And I was here to share that power with others.

I was also my own woman and I was not going to join some feminist cult.

The rebel in me firmly resurrected by a cup of coffee, some fruit and nut chocolate, and a jolly good venting at minister of religion, I strode up the mansion's steps, two at a time.

CHAPTER SIX

The Creation and Redistribution of Mass

Day Three

I had five students in my first Friday class – all mature women. Following introductions, I made them do some loosening up exercises on butcher's paper. After pulling out a collection of white models of platonic solids and an orb I'd found in a cupboard, I told them about positive and negative spaces and showed them how to create shaded shapes and create the illusion of mass by identifying the source of light. I spoke about finding one's personal style.

I listened to their stories as they sketched. There were mothers taking a break from husbands and teenage children, widows and divorcees like me trying to re-discover their places in the world. They were all women defined in varying ways by the absence or presence of men in their lives.

When they asked me about my artistic background, I glossed over, told them I'd been to art school. Worked as a graphic artist. Taught art classes here and there. I omitted the story of my exhibition. And my divorce. A teacher must retain a level of dignity, composure and control. I wasn't here to be pitied or to seek empathy. I was here to share the palate of my creative knowledge. Resolving to conduct an excellent class, I embraced my role as educator.

During that class, I came to define my students by their artistic styles. There was Stick-figure Saniya, who was incapable of drawing a single, relaxed line. At the other end of the spectrum, was Loose Judith, who was so expressive, her marks fired off the page and onto the sketch-board. Other students tucked their drawings up on the edges and corners of the paper as if terrified of the boundless space in the middle of the sheet. Some began in the middle of the sheet, fearful of going near the edges. One was just terrified of making a single mark on her paper. Her name was Mary and she smelt of Christmas. Mary – a day-guest – wore both a wedding band and engagement ring. Carefully groomed, not a wayward hair escaping her tight bun, she had sparrow-brown colouring with a matching wardrobe, as if she were trying to hide in life's undergrowth. For most of the class she remained quiet and didn't share her story, only shyly mentioning she lived locally. I encouraged Frightened Mary – as I came to think of her – and coaxed her into making her first marks.

Over the next two hours, the inhibited found their inner courage. Loose Judith tempered her wild expressiveness with some structure. Stick-figure Saniya produced a charmingly quirky drawing of a collection of slightly erotic-looking platonic solids. And Frightened Mary glowed with delight as she delicately shaded her first platonic solid – a cube.

Towards the end of that class, another student squeezed out more of Frightened Mary's story. She was a pastor's wife, she confessed. The wife of Watson's Reverend Quentin Nader. She didn't look at anyone when she spoke, just stared out the window as if wishing, now her secret was out, that she could fly away and hide. At the sound of that man's name, a cold stone plunged through my stomach.

Despite delivering a successful first class, after my students' farewells, I felt deeply embarrassed. Guilty. Ashamed. Puzzled. Had Reverend Nader shared the story of our encounter with his wife? Was Mary Nader a clever actress in cahoots with her husband? Had Mary come to sabotage my class?

Yet I never glimpsed a moment of disapproval or contempt in Mary's eyes. She exuded a pure, forgiving, and virtuous air of humility.

Wishing I could go back in time to yesterday in the Café and practice some restraint as I listened to Reverend Nader's words, I felt sick with remorse. It occurred to me I may have been able to get away from my past life, but I could never escape my destructive self. Why couldn't I, as my ex repeatedly asked, *just shut the fuck up?*

Inside me, another familiar, hollow feeling returned. My inner flagellant grew restless. Who was I to teach art? I wasn't good enough to teach what I hadn't mastered myself. I was a hypocrite. A fraud. I tidied away the last of the papers and pencils, convinced my students had seen through my façade. They'd promised to return, but they were just being polite. *Fucking retarded, lying bitch. You are a bad woman. You are useless*, snarked that unwelcome, chastising voice that still haunted my psyche. The shame came over me like a burst dam. My ex was right. I was a disaster. A raging incompetent. And abuser of ministers. What I had started, Mary Nader would finish off. And tomorrow, I would have no students.

Exhausted by the energy I'd put into my class, and the shock of Mary's revelation, later that same afternoon, I took another long solitary walk through the marked bush trails surrounding the retreat. I reflected on my exhibition and those unsold artworks now cluttering my walls and attic. If all created acts are, on some level self-portraits, then, through those generic 'public toilet people' I had depicted myself as an empty shell delineated by my surroundings. Despite my aversions to leaf blowers and religious zealots, I was still a negative space. A blank human-shaped canvas craving serendipity. A woman longing to be filled and led.

Over the years, I've come to understand that teaching is as much about discovering ourselves and learning from our students as it is about sharing our knowledge. My thoughts snapped to Mary Nader. Her fragrance, her clothes, her demeanour and the way her shoulders hunched under her off-white cardigan niggled at me. Something about that woman didn't add up.

I sat on one of the park benches dotted along the marked bush trail, perfectly placed for middle-aged matrons to rest and recuperate. Inhaling nature's orchestra of odours, from the soft scent of warm honey to the sharp, hot green of active photosynthesis, listening to the chorus of crickets and birds, I watched a skink at my feet tackling a caterpillar. In the battle of its life, the squirming caterpillar trapped by the skink's jaws, vanished along with its captor under a rock. Again, I thought of Frightened Mary. Did she find solace in her husband and his faith? Did she find belief in a higher order comforting? Fortifying? In the surrounding trees, a family of kookaburras suddenly erupted into shrieks and laughs like demons enjoying a damn good joke. With a squirming sensation deep in my core, I sighed, rose and returned to my cottage feeling as though I'd overlooked something enormous sitting right in front of me.

※

Tonight – Friday night – after dinner, the retreat was hosting a fundraiser for a women's refuge. I'd been told to pack a glamorous outfit and, although I'd complied, I had no intention of wearing it.

In the fourteen years since my divorce, I'd turned into a bit of a hermit. Loud, bucolic public events only reinforced the pain of my solitude. They also aggravated my tinnitus.

I gazed at the cheerful invitation. This was a charity event. A good cause. And how long had it been since I attended something that was fun?

As a new teacher, I decided it would be best to attend, so I pulled my black Carla Zampatti dress out of my suitcase. It still fitted me. Just. With the help of my black tummy flattening panties and black lacey underwire bra.

I appraised myself in my cottage's full-length mirror. Apart from the unwelcome mass, I was looking more and more like my mother. The last time I wore this dress – well over fifteen years ago – I'd been at a dinner party with my ex and some of his colleagues. I recalled the moment the conversation segued into murder and domestic violence, as dinner party conversations sometimes do. I turned to him and said, 'What about those times you've told me you're thinking of ways to bump me off?' I asked.

The table fell silent.

I smiled chirpily at the other guests and raised my glass of wine, toasting my husband. My inhibitions loosened; I was a little tipsy. 'Here are our witnesses. If something happens to me, you will be the prime suspect.'

I said it half-jokingly, using the same tone he used when he said he was thinking of hiring a contract killer or telling me to commit suicide.

Around the dinner table, a swift subject change followed awkward smiles and uncomfortable snickers.

Our drive home that night was equally memorable. I sobered

up fast. 'You are so fucking *stupid*. What the hell did you think you were doing talking about our marriage, our private stuff at the dinner table?' he hissed.

I regarded his hands gripping the wheel – beautiful hands – a pianist's long fingers on a man who played with money for a living. I hesitated, feeling that lean and tall man next to me bending like a willow in the wind of his rage. A single butterfly breath from me might make him snap.

'It was a joke. You know – just like the way you joke about bumping me off.'

He didn't reply. Those big grey eyes I'd once fallen in love with took on an unhinged look. He ran a hand through his thinning mane of lion-yellow hair and swore under his breath. 'Fucking bitch.'

I realised then that not only wasn't I behaving like a proper wife, I also wasn't behaving like a proper victim.

While viciously deployed words were his arsenal of favour, another strategy he used was festering silence. He began to drive erratically, screaming too fast around corners. He even drove through a red light.

Thinking of Sophia, orphaned at the age of eight, I told him to slow down – an invitation, of course, for him to tell me to fuck off. He drove even more recklessly.

Not a word was needed for me to know he was furious enough to kill.

Luckily it was late and the traffic was light.

We didn't go to many more corporate dinners after that. On those increasingly rare occasions, he made a point of deploying crucifying post-mortems. I was always embarrassing. I talked too much or wore too much makeup, showed too much leg or cleavage. I drank too much. And if I ever showed even a hint of flirtation or spent too much time in conversation with another man, he would fly into a rage afterwards, looking for reasons to belittle me.

I see it so clearly now. It was all about control. He was always right. I was always wrong. But at the time, I still loved him. He was the father of my child. The provider of my material security. My husband.

And then, one day, he hit me.

I should have immediately taken Sophia and run. But I wanted to keep things civilised. I excused him. I'd antagonised him. I had slapped his face after he called me a cunt. He had retaliated. It was my fault.

Instead, I took on a secret, other life. I read about domestic violence. Visited a counsellor.

As predicted in the self-help books I'd read, his aggression escalated. After I woke one night to find him hovering above me with a pillow ('it's your fucking snoring!' he said) after he tried to run over me in the driveway, claiming it was an 'accident,' after he threw some hot minestrone soup he didn't like at me (soup was off the menu after that), I found a lawyer, a small rental. Along with a modest inheritance I eventually used to buy my post-divorce semi, one of the gifts my mother gave me was a hard nose when it came to money. She was a widow and had to be tough – particularly when my father's life insurance company tried to wriggle out of paying up. 'Money can't buy you happiness, but it can buy you freedom,' she once told me. 'Manage your money and you can manage your life.' And then I still married a man who considered the management of money – even money I had earned – male territory. What a fuckup.

When I tried to negotiate the terms of our financial separation, custody arrangements and my release from our marriage, my ex wept and yelled and punched his fist through the pantry door, all while Sophia – far too young to understand what was going on – looked on, wide-eyed with horror. 'Take all my money!' He wailed, ripping the notes from his wallet, scattering coins across the hall's wooden floor. He looked at little Sophia. 'Your mother is a greedy bitch!' Then, he locked himself in the bathroom, sobbed convulsively and threw bottles of hair care products at the walls. 'You're taking my daughter from me!'

It certainly wasn't a performance worthy of an Oscar. It was so over the top he would've been laughed out of the audition. And behaving like that in front of his young child? Inexcusable. After he stormed from the house, I spent the next hours comforting Sophia, making light of his drama as together we picked coins out of the cracks in the floorboards and wiped shampoo and conditioner off the bathroom tiles.

To his credit (which in hindsight, just goes to show how much my expectations had been lowered) beyond that tantrum, he didn't try to imprison me or stalk me. He didn't try to kill me. By that point, he already had someone else lined up to take my place. Someone who believed his story about the hard, cold bitch who took off with his child and his money. After all, my ex had no trouble making friends, enticing lovers. He could play the wounded, vulnerable man with just the right amount of nuance and delicacy. Publicly, he was a man of charm, humility and intelligence. Privately, he was vicious, manipulative and insane.

Feeling like an antique riddled with the borer of life's defeats, I slipped into my pair of twenty-year-old black suede evening shoes. There hadn't been much need for glamour since my abdication from the role of corporate wife.

Once upon a time, I'd loved to dress up. Before the tumult of divorce and the subsequent soul searching, I subscribed to the adage that a woman should dress to please a man, that she should be demure or sexy depending on the circumstances (again, to please a man.) Written into my subconscious, branded into me by a European mother who believed that reputation and social status and good grooming – brushed shoes and well-pressed clothes – as well as a reputable man by my side – were the roots of happiness and the foundation stones of civilisation, I tried to please. I frequently failed. My mother only wanted what was best for me. She had, after all, flourished in her marriage until it came to an abrupt end at a North Shore beach. I tried to have a happy marriage. I tried until it nearly killed me.

One last time, I surveyed myself in the mirror. This was a haunted dress. But I liked it and it had been dry cleaned. A pair of long, flamboyant earrings dangling from my lobes, anticipating a room full of gorgeous men, I sashayed from my cottage. This was the new me. Independent. Sassy. There was a Goddess in me somewhere. All it took was a redistribution of mass.

CHAPTER SEVEN

Hothouse Flowers

Day Three – Evening

On my way to the fundraiser, I stopped at the main desk. I had given Sophia the retreat's phone number in case of emergencies and wanted to check for messages.

When I arrived, a woman somewhere in her seventies with close-cropped grey hair and an overnight bag by her feet stood at the desk looking disgruntled.

'What happened to him?' The woman complained. 'He was my favourite!'

'He has moved on to other employment,' the receptionist calmly replied.

The woman looked irritated. 'He never even called me,' she muttered as she grabbed her key and overnight bag.

I watched her turn towards the stairs opposite the reception desk. The top story of this main building had rooms rented out on a nightly basis – hotel rooms for people passing through. Although where they were passing through from or to, I had no idea. Yindisha wasn't exactly near a main thoroughfare. She flounced up the stairs, two at a time, sprightly for someone of her age. And I casually wondered if some of the guests were coming to the retreat just to sleep with the men. *Gigolo School*, I thought.

The receptionist checked my records. ' No messages for you,' he said. ' No news is good news,' he added cheerily.

Staring hard into his eyes, I smiled back. A faint alarm bell rang deep inside me as I regarded the whites of his eyes – bright and clear, just like Mathias. My gaze dropped to the mauve and green carpet, patterned with waratahs and eucalypts. In times of confusion, I am comforted by patterns. I seek them out. And luckily for me there are patterns everywhere – in nature, in science, and therefore, in art – those transcriptions of the natural and unnatural world.

It occurred to me there was – despite their apparent racial diversity – an unnatural similarity among the men which implied, rather than natural variation, intelligent design. It was, among other things such as their similar gaits and physiques, in the whites of their eyes. Not a single vein broke the surface of those pearled surfaces. They all had orthodontist-even teeth. They all had attractive, low and modulated and occasionally husky voices. Deep under the men's superficial differences and variations, there was a pattern, as if they had all been shaped from the same template. *Androids?* this reader of science fiction, this middle-aged woman with an over-active imagination, thought to herself. And then, I recalled that triumphant Gnostics lecturer speaking of how archaic knowledge once dismissed as ignorance and superstition was now in the hands of those who understood its power. So, who was *really* in power around here? The men? Or the women? Or something or someone else?

Potted palms and urns of flowers flossed the ballroom. 'Spring' from Vivaldi's Four Seasons piped from speakers discretely hidden in the foliage. I inhaled an intoxicating fragrance of ginger and lemongrass. A heavy red curtain was drawn across the stage. It transpired the fundraiser was an auction. But for what, at this point, I had no idea. New guests had arrived, all women, all dressed up in their finest. A few men served virgin cocktails and mingled with the women. Uncomfortable in crowds, I retreated to the least populated corner of the hall near a table of nibbles and joined my student Loose Judith, who was in conversation (and, I could tell, discretely salivating) with a blond surfie type called Steve. He was telling her about his background, how he was born in Darwin and hated the heat. He was studying horticulture and was helping with Yindisha's gardens. Eventually, he hoped to move to Sydney and run his own gardening business.

We were discussing how expensive it was to live in Sydney when Galilea strode onto the stage at the front of the hall and tapped on the microphone. Elegantly dressed in pressed black linen pants and a high-collared white silk shirt, I wondered again at the contradiction of this woman with the liver-spotted hands who dressed like a puritan and shagged her much younger personal assistant.

Warmly, she welcomed us all – the current guests, the new guests and the employees. Following a brief introduction to the retreat, its focus on both our physical and spiritual well-being, its philosophy of sustainability, zero carbon footprints and a reconnection with our true selves, her eyes lit with evangelistic flames. 'This is the future. *We* are the future. Strong women and men...' she paused, regarding the room. '...*Good* men by our sides. Companions in this creation of a new, healthier more sustainable way of life.'

She spoke of the current political climes, the mindset of conquests, competition, of disrespect for diversity, of government interference, mistrust, and paranoia.

'All this must cease,' she said. 'We are better than that. Wiser than that.'

Claps rose through the hall like hail on a tin roof.

She spoke of the systemic oppression of women and how we were still oppressed. 'Here, we are working to redress those injustices and imbalances,' she added. 'We must change the system. Instead of simply trying to succeed in a hierarchical system perpetrated by men, we must feminise the world.'

I glanced at the men, smiling and nodding in assent. There was not a single disgruntled masculine face in sight. Where the hell had Galilea found such *compliant* recruits? I wondered.

'We must place as much value on compassion as we do on innovation and technological progress. Countries must focus on happiness as much as productivity. Continued economic growth in the form of gross domestic product is neither a healthy measure of a country's wealth nor a future option for society or our planet,' she continued.

She paused. Jock stepped forward and handed her a glass of water. The audience waited in silence while she thanked him and sipped.

'Now, there's only one way to mitigate the damage we have already done to this planet,' she continued. 'Women must be in charge economically, emotionally and spiritually. It is the only hope for Mother Earth.'

She paused again and inhaled. A severe look in her eyes, she regarded the women and raised a scolding finger. 'No more pandering to outdated patriarchal systems. Yindisha is about change.'

More claps and cheers and titters of approval followed.

Then, she addressed the men. 'And good men must be role models for other men. Toxic masculinity has no place in Yindisha's new world order.'

'Hear, hear,' said Surfie Steve. I glanced at a few of the other men nodding eagerly.

Although I had no quibbles about her talk, I wondered how the men really, truly felt about playing such subservient roles in this matriarchal theatre. And a *new world order?* Surely underneath all that polite compliance lurked at least a little resentment? Surely among all these men were a few bastards and imposters who wanted to see Galilea and women like her disarmed or even dead?

The curtains behind Galilea parted to reveal a band of musicians. As this was Luddite Land, there was not a synthesizer or electric instrument in sight. The piano had been moved onto the stage. There was a guitarist, drummer, violinist, trombonist, flautist. All men. All divine.

Galilea stepped off the stage. The lights dimmed. Murmurs of anticipation rippled through the audience as an elegant, shadowy figure appeared and sauntered towards the microphone. A spotlight roamed across the stage, stopping here and there: on a musician, a pot plant, the edge of the mysterious figure's trousers. The light, in its taunting glimpses, revealed enough for the audience to realise the figure was male.

The spotlight switched off and in semi-darkness the musicians began to play the opening lines to 'Halleluiah.' Out of the blackness, an angelically beautiful masculine voice rose and soared. The voice touched the heavens and moved the earth beneath the audience's feet. What a breathless wonder! Who or what was the owner of this divine voice?

When the song reached its peak, the figure emerged under the spotlight like an unfolding dawn. Like a revelation. The audience gasped. I doubt there was – in that room – an expanse of skin without goose-bumps. Not only could he sing but he was perfect, the epitome of male beauty. Gentle green eyes, sumptuous lips, licks of tawny hair sat above a high forehead and chiselled cheekbones. Gasps of pleasure blew through the audience. He finished the song with sunbursts of trills, starbursts of staccatos that sent us into a frenzy of exuberant clapping.

I took in his humble bow, his wide, generous, toothsome smile of thanks and swooned. Why was he here at Yindisha Retreat?

Why wasn't he singing for Australian Idol or some other high-ratings fame-hunting program? I realised my question had provided its own answer. This man was not hunting fame, nor looking to burnish his ego. He simply wanted to sing and to please. *Impossible,* I thought. This man, these men, were just too good to be true. They were hothouse flowers. They would neither survive nor thrive in the real world. *Unless...*

I thought of those radio waves my father studied, those invisible forces that weave around the earth and sing their elusive messages from the heavens.

Aliens?

The impossibility of it all descended over me as though I was losing consciousness and falling into a dream.

He sang four more songs, each a demonstration of his range, his capacity to be divine, raunchy, sincere, erudite and loving. His eyebrows rose and fell with exquisite expressiveness, dispatching humour, empathy and passion into the hall. The audience swooned. I swooned. While he sang, nothing in the world existed except that beautiful man and his magical voice. Every woman in that hall was in love. Mesmerised and struck into silence by his otherworldly harmonies.

After a finale that swelled the audience into another round of clapping and cheers, hearts sank as the light waned and shrunk, until all that remained was the incandescent pearl of his smile. It hovered, seemingly in mid-air before vanishing, along with its owner, into the shadows. A hush descended.

Once more Galilea appeared – a disappointment after that beautiful man attached to that sublime voice. 'As some of you may have guessed, you are bidding for the singer.'

Murmurs fed through the crowd as Zane reappeared, grinning generously.

'Whoever wins Zane will have him as their personal butler all weekend. He will be at your beck and call.'

The music and that singer's succulent beauty had the same effect as wine at art openings. Inhibitions were loosened. Open wallets followed. And here, in this ocean of estrogen, every participant was intoxicated. Enchanted.

The bidding started at one hundred dollars and quickly escalated. Loose Judith flung up her hand, offering eight hundred.

The sprightly, grey-haired new guest I had seen earlier at the reception desk countered with a bid of one thousand.

I observed all this in a frozen state of detachment. The bidding was already well beyond my budget.

Yet those bids still came thick and fast, stalling at two thousand. Everyone chuckled magnanimously when Steve made a bid. He pushed the bidding up to over three thousand dollars.

Loose Judith bid with increasing vigour. She had a hungry look about her. I thought of her vigorous charcoal strokes in class today and imagined the energy she displayed wasn't just confined to drawing.

Again, that grey-haired senior countered Judith's bid.

Eventually, Loose Judith won, donating five thousand dollars to the women's refuge.

The room erupted into a chorus of whoops and cheers. The tinnitus in my right ear shrieked in protest.

I nibbled on a rice cracker, watching Loose Judith stride to the stage to claim her prize. The retreat had our credit card numbers so there was no backing out.

I regarded that perfect, singing sculpture of a man. My questions niggled. My ear rang like a siren. Some things were just too good to be true. There were things about Yindisha I wasn't being told.

But there was no secret about what Loose Judith wanted. Tonight, she was going to have sex.

CHAPTER EIGHT

Fachidiot

Day Four

Three extra women joined Saturday's class. I now had a total of eight students. Mary Nader had not sabotaged my class. Instead, she was back, looking as innocent as ever, as if she knew nothing, or didn't care about my encounter with her husband.

Reassured, I began my class by telling my students that often when it comes to artistic expression, we are our own worst enemies. We criticize ourselves before we have even started, tell ourselves we are hopeless. We become fearful of that blank page or canvas in front of us. That first mark, that first soiling of the virgin surface, is usually the most terrifying. But once we have defiled that waiting expanse, the creative journey can begin. And after all, isn't life an art form? Life doesn't come with a manual and troubleshooting section. We are human. We all make mistakes. Even as we dream of perfection.

When I say such things to my students, I am also reminding myself of that terror of facing something new. Our fears become self-fulfilling prophecies. We allow what we fear to destroy us.

We submit to the darkness. Yet every moment we move through existence and touch the world is an act of creation. An adventure. I told my students they all had the potential to be excellent artists. It was all about attitude. Confidence.

My students drank in my words as though I was a sage. For a few hours, I kept my inner flagellant at bay. After all, if the whole truth be told, moving through the world can also be an act of destruction.

After loosening up exercises which involved wild charcoal scribblings on pieces of butcher's paper, I started the new students off shading circles and platonic cubes. I directed yesterday's students to the still life in the middle of the room. It comprised flowers I'd been given permission to pick from the resort gardens and some fruit – apples and bananas – I had purloined from the breakfast table.

'Fill the page. Start with the whole composition before moving on to the details,' I reminded my students as I watched Frightened Mary back to her old habits – still struggling to loosen up, retreating to a corner of the page. 'That may be the apple of knowledge,' I quipped to her as she zeroed in on one of the still life's apples, 'but today, we're focusing on the whole fruit bowl of wisdom.'

'I'm just so hopeless at this,' Mary sighed as she reached for her eraser.

'No,' I replied. 'You are not. Don't undermine yourself. I once felt like you, but I persevered.'

I sat beside her and showed her how to work with the positive and negative spaces, cheering her on as her gestures became broader and more confident. Her face lit up as she took control of her page.

Of course, several of the guests who had attended last night's auction wanted an account of Loose Judith's first night with the delectable Zane.

'Was he good in bed?' asked a new guest who had been one of last night's bidders.

Loose Judith rolled her eyes. 'He was adequate,' she replied. 'I've had better. I've had worse.'

'So, he wasn't as good at sex as he was at singing,' the unsuccessful bidder – whose name was Olivia – persisted.

Loose Judith gave the room a big-toothed wide-mouthed grin. She turned her still-life sketch to face us, pointing to, amidst the proportionally accurate sketch, the tiny banana.

The room shook with guffaws. Mary Nader's chin dropped closer to her drawing, a smile of tolerance twitching her lips.

'It could be worse,' replied Olivia, now looking vaguely pleased she'd lost last night's bid. 'He could have been watching television all the time. Drinking beer. Playing with himself.'

To which Loose Judith reminded her that not only were devices and alcohol banned at the retreat, he was also supposed to be her *butler*. 'He's not too good at that either,' she added. 'Although he sings while he works.'

All of us except Mary Nader laughed. During the conversation, she'd regressed and was now back carefully shading her apple.

Somewhere between my stomach and heart, a dark gap opened. Chasing away that black place where it seemed something wanted to take root, I told my students a German word my mother had taught me. *Fachidiot*. She used it sometimes to describe my father – a man of great intellect so absorbed in his science, he would sometimes forget basic tasks like returning milk to the fridge or putting the dirty cups that piled up in his office into the dishwasher. He was hopeless at supermarket shopping (but he always came back with chocolate for me), awkward around guests and occasionally, even forgot to zip up his fly.

'They are people who have extremely specialised knowledge, but know nothing of life's practicalities,' I added. 'The word loosely translates as: 'knowledge idiot.'

Several women chuckled, saying they knew men like that who were lucky to have practical women in their lives.

While I agreed, adding my mother had been one such woman, I didn't mention that my father had been so impractical he had swum beyond the flags and drowned. I didn't mention I'd inherited his absent-mindedness, his *fachidiocy*, but not his magnificent scientific brain.

Out of the corner of my eye, I saw Mary, her face tight, hunching over her drawing, still darkly shading her apple.

Once more I reminded her to consider the whole picture and not just the apple. Sensing her fragility, I spoke gently. 'I know it can be hard to change deeply ingrained habits, Mary. But use this opportunity to go a little wild. Have some fun. Make your apple *sing*.'

Oh, how little I knew back then. When she gave me a tired, hopeless look, I thought how some people – when confronted with an insurmountable problem – focus on something small and manageable. I reminded myself that everyone has their own style and perhaps Mary was one of those artists who wanted her work to marinate in the heavy shadows of melancholy. Deciding to let her tackle her still life and that apple in her own way, I turned from her, niggled by a half-formed thought.

Briefly, the class discussed Yindisha's good-looking men. Apart from acknowledging the retreat's fastidious recruitment policy, no one seemed excessively curious or had any alternate explanations. The guests were all happy. A surfeit of polite, respectful and beautiful men was not something to complain about.

I thought of my ex. He had been beautiful too. Outwardly, at least. That dark spot between my stomach and heart throbbed and ached.

When Loose Judith used the phrase 'Eco-feminist' to describe Yindisha Retreat's ideology, I noticed Frightened Mary wince as if she'd been slapped.

Near the end of the class, someone's mobile phone rang.

'Who's violating the digital detox rules?' Loose Judith snapped.

'I'm sorry,' Mary replied, pulling her phone from her handbag, colour draining from her cheeks. 'My husband has been away at an Anglican Bishop's conference. He doesn't know I'm here. He must've come home early.'

I heard panic in her voice. Swiftly, she packed up, grabbed her handbag and rushed from the class, apologising once more to me and looking pale as she bustled out the door.

I called to her. 'Tomorrow, Mary, we are going to start on colour!'

She turned and gave me a grey, sorry look. And I knew in that second, she wouldn't be back. And deep down inside, another part of me knew exactly why. It came to me then. I saw the whole picture. Once, I had behaved just like Frightened Mary.

CHAPTER NINE

The DNA
of the Soul

Day Four (late afternoon)

Disconcerted by Mary's hasty retreat, I had just finished tidying up the art room following the departure of my students, when I noticed a small dark square underneath a storage cupboard. It was a wallet. I opened it to identify the owner. It belonged to Mary Nader. She'd been sitting near the cupboard and must have, in her panic to grab her mobile phone, knocked it from her handbag. In addition to a picture of her husband looking holy, respectable and approachable, photographs of Mary's two young adult children – one on each side of the open wallet – looked out at me. She'd talked about them fondly in our first class when we all introduced ourselves. Her son was studying law and commerce at Australian National University in Canberra. Her daughter, in her last year of high school, was boarding at a school for young ladies in Sydney. My heart squeezed as I gazed at those groomed children – beautiful in that bloom of youth. But their eyes told me another story. I'd seen those same hard, hurt flames deep in Sophia's eyes. I wrestled with my imaginings. Was I – a damaged woman – reading too much into those expressions? My gut told me no. These children were, underneath those benign smiles, confused, hurt and angry.

So, I dug deeper. I am inquisitive (*a nosey bitch* – to once more quote my ex). Amid the usual collection of cards which included a Medicare card and driver's license with Mary's address at the Watson village rectory, buried deep in a pocket under her card-holders, I found a business card from Relationships Australia in Sydney. I flicked it over. She had been to an appointment just last month.

There it was. The answer. Deep in my marriage troubles, I had also (secretly) resorted to the counselling services of Relationships Australia. The councillor gave me some tools for managing my rocky marriage. Our marriage temporarily improved. My behaviour changed. But his behaviour didn't. As far as he was concerned, *I* was the problem.

I thought of Mary's heavily shaded apple, her fidelity to the boundaries of the shape, her respect for the source of light, but her obsession with the heaviness of shadow. Her drawing spoke of complete and utter obedience to form. I thought of her husband – the splendidly presented, most holy Reverend Quentin Nader – and that day I first met him with his bag of stakes for Mary's garden. I knew the script. Ostentatiously generous in public, the husband makes a point of being seen to support and adore his wife. Men are impressed by his status and his apparently happy marriage. Women envy his wife. But some women – women like me – know it is all just an act. Underneath all that magnanimity lives another creature – a creature that in private, in the secrecy of one's own home, is a complete and utter bastard.

I stared at that card. Was I reading too much into this? Was my wounded self and my far too active imagination over-reacting again?

No. My hand shook. I thought of Mary's panic when her phone rang, the look of terror in her eyes when she saw the caller ID. I thought of her panic when she discovered her wallet – that important piece of herself – with its secret – was missing. I knew how she felt. The bastard's wife must always be at his beck and call. She must never fall from grace. She must never make mistakes. That is his expectation of marriage.

I rose from my knees and marched to the door. I had to return Mary Nader's wallet immediately.

He doesn't know I'm here.

Mary's words kept snapping into my thoughts as I raced down the bush-flanked gravel pathway that led to Watson. I'd worked out I could be there within twenty minutes and back in time for dinner. Mary told me she had bicycled to the retreat and I could see fresh tracks on the path. My greatest hope was I would catch up with her before she even realised her wallet was missing and certainly before she reached home and husband. Even though my legs were no competition for a fearful, cycling woman desperate to reach home, I sped up my pace.

He doesn't know I'm here. It was the way Mary said those words as much as the words themselves. She was frightened he would find out she had visited Yindisha – even worse – attended a class. Mary Nader, who had desperately embraced a few hours of freedom, was now trying to avoid her husband's wrath. Again, I wondered if I were reading too much into her words. Damaged as I am – I see the world through the lens of my very particular pain and persecution. *No*, I told myself. My suspicions were correct. After my own experience, I notice signs and patterns the oblivious might miss. Reverend Nader was another wife abuser.

Under no circumstances could I let the cat out of the bag by arriving at the front door with a big smile and handing her wallet to her husband – who would probably – as the man of the house – answer the door. Mary would want to keep her visit to Yindisha a secret. I realised as I jogged, the situation was going to be tricky. I had to work out a way to find Mary alone and hand her wallet over in private. I didn't want to get her in trouble. And, as I thought that, my heart bent as I recalled the number of times my husband had berated me for the tiniest misdemeanours. Married to him, I was always in trouble.

I was out of breath and my heart was pounding by the time I reached that pretty, hydrangea-flossed path that led to the rectory.

I walked down the path, a part of me still hoping my suspicions were wrong.

When the house – a grand sandstone and brick residence that was probably as old as the village – came into view, my stomach knotted. I crept towards a soaring oak overshadowing the front veranda. A window was open and inside, I heard a chastising man's voice.

'If you had some important event to attend, I would support *you*,' he said. 'I would be there for you, waiting with a nice hot dinner when you got home!'

Ah, yes. The derailing strategy. The man makes himself sound as though he is supportive, feminist even. But the truth is, nothing is more important than him, and he will engineer his household to ensure everything revolves around his needs. An important event demanding his wife's attendance is pure illusion. Nothing will ever match his grandeur.

'I wouldn't be off on some bush walk away with the fairies, so lost in my indulgent, ungodly thoughts that I forgot the time!'

As I suspected. Mary hadn't told her husband she had been at an art class at Yindisha Retreat. And he hadn't told her about our encounter in Watson General Store. This was a marriage of secrets and recriminations.

I heard Mary reply. 'I didn't forget the time. You were home early.'

I held on to the tree as if it were an anchor. Answering back. Never a good idea.

His voice rose. 'I was home early because I had a sermon to write for tomorrow. Some of us have important work. Some of us have a community to serve!'

'I'm sorry,' said Mary.

'When you are disobedient, you dishonour me and you dishonour our faith!'

'I'm sorry,' Mary repeated.

Cringing behind that tree, I began to feel sick. I had said sorry so many times in my marriage. Sorry for my mistakes. Sorry I have upset you. Sorry I exist.

'Stop saying sorry!' His voice rose. 'Sorry is no excuse for carelessness! I am serving God and you, as my wife, are serving *me*! You should have been here when I got home!'

My stomach clenched. I had heard words, or words like this so many times throughout the twelve years of my marriage. The message behind them is always the same: 'Behold my munificence!' the husband crows from his perch of male righteousness. 'And what are *you* doing worm of the earth? While I toil and do good work, you leech and sponge. You use our credit card to buy silly, womanly things. You gossip with your friends about nothing and complain about everything. You stupid woman. You foolish piece of frippery. You are lucky to have me. You are lucky I tolerate you because no one else would want you.'

Again, I heard that so-called reverend, that patronizing shit's voice. 'I will be in my office.' Call me when dinner is ready.'

A door slammed.

My opportunity had come. I made my move.

Mary would be in the kitchen preparing a dish which probably wouldn't meet her husband's satisfaction. Even you are a brilliant cook, your husband – perhaps a frequent restaurant-diner – like mine – will find flaws in the temperature, the ingredients, the way in which it wasn't made with enough love. Occasionally, he will even choke dramatically and accuse you of trying to poison him. 'Your cooking is *awful*,' he will say.

I drew a fortifying breath. I had a wallet to return.

I crept out from behind that tree and tried to move in the opposite direction of the sound of that slam. I had to find the kitchen and a back door.

Like a thief in the night, I crept past a fragrant border of gardenias. Such a pretty rectory garden, protecting such a dreadful secret.

Fortunately for both of us, Mary Nader stepped outside the back door, heading for her vegetable garden just as I navigated my way across the lawn.

She jumped when she saw me, put a hand over her heart as if I had given her the most terrible fright. That's another thing constant abuse does. It makes you permanently terrified.

I held out my offering. 'Your wallet,' I quietly said. 'I found it.'

I didn't say where or when. Who knew whether this garden had ears?

She bustled over to me, quickly took the wallet. 'Thank you. I didn't even know it was missing.'

I smiled with relief. That had been one less thing for her to worry about. I noticed the way she stood – shoulders hunched as if protecting her heart. I once stood like that too.

'I'm sorry,' she said, her eyes darting to the back door, clearly terrified her husband might suddenly appear and demand to know who she was speaking to. 'I'm very busy at the moment. I can't talk.'

Her voice sounded shrill and shaky.

'I know you can't, Mary.' I kept my voice low. I caught that sparrow of a woman's frightened eyes. 'I understand.'

I turned to leave and stopped. I couldn't leave without offering some kind of support. *Interfering bitch.* My ex's words slammed into my thoughts.

'Your husband doesn't know you've been at Yindisha Retreat, does he?'

Frightened Mary paled, glancing from her vegetable garden towards her back door, her hand tensely winding the edge of her apron into a tight spiral. 'No.'

I gave her a soft look. 'Your secret is safe with me. If you need to talk, you know where to find me.'

She looked right then as if she were about to fall apart. Her eyes turned watery and her lower face puckered as if she could barely contain the words she wanted to say.

And I wanted to cry as well. I wanted to take her in my arms and say *I understand. I understand. Mary, you have to leave.* But I knew she couldn't. Her husband was a pillar of the community. What chance did this humble, bullied woman have against the word and unsullied reputation of her Godly husband? What chance did she have against her husband and his imaginary friend?

'Thank you,' she managed. 'I need to go,' she added already turning towards her vegetable garden, the tomatoes, bright, plump and red on their stakes.

My heart somewhere near my shoes, I quickly left before I got Mary into trouble.

Evening fell and the bush flanking the path seethed with dank shadows. Thinking of Mary, I walked back to Yindisha Retreat in a black rage. I knew from personal experience it was hard to help a woman who was being abused. Mary Nader wanted to hide her secret because she was both ashamed and afraid.

The abuser feeds on this shame and fear with the relish of a wolf devouring fresh kill. And, even though he has driven you into this cringing state of existence, he will hate you for being an apologetic worm. You – the besieged wife – are, after all, his warped creation. And he hates you – his creation – because deep down, below the surface of his thoughts where his shrivelled conscience still shows faint signs of life – he hates himself. He feels shame. But he hates and fears his shame and masks it with fury. And so, once more, his raging sense of entitlement regains its dominion. His shame is deflected back on to you. *That* is his definition of intimacy.

I imagined taking that so-called Reverend by the throat and trying to shake some kindness and humility into him. But a man like that cannot be shaken. Image is everything. His certitude must be rock-solid. His belief in himself must be beyond reproach. And – Reverend Nader – that man of the cloth – had God on his side. Just as my ex had the world of big business and big money on his side. Money and God. The two unshakable male powers that still rule the world.

My heart bled for poor Mary. My heart bled for her children. Those beautiful souls, their eyes holding those angry secrets.

When I first left my marriage, my ex used our daughter Sophia as collateral. Eight-year-old Sophia still adored her daddy. She hadn't yet learned to answer back and challenge him. For a long time, I was the evil parent in the equation – the enemy who had torn the family apart. On top of a marriage breakup, I had to carefully negotiate with an angry daughter who parroted her father's words. I was a bad mother, a terrible mother. A greedy, lying bitch. For a time, she even thought that was my other name. *Bitch*, she would say, looking at me guilelessly, *Bitch*.

But I knew the time would come when he would turn on our child.

Meanwhile, I consulted enough counsellors, lawyers and friends to understand that without physical evidence of mistreatment – wounds and physical bruises – emotional damage is invisible. I had no evidence to petition for full custody. I was also warned by several wise and experienced professionals about involving the family court system where I would be branded as the conniving, vindictive parent and full custody would probably be awarded to my ex. Instead, I had to take the long-term view, build self-esteem in my daughter and help her understand the emotional and physical boundaries beyond which an abusive parent must not step. In the meantime, as if I harboured some virulent virus, he barred me from entering what had once been the marital home and, when he dropped Sophia off at my rental, mocked my 'cockroach infested shack' and did everything he could to turn Sophia's heart.

Biting my tongue and regularly wishing him gone from the world, I remained on high alert, watching for behaviour changes in my daughter, preparing for the moment I knew would come when she answered back, challenged her father and was punished for her insolence and spirit.

My body ached with resurrected pains. Damage like this never goes away. These invisible wounds hide inside the DNA of the soul. Patterns repeat.

Somewhere in the distance, an animal wailed into the waning light. My jaw cramped. I thought of the way Galilea had introduced me to Reverend Nader and her facetious comments. She knew, or at least suspected he was not the man he pretended to be.

My ex had not been the man he pretended to be either. Charming in public, emotionally violent in private, the abuser needs the complicity of the woman who loves him. Intimacy is for the abuser, an opportunity to filter his rage. In the last years of my marriage, I had agonising stomach pains which turned out to be stones in my gall-bladder. In Chinese medicine, the gall-bladder is called the body's Minister of Justice. How long before sparrow-brown, hunted and Frightened Mary became physically ill? Perhaps she already had something malignant growing inside her. Perhaps *her* gall bladder was also full of stones.

Pausing under a black bough overhanging the road like a giant reaching hand, I realised I was grinding my teeth. I could no longer see my feet. Engulfed in darkness, again, I thought of Mary the sparrow. Mary the prey.

Surrounded by angry shadows, I balled my fists. Why do women – or at least women like me – feel so vulnerable alone in the bush? I glanced up at the sky still starless in the dying day. Ever since my marriage breakup, I'd been afraid of the dark. You get like that when you know someone wants to destroy you.

Alone in that pocket of darkness, my rage warped into fear. I'd been in such a rush to return Mary's wallet I hadn't collected my phone on the way out of the retreat. If I fell, if there was an emergency, I wouldn't be able to ring 000. Out here, I could just vanish into the wilderness to never be seen again. I thought of the police interviews, Sophia desperately trying to find me. Mary Nader would be an unreliable witness. She wouldn't want anyone to know I visited her in case it made her husband angry.

I paused for a moment listening to the sighs of the bush, the frenetic twittering of birds settling down for the night. I needed to pee.

Edging to the side of the path, I dropped my pants. Mid-pee, I stopped. Held my breath. Something or someone was watching. I could hear breathing.

The long grass flanking the path restlessly shuffled. I felt a sinister something curdle the night air into menacing whorls of evil. My heart galloped. Swiftly, I yanked up my pants and stood upright.

My heart palpitating, my gore rose into my throat. My bellow shattered the stillness. 'Come out of your hiding place, you coward!'

An exhalation of breath replied. I drew in a deep intake of the night air. 'I'm not afraid of you, you *fucking moron*!'

Panicking, I looked around for a rock or stick to use as protection. But all I could see under my feet was evenly swept gravel. Not a stone in sight. Only boulders flanking the road and far too heavy for me to lift. Too big, too small... All around me vines strangled the bush.

To my right, I heard a violent crackle of dried leaves. My heart jumped to my throat. I stood frozen, my fists still balled, my body tight. The tinnitus in my right ear wailed like a police siren.

The sound of snapping twigs and crunching undergrowth faded. Whatever it was, it was large enough to make a racket as it retreated.

I stood for a moment, trying to calm my heart, my ear still ringing. Why was I so terrorised by nature, wildlife and the darkness? Why could I not embrace the beauty and magic of this glorious night? The answer was as old as human civilisation. I was afraid of men. I was afraid of rape. That threat of violence curtailed me, cautioned me about stepping beyond society's prescribed boundaries. It was the existential equivalent of the glass ceiling – a glass box that imprisoned me, disconnected me from my inherent wildness, my freedom, my true untethered self.

And oh, the irony of my marriage, that my protector – the man I should have trusted most – was the man who made me feel most afraid.

I sped my pace. Under my feet, gravel noisily crunched. For my daughter's sake I had to survive. Master this irrational fear. Every few steps I stopped. Behind me, I thought I heard a rustle stop as well. I was sure that something out there was still following me.

I broke into a run.

Moments later, out of breath, I paused. Listened. Beyond my gasping I heard nothing but the evening songs of birds. The bush here was more groomed and open. Less unruly. Grevilleas and banksias flossed the path. In the distance, I saw the lights of Yindisha Retreat.

Wanting to be alone, I scuttled to my cottage and ordered room service. The man who delivered my light salad took one look at me and asked if I was all right. Brusquely, I thanked him for his concern and said I was fine.

After dinner, I visited the retreat's library. The lone man issuing and shelving the books would have looked more at home on a rugby field. He told me as he checked out my Robert Galbraith thriller, that he loved books and was enchanted by the Dewey system. He also asked me if I was all right. Yes, I replied again. Was my distress that obvious? Right then, I felt faintly annoyed by all those caring men, the apparent antithesis to men like my husband and Reverend Nader. I couldn't believe those men were being honest. I didn't trust their in-your-face friendliness. No one was nice for the sake of it. Yindisha's men had to have an agenda. Was it money? Good references? If this was Gigolo School, perhaps they were fine tuning their seduction strategies and we women were their test subjects. And had one of them been following me in the bush? Observing my behaviour?

With nothing better to do except read, I had an early night. Disturbed, and still wondering about Yindisha's men, I hovered on the cusp of sleep. Perhaps they wanted women's souls? I wondered as I dropped the book and fell into my dreams.

CHAPTER TEN

The Skewed Perspective

Day Five

I woke the next morning abruptly, recalling a fractured dream about muscley, submissive men, authoritarian woman and a righteous minister with glacier-blue eyes. Mary Nader had featured as well, quaking in the shadows of fire-scorched trees bent like crones.

My thoughts finally reassembling, I planned my day and made my way to the breakfast room which, to my relief, was empty. Afterwards, I browsed the breakfast room's notice board. The early morning guided bush walk I'd planned to go on had been cancelled due to 'unforeseen circumstances.' Another sign reminded guests to not go on unmarked trails alone because the bush around the retreat was dense and it was easy to get lost.

Recalling last night's walk, sensing something more behind that cursory warning, my insides squirmed. Was there a serial killer somewhere out here on the loose? The back office of my brain in a state of turmoil, I headed to reception to collect my phone.

Sophia and I had agreed we would chat at around eleven o'clock on Sunday mornings. Phone in hand, I stepped outside the retreat's gates so I wouldn't be violating the rules of digital detox.

I punched my password into my fully charged phone and heaved a sigh of relief. Finally. A chance to reconnect with the real world.

Sophia answered after the first two rings. Seeing her on FaceTime reassured me that everything was right with the world. She had my father's curly black hair, but her eyes – a beautiful hazel green – were all hers. How I loved those eyes.

Sophia told me she was enjoying her job. She had started dating someone called Dave. He was doing a PHD in computer science at ANU.

I was about to ask her how they met when she changed the subject, asking me how I was enjoying the retreat. I immediately told her about the impossibly beautiful, gracious men.

There was a long pause at the other end of the phone.

'Mum, not all men are arseholes like dad.'

I flinched. When Sophia was twelve, she told me he had grabbed her hair and pushed her when she had challenged his discipline and answered back. He told her she was turning into a bitch like her mother. After refusing to return to his place following one of my custody weekends, she never spoke to him again.

Over the following years, I'd told her – again and again – that her father was not a typical man, and there were beautiful, good men in the world.

Now she was boomeranging my words back at me.

'It's just there's something about them that doesn't feel right...' I bleated.

Another sigh from Canberra. And an eye-roll. 'Mum listen to yourself. You're feeling suspicious just because men are being nice to you? Get over it!'

I managed to laugh. Sophia was right. I'd spent too long married to that arsehole and now, my idea of normal was skewed.

Unable to resist the temptation to give mum a hard time, Sophia dug in harder. 'God, Mum, you're so paranoid!'

I gave in and agreed. I had been shocked, although not surprised, by Reverend Nader's treatment of his wife. Yet the respectful men at Yindisha Retreat disturbed me.

'Have some fun, Mum. Stop thinking so much and just enjoy yourself.'

I laughed again, telling her she sounded just like her mother.

We left on a good note, with me taking a good hard look at my ridiculous self.

Was I so hurt and damaged I was unable to recognise male sincerity and goodness when it poked me right in the eyeballs?

Of course, I didn't stop thinking. I didn't take my daughter's reconstituted and sage advice. An emotional hoarder attached to my inner rubbish – my brain was full of more waste than a landfill.

Like a wary toddler, I'd dipped my toes into the post-divorce dating world before squealing and scampering back to the beach of solitude. At my age, those slim pickings included divorced men with more baggage than a cargo ship, others who approached life with the philandering zeal of a bonobo, and others so brooding, silent and secretive they had to be porn addicts or serial killers in their spare time.

No. I wasn't going to deny myself my suspicions. Some kind of fakery lurked below the subservient charms of Yindisha's men. I wasn't being paranoid.

Besides, I thought as I climbed the main building's steps, Sophia was in love. She was young and full of dreams. *Her* perspective was skewed.

I marched through the mansion's grand, double doorway, trying to sweep all my emotional detritus aside. I had a class on colour to teach today. I had to pull myself together. Inside the retreat's well-stocked library, I hunted for some books on expressionism, symbolic imagery and the work of the Surrealists.

Armed with books about artistic illusions, I arrived at a class with everyone from yesterday present. Except Mary Nader. Again, I reminded myself to trust my instincts.

The Illusion
of Depth

Day Six

The following morning opened into a perfect, cobalt-blue-skied autumn day. After yesterday's class on the Fauvists, the Surrealists and the Dadaists, I felt as though something inside me had turned on its axis. Charged up by the morning's beauty, energised by the echoes of dreams I couldn't recall, I felt cheerful. Hopeful. Brave. Ready to change the world one brushstroke at a time.

At the civilised hour of eleven in the morning, after farewelling my predecessor Camilla and watching her depart for Melbourne in a white electric car with one of Yindisha's fine manly specimens, I was filled with optimism. My class and I – armed with canvases and portable easels – made our way to the lookout for a few hours of open-air painting.

Again, Mary Nader was absent. I ignored the squirm in my stomach and told myself to focus on the here and now. I had a class to teach. I would think of that poor woman later.

One of the retreat's men – a square-jawed, black-eyed fellow called Trevor – accompanied us. He carried a backpack with refreshments, water and spare paints and brushes and told us in a jocular tone that he was our Sherpa.

Resolving on this gorgeous day to follow Sophia's advice and to burn away those memories of my arsehole ex that continued to play havoc with my confidence, I was determined to focus only on the world's beauty and unearth my deeply buried independent, capable and assured self.

I told my students everything in life we see and feel is a matter of perspective. I spoke about optical illusions and how we can use colour to trick the eye. I expounded on the golden mean and the Fibonacci sequence in nature. Finding a patch of fading sunflowers, I was able to illustrate the sequence with the patterns of their seeds. I told my students about fractals, pointing to fern fronds unfolding in the undergrowth. As I spoke, I felt my closed inner landscape of fences and walls open up. I enthused. And there, in my words of exaltation and my infatuation with the natural world, I heard my mother's voice.

While my fascination with science comes courtesy of my father, my love of beauty comes from my mother. After the devastation of the war, that daughter of Germany found solace in nature. Wherever she lived, she planted trees – banksias, grevilleas, magnolias – forests of them. I drew in the beauty she had revealed to me, channelled her amazement and silently praised her. My heart filled with love.

When we arrived at the lookout, we all oohed and ahhed at the gorgeous view framed by orange and red flowering gums. It had rained overnight and the world had a freshly washed feel. White clouds fluffed the sky and a mist hung low in the valleys.

As we unpacked, I pointed to the distant, purple hills and explained the principle of areal perspective to my students; how the atmosphere dilutes colour and how we can use bright foreground colour and dilute background colour in our artwork to create the illusion of depth.

After he had helped us set up our easels, Trevor excused himself saying he was going to look for mushrooms and wildlife. 'Remember ladies,' he called to us as he departed into the bush, 'you are the hope of the world!'

We all giggled at his flattery, with someone mentioning wasn't it wonderful there were so many lovely men at Yindisha Retreat. Inhaling a waft of his aftershave, another student commented on how all Yindisha's men smelt the same. Stick-figure Saniya replied the retreat bulk-bought the stuff. Economies of scale, she explained before pointing into the bush and saying: 'Ooh! Did I just see a wallaby?'

We began to see patterns, beauty, wildlife everywhere. Imaginations were fired, small details pulled together to create new realities. I showed my class how to dilute their acrylics, starting with washes, then gradually building up the layers of paint. Spirits exalted in that painterly patch of paradise. Our creations took shape.

In the end, it was a casual anecdote that sent a black cloud across my thoughts.

As we paused for snacks, one student told us a story. She had made a wrong turn on her way to the retreat, she said. Instead of going to Watson, she drove straight ahead. About two kilometres along the road, she started seeing 'No Trespassing' and 'Restricted Area' signs. And then the road stopped at a boom gate. In the distance, between the trees, she saw a mesh fence topped with razor wire. She told us how a big, gormless-looking fellow who resembled the incredible hulk came over and told her she had to turn back. He told her it was a security area. When she asked him why, he said it was confidential.

'It's a government-owned agricultural research station,' said Stick-figure Saniya. 'They are doing studies into soil carbon capture.'

With a high, shaky voice, as if she were struggling to contain some inner turbulence, she pointed skywards asking if anyone could see familiar shapes in the clouds. We all looked up and forgot about the mystery of the research station. Later, I realised it was a skilled deflection deployed to avoid further speculation.

Something inside me pinged as I regarded Stick-figure Saniya's fragile beauty. Her black hair was so straight it looked as though she fastidiously took to it every morning with an iron. In addition to her lime-green fingernails, I noticed – in the bright light of day – her eyebrows were skilfully painted on.

I thought of illusions and how outward appearances can disguise inner turmoil. When I thought again of poor, abused Mary Nader, my joy evaporated, leaving behind a trail of doubt, sorrow and discontent.

The artist, as an observer, must always remain detached from the world, but so often, we fail to detach from ourselves. I spent the next hours teaching in a distracted way, thinking of that research station, and dwelling on Saniya's eyebrows, feeling as though I was avoiding facing something head-on because, despite the fact I was teaching others how to open up and see – *I* was the one with tunnel vision.

As I showed my students how to lighten their purples and blues to mimic atmospheric effects, I thought how, underneath the dilutions of distance, lurked a writhing, dangerous world. A world of brown snakes, crocodiles and funnel web spiders. A world of men like Reverend Nader. And my ex.

I felt the impossibility of our collective endeavours, the futility of trying to capture this evanescent quality of the natural world and pin it to a canvas.

Over the next few hours, my imagination plunged into freefall. My lessons on atmosphere and aerial perspective transformed into private metaphors. Inwardly, I dwelled on how what we see is always blurred and distorted by the atmosphere. Outwardly, I prattled on, explaining how there were no wrong or right ways to paint and how a teacher's job was to guide students, bring out what was already within. I was focusing on one particular student's work when I connected a few more mental dots. This student's trees looked like pieces of green popcorn sitting atop empty toilet rolls. Her clouds resembled balls of wool. When I asked her if she had seen the work of any of the naive artists and symbolists such as Rousseau or Chagall, she said she hadn't. I told her how this simplification of the natural world displayed a joyfulness. The artist refuses to be bound by traditional techniques and returns instead to the innocent, simple and joyful perspective of the child.

As I spoke, my inner landscape protested. Happiness was a flight from depth, a strategy to avoid our interior lives. Joy was dangerous. Simplicity was a cousin of stupidity.

And then, Trevor returned, bouncing back with a big smile on his face.

He told us he found some mushrooms. And, he'd seen a lyrebird. His enthusiasm was infectious. Simple. Joyful. Like a child.

It hit me then. That was Trevor. Shallow. Oblivious. Innocent. Simple. This man was a trick of the eye. Not all there. An illusion. I regarded my students, laughing and engaged, wondering why no one else had noticed this quality of perilous and naive joy in all Yindisha's men.

And then, my gaze returned to Stick-figure Saniya's eyebrows and I wondered if I was – ever so slowly – losing my mind.

Late afternoon, my throat raw from talking, I walked in silence amid my chatting students, my mind contracting into a singularity of suspicion. I observed Trevor flirting and chortling with them. They drank in his cheeriness and beauty with a joyous oblivion borne – I suspected – of a desperate need to be adored.

At that point, Yindisha's wrongness still felt like a vague, unsubstantiated thing I was determined to shape into something solid. Perhaps that research station was a re-education camp for criminals, refugees or religious fundamentalists? That would explain the retreat's perfectly polite, perfectly behaved men. And the research station's strict security. Perhaps Galilea visited Manus Island, selected all the best-looking men and brought them back to Australia under some secret immigration plan.

No. I thought of Steve the surfie, Tamati the New Zealander and decided this didn't make sense. That diverse collection of men had stories. Spoke of local homes and families. They weren't refugees.

As my companions happily chatted, my thoughts travelled deeper to more gloomy and suspicious realms. A gay conversion centre perhaps? That might explain Galilea's puritanical garb. Members of a fundamentalist religion that thought gays were sinners would regard conversion as an act of morality.

If thought has colour, mine at that moment turned viridian green. *Brain washing.* I looked back at Trevor, noticing for a moment his walk was faintly stiff. *Or robots?*

Why do you immediately assume that men who are gentle and respectful have to be brainwashed criminals, refugees, converted gays or robots? A voice that sounded like Sophia's intruded on my thoughts.

I regarded Trevor, seeking more signs he was something other than human. Of course, I could have asked him if any of my wild imaginings were true. But right then, this woman who had slammed a book down under a minister's nose and accused him of evil wasn't in the mood for bluntness. I was tired. I didn't have the courage to ask Trevor if he was a refugee, a converted gay or a robot. To my companions I was, after all, just a polite middle-aged woman teaching outdoor painting. I didn't want to upset this delightful, enthusiastic man. Here, amid this natural beauty among the flowering gums, among students who thought I was a creative sage, it would have been rude. And besides, if I asked Trevor, he probably would have lied. And I would have sounded like a lunatic.

The sun sank along with my mood. Here and now, separated by time and space, I see my wild, emotional oscillations more clearly. It was in those moments – in my Icarus-like plunges into the valley of life's shadows – that I realised how little humankind understands the workings of the cosmos. My short-sightedness wasn't just a physical defect, but a reflection of my inner landscape. I was blind to the universe's greater truths.

Closer to the retreat, the bush trail plantings became less unruly and more landscaped. Yet, underneath all that orderly beauty was a system of predation. A war of survival. Ecosystems adapting, changing, falling in and out of balance.

And here – above – on the surface of the world, on this canvas of civilisation, we were all pretending to be creatures we weren't. We were all inhabiting a superficial realm of images, social conditioning, traditions and habits. We were all playing roles. Creating illusions.

Recalling Mary Nader's haunted gaze, my thoughts strained, as if suffering some form of intellectual constipation. If I just tried harder, thought harder, looked harder, squinted at the mysteries of existence, perhaps I would be able to see everything in a new light.

At the entrance of the retreat, nursing a dull headache, I farewelled my students with a cheery smile. Ever so breezily, I told them what a pleasure the day had been and how I had enjoyed seeing them all improve. Once more, I took in Stick-figure Saniya's fake eyebrows, her impossibly straight hair, those bold green fingernails. Now, I felt a welling of tender protectiveness. Something about her felt frail and endangered. She was like an exotic bird that might any day become extinct. We all exchanged platitudes, hugs and laughs. But for them, I wouldn't have a job, I reminded myself. I kept my other thoughts to myself. Because, like everyone in this world, I was also trained to pretend.

CHAPTER TWELVE

A Brief History of Snoring

Day Six (night)

The air as still as a held breath, I lay in bed listening to the night birds' shrieks and wails. I stared at the night shadows dancing over the ceiling and tried to shake off my restless thoughts. I'd just spent a lovely day sharing my knowledge and making a few women embrace their inner artists. *Why couldn't I just enjoy this place? Feel satisfied? Be simple like Trevor?* I mused as I fell asleep.

Waking suddenly after what seemed like only a few minutes, I heard a low sound, like the rumble of a machine. I rose from my bed and opened the window. The sound came from the barracks behind my cottage.

Perplexed, I put on the retreat's complementary slippers and dressing gown and crept outside. Behind the hedge, that cacophony grew louder. It was definitely coming from the men's quarters. It sounded as though a fight was going on inside. But I heard no crashing furniture, no crunching sounds of fists against bone or manly cheers. No. The men were simply snoring in a kind of weird, disharmonious unison. It was as though they were speaking a strange language in their sleep.

I shook away those wayward thoughts. There are clinical explanations for snoring – blocked airways, sleep apnoea. I listened harder. The snores sounded ugly, violent. But seriously, did all those fit-looking, trim men have sleep apnoea? Is that why they were here? Was Yindisha a sleep apnoea retreat for men? One thinks these things in the dead of night, standing in a patch of perfectly mown moonlit grass surrounded by the deep shifting shadows of ancient trees and alien noises.

Another explanation of snoring, I told myself, harks back to our ancient history, to a time when a sleeping human was vulnerable. Snoring is the body's way of warning predators to stay away.

The snores grew louder until they seemed to shake the full moon from its perch in the sky. The sound reached a violent, rasping crescendo.

I looked around. Had no one else heard this dreadful sound?

Fleetingly, I considered my own apocalyptic snores, which seemed to get worse as my marriage deteriorated. Towards the end, it was hard to get a good night's sleep with my ex constantly prodding me and telling me to shut up in the middle of the night. Eventually I retreated to the spare room where I could make the windows tremble and shake dust from the picture rails in perfect peace. My mother told me that my father had also snored so loudly she eventually banished him to the spare bedroom. What a delightful gene to inherit from my father.

Suddenly, the snoring stopped. I imagined the men in their narrow beds, turning over in unison, now sleeping on their sides.

A chill dribbled down my back.

Thirty men wearing the same aftershave. Thirty men snoring in unison. Turning together in their sleep.

I crept back to my cottage utterly spooked.

CHAPTER THIRTEEN

Framed and Hung

Day Seven

The pale woman staring back at me in the mirror looked bitter and miserable. She looked as though she had spent the night loosing battles with vampires, viruses and malevolent politicians. Wincing, I turned from that early-morning, haggard, bags-under-the-eyes face. Despite seven days without even a sip of wine, I felt as though I had a hangover.

After breakfast, I made my way to the massage quarters for a free hot stone massage. In the massage room's reception area, Saniya – of the lime-green-fingernails, but now dressed in the Yindisha Retreat uniform – greeted me effusively.

'You work here?' I asked, shocked. Why hadn't she told me during our classes?

My gaze kept flicking between her lime-green fingernails and her perfectly painted eyebrows as she explained she hadn't thought it important and didn't want to change the teacher-student dynamic. In her breathy tones she said that Yindisha's massage therapists worked on three weekly rosters – last week was her week off. 'I've been wanting to take an art class for ages,' she said. She handed me a robe and a pair of black disposable panties as she guided me to the changing room. Her smile glowed. 'And I've loved every minute of your fabulous classes. You're a fantastic teacher.'

Then she left me, feeling chuffed but still unsettled, to undress. My thoughts returned to yesterday – to Saniya's skilled deflections of our conversations. *Was the retreat covertly assessing me? Spying on me?*

Outside the changing room, I heard her speaking with one of those snoring men about the aromatherapy. When I came out in my disposable panties and robe, yet another Mr-Gorgeous sat me down in front of a line of vials and asked me to select the scent I liked best.

Recalling those snores, my body tensed as I sniffed.

Gripping my chosen vial, I followed Saniya into a softly lit room. Unable to contain myself any longer, I mentioned the snoring I'd heard last night.

Instead of looking perplexed or worried, she laughed. Effusively. Yes, she said, she'd occasionally heard them snoring and wasn't it a dreadful sound? 'A shame we can't make men who don't snore,' she added.

I persisted. I commented on the men's beautiful skin and pointed out I'd never seen one with a single blemish or pimple.

'Healthy lifestyle and healthy attitudes,' replied Saniya. 'The skin is the largest organ in the body. It reflects our inner health.'

Of course, she was going to say that. She was a therapist. And this probably wasn't the time to disagree. But. Was there something cautious in her tone? Something too forced and blithe?

Trying to tune in to the room's cloistered peace, I lay down on my stomach and she placed the first hot stone on my back. The stone felt good and the room smelt of freesia and bergamot.

My thoughts restless, I still struggled to relax. I thought of all the men, dusting, vacuuming, gardening, keeping the retreat in immaculate order. They had to pay them salaries. Aside from that snoring and absence of pimples, the retreat's business model didn't make sense. At the moment, towards the middle of the week, there were only a few guests. All the people at breakfast this morning had been staff. There was no way this organisation could possibly be making a profit, let alone breaking even.

Another stone settled on my back. Slowly, my thoughts folded in on themselves. Deciding there was probably some kind of corporate sponsorship, some infrastructure underpinning the retreat, soothed by Saniya's dismissal of my suspicions, deliciously kneaded into a state of submissive abandon by her skilled and gentle touch, I relaxed into that fragrant massage. I even forgot about those lime-green fingernailed hands probing my back.

Afterwards, I collected my phone from reception and made my way to Watson. Feeling soft and floaty, I walked down that path that a few evenings ago had so terrified me. Today, basking in the throbbing greenery, I inhaled the sharp autumnal air and listened to the percussion of birdsong, my post-massage body still feeling as boneless as a jellyfish. But deep in the back room of my brain, that unsettled voice still bleated. *Something about Yindisha doesn't feel right.*

Watson Gallery of Art and Craft was my first stop. After sizing up the low standard of the exhibited artwork, I deployed my most charming smile to the man behind the counter, all while thinking how pot-bellied and unfit he looked. In contrast with Yindisha's men he looked like a lesser being. Reminding myself I wasn't one to judge, I explained I was an art teacher at Yindisha Retreat and was wondering if he would consider displaying some of my students' works.

He gestured to a wall covered in elaborate frame and moulding samples. 'Sure. If they are properly framed,' he said.

'We can do the framing,' he added.

Inwardly, I bristled. While I understood he was trying to rustle up some business, I never framed paintings on canvas. The artwork should speak for itself. It should not require enhancement. My mother – firmly the traditionalist – once told me a husband was like a frame encasing a pretty picture (his wife). The husband protected that pretty picture from getting tarnished, kept her in place on the gallery wall of society. In other words, once a woman was married, she was framed and hung.

Feigning polite innocence, I told the gallery owner that, unlike delicate watercolours on paper, I was under the impression painted canvases needed only simple frames or none at all. I told him that acrylic paint – which I was using with my students, was – being plastic-based – as resilient as house paint. After giving me a patronising look, he said he would only exhibit works he had framed. I forced a smile and told him I would discuss his offer with my students.

The man gave my naked marriage-ring finger a parting shot. I knew what he was thinking. Unmarried. Divorced. Spinster. Unframed. I was a member of the *Salon des Refuses*. Rejected, dusty and irrelevant. He probably thought I was a lonely woman who lived with ten cats, ate mince for dinner every night and had come to Yindisha for sex.

'I heard Yindisha Retreat had a bachelor auction the other day.' His tone had a slight sneer and I wondered how ordinary men might feel about Yindisha Retreat's delectations of manhood. Not good, I was sure. He pointed to a jar on the counter labelled 'Watson Parish Church Fund.'

'The church needs a new roof,' he said. 'Care to contribute?'

Thinking of Yindisha's auction and the five-thousand dollars raised for the women's refuge, feeling irritated at the thought of funding a wife-abuser's parish, but not wanting to burn any bridges, I reluctantly dropped in a two-dollar coin, gave him a curt, polite thanks and made my way to Watson General Store.

A silver car was diagonally parked outside the store. A group of women had just arrived. Professionally dressed in a relaxed, untucked way, an aura of seriousness enveloped them. The oldest woman in the group had a distinctive port-wine birthmark that covered the right side of her face. I stared, certain I recognised her. A couple of years ahead of me at art school, I think she had been studying sculpture. Alison, wasn't it? Were they on their way to the retreat? I noticed most of them looked younger than the average Yindisha Retreat demographic.

I gave the young woman ahead of me in the line a warm smile. 'Are you on your way to Yindisha Retreat?'

She gave me an opaque look. Then suddenly looked uncomfortable. Her eyes darted towards Alison, now at the counter. 'No,' she said. 'Just visiting.'

She turned her back on me. I felt faintly hurt at her rudeness. Also, puzzled and suspicious. From what I'd seen so far, you didn't just come to Watson for a visit. You either came to Yindisha Retreat or worked at the research station.

Alison turned, saw me and quickly looked away. Yes, it was definitely her. Either she didn't recognise me or she was avoiding my gaze.

Now feeling annoyed and confused, I watched that unapproachable group of women buy takeaway muffins and coffees. None of them spoke to one another or any of the café's other guests. It was as though they inhabited some mysteriously coded world from which ordinary beings were excluded. They made me feel faintly ashamed, although I couldn't parse exactly why. *Snobs.* The word came from a bitter part of me – the schoolgirl Alethea teased by the cool, partying cohort because she was strange and quiet and drew on her desk.

I found pots of Mary Nader's aioli for sale at the counter. I bought a pot and when I inquired after her, the proprietor told me she was in Sydney with her husband visiting their daughter who was playing the cello in a school concert.

After I left Watson General Store with my takeaway coffee and little jar of aioli, I paused, watching art-school Alison and her three companions climb inside the silver car.

Instead of heading towards Yindisha, they drove back in the direction of the fork in the road. My gut told me they were headed for the research station.

But what was art school graduate Alison doing at a government research station? Had she had a complete career change?

My thoughts raced. The women's noses-in-the-air exclusivity irritated me. Pondering Yindisha's apparently unsustainable business model and how surely it had to be financially underwritten to stay afloat, I recalled Stick-figure Saniya's mention of soil research. I remembered now. Alison had worked with clay. She had sculpted human figures.

And then, Stick-figure Saniya's odd phrasing bulldozered into my thoughts: *A shame we can't make men who don't snore.*

Invigorated by coffee, gripping Mary Nader's aioli as if it were some restorative potion, I strode back to the retreat filled with resolve. Something didn't add up. And I was damn well going to find out what the hell was going on.

CHAPTER FOURTEEN

The Mighty Must Fall

Day Eight

With my mobile phone, an apple and sandwich tucked into my travel-worn backpack, I threw back my shoulders, pulled in my stomach and strode into the bush.

Dressed in sturdy shoes and an old hiking outfit, ignoring the retreat's advice to hike in pairs, I carried a stick to scare away snakes and had doused myself in insect repellent.

The morning sun warming my back, I began my walk on a marked track that headed in the direction of the research station. As soon as it veered away, my plan was to enter the bush or hopefully find a narrower, unmarked path heading north. Looking at the map of the area I had downloaded, the research station – or at least the patch of bush where it was supposed to be – was less than two kilometres – or under an hour's direct walk from Yindisha.

In case I vanished, I had left a note for Sophia in my luggage explaining where I was going so the authorities would know to search for me somewhere in the bush between Yindisha Retreat and that research station. I apologised to her in advance for my reckless curiosity. I told her I loved her.

The first part of the marked trail was pretty and groomed – flanked by grevilleas, banksias and flowering gums. It's true what they say about the healing power of nature. Here, strolling along swept and shaded paths I felt at peace with the world, at one with the universe. Here, entropy – that second law of thermodynamics that dictates everything in the universe descends into a state of maximum disorder – had been reduced and tamed by the hands of human consciousness. Nature here felt wondrous, exhilarating. Managed. Safe. Yindisha's men had swept and clipped the nature surrounding the retreat into a state of pretty submission.

Submission. Yindisha's men. Those words grated against each other. A sense of urgency suddenly overcame me. My heartbeat accelerated and I sped my pace as if I wanted to retreat towards or away from something.

About fifteen minutes later the marked trail veered south, away from the direction of the research station. Unsure what to do, I followed that safe path, becoming increasingly irritated at myself. At this point, I should have been breaking into the bush.

I thought how adventure stories invariably have male protagonists. Danger and an interesting life is a man's business. Uncovering espionage is a man's business. Even if that man, like Galbraith's Cormoran Strike, has only one leg. When it comes to taking initiative and righting the world's wrongs, having only one good leg is preferable to being a woman.

I thought of Sophia and how, despite my intolerable marriage, I had adored being a mother, loved nurturing and caressing my delicious baby. I wanted to stay safe for my daughter. I thought how women don't fight or challenge or subvert because their priority is their offspring. Tahire – the woman after whom my cottage was named – had been an exception. She had painfully chosen justice and death over the mothering of her children. What a gut-wrenching choice.

I hesitated in the shadow of a tormented-looking eucalypt, skirts of bark hanging from its trunk. I took a sip of water. What the hell was I – a middle-aged, unfit woman – doing?

I thought of how those rare female protagonists in thrillers are invariably young, attractive, courageous. Childless. And inevitably buxom.

Apart from my ample bosom, I was none of those things.

In the midst of my flagellating thoughts, I noticed a faint trail wending north towards the valley and the research station. The bush beyond looked wild and unruly. Dangerous. I had a decision to make. My insides hardened.

Banging the bark and leaf-covered ground in front of me to scare off snakes, I stepped off the marked trail and into the unknown.

The bush changed. The orderliness of the marked trail was replaced by a funerial chaos. This was the Australia depicted by those first British visitors as a place of terrors – the agonised contortions of eucalypt limbs, demonic shrieks of birdlife and dank and dangerous shadows where venomous and alien creatures lurked – a nightmare of Gothic proportions. This nature wasn't healing. It was wild. Threatening. Deadly.

The ground dropped, became steep. Several times, I lost my footing and tripped over tree roots. Mossy boulders jutted from the floor of leaf and bark forcing me again and again to change my direction. I stopped and checked my phone. There was no reception.

My stomach taut with nerves, I headed towards a clearing on a patch of high ground ahead. Perhaps there would be reception up there. On all fours, I crawled to the top of a mossy mound, lost my grip and skidded down the other side on my backside. I scrambled for my phone, finding it under some dead leaves, the screen cracked. A great muddy streak down the inside of my leg made it look as though I had shat myself.

I sat for a moment, paralysed, my heart palpating in shock.

You stupid, stupid, woman. Who do you think you are? Lara fucking Croft?

I lost track of the number of times my ex told me I was stupid. Sometimes he would saw it slowly: 'Stuuuupid', as if I were too dense to even understand the word. I looked through the tree canopy feeling defeated and confused. What did I hope to find? Did I think I was some kind of hero? Who was I kidding? Forty-five minutes into my investigation I felt ready to scuttle home. Just as I had been out of my depth in the corporate environment, I was out of my depth now. The corporate environment – like nature – is Darwinian – only the fittest, the most cunning thrive. Darwin's law rewards predators. Exterminates the weak. And moral codes, ethics and compassion are indulgences that have no place in this battle for survival.

My ex thrived in that corporate environment. Reflection, introspection and morality were not qualities I would associate with that toxic oil-slick of a human being.

Thinking of him made me shudder. I checked my phone. Despite the crack, despite the absence of reception, my phone was still alive.

I was still alive. I patted myself down. Nothing was broken. Extra padding had its benefits. And my ex wasn't here, trying to stalk and kill me. He was somewhere in Sydney, trawling dating web sites, courting and charming his latest female victims.

I looked around, still quailing at bush's damp and lonely gloom.

Realising I probably had low blood sugar, I found a spot under a rocky overhang and, my hands still shaking, pulled out my sandwich, which had been squashed in the fall.

As I ate, I thought of predatory beasts and the Darwinian environment of the corporation. The beast learns from his surroundings and, as he gains power, shapes his environment to serve his needs. Swallowing hard, chewing angrily as if eating my fear, I considered how, above all, that beast is a master delegator. Secretly lazy, (although he struts and crows like a rooster when people he wants to impress are watching) he charms his victims into thinking serving him is an honour. He brings those finely honed skills home. He has a way of persuading you that you are the chosen one, privileged with the task of laundering his skid-marked underwear, washing his dishes, wiping the corn chip crumbs off the coffee table after he spent Sunday afternoon watching rugby, drinking and cheering.

My jaw cramped. Recognising my agitation, I tried to eat more slowly. My sandwich made me feel better. Braver. I felt disgusted at those memories. I felt angry and disappointed in that younger self who ironed the predator's work shirts and even packed his suitcase for him when he went off into the corporate savannah on business trips or to attend conferences and have one-night stands with glamorous professional women who were unoppressed and free of family obligations. I inwardly slapped my cheek to pull myself together. Was this new, tougher woman – the independent, divorced Alethea Braxton – going to let nature defeat her? Was she going to let trees and fresh air and a bit of wilderness give her the shits? I rose in defiance. I was not a victim. I had survived. If the bush and the corporate world were Darwinian, then, as a thinking, intelligent (or at least sentient) woman, I had to transcend Darwinism. Besides, Darwinism was a male perspective and nature was a leveller. I had to apply the taming powers of my uniquely cunning and female consciousness to the chaos of nature. I had to battle entropy. Create order from chaos. Master the beast. The mighty had to fall. That was another law of nature.

I balled my sandwich wrapper tightly in my fist and shovelled it into my backpack. No. I would not be defeated. I was an artist. A worshipper of beauty. A seeker of truth.

A sudden crash in the bush broke the silence. My breath stuck in my throat, I slid back under the overhang, cringed and hid.

A man in a white singlet and beige pants appeared between the trees, running for his life. The whites of his eyes were huge, as if he were in possession of a wild, animal terror. As he tore past my hiding place, I caught a glimpse of a circular motif on his arm. A tattoo? A short-haired woman in black tee shirt and black pants pursued him, holding in her hand something that resembled a paint spatula.

It was then I realised I was close to the road that led to the research station. Below, through the trees, an electric vehicle drew up. The driver – another woman dressed in black – stepped out and spoke into her earbuds. She was too far away for me to hear what she was saying. In her hands, she carried a sack and some other machine that looked like a leaf blower. Furrows of anxious fury crossed her face. I noticed her tee shirt bore the same motif I had seen on the man's arm – an orange-brown circle breeched diagonally by a curling flourish, and, inside the circle, two sans-serif letters I couldn't quite make out. The motif looked faintly familiar.

My heart hammered and I released my held breath. Nearby, I heard the crashing through the undergrowth suddenly stop. A sound like falling stones followed. Listening to her earbuds, the face of woman with the sack relaxed. She strode towards the spot where I assumed the pursuit had ended and a moment later, I heard that all too familiar sound of a fucking leaf blower. I ground my teeth and waited for the women and their quarry to emerge. Moments later, they strode into view holding a limp sack between them. I've seen enough crime movies to know that what they carried wasn't body-shaped but resembled more a sack of potting mix. My gut clenched. Had they, in that short time, hacked that man to pieces?

'Phew,' I heard one woman say. 'That was a feisty one.'

After they had left in their vehicle, I descended closer to the road, creeping to the area where I thought that pursuit had come to its end. I found nothing. Just a patch of wet dirt. I sniffed. Not blood. Water. And the faintest scent of lemon geraniums.

All evidence of their crime had vanished.

My heart drumming in my ears, my tinnitus shrieking like some infernal inner orchestra, I looked up and noticed something I hadn't seen before. A camera. In the knot of a tree. I looked around. Wedged into the knots of the trees, discretely perched in branches, sat the black orbs of cameras. Everywhere. *Shit.*

I had witnessed a crime. And those cameras had seen *me.*

Hearing the sigh of another electric vehicle approaching, I slunk behind a tree. A black car passed, Galilea, in another of her crew necked shirts, at the wheel.

Double shit. I turned and quickly scrambled away, back up the hill.

CHAPTER FIFTEEN

Robots Who Weep

Day Eight (evening),
Day Nine (morning)

Paranoid and dishevelled, I stumbled back to the retreat. After checking the Wi-Fi still worked, I handed my cracked phone to the receptionist saying I accidentally fell on it during my walk. He knew I was fibbing. *What was it about these men that felt so strange?* I wondered again as I gazed into beautiful eyes as empty and deep as space. Were Yindisha's men terrorised into submission? No, aside from that man in the bush, I had never seen even the faintest hint of fear in any of the men's eyes.

What then? Brain washed?

I scuttled back to my cottage, had a shower, changed and washed my clothes.

I pulled the note I had left for Sophia out of my luggage and, hands shaking, tore it up.

Following a solitary early dinner in an empty dining room, I returned to my cottage while it was still light. Then, I put the chain on my door, checked all my windows were firmly locked and even looked in the wardrobe.

I mulled over the incident, tried again to make sense of what I had seen – the terror in the man's eyes, the women pursuing him. He'd been tall, good-looking, just like Yindisha's men. And he had just vanished. Or at least reduced to some different form that could fit in a sack.

A feisty one...

A feisty *what?*

And why were those cameras there? Who was watching?

And, whatever this was, Galilea was involved.

Again, I checked all my windows were locked.

How long would it be before someone in a trench coat knocked on my cottage door and arrested, chloroformed or assassinated me?

I felt very, very, alone. And indescribably tired, as though I'd been struck by a demolition ball. I even wondered if I'd knocked my head during my fall and hallucinated the whole episode.

And then, I recalled something else I'd glimpsed as the man fled past. At the time, I thought it was just a pattern of shadows. Now, in reflection, I realised his forehead was covered in strange marks. Script, or coding of some kind.

And the motif on his arm and on the women's shirts? I realised why it looked familiar. That curlicue I'd seen reminded me of the 'S' in Yindisha Retreat's logo. The retreat and the research station *were* connected.

Even though the evening was still warm, I shivered. I crawled under the covers and curled into a foetal position. Despite my anxiety, I slept. And dreamt.

In that untethered world, I was back in the bush. A man appeared – not the frightened one I'd seen, but one filled with sexy self-assurance. He too, had odd marks on his forehead and that motif on his arm. He stared at me intensely as if he were penetrating the deepest recesses of my soul. He wasn't someone

I knew and, although I couldn't discern his features, I beheld a creature of luminous beauty. Gentle. Passionate and fathomlessly wise. Lured by his gaze, titillated by a sense of danger, I let him push me onto a patch of mossy ground under the shade of a soaring eucalyptus. Inviting him in, I was young in that dream. Or perhaps not so much young as ageless. Happy with my body. Our union escalated swiftly into a bestial physical encounter, with none of the emotional detritus and insecurities that frequently contaminate middle-aged liaisons. It was mindless, glowing sex. A timeless, all-consuming animal passion. A forgetting. A reset of my weary, self-flagellating brain.

I woke the next morning feeling alert, refreshed and *alive*.

Replenished by a night of imaginary sex (surrounded by all this male beauty, I couldn't really blame my yearning subconscious) and determined to bravely face whatever was coming my way, I stepped out of my cottage into a briskly cool morning.

Immediately I felt the despair. Three women huddled together on the path ahead. One wept.

'Elise Cranston died last night,' one of the retreat's yoga teachers said to me as I passed.

Still half-suspended in that post-coital dream-world, I blinked several times, taking in what she was saying. Reality in all its heavy sobriety slammed me back to the present. The old woman I'd spoken to on my first day had passed on.

I thought of my mother, also no longer of this world.

'She died in her sleep,' another said. 'She went in peace.'

The man I saw yesterday hadn't gone in peace, I thought.

And I had sex in my sleep.

'Oh. I'm so sorry,' I managed to reply. Last night's encounter shimmered into my consciousness. While I was having a raunchy dream, an old woman had died. Despite having no control over the workings of my unconscious, I felt embarrassed. Ashamed.

Five minutes later, I stood on the front steps with a group of other teachers and watched a funeral director from Bowral wheel Elise Cranston's stretchered and shrouded body into his hearse. Jerome – her caregiver – hovered and wept as the driver closed the doors. In those quiet tears I sensed he wasn't just doing a job – he really loved her.

'Elise died with an angel by her side,' someone behind me said.

Another mentioned Jerome had been with her for nearly twenty years. The two women – a yoga teacher and that handsome woman in her seventies who'd given the Gnosticism lecture on the day I arrived – exchanged knowing glances.

All the tiny hairs on my skin stood on end. What the fuckitty-fuck was going on here?

Galilea arrived, hugged Jerome and guided him into her car. They left together. I wondered if she was taking him to the research station. Perhaps to wipe his memory. Or do to him whatever they had done to that fleeing man in the bush.

I thought again of that wet patch of soil, that negative space where a man, or a creature resembling a man, had fallen and vanished. I glimpsed Jerome in the passenger window wipe a tear from his eye. *An angel.* Whatever Yindisha's men were, they certainly weren't robots. Unless of course, someone had found a way to make robots weep.

A cold autumnal wind swept through the trees, making me tremble. Feeling the icy hand of death waving too close for comfort, I turned and made my way back to my cottage.

CHAPTER SIXTEEN

Lucas

Day Nine, Day Ten

Still shaken by death's uncomfortably close hand, I spent an hour of my next free day at a yoga class. Afterwards, my brain full of chattering monkeys, I spent another hour trying, and failing, to meditate in a room full of middle-aged women and two beautiful, fragrant men. Fretting over those cameras in the bush, feeling like a naughty schoolgirl, I waited for the inevitable summons from Galilea – the headmistress. My gut in a knot, constantly glancing over my shoulders, I pretended I was fine.

After my yoga and meditation failures, I socialised with the other teachers, heard stories about how childless Elise Cranston had no family and doted on Jerome, her caregiver. And how the heartbroken Jerome, after attending Elise's funeral in Bowral would return home to his family in Perth. I wondered facetiously if angels had families in Perth.

Thursday arrived and I was still free, un-summoned and un-chloroformed. My class had four new students including one of Yindisha's men – a slender, amber-eyed, high-cheek-boned man of indeterminate age called Lucas. The word *chiselled* came to mind.

He told me he worked in the orchards and was having time off to take some classes. I took in his attractive, unusual square-jawed, full-lipped features. Something about him glowed; he made me think of gold nuggets and vampires smouldering in sunlight.

Probably another spy, my department of endless suspicions added.

Nevertheless, I let my guard down. He was beautiful and smelt sublime.

When I pulled out the collection of white platonic solids, someone mentioned agape – the concept of platonic love.

'Why do some women feel ashamed or guilty about sex?' Loose Judith asked, glancing covetously at Lucas as he shaded his platonic solid – a tiny, perfect tetrahedron. 'I mean it's a perfectly natural bodily function.'

I suggested that perhaps our guilt is residue from a time when sex meant exploitation, power and unwanted impregnation.

Lucas paused from his shading. 'What would happen if we removed all that conditioning and constraint from the equation?' he asked in the same neutrally attractive accent as Galilea. 'Isn't pleasure without pain possible? Isn't it all a question of personal attitude and perspective?'

I was sure he gave me a mischievous look as he spoke. I ignored it, trying to stay professional. I failed. I thought of my naughty dream and now, that anonymous face was replaced with his. My insides did a little dance. He may have been a spy, but he was a charming spy. And, following that erotic dream, my slumbering hormones had been resurrected.

'There is no pleasure without pain.' I replied. 'Life's greatest accomplishments involve trial and suffering. We won't learn if we have only endless fun.'

Lucas gave me a deep look which made that gap where my

gall bladder had once sat, quiver. 'Perhaps some people conflate suffering and criticism with learning,' he said. 'Learning should equate with reward, not punishment. Learning should be pleasurable. We learn more if we feel safe and happy.'

I studied him as he spoke, wondering how it would feel to run my hands over his chest. Now, *that* would be pleasurable.

'I live in hope,' I replied, giving him what I hoped was a mildly saucy, but not predatory, grin.

When he gave me an undaunted smile back, my willpower took another backwards step. In that moment, the resistant Alethea Braxton went into temporary retirement. I started to feel intrigued. Curious. Attracted. For the first time in ages, I felt zesty, desirable. Confident. Flirty.

That inner voice of chastisement bleated like a dying lamb. *You are a bad woman, Alethea Braxton. You are utterly deluded.*

Fuck off, my resurrected department of physical desire retorted.

Lucas joined the dinner table that evening and sat next to me. We talked about life on other worlds and under the sea. We both, it turned out, loved Star Trek. Lucas had a similar, sensuous look overlaid by a kind of fierce stubbornness that reminded me of that comely Captain Kirk.

'You remind me a bit of Captain Kirk,' I said in a moment of giggly weakness.

'I assure you I am able to resist alien women,' he said, grinning back. 'But show me a piece of beautiful ripe fruit and I'm a lost cause.'

I looked away, laughed and hotly blushed. When I made some paltry reply about ripe fruit making good preserves and being tasty in stews, he chortled back.

During that dinner, his eyes never left mine as if I was the most beautiful, most exotic piece of ripened fruit in the room.

I revisited my assumptions about Yindisha's men being simple. Lucas had a worldly sophistication about him. He was erudite, knowledgeable. Witty. All of which blew apart my theory that Yindisha's men were simpletons; feeble-minded dropouts from the university of life.

I lay in bed that night, staring at the moonlit shadows dancing over my walls and wondered if I might be developing a crush. Lucas's face dancing in my mind's eye, I fell towards that unknowable world of slumber, sleeping heavily, as though I'd been drugged.

The next day during the still-life exercises, Lucas produced a tiny, pathetically inhibited drawing.

'You need to loosen up,' I told him.

Following my words, he tore that inhibited still life from his butcher's paper block and covered the next sheet of paper with dark and vigorous scribbles. 'You mean like this?' he asked, his eyes teasing.

My insides turned soft and squishy. Is there anything more charming than a man who makes you laugh? A robot he was not. And he was too naughty to be an angel.

'Somewhere in between the two,' I said, grinning.

Towards the end of the class, he showed me his final offering – a lovely expressionist still life, full of energy and attitude.

'Better?' He asked.

'Splendid,' I replied enthusiastically.

'Good enough for you to take up my offer to make you dinner tonight?'

My mouth went dry. I felt as though I'd been hit in the solar plexus with a scented feather pillow. *What? Why?* I wanted to ask him, but I managed to bite my tongue.

By this point, I still wasn't entirely sure how I felt – but I was deeply attracted and even more surprised by his attentiveness. He was also a quick learner. Smart. Witty.

And what fabulous teeth. What a glorious smile.

But what did this gorgeous man see in frumpy middle-aged me?

Ah, what the hell, I told myself. *Have some fun Alethea. Don't you deserve it after all this time? After all the shit you put up with in your marriage? So what if he's a gigolo-in-training and you're his lab rat?*

With an uncharacteristic absence of consideration, I recklessly took up his offer.

He's going to kill me, I thought when he beamed in delight.

An hour after my class ended, I was summoned to the front desk.

The receptionist told me Lucas had to cancel our dinner – something to do with an emergency at an orchard.

Sophia had left a message as a well, cancelling her Sunday morning call as she and Dave were going on an endurance horse ride for the weekend. They would be out of mobile phone range and she would call on Tuesday morning instead. I spent Saturday night feeling all at once relieved, abandoned and restless. The police/secret service weren't at the front desk to arrest me for nosiness. Good. But I would miss tomorrow's call with Sophia. Bad. And had Lucas simply got cold feet? Annoying.

I went to bed feeling sorry for myself. As sleep washed over me, my subconscious deployed images of Lucas in the bush fleeing a pair of women with paint spatulas. When they caught him, they painted him, covering him in coloured patterns that made him merge with the undergrowth. He turned invisible. I dreamed I was kissing one of the two-dimensional hollow men in my paintings, and, as I kissed him, he came to life. Then, I turned invisible. I woke feeling dull, addled and rejected.

Lucas wasn't back for the Sunday class on colour. Disappointed, I told myself I didn't give a damn.

Sunday night, at dinner time, he was back in the dining room. He came over to me and apologized, saying there had been a suspected outbreak of coddling moth in one of Yindisha's orchards.

Would I be available for dinner tomorrow night? He asked. He would bring a special coddling moth-free applesauce to go with the fritters which were his specialty, he added. His eyes were a perfectly calibrated combination of earnestness and vulnerability. How could I say no? I was charmed. Lured. Of course, I replied. I just happened to be available. Intoxicated by his obvious delight, I watched him leave the room, my insides a riot of quibbling apprehension. *Ooh! Am I going to have sex with him?*

Alethea, you fool! How old are you? Sixteen? Asked a prissy voice I swiftly banished from my mind.

CHAPTER SEVENTEEN

Melting Point

Day Eleven

The day I lost my virginity for the second time began with a final wave of belting summer heat. I'd slept badly. Feeling bleary eyed and out of sorts, I spent an hour weeding in one of Yindisha's community gardens, took a Vegan cooking class and learned how to make raw fig bars which came out soggy and crooked. Afterwards, I restlessly attended another yoga session.

I held my afternoon class on the grounds of the retreat, where we sat under the shade of a silky oak and painted pictures of the lawns, fallen leaves and flowering shrubs. Again, Lucas was absent. Those coddling moths must have been serious. My thoughts were all over the place. I wasn't in my best teacherly form. I was becoming increasingly anxious about my dinner date. I hadn't been on a proper date in ages. I hadn't had sex in well over ten years.

Lucas arrived that evening at one minute after six o'clock carrying a straw basket filled with ingredients for dinner. An evening bird shrieked in the pink rhododendron behind him as he strode into my cottage smelling of that musky-citrus fragrance along with a faint whiff of the clump of chives sticking from his basket.

After saying, yes, the coddling moth issue was now dealt with, he pulled out a flask of lemonade, poured me a glass and banished me from the kitchenette. Telling me to relax on the sofa with my drink while he prepared dinner, we chatted as he cooked.

I asked him if he had a girlfriend (best, I thought, to get this out of the way sooner rather than later). He explained how he'd had one long-term, serious girlfriend and had travelled to Europe with her. Then, in Paris, she'd dumped him for a Frenchman. 'She's married now and living in Marseille. We managed to stay friends,' he said. 'She has a little girl. I've seen pictures of her.' He smiled kindly. 'Very cute.'

I was impressed with the way he seemed to have tidily and wisely moved on. Or perhaps he hadn't? Perhaps that's why he was now here in Yindisha working in the orchards and making dinner for a middle-aged woman.

Yet I also sensed as he spoke there was still hurt there. He didn't seem to want me to dig deeper and I respected it. Perhaps I fleetingly mused, all Yindisha's beautiful men were heart broken and had come here to heal. And bonking middle-aged women was part of the therapy.

Briefly, having been married to a pathological liar, I also wondered if he was making everything up. Perhaps he was a reformed wife beater. I still had the niggling feeling something about him was wrong. So, in the interests of openness and sincerity, I confided to Lucas that when I first arrived, I'd wondered if he and his fellow colleagues were androids or robots.

He laughed this off saying his ancestors were Greek, he wore a size ten shoe and had a genetic predisposition for baldness. 'I don't know any robots with Greek ancestors and looming baldness,' he said as he tossed a batch of the fritter-batter he'd made into a frying pan.

When he asked about me, I sketchily described my bad marriage and subsequent divorce. Even after all this time, I still wasn't sure how to tell my story without appearing too bitter or excessively insensitive and blithe.

After he had listened to my story (truncated and probably a little on the blithe side because I didn't want to come across as a permanently and unattractively damaged woman) he regarded me thoughtfully with those intense amber eyes.

By this point, I was thoroughly enjoying watching him cook. My body shimmered with a long-lost feeling of desire. Not wanting to be another of those older women shagging a younger lover, I fought that bodily desire with every morsel of my waning will. Silently, I snapped at myself. *Alethea Braxton, you are not a cliché!*

When we finally sat together to eat (delicious corn and capsicum fritters and fresh tossed salad greens – he was an excellent cook – another thing my ex wasn't – not that I'm comparing) we spoke about how marriage was another manifestation of female submission to outdated hierarchies, how women's self-esteem was entangled with male desire. And yes, somewhere in that conversation, he told me I had beautiful eyes. It might have been just after I praised his culinary skills.

I knew I was being played. Each of his amorous phrases was skilfully deployed. He charmed me and I fell for it. By the time he'd done the dishes, I had descended into a nymphomaniacal state of boiling desire. I was no longer tired. I was alive and on fire.

But let me add here, it was a controlled burn. There was never a moment when I doubted who was in charge. He made me feel as though I was the orchestrator of this encounter. Everything was my choice.

Still battling my escalating urges, I told him about what I had seen in the bush the other day and how the man had vanished.

He looked just as puzzled as I felt. He didn't have any explanation either. As far as he knew, he said, the research station was indeed a government-owned agricultural facility investigating soil and carbon capture technology.

I can barely recall now how smoothly he changed the subject. And I was so caught up in that strategic seduction, I let the mystery lie.

I surrendered.

When he offered the inevitable massage after he had washed up (and let me tell you, watching him wash up – something else my ex had never done – was the final straw that broke this covetous camel's back) he made me laugh when he pointed out I was tense. 'You need to loosen up,' he said, repeating my words about his artwork.

As his hands caressed my neck and shoulders, that great gap of longing finally fully opened. I yielded. His eyes never left mine as I disrobed. It seemed as if in his looking at me with those intense amber eyes, he understood me in a way I didn't understand myself.

My thoughts collided like debris backing up a drain. I realised I wasn't going to be ravished. I was going to be loved. And I was going to enter a place of no return.

Feeling charged with power, yet simultaneously bent into submission, I let him guide me to my room and push me gently onto the bed. I shook like a terrified new bride.

Of course, I opened my mouth one more time, because I *wasn't* a new bride.

'Why?' I asked.

He looked affronted, puzzled, as if my appeal were utterly obvious.

'I'm *old*,' I reminded him.

'You have lived,' he replied. 'You have experience, maturity. You know your own mind. You are strong. Wilful. You have created *life*. I find that irresistible.'

When he planted his lips on mine, as if to shut me up, I thought *Well, what the fuck. There's obviously something seriously wrong with you*. And with that, my overthinking brain went blank and I yielded to my body.

Now, reflecting back on that moment, I still struggle to give the experience shape. I recall how the curlicues of that citrus-musk fragrance wrapped around me like unseen silken ties, binding me yet bestowing me with a lightness I felt in the furthest reaches of my limbs. After he breached me, my flesh felt as though it had fallen away from my bones and my body fragmented, turning indistinguishable from this man, as if I had been softly buried and decomposed. Finally, I cried out in a great shudder of pleasure. Above me, he shivered and moaned as well. It felt real and true.

Afterwards, I lay on my salmon-coloured pillows and stared at that bight-shaped crack in the ceiling above the bed. I still had my contact lenses in, so it was nice and sharp.

Next to me, Lucas snored lightly. As my thoughts reassembled, I recalled something someone had once said: 'After sex men want to laugh and women want to cry.'

And yes, I suddenly wanted to wail. It was as if in plumbing my depths, digging below the frail crust of my composure, sex with Lucas had unearthed some underground ocean of my soul. There, sex uncovered fossils. Far too many fossils.

I thought of my ex – those early years when we had been so much in love and so happy. I recalled the falling, the wonder and mystery of it all, that feeling of being utterly stunned by love. There were so many good times early on. We had such fun. We had such an easy rapport. I admired the way he seemed to tread through life so very lightly. In the beginning, he love-bombed me. He knew which strings to pluck on that heart yearning to be played.

And then, we got married. Those first tender shoots of love replaced by expectations and obligations; I no longer knew my role. I didn't know how to be a 'wife.' I recalled the times my ex said to me – 'You are my wife! Behave like a wife!'

Eight years later, that man who had once been my great love ripped my heart from my chest, pummelled it with a meat tenderiser, threw it back at me and then asked me to fry it up so he could have it for dinner.

My heart ached and my lower lip trembled. How does a man who is supposed to be your dearest friend, the parent of your child, your companion as you navigate life's trials, turn into someone you no longer recognise? *And wouldn't Lucas, if I let him into my heart, do the same?*

The hurt erupted, the grief bursting forth like a volcanic eruption. I shook the bed with my shuddering sobs.

Lucas woke as I sprang from the bed and grabbed my robe.

'Are you OK?' he asked.

I kept my back to that beautiful creature who had opened the door to an overcrowded, cobweb-infested attic of memories, insecurities and hang-ups.

'I think you'd better go,' I said.

CHAPTER EIGHTEEN

The Persistent Puritan

Day Twelve

Is there any more perfectly placed item on the menu of life than regret after sex?

I woke the next morning with echoes of Lucas's touch still vibrating through my flesh and my brain in chaos. Considerate and respectful after last night's conniption, neither probing nor offended but looking softly concerned, Lucas had simply and politely accepted my request for him to leave.

Determined to pull myself together, instructing myself Lucas had been nothing more than a pleasurable one-night stand, I dressed and made my way to breakfast.

Insistently, memories of pleasure – Lucas's touch, the tender look in his eyes – licked my thoughts.

I sat at the breakfast table pretending nothing was amiss, making casual conversation with the Zumba teacher about the cooler weather, all the while convinced the other diners could tell I had had a night of electrifying sex. I felt simultaneously enervated and ashamed.

How could this be? I kept wondering. How could Lucas, that beautiful man, respect this damaged, dense woman? This had to be some kind of ruse! He had to be mentally defective to take me on. Deluded. Brain washed.

Reality checks consumed my morning's thoughts. *Yes, it was the best sex you've ever had, Alethea. But don't fool yourself. This place isn't the real world. In the real world of younger, more succulent women, you wouldn't have stood a chance with him. Here in Yindisha, his meagre pickings comprise varying selections of tough old meat and emotionally diseased bog-witches like you, Alethea Braxton.*

My thoughts see-sawed. I felt as though I'd been dismantled, then carelessly put back together. I felt fabulous. Terrible. Fabulous again. Sexy. Hideous. Gorgeous.

With a wilful effort, I hung on to the gorgeous feeling and, after breakfast, made my way to reception to collect my mobile phone.

Outside the gates of the retreat, I took a long deep breath of the morning's cool air and called Sophia.

She answered immediately. Beyond the cracks in my screen, she looked ruffled, sleepy and happy.

She spoke about their endurance ride, how she and Dave slept in a tent beside the car. She told me that in the middle of the night they thought it had started raining, but it turned out to be a possum peeing on their tent. I laughed more heartily than I should have. Sex had unhinged me. I was far too happy. Unstable.

When she asked me how my second week was going, I hesitated.

'And how are you dealing with all those gorgeous men?' she added with a twinkle in her eye.

I bit the inside of my cheek. I thought of those cameras in the bush. I thought of spies. How much should I tell her? I didn't want her to worry. I thought of Lucas. I wanted to stay in her eyes, the composed and restrained mother I had tried to be as I raised her. Sexual indiscretions were her father's department. I was the mother figure, the grownup in charge of my life and desires. I had, in my mature years, turned chaste and sensible. And I wished to stay that way in Sophia's eyes.

'I'm dealing with it,' I replied, my gaze tracing the cracks in my screen. 'They're all very young. Little boys, really.'

When Sophia mentioned that the French president had married his English teacher – a woman twenty years his senior – I realised she might be open to hearing about her mother's shenanigans. But still, I resisted.

I changed the subject and indulged my niggle about her latest boyfriend. 'How did you meet Dave?' I asked.

When Sophia paused, I knew. The silence between us prickled.

I persisted. 'Did you meet him on Binder?' The word *Binder* spat from my mouth.

Another silence followed. Sophia knew how much I detested those gross dating platforms. Her father – once our relationship died – had Bindered and RUFPeed like a lost soul embracing religion. Dating sites were full of men like Sophia's father.

I opened my mouth, but Sophia interrupted.

'Mum... *Stop.*'

My inner puritan bristled. We'd had this conversation before. I'd warned her those sites were hunting grounds for arseholes. And Binder? It might as well have been called *I'mlookingforacasualhotfuck.com*.

'Just be careful,' I managed, thinking about how I had never met a man called Chastity. Sex offenders, fakers and shallow fuckers stalked those sites.

Sophia's look said it all. *Get with the times, mum. This is the way people hook up these days.*

'Perhaps it's time *you* started to relax a bit more, mum. Isn't that why you are at that retreat? To have some fun?'

This time, *I* paused. I could have told her, but my mouth went dry. I was the mother, supposed to be setting an example. I was not one of those women who raced from man to man, hunting for love and solace, finding only disappointment and rejection. Besides, men couldn't be trusted. My thoughts scrambled over one another like a panicking crowd trying to squeeze through a narrow exit.

Across the airwaves, my daughter was reading me. 'A bit of sex might do you good,' she added.

The words came out before I could stop them. 'I would never do that,' I said primly.

There. The universe had served up an opportunity to be honest. And I had lied.

Right then, I wanted an excuse to hang up. I wanted to run into the bush and hide and never return.

Sophia rolled her eyes. 'Fine then.'

And just like that, the climate of our conversation turned. Sophia was suddenly in a hurry to sign off as well. She looked as though speaking with me now was about as pleasurable as a smear test.

'I love you,' I managed just before she said goodbye and vanished.

The back of my neck burned. The inside of my cheek stung where I had bitten through the skin.

I walked back inside the retreat's gates feeling like a disgraceful, lying bog-witch who deserved to be burned alive.

CHAPTER NINETEEN

The Pretender's Map

Day Twelve (early afternoon)

As I handed in my mobile phone, the gorgeous receptionist gazed at me as if I reeked of hypocrisy and shame. He looked away quickly, as if the sight was just too hideous to behold.

Glancing at the cracks in my screen, he asked me if I wanted to arrange to have my phone fixed. No, I replied. It was working just fine.

Slapping the phone on the reception desk a little too hard, I walked away. I didn't want anyone fiddling with it. I didn't want anyone fiddling with anything that belonged to me. Including my thoughts. I hated myself right then. In the space of twenty-four hours, I had slept with a man too lovely to be true and lied to my daughter.

It was almost as though that great conductor in the sky, in whom I didn't believe, was orchestrating these events to torment me.

After lunch, still wading in that fug of self-loathing, I once more retrieved my cracked phone and made my way to Watson.

I tried to soothe myself as I walked. The day exhaled a cool autumnal breath and the bush surrounding the path to Watson was pungent with the fragrance of eucalypt and heather.

I told myself the only way to stop Lucas – with his lightness and beauty – from turning into a narcissistic abuser like my ex – was to keep my distance. After all, abuse always starts with love and intimacy, or at least a very convincing facsimile. And, as his behaviour deteriorates, you excuse him. Oh, you think when he comes home from work in an evil mood – something bad happened in the office. Or perhaps he's getting a cold. Or maybe he's hungry or tired. No doubt, Lucas would undergo a similar transformation if I gave him the opportunity.

My thoughts groused and tumbled like tattered smalls in an overheated drier. Once upon a time, my heart was a limpet – cemented to the rock of love and refusing to let go – even when that rock turned out to be the malodorous hide of a sea-monster. Why couldn't my heart be more like a dandelion puff drifting lightly on Binder's breezes? Why was I so damned *stuck*?

This morning's conversation with Sophia stabbed at my heart. I was such a hypocrite. If she found out I had lied, she might never trust me again. Just as Watson came into view, I stubbed my toe on a rock. The words arrived, attached to the voice of my ex. *Lying bitch. You are the scum of the earth. You deserve all this shit.*

I found Mary Nader inside the Watson General Store speaking with the young woman serving at the counter. Shovelling aside the sewerage system of shame backing up my thoughts, I greeted her warmly. She responded coolly, looking faintly embarrassed.

I ordered my takeaway coffee and sped after her as she scuttled from the shop, as if she didn't want to know me. I was having none of it. I knew exactly why she was avoiding me.

Shoulders hunched, she made her way down the footpath, heading back to the parish.

'Mary!' I called. She stopped and turned. Her eyes were filled with the same hunted fear I'd seen in the eyes of that man in the bush.

She wore a loose summer cardigan and had a French market basket slung over her shoulder. Its strap pulled at the collar of her cardigan and, just as I caught up with her, it pulled the sleeve down, revealing – on her upper right arm – a large bruise.

I caught only a fleeting glimpse. My heart jumped. Hurriedly, she pulled her cardigan back up. 'I'm sorry,' she said, 'I don't want to be rude but I'm in a bit of a rush.'

Her eyes darted, as if looking for ways to escape me.

'I know exactly what you mean, Mary,' I replied. 'Once, I was always in a rush too.'

I looked at the place on her arm where the bruise was once more hidden. 'I once covered my bruises as well.'

She stepped back as if she'd been hit again. The fine, translucent bags under her eyes made me think of battered rose petals.

I knew exactly why that bruise was there. Upper arm. Passenger seat driver side. I'd been hit in that same spot when we got lost traveling to Coffs Harbour. I was navigating. Poorly. The turnoff was hidden deep in the crease of the map. My ex kept punching me with each wrong turn. 'All I'm asking you to do is read that fucking map!' He yelled, deploying yet another punch to my upper arm. 'You are so fucking stupid!' Of course, we have satnavs now – less women – fewer poor navigators are getting their arms bruised. Abusers will have to find other ways to blame their victims when they get lost on Australia's back roads.

Mary blinked rapidly, avoiding my gaze. She greeted a passing woman and her drooling toddler with a beaming smile. I waited until they were out of earshot. I tried to keep my tone lightly inquisitive. 'So how did you get such a whopping bruise?'

She gave a forced laugh. 'Oh *that*,' she said. 'I bumped into a pew the other day.'

A pew? Was she on her hands and knees at the time? *Bullshit.*

Yet once, I had done the same thing. When an acquaintance asked me how I got *my* bruise, without even a second thought, I blithely told her I walked into a hat-stand in the middle of the night. Social instincts kicked in. To do anything different would have made her feel uncomfortable. It would have been awkward.

Afterwards I felt ashamed. I had let myself down. Of course, this is all part of your abuser's modus operandi. You, the victim feel shame. And your abuser feeds off this shame with the same relish as a parasite sucking its host's blood. He knows your weak spots. He knows exactly where to target his wrath. That incremental erosion of the spirit, that infestation of doubt, is part of his strategy. You destroy yourself to please him.

It still pains me to write these words. I can feel that phantom gall bladder, that ghostly Minister of Justice, still writhing in that gap under my ribs.

My blood heated. I felt angry on Mary's behalf. Unlike deceitful me, I could tell Mary was a good woman. A kind woman. She deserved none of this.

'Oh, I see,' I replied, giving her a look that I hoped was both loving and supportive, but also conveyed I knew she was lying.

Mary took another step back, trying to create more distance between us. I felt torn between the obvious torment I was inflicting on her and my frustration over her predicament.

Another passer-by greeted Mary, the man glancing at me with benign curiosity. They exchanged brief words about his daughter who was recovering from an early bout of flu. It was clear Mary was well-liked, well-known and respected in Watson.

'And how is *your* daughter?' I persisted, once the man had left. 'I hear you were up in Sydney visiting her at a concert?'

Her eyes lit up at the mention of her daughter. Yes, she said, she and Quentin were so proud of their daughter, who had performed a solo piece on her cello.

'It must've been lovely to have a break with your husband,' I added, knowing it was probably more like a trip through the nine circles of hell.

'Oh, yes,' Mary said crisply in a high voice. 'Quentin is such a hard worker. So busy. Such a good man. He's doing so much for the community. He really did need the break.'

I'll bet he did, I thought. *Two hours in a car to abuse and punch his wife.*

I raised my eyebrows. She knew I was baiting her. We both knew how that public persona that was her husband, that *reverend*, was so finely crafted it seemed impossible to imagine that such a charming beneficent man could be the perpetrator of such evils. It was clear she also knew that I knew she was lying.

'And now, I really do need to go,' she added again. She took a shuddery breath that spoke volumes. 'I'm meeting my husband,' she added.

I nodded, understanding. I had once rushed around at my husband's beck and call as well. After all, your abuser has succeeded in persuading you of his importance. Above all, you will deny your unhappiness. You will present to the world a happy face. You are a capable woman. You dress well. You smile graciously. You hide your pain. Eventually you turn invisible. The crime vanishes. It will be buried along with you when you become ill, go mad, or die. Or are murdered.

And of course, by taking his name, Mary Nader was already branded as her husband's possession. It was only a few more blows before her complete annihilation.

Behind me, a car pulled up into the car park. Mary – already pale – turned white. She looked at me then as if she hated me, as if she hated that I had intuited all the ghastly details of her marriage. She looked at me as if *I* was the problem.

I understood it all in that moment. I had stepped over the invisible line. I knew she would do everything now to avoid me. Mary wanted to turn invisible. And, if her husband was successful, she would vanish entirely.

Across the road, through the four-wheel drive's tinted glass, I saw Reverend Nader sitting in the car watching us with eyes as hot and blue as gas-lit flames.

CHAPTER TWENTY

Uninvited

Day Twelve (late afternoon)

My heart aching for poor, bruised, abused, Mary, I arrived back at the retreat feeling addled and restless. I wanted to help her but I had no idea how.

After I'd handed my phone into reception, I saw two elderly women shuffling into a conference room down the corridor. Inside, I heard Galilea's voice, just before the door slammed shut.

I strolled to the noticeboard, but saw no mention of an afternoon lecture.

The receptionist was distracted by another guest, so rather than asking, I decided to investigate. After striding purposefully down the corridor, I gently opened the door and peeped inside.

In the room, I saw a surprising amount of technology for a retreat that banned the stuff. A large screen engulfed the back wall and a laptop sat on the desk in front. A scattering of women sat facing Galilea who was standing at the far end of the room. Among the audience, I recognised several of the long stay residents, minus the men I saw frequently keeping them company.

Galilea's face was turned towards the screen, so she didn't see me as I entered.

On the screen was a picture of an African woman standing against a backdrop of parched soil and half-dead trees. 'Bolanle has no access to clean water,' Galilea was saying as I crept inside. 'Her husband was killed in a local war and she has four children to feed. In addition, Kalifa, her oldest daughter – along with an entire class of young girls – was kidnapped by a local militia group. Kalifa is now pregnant with one of her kidnapper's children.'

Mutters of indignation and disgust rippled through the room.

Ever so quietly, I slid into a chair behind a tall woman with big hair taking notes on a clipboard.

Galilea spoke about female poverty and the way in which the most vulnerable countries and communities were suffering the greatest effects of climate change. She spoke about exploitation of the environment, oppressive traditions such as clitorectomies, women in impoverished communities resorting to prostitution to feed their families.

When she looked up, I moved my head, so I was directly behind the woman with the clipboard. Hidden.

Even as I cowered in my chair, I felt a stab of envy as I regarded Galilea. Up there, facing her audience she was in command. Powerful, passionate and righteous. I coveted her poise and confidence, her straight back and a perfect posture I could only dream about. I could only hope that when I reached my sixties, I would look as good as her. Be as assured as her.

Behind her, images of planetary devastation – parched soil and bleached coral reefs and human deprivation – emaciated mothers holding their starved babies – populated the screen. Galilea explained how climate change, global politics, economic systems and human rights were inexorably intertwined. 'We cannot carry on like this,' she said fiercely. 'We must stop this rapacious plundering and abuse of women and our planet.'

I pressed my thighs together, trying to remain small and insignificant. *I shouldn't be here,* a little voice at the back of my mind bleated. *Why the hell not?* I replied to my eternally doubting self.

I peered over the shoulder of the woman in front of me. The sheet of paper on her lap said: *Seminar for Week Five Guests* followed by a list of names. Some of the names had handwritten notes beside them. No, I wasn't supposed to be here. I was a week two guest and employee.

Galilea addressed a woman in the front row. 'We have forgotten how to act as good guests walking gently over Mother Earth,' she said. 'And this is because human civilization is currently defined by a male paradigm. A system of domination and conquest.'

The woman Galilea was speaking to nodded vigorously. 'Yes, corporate hierarchies, planet-screwing industries and profit-driven businesses are all diseases of righteous, wealthy, middle-aged white men,' the woman said.

'And my ex-husband was one of them!' shouted another.

Claps scattered through the room. *So was mine,* I thought.

The air in the room seemed to heat. This room was *angry.* I thought of Mary Nader's bruise and my back heated as well.

'We cannot heal our planet until we address this assault on the welfare and dignity of women,' Galilea continued.

Another image appeared on the screen – a woman and two children holding bundles of possessions and wading through floodwaters against a hurricane-shredded backdrop.

'Overwhelmingly, the victims of war, political corruption and climate change are women and children,' she said. 'Human rights are women's rights. And the planet, our home, is out of balance.'

Even though all the images I'd seen were heart-rending, I felt in that moment as though Galilea had a distinct agenda – an agenda that was more than just a diatribe about climate change, economic inequities and human rights. She was up to something else. Subtly manipulating.

'Men have made a right cock up of things!' someone shouted.

'The patriarchy is raping Mother Earth!' another added.

'Blame religions! They're the worst!' A woman at the front of the room shouted. 'If this were the middle-ages, we would all be put to the stake! Burned for our independent thinking!'

'Witches!' said one woman.

'Yes please!' said another.

Women laughed. Someone cackled loudly, which made everyone laugh even more. I quietly smiled and thought of Reverend Nader's gas-lit gaze. This gathering would be one of his worst nightmares.

Galilea gave a measured smile. 'The patriarchy – that male competitive, oppressive and entitled mindset – has overwhelmingly replaced a desire for truth, respect and human progress,' she said.

I wanted to put my hand up, challenge Galilea and ask about all the men equally disadvantaged by the patriarchal system. But I knew it would derail her agenda. She was carefully stoking her audience's fires. Leading them to a destination I had yet to discover.

'Instead of submitting to fossilised doctrines and deeply ingrained misogyny, we must look for feminine solutions to man-made problems. We must address the way in which men treat women personally. Professionally. Globally. We must work directly with Mother Earth. Consult with her. Respect her.'

I leaned forward, peered over the woman's shoulder and squinted at her clip board.

Under each of the women's names was the first name of a man. *Geoffrey, Thomas, Aaron.*

Something cold shuddered through me. Those were *Yindisha's* men. Every one of these women in the audience had their own personal *boyfriend? Butler? Man-whore?* I wondered.

I shouldn't be here, I thought again. *I haven't been invited.*

'Yes, men are overwhelmingly responsible for our planet's ills, but perhaps we women are going about this in the wrong way as well?' Galilea offered. 'Perhaps it's time for women to stop blaming their problems on men?' she continued.

She smiled warmly. 'Perhaps it's time for women to take charge.' She paused, waiting for her words to sink in.

'How? Most men in power aren't ready to listen to the voices of women...' a woman at the front said. 'They're too stuck in their ways. So many men pay lip service to women's emancipation. But underneath – just give them a bit of time, familiarity and contempt – and they all lapse back into their old habits.'

I shuddered as a silence filled the room. Yes, I knew the script. That was what my ex had done when we first met. Pretended. And then lapsed back into his default setting.

And then, another woman – one I hadn't heard before – spoke. She sounded ancient – her voice quaked, but her words were loud and clear.

'But not *Yindisha's* men,' she said.

'No.' Galilea said swiftly and firmly. 'Not Yindisha's men. Yindisha's men are... *different.*'

Another silence followed, as if all these women were thinking the same thing – about those beautiful men with whom they shared their thoughts and no doubt, their beds.

A bodily memory of Lucas pounding me into my mattress sideswiped me, along with a tiny orgasmic echo. I shuddered, suddenly feeling weak and exposed.

I crouched back into my chair as Galilea's gaze once more scanned the audience.

'Women have a duty to hold men to higher standards,' continued Galilea.

I could feel a great welling of approval swell though the room.

I shifted in my seat as a hollow opened in my stomach.

'And here in Yindisha we have both a very selective recruitment policy and an exceptional training program which holds our male employees to these higher standards...'

'Imagine if *all* men behaved like Yindisha's men,' one of the guests said. 'We would live in a different world.'

The woman in front of me wrote a note beside another name.

They're recruiting women, I thought. Monitoring them. *But why? And for what?*

'The world would be unrecognisable!' another offered.

The whole room seemed to purr like a collective of contented cats.

Galilea gazed at her audience, nodded firmly and then drew a long breath.

'So, instead of women trying to fit in to a men's world, *why not change the men?*' she asked.

Unfortunately, my stomach decided in that moment to emit a long, low growl. The woman in front of me spun around. Her eyes widened in alarm.

'Alethea?' She knew my name. But I didn't know *her.*

She glanced back at the door.

'The door was supposed to be locked,' she hissed.

Her gaze softened into a kind but concerned look. 'It's a seminar for week five residents. A private session...'

'I'm sorry,' I blathered as I rose to leave. 'I was curious. It sounded interesting...'

Why not change the men?

Those words echoed inside my head as she rose and ushered me out the door. When I briefly turned back, I saw Galilea looking at me. Half the women in the audience turned as well.

Fuck.

I strode back to my cottage feeling shaken and stirred.

What was the difference between me and those women who had been at Yindisha three weeks longer? What had changed in them? Why wasn't someone like me – someone coming up to my second week – allowed to attend?

And why did that woman I had never met know my name?

Why not change the men?

How? I wondered as I made my way to the dining room for an early dinner.

There was no one else at dinner, just a cheerful hunk called David setting up the servery.

As I ate, I considered how I couldn't argue with Galilea. A lot of the issues she covered were common knowledge. Yet she had been stirring and steering those women. And most of them seemed willing to be guided to where she was taking them.

This was how cult leaders behaved. They nibbled away at our insecurities, fed our soulful hungering with suggestions and ideas that seemed – on the surface – reasonable, world-changing and wonderful. But underneath it all, invariably, was a more sinister agenda.

Why not change the men?

After dinner, I went for an evening walk where I was bitten by mosquitoes.

How were they changing the men? Where were they changing the men? I wondered as I walked. As I looked deep into the bush's north-west shadows, I knew right then the men were trained and *changed* at the research station. Which meant Lucas was lying.

That thought made me feel utterly weary and heartbroken.

I swatted the mosquito dining on my elbow and turned back to my cottage.

By the time I got back, my skin was on fire and my feet felt as though they were encased in concrete gumboots. Hoping that wasn't a premonition, overwhelmed by my day, I wearily undressed and showered. I thought how I had no choice now. I had to ask more questions. Dig deeper. But always, always, remain resolutely detached. A part of me still anticipating that inevitable knock on the door, overwhelmed by today's dramas, I put on my nightie and crawled into bed. *Why not change the men?*

My thoughts dipped and circled, like a wary bird trying to find a safe place to land.

What had they done to Lucas?

CHAPTER TWENTY-ONE

Entropy

Day Thirteen

There are days in life I call entropy days. These are the days when the entire universe seems to conspire against you and all your efforts to conduct life in an orderly manner are stymied. These are the days which begin, perhaps, with a blocked toilet. Maybe a flat car battery follows and a long over-due mammogram must be cancelled. At this point entropy – that second law of thermodynamics that states closed systems always degenerate towards maximum disorder – is just getting started. The toaster explodes in a blaze of sparks and short-circuits the fuse box. The cricket-obsessed boy in the property behind yours hits his ball over the fence and smashes the pane of one of your French door windows. Instead of apologising, his father – after he's climbed the fence and trampled over your azaleas – implies this is all your fault for having French doors blocking the trajectory of his son's magnificent strike. For a fleeting moment, you understand why people who own guns are tempted to use them.

Chaos builds, feeding on itself like some self-sustaining, toxic, and fucked-up ecosystem.

After a night in which all my dreams seemed to contain some version of a stark-naked me barging into private gatherings, I woke feeling headachy and bilious. Outside, a restive wind fidgeted with the trees. Pools of morning light danced across my cottage floor and when I rose, the ground seemed to shift under my feet. I stubbed my toe on the kitchen's island bench. I felt agitated. Dithery. My mother would have called it getting up on the wrong side of bed. My ex, if he had been in a good mood, would have laughed and called me a dumb and ditsy twat.

Today was nearly two weeks since I arrived at Yindisha Retreat. A day since I lied to my daughter. Two days since I had sex with Lucas. *Lucas.*

Despite suspecting he was a liar, every cell in my body sparkled when I thought of him. Already, my body felt hungry for more. Not only was I addicted to coffee, but I had added another need to my repertoire of bad habits. I wanted Lucas again. He had woken something inside me. The emotionally needy woman. The desperate divorcee. The insecure depressive. The self-destructive artist. The nymphomaniac.

After dressing in slow motion, I stepped out into a cool autumnal day. The sun sparked and winked between the canopy of trees. Clouds blown into eccentric whorls and feathers dusted the sky. Birds quarrelled in the trees. The air smelt of nutmeg and lilacs mingled with intermittent whiffs of concentrated compost.

Determined to keep that second law of thermodynamics firmly in its place through the application of a disciplined consciousness, after breakfast, I joined a meditation class.

Trying to focus on my breathing, putting my monkey thoughts in bubbles and blowing them away, I happened to glance out the window just as Lucas walked past. Although he didn't see me, when I drank in the sight of him, my nether regions broke into a full-blown and psychotic flamenco. In that moment, meditation was off the menu. I felt hungry for him. I wanted a second helping. I also wanted to force him to tell me the truth about his relationship with Yindisha.

Entropy rubbed its hands in glee.

Trying to wean myself from my lusty thoughts, I spent the next hour in the retreat's library looking at art books. I spent an additional good half hour looking through an attractive volume on the Goddesses of ancient Greek and Roman mythology. Afterwards, I went for a walk with my sketch book and spent a few hours drawing leaves and flowers and trees. Nothing seemed to work. My leaves looked dead on the page. I couldn't catch the rhythm of the flowers, or the power of the trees. I returned feeling dissatisfied. With my art. With myself.

On the way back to my cottage, a bird shat on me.

At lunch, I noticed several new male staff members. I noted I hadn't seen Tamati the New Zealander or Kayden the Iranian refugee for several days. Had they already moved on to other jobs? Or had they been fired? Rising panic followed. Perhaps Lucas would leave without telling me?

To calm myself, I observed the new guests more closely as I made light chat with them. They were all painted in the same broad brush-strokes. Middle-aged. Wary and damaged-looking. My imagination went into overdrive. In all their eyes I could see the same simmering secrets, lingering pains and resentments. In the ones chatting to Yindisha's men, I saw pathetic gratitude for the attention of these beautiful specimens of manhood. I realised I was no different. I was one of them. Pathetic. Desperate.

Passing the reception desk, I noticed the receptionist was new as well. Another gorgeous male. Just a different shape and colour. He was talking to Galilea. I watched as she leaned over the counter, put her hand on his chest and drew her face close to his. He looked back at her as if completely held in her thrall.

That strange moment of intimacy confounded me. What was

she doing? Was she seducing him? Hypnotising him? Did she fuck all the male employees? Had she fucked Lucas? Was that how she *changed* them?

Quietly, I slipped past, feeling a kind of slow and bitter unravelling.

Down the hall, I heard sounds of bucolic laughter. Wondering what was so funny, I paused outside a classroom. A sign on the door said: 'Hasya Yoga.'

Inside, I heard all manner of laughs, titters and guffaws. *Ho ho. Ha, ha, ha...*

'It's contagious, isn't it?'

I swivelled towards the voice. My heart lurched as I looked into Galilea's smiling eyes.

She had crept up silently behind me, like a stalking cat.

'It's called laughter yoga,' she explained. She went on to say it encouraged positive thinking, and how a man called William Frey – a psychiatrist at Stanford University – had documented the health benefits of mirthful laughter and discovered it increased circulation, reduced pain, assisted cardiopulmonary rehabilitation and lifted depression.

I listened, feeling tight and combative. *Where are the quality studies, the absolute scientific proofs?* I wanted to ask.

I felt a firewall rise between us. I waited for her to mention my unwelcome presence at yesterday's seminar, because I damned well wasn't going to apologise. I thought of my foray into the bush and what I'd seen and felt even more defiant.

Galilea regarded me and her expression sobered. 'I'm sorry I haven't had a chance to catch up with you, Alethea. I've been busy.' She glanced away, back towards reception. 'It's been a very hectic week...'

Problems with the staff perhaps? With the untrainable men? Men who don't want to be changed? I wondered. I thought then how she had more of the air of a ruler of some expansionist empire than the owner of a small and quirky Southern Highlands retreat.

In the Hasya Yoga room, everyone laughed even louder.

Something in Galilea's gaze shifted and she smiled again. 'The body doesn't know the difference between real laughter and fake laughter. At some point, the make-believe version transforms into the real thing,' she added.

Another shriek of fake laughter replied.

'It's about flexibility. It's about embracing experiences we find strange,' she added. It's about looking at the world in a new way.'

I felt then as if she were speaking in code, trying to explain something obliquely.

She looked away for a moment, as if carefully considering her next words.

'A fair number of the women who visit Yindisha have been emotionally and physically abused,' she said. 'Everything we do here helps them heal.'

'Including the men,' I muttered before I could stop myself.

'Yes. The men,' Galilea replied. I heard a note of satisfaction in her voice. Again, I wondered if she seduced them all.

I mentioned there seemed to be quite a turnover of male staff.

Instead of agreeing or denying, her face darkened as if sideswiped by some ugly memory. 'There are men in the world who despise gentleness. They see it as weakness. And, so great is their indignation, so profound is their righteousness, that they destroy everything that is beautiful.'

I felt unsteadied by the force of her words. To whom was she referring? The men that had left? Had they not met Yindisha's high standards? Had they been scoundrels? Secret arseholes?

My coffee withdrawal headache throbbed.

'The legacy of relentless male abuse is long and wide and deep,' Galilea continued. 'Abuse makes women lose confidence. They lose touch with themselves, their hopes, their talents, their capacity for self-love and the love and nourishing of others.'

My thoughts jumped back to that man fleeing in the bush, followed by an image of Diana the Huntress in the mythology book I'd read earlier. *So as revenge for that abuse, you invite women to hunt and kill men? Is that what Galilea did with the men who failed to make Yindisha's grade? Had those women chased that man through the bush as a sport? Like some kind of feminist fox hunt?*

My insides chilled.

'Women have fed the beast of the patriarchy for millennia,' continued Galilea. 'We have been condemned to ride it for fear of being eaten if we dismount. But now that beast is weakening. And a weak and frightened beast is dangerous. The threatened beast lashes out irrationally. Destroys indiscriminately.'

Although I had no trouble yelling at an Anglican minister, Galilea's passion rendered me speechless. In her words, I sensed a veiled and strange religiosity that made me uneasy. I listened as she spoke of how men's taming of women had isolated us from our spiritual roots. She told me Yindisha aimed to protect, resurrect and channel what was wild and innate in women.

I was considering asking her whether wild and innate included fucking all her male staff, when the new receptionist strode up to us.

'An urgent call,' he said to Galilea. 'At the front desk.'

When she excused herself and turned, I noticed Galilea moved slightly stiffly, as if managing some old wound or hidden pain. Arthritis, perhaps. Or some other illness she covered well. I watched her walk down the hall, the receptionist close by her side. I watched her reach up and ruffle his hair. My insides heated.

Man eater, I thought. *Cult Leader...*

'Laugh louder, from the belly. From the heart.' I heard the yoga instructor say.

Recalling that man I had seen in the bush, my insides hardened. I turned away. Nothing about this place was funny. Everything about this place was strange.

I arrived at my cottage and couldn't open the door. My key was stuck and refused to turn.

Returning to reception, I arrived just in time to see Galilea with a set look on her face step into her car and drive away. The only place she could be heading in such a rush was the research station.

Meanwhile, the receptionist looked at my key and then checked my paperwork. 'Ah,' he said. 'You've been here nearly two weeks. Tomorrow your trial period will be over.'

I nodded feebly. *Thanks for reminding me*, I thought. *I'm about to be told I'm no longer wanted.* A memory of Lucas's touch stroked my insides. *I still have unfinished business.*

After taking a harder look at my key, the receptionist pulled open a draw behind the desk, saying that, with older locks, Three in One oil usually did the trick. He oiled my key, daintily placed it in a paper bag so I wouldn't get greasy hands and told me to return again if it didn't work.

I walked back to my cottage with a storm in my brain. I wiggled the key in the lock. My door opened. With a great sigh, I looked around, thinking how my trial period at Yindisha was nearly over. In the next few days, I would receive my sentence.

I opened a window to let in some fresh air. Seconds later, a tawny frogmouth flew inside. It flapped around, knocked over the vase of flowers on the dining table, briefly perched on the standing lamp next to the couch and stared at me with that expression animals have of knowing exactly what's going on in your soul. Just as I pulled a towel from the bathroom to shoo it outside, it gracefully rose and flew back out the open window.

I stood for a moment in my swirl of entropy, staring at the retreating shape of that strange, wide-mouthed bird that looked like an owl, but wasn't.

Inhaling the scent of some heady dusk blooms, memories of Lucas's touch flared into an eruption of desire. *When you can't beat entropy, go with its flow. Embrace chaos.*

I exited my cottage in a state of surrender. I found Lucas in the dining room, having an early dinner and hustled him aside. 'Lucas. I need to speak to you. Alone. In my cottage.'

CHAPTER TWENTY-TWO

Wild and Innate

Day Thirteen, (evening)

Back in the privacy of my cottage, I told Lucas I was concerned for his safety. 'Something about Yindisha doesn't add up,' I explained. 'In the two weeks I've been here, I've seen a high turnover of male staff. I'm worried you might be next to disappear.'

When I mentioned Tamati and Kayden, he chuckled and said they had both been at Yindisha for years. It was just an unfortunate coincidence they had left for other jobs within a week of my arrival. He added that he wasn't planning to go anywhere soon.

I replied that perhaps that wasn't his decision to make.

When I asked what he thought of Galilea, he smiled benignly. 'I don't have much to do with her. She trusts us. She leaves the managers to do their jobs.'

I looked for secrets deep his eyes and saw nothing but authenticity. Beauty. Kindness. Sex. Fronds of desire unfurled deep in my belly. I was hungry. But not for food.

I drew a deep breath. Business first. 'I recently heard Yindisha has a unique training programme for its male employees.' I looked hard into his clear amber eyes. 'And I wondered. Did you have some kind of induction programme before you started working here?

'Yes. of course. I did a week's training. We covered feminist theory. Climate change. Sustainability philosophies.'

'Where?'

'Here. At the retreat.'

I stared into his eyes. I'd learned to recognise that shifty, defiant look my ex got when he was lying. But everything about Lucas seemed genuine.

'You weren't trained at the research station?'

'No.' He looked genuinely puzzled.

I looked away. My coffee withdrawal headache pounded at the back of my skull.

So, what are they doing to the men? I thought. *Giving them some super-vitamin that enhances their learning capacities? Makes them more receptive? More pliant? And was that all it took? A week?*

'You seem upset about something,' Lucas observed. He moved closer.

The proximity of him was making my insides tingle with desire.

Stop overthinking everything Alethea, I told myself. *There's a beautiful man in your hall. Yield to your wild side. It's what Mother Earth wants...*

'I'm fine,' I lied. 'Just curious about how this place really operates.'

I stepped towards Lucas and, as I had seen Galilea do, ran my hand through his hair. He responded with a kiss on my cheek. I moved my face so our lips touched and we plunged into a long, delicious kiss that made my insides erupt.

Lucas pulled back and mentioned he was due back in the orchards for an evening meeting with his manager.

'When?' I murmured, hungrily tracing my hands over his perfect breast.

'In half an hour,' he replied.

'Plenty of time then.' I reached for the bottom of his tee shirt and began pulling it off.

'You want to hurry through this?' He said as if concerned about the quality of our encounter.

Still gripping his shirt, I gazed into his eyes. What red-blooded man ever said no to a quick, hot fuck? But Lucas seem to care. He was prepared to forgo an opportunity for sex to make sure it was really what I wanted, or at least of a standard I wanted. *Who was this man? What was this man?* I wondered.

I wanted him right then even more. Even if it only lasted five minutes. Five minutes with him would eclipse a lifetime of pleasures. Oh, the ways we think in the heat of desire.

'Do *you* want this?' I managed, uncertain how I would react if he said no. I would probably die on the spot. Or spontaneously combust.

'If it makes you happy, of course.'

'Then let's not waste any time.' I ripped off his shirt.

I paused, noticing a scar below his left nipple. I ran my hand over the ridge. 'You've been hurt.'

'A long time ago. I was mugged. In New York.'

He told me how, while visiting New York one autumn, he had come across an old couple being held up at knifepoint in an alley and had intervened.

'Luckily the knife went in just below my heart. Luckily I had travel health insurance.'

'Wow,' was all I could say, even as I thought: *Not only is he sexy, he is also brave and chivalrous. And canny enough to have health insurance while traveling through the USA. This man is just too perfect to be true.*

Desire put a roadblock on further questions. I continued to undress him, more gently now, because once upon a time he had been injured. And I cared. He responded in kind.

'You are so beautiful,' he said as he unhooked my bra and ran his hands over my bare breasts.

Stars sparkled over my skin. When had I last heard a man say I was beautiful? It had been a while. 'So are you,' I managed.

We didn't make it to the bedroom but instead crumbled onto the runner in the hall. As I swayed to his exquisite rhythms, I thought of the ghosts of those Methodist Girls School mistresses watching over us, clucking with disapproval.

Time expanded and contracted like a universe collapsing and being reborn. I was a brilliant lover. I was a genius. A gymnast. And oh, I was beautiful!

His poundings grew more insistent, more powerful. Now, I was a worm under a rock. Some legless crawling creature – wretched and bad, wicked and evil and deserving of this violent, punishing, flagellation. When I straddled him, I was a wild creature, in touch with my inner brute. In total control. Filled with a sensual potency, I snarled and rutted like a beast on heat until my insides seemed to turn liquid. My body felt open and fluid. Pleasure broke though me, sharp and sweet, like some wondrous nectar. *Take that all you repressed Methodist ghosts watching from your pious, saintly realm!*

A sensual power rose through me, welling outwards like some locked up creature bursting from an ancient skin. *This is heaven,* I thought as my body, annihilated and reborn, rose to a peak of ecstasy. For moment I felt whole, as if our coupling had been a reunion with some ancient, divided self.

A delirious all-enveloping magnanimity filled me and seemed to ignite the room in a fiery glow. My soul's wings broke free. A great, welling generosity of spirit soared through me.

After Lucas pushed me on to my back, taking me once more from above, I released a primal scream. I was a creature cleaved and re-joined into an infinite, fiery form. Above me, Lucas shuddered like a leaf caught in my blaze.

After it was over, I felt the loss of him as he moved off me. Yet my body still felt heavy, as if sinking in quicksand.

For a few seconds (or perhaps it was hours – I no longer had any sense of time after such incandescent pleasure) I lay on the runner, filled with an inner shimmering, feeling like a newborn star. Something resembling a thought – something with no more substance than a neutrino – shot through me. I turned onto my side, my gaze trailing over the ivy and poppy pattern on the runner – ivy for hope and immortality. Poppies for sleep.

I tried to keep my tone light. 'Do you supply any other guests with such personalised service?'

He turned and gazed at me. 'There is only you.'

I didn't know in that moment how to reply. Terror and delight shot through me in equal measure.

Something half-formed and blurry blipped, resurfaced and vanished into the fog of my thoughts. This time, I hadn't cried. I felt pleased with myself, as if I'd taken back a morsel of the power I'd lost in my marriage.

'I'm sorry...I have to go,' he said when I didn't respond with an equally amorous, post-coital platitude. He rose and we both dressed in swift silence.

Happy to have my body back, separate and whole, I gave him a tender kiss goodbye. I felt faintly relieved he was leaving, giving me time to re-group my thoughts.

Yet as I watched him stride down the path, my entropic storm returned.

Love like this would spoil me. Pleasure like this would ruin me. A cascade of jealousy and suspicion followed. My thoughts suddenly turned phthalocyanine green – a poisonous, insane green that could wreck an entire painting with a single misplaced brushstroke. Lucas was lying. Of course, he was lying. Who else at Yindisha did he fuck?

Feeling all at once possessive and possessed, I realised in that frightening moment how deeply I had fallen under Yindisha's spell.

There is only you. Smoothing my ruffled clothes, I mulled over those words – both terrifying and exhilarating in equal measure – and wondered at that human capacity to hold simultaneously conflicting thoughts without one devouring the other.

I was the only one. Lucas's words suddenly frightened me. I thought of an old boyfriend and how I enjoyed his obsessive attention until it became too much. When I broke off with him, he wept and hounded me then went into a major depression and threatened suicide. After I told him he didn't need a girlfriend but professional help, he suddenly stopped stalking me. He moved on to a new woman he eventually married. I heard they're divorced now. They have three children. Probably all of them in therapy.

I thought of all those stalkers and cheaters and dumpers and how anything in between is called a relationship. I thought of the way that men always want to appear as if they are in control. Even when they aren't. They've always called the shots. And they're always trying to prove you are wrong. And then, there was Lucas. And then, there were Yindisha's men. Different. But perhaps underneath just the same, just more skilfully disguised versions of typical, treacherous manhood.

Suddenly feeling ravenously hungry, I went to dinner and, alone in the dining room again, ate an enormous and healthy meal.

A few minutes after I returned to my cottage, there was a knock on my door. I thought perhaps Lucas had returned. For more. Because it had just been so damn good. A man I didn't recognise stood on the threshold. Handsome, of course.

He handed me a note. 'A message from Galilea,' he said, giving me a sage look. He nodded respectfully, turned, and left.

Alethea, I'm sorry I didn't get a chance to have a proper catch up this afternoon. It would've been nice to have had time to sit down with a cup of tea. We have some things we need to discuss. If you are available, please meet me in my office at 10:00 AM tomorrow morning.

My insides went cold at the painful inevitability to come.

Everything had repercussions. Time grew from a process of cause and effect. Sex with Lucas had consequences. My curiosity had consequences. I would be punished for being nosey. This was the way the world turned. Every intake of breath, every step I took gave me tiny glimpses of life's tapestry. Every moment of pleasure, every childhood joy was nothing but another fragment building towards tragedy. Pleasure always gave way to despair. Death followed rapture.

An overwhelming and heavy tiredness came over me. I undressed as if my body had turned to lead. I didn't put on my pyjamas, but instead, went to bed naked, wanting to relive those moments with Lucas, as if some part of me knew it was the end of something that had just begun.

As I lay and stared at the wavering shadows thrown by the bitten moon's silvery glow, more of William Blake's words came to me:

The lust of the goat is the bounty of God.

I noticed then, I had gone a whole day without coffee and my headache had gone.

I thanked my orgasm.

Once more, memories of pleasure swarmed though me. This tiger's tank was filled. This goat was content. Tomorrow I would tackle this all head on. I was Alethea Braxton. Woman. Beautiful. Powerful. I would take what was mine and discard the rest. A half-formed plan took root.

Filled with the drowsy syrup of satisfaction, I gave in to sleep.

CHAPTER TWENTY-THREE

The Threatened Beast

Day Fourteen, 8am

Refreshed after a heavy sleep, I woke early. My thoughts were tangled up in erotic memories of Lucas and dreams I couldn't recall. I rose lightly, feeling as though my shoulder blades had grown wings. I felt lightened, powerful, sated. The world felt different, as if I had stepped into some parallel universe in which I was a better, stronger, sexier version of myself.

Resolving to walk into today's meeting with Galilea with confidence, ready to negotiate, ready to confront what I had seen in the bush head on, I dressed and stepped out into the morning's cold autumnal blast. Curling fingers of mist rose from the lawns. My breath fogged the air. The world felt clean, alive and sharp. Ready for the challenges that lay ahead, I made my way to an early breakfast.

When I arrived in the dining room, there were no men, just four female staff members including Saniya. They were deep in conversation at a round table in a corner.

Saniya looked up, saw me, gave me a cool hello and returned

to her conversation. The other staff members – women I didn't know well – glanced at me and quickly looked away.

It was a small thing, but the shock of it hit me like a punch in the stomach. I saw mistrust and fear in their glances. I felt in that instance as though I was no longer one of them, but a stranger and a possibly a traitor.

Recalling those cameras and how they had witnessed me ignoring the retreat's warnings to not wander off the trails, and my more recent seminar gate-crash, my stomach squirmed. While I was at the servery, the four women left. Those wings that felt as though they have sprouted from my shoulder-blades shrunk into nubs – embryonic devil wings, pointed, leathery and dark.

My legs shook as I sat down at the main dining table with my bowl of Bircher muesli, vanilla yoghurt and berries. Alone at the table like a diner inhabiting some brooding Edward Hopper painting, I suddenly didn't feel hungry. I felt ill. The room felt shadowy and filled with forebodings. I had seen and heard things I wasn't supposed to see and hear. And I knew in that instance I was about to be fired.

I ate without pleasure in maudlin solitude, now convinced everyone at Yindisha had heard about my spying. And perhaps there were even cameras in my cottage – tiny things I couldn't see? Had they been watching? Judging? And who exactly, were *they*?

There was something pure, almost virginal about Lucas. Perhaps part of my test was to not exploit these fragile, beautiful men, to not defile their gentle innocence. Lucas had been a test of my restraint. And I had failed.

My mother once told me middle age was a dangerous time for women and love. Women can go a bit crazy, she said. I considered the biological mechanisms behind that craziness, the mechanisms behind *my* behaviour with Lucas. Perhaps it had something to do with my menopausal hormones shooting all over the place. I was farewelling a fertile youth. Amidst the dying cries and convulsions of my reproductive life, I was desperately holding on and trying to resurrect the past.

I recalled Galilea's words. *The threatened beast lashes out irrationally. Destroys indiscriminately.*

Was that me? A woman threatened by loss of her sexual power? Lashing out? Like a beast?

What about middle-aged women who left marriages for teenage boys? Who visited nightclubs, danced until dawn flashing crinkled cleavages, varicose-veined legs, crow's feet and bags under eyes, liver spots and moles all masked with foundation? Although I no longer had a husband or a dependent child to abandon or embarrass, was I any different?

Perhaps, through fucking Lucas, I had destroyed beauty and purity and corrupted innocence. Perhaps I had desecrated an angel. *Raped* an angel. And, now Lucas was fallen, that polluted creature would be hunted and brought down before he turned into a monster. That was Yindisha's secret. They killed what other women – horny women in the grip of menopausal madness (like me) – had defiled.

By trying to protect Lucas, I had inadvertently destroyed him. *You are a bad woman.* So said the voice of my ex.

I rose, slammed my bowl and empty orange juice glass into the hatch that separated the dining room from the kitchen where beautiful men washed and dried dishes and replaced empty serving bowls. I strode from the dining room.

Telling myself I was using religious tropes and unconscious indoctrinations to chastise myself for what had simply been an encounter of pure pleasure, I tried to pull myself together. Yindisha's men could just as easily be criminals, scoundrels and liars as innocent angels. Probably, like most of humanity, they were mixtures of both. And besides, angels didn't exist.

I walked through gardens now weeping with dew, cursing

my ridiculous imaginings, anticipating what was to come and pondering the practicalities.

Once I had been fired and perhaps walked off the premises by a security guard before I inflicted any more damage, I mulled over what I would do once I returned to Sydney. I would have to find a rental until my tenants' lease expired. Perhaps I would apply for a part time job at Bunnings. They hired older people and I've always liked hardware stores. I might get a job in the paint mixing department. I knew my acrylics from my enamels. I knew about solvents and colour mixing.

Or perhaps I would go back to university and study horticulture. But how could I afford to do that? I doubted at forty-eight years of age I would get a student loan. I would have to mortgage the house.

On my way back to my cottage, I passed one of those beautiful men beheading dead hydrangeas. He greeted me by name and asked how I was.

Fabulous, I lied.

And how would I cope on my own again after all this delectable, attentive company?

Perhaps I would get a puppy.

By the time I arrived back at my cottage, I was feeling despondent and depressed. I slumped onto the sofa in my lounge, brooded and gnawed at my nails.

I glanced down at that runner on which last night, Lucas and I had so deliciously fucked. *It had been mutual. We were two fully consenting adults.* My insides hardened. My time at Yindisha had, in many ways, only just started. I enjoyed teaching my classes. I wanted to know what was going on at the research station. I wanted to see Mary Nader have the courage to leave her husband. I sat upright and drew a resolute breath. No. I wasn't going to leave Yindisha Retreat without making a mark. I wasn't going to leave without exposing their skulduggery. I wasn't giving in without a fight. I left my cottage and marched back to reception to collect my phone. I had two hours. Two hours to take back control.

CHAPTER TWENTY-FOUR

The Rabbit Hole

Day Fourteen, 10am

Two hours and a flat phone battery later, I arrived at Galilea's office ready for war.

I intended to keep my dignity when I was fired. I wanted my questions answered. I willed the courage to negotiate and call the shots.

My googling had revealed nothing about the research station. And beyond her role as director of the retreat, I had found nothing on Galilea either. No work history. No LinkedIn membership. No Facebook page. Zilch. It was like she didn't exist. This lack of information was, in itself, suspect. In the digital world, absence was just as incriminating as presence.

Our meeting began very pleasantly. Wearing another of her puritanical crew necked retreat sweaters, urging me to make myself comfortable, she gestured towards a pair of seafoam-blue linen couches with puffy pink cushions.

Placing herself in the upholstered armchair to my right, Galilea told me I was doing a wonderful job and my students were all very happy. The feedback was positive.

As I prepared myself for the moment when she said: 'but...', Jock arrived with a tray of tea, scones, cream and jam, which he placed on the glass coffee table between the two couches.

After he had poured the tea, Galilea drew a long, faintly impatient breath and thanked Jock, watching his back as he left the room. My jaw hardened. I wanted to pre-empt her. I didn't want to quietly sit and wait to be fired. I was tired of being rejected. I was tired of being manipulated.

My eyes dropped to the faded Persian rug decorated with plants and birds under my feet.

'I've very much enjoyed working here,' I said. 'But...'

I paused. Out of the corner of my eye I could see her freeze as she brought her teacup to her lips.

'This place just isn't the real world.' I gestured towards the door Jock had just exited, the fragrance of his aftershave still infusing the room. 'Everything here seems to be too good to be true. I have a feeling I'll struggle to adjust when I return home. I'm feeling too out of touch with reality. Too spoiled.'

Without even taking a sip, Galilea put down her cup. She gave me a dark look. She seemed inappropriately angry at what I thought was a light comment. 'Spoiled? How exactly? By being treated kindly?'

Unsure how to reply, I glanced away, out the picture window, my gaze resting on a hibiscus tree, thinking how the flowers' stamens resembled radars, wondering who or what might be eavesdropping on our private conversation.

'Are you saying that you don't think you deserve to be treated with respect?' Galilea persisted. She sounded irritated. 'And I presume you mean by saying you feel spoiled, that you are speaking of Yindisha's men?'

Her irritation sloughed away the thin skin of my assurance, leaving me feeling naked and raw. Already, this conversation was not going the way I had planned.

She gave me a firm, chastising look. 'Yindisha's men are showing us how we deserve to be treated. They are helping us grow by acknowledging our femininity. They're empowering us, helping us fulfill our potential by treating us with respect. Restoring our stolen spirits.'

We both sat through a few seconds of silence. It was as though we were both circling around something smelly and dangerous – we both knew it was there, but couldn't acknowledge it to one another.

Ask about the research station, I told myself. *Confront her about that incident in the bush.* My mouth went dry as Galilea picked up the purple folder sitting on the side table next to her chair. When she turned it over, I saw my name written in black marker across the top.

I prepared to speak, but she cut in. 'Alethea,' she said as she placed it on her lap. 'Your name means truth.' She paused and her eyes darkened. 'And sometimes truth can make us uncomfortable.'

She opened the folder and pulled out an unflattering photograph of me in the bush on my knees, by that wet patch of soil where the man had vanished. I was glancing up at the camera, looking slack-jawed, goggle-eyed and stupid with surprise.

My heart lurched. There it was. Evidence. 'That certainly won't make the cover of Vogue Magazine,' I said, trying to appear composed.

A token smile quirked her lips. 'You have a choice, Alethea. You can either leave Yindisha Retreat now and never mention what you saw...'

She pulled another document from her folder. She leaned forward and offered it to me. 'Or you can sign this non-disclosure agreement...'

When I took it, she leaned back and steepled her hands. Her gesture was forced. Everything in the room suddenly felt uncomfortable. Prickly.

'What exactly did I see?' I asked, noticing words such as: 'confidential', 'bond of trust' and 'penalties' in the document I was holding.

'If you choose to leave us now, you saw nothing,' she replied.

That man's wild look of terror shot into my mind's eye.

I persisted. 'I can't forget what I saw.'

A lightning-fast look of affrontery flashed across Galilea's face. 'What do you think you saw?'

'I saw two women kill a man.'

'You saw two women chasing someone,' she corrected. 'Everything else, you inferred.'

I recalled those women carrying that limp sack and gave her a sour look.

She sighed. 'It wasn't what it looked like, Alethea.'

Unconvinced, I looked down at the NDA, my gaze stalling when I read: *Under no circumstances must you discuss what you have seen with any of Yindisha's male staff members.*

I looked up at Galilea. 'Was what I saw legal?'

'There are no legal precedents.' She paused as if carefully considering her words. 'This is...new technology.'

I persisted. 'Is it ethical?'

'It is sacred.' There was no hesitation this time.

My neck heated. 'Sacred isn't always ethical,' I replied. 'Virgin sacrifice was considered sacred by the Incas. Some voodoo sects ritually kill puppies and kittens. Some sick people practice cannibalism because they consider it *sacred.*'

Galilea looked patronisingly amused. Smug. 'I don't think we've ever had such a forensic recruit, Alethea. I've never had anyone ask so many questions.'

My insides heated. A recruit? I wasn't a recruit. Nobody recruited me without my permission.

'We are obeying a cosmic law,' Galilea added. Stiffly, she leant forward and picked up her teacup as if it was some holy object.

Cosmic law. I didn't like that phrase either. Cosmic laws were vague things open to myriad interpretations, usually involving woolly, fairy tale thinking, baying at the moon and nutty rituals like dancing naked around magical stones.

'We have ethicists examining the ramifications of this... technology,' explained Galilea, nursing her teacup. 'We have lawyers drafting legal frameworks.'

Ever so carefully, as if she were trying to also cool the rising heat in her office, she blew on her tea before taking a sip. Waves of intensity rolled off her. I realised in that moment she wanted something from *me*. She wanted my compliance. Desperately. *Good.*

Gently – as if it were as brittle as the atmosphere in the room – Galilea placed the teacup back on its saucer. 'Alethea, I applaud your inquisitiveness,' she said. 'So many women just blindly accept what they are told. When it comes to rules and governance, what we sometimes call respect for authority is simply submission.'

She lightly cleared her throat. 'This blind acceptance of the laws of men is what caused the dreadful state the world is in now. Conflict. Political unrest. Global warming. Pandemics. There are too many men in the world with too much power. There are too many women enabling them.'

Her eyes darkened. 'Men and a patriarchal system are destroying Mother Earth.'

I thought of that terrified man running through the bush. *What? So that gives women an excuse to hunt and kill them?*

I sat silently for a moment as the full force of my dilemma crashed through my thoughts. I mistrusted Galilea. I found her too forced, yet simultaneously, too smooth and reassured, her ideological tendencies worryingly inflexible, her compliments false. But so many of her words made sense. And here she was, buttering me up. She wanted me to sign that non-disclosure document.

'And if I sign?'

'Then everything will change. You will be fully employed by us.'

'Do I have to decide this now?'

'Yes.'

I thought how out in the real world, I would have time to find a lawyer to look over the document.

'I might not be the kind of person you want. I might be more trouble than I'm worth,' I managed.

Galilea laughed lightly and pulled another sheet of paper from the folder.

'Your mother – maiden name Ursula Fischer – was born in Munich and, after moving to the United Kingdom and then Australia, worked for fifteen years at the Sydney Goethe Institute.'

She gave me a sympathetic look. 'Before he tragically drowned, your father – Conrad Braxton – was a lecturer at the Macquarie University Department of Physics and Astronomy.'

That mention of his premature passing made my heart squeeze. I swallowed the lump in my throat.

'You have a daughter called Sophia Malinov. She has a degree in political science and works as a policy writer for the Federal Department of Environment in Canberra.'

My stomach, settled after all Yindisha's healthy food, now churned like the inside of a blender.

'None of this was on my resume,' I interrupted. But now I knew why that woman in the seminar knew my name. I was definitely being *watched*.

Galilea shot me a cool look. 'Most employers venture beyond the resume when considering a new applicant,' she said.

My churning gut hardened. This wasn't just going beyond the resume and having a sniff around social media. This was serious digging. An invasion of privacy. Frozen in my seat while my blood heated, I didn't say anything further. I wondered what else this woman whose own life was a mystery knew about me. Did she know about Lucas? Had he told her? Confessed his indulgences as if she were some feminist high priestess?

She dropped her eyes back to the sheet of paper in her hands.

'You were married for twelve years to Jordan Malinov.'

I winced at the sound of that name. At this point, I feel compelled to mention that an ex with an exotic name does not give him permission to hijack this story. Despite his surname, (which incidentally translates from Russian as small or raspberry), he was a weak and insignificant man with an ego the size of Jupiter and more insecurities than there are stars in the universe. I never took his name. I was much happier with a surname attributed to a pregnancy contraction than a small Russian (in his case, Bulgarian,) raspberry.

'Jordan Malinov was, for five years, a partner at Ernst, Kensington and Whitehouse Financial Consultancy,' Galilea continued.

Yes. That was his longest stint in one job. He eventually left in a sulk because a more successful narcissistic sociopath who managed to buy himself a BMW with client money got promoted ahead of him. I didn't say anything out loud. By this point, my anxiety was overflowing into breathlessness and hot flashes. I wanted to move on from the topic of my ex. I wanted him and his name neutralised from my story.

I felt right then like a cornered possum – angry, frightened and confused. Had I been a possum, I probably would have bitten Galilea right then and fled, only to crash into her office door which was no doubt at this point – locked.

'I don't appreciate being blackmailed,' I said.

I gave Galilea a firm look when she opened her mouth – no doubt to deny my accusation. 'I looked *you* up on the internet as well,' I said. 'Unlike me, it's almost as though you don't exist.'

When Galilea gazed at me, reality seemed to shift and buckle.

I felt as though my words had opened a vortex. As she regarded me in burning silence, in her eyes, I saw a singularity of pain and rage so potent, I had to look away.

Slowly, Galilea put down that sheet of paper. She raised her chin, lifted her liver-spotted hand and hitched down the neck of her sweater. Below the line of the sweater, her skin was pocked, puckered and ridged like a landscape ravaged by fire and drought.

I gasped in shock at the sight of those ugly scars.

'My husband – the man who was supposed to love me – did this,' she said. 'He set fire to me. Then tried to pretend it was an accident.' She blinked rapidly and drew a shallow breath. 'He's in jail now. But he's due out in three years and I know him well enough to understand he won't give up until he kills me. In the meantime, I have changed my name. I had reconstructive surgery and took the opportunity and to alter the way I look so he can never find me.'

It seemed the world in that moment turned upside down. Too ashamed to look at her, I sat for a moment staring at the rug's patterns of repeating black arabesques under my feet. When it comes to domestic violence, there is always a worse story. This is one of the reasons so many women stay in abusive marriages. Instead of leaving, they count their blessings. *He doesn't drink or do drugs. He's employed. A good provider. He doesn't hit me...*

My heart felt as though it was trying to hide in the folds of my lower intestines. 'I'm so sorry, Galilea,' I managed. 'I had no idea.'

The room seemed to contract and shrink. My body felt light and floaty, as if in that moment I was watching everything unfold from a distance.

After raising a hand dismissively as if attempted murder were of no consequence, Galilea gave me a quizzical look. 'Alethea, didn't you come to Yindisha to shake off old habits? Didn't you come here because you wanted something to change?'

Well yes, I wanted to say, but not quite like this. I hadn't come to be sucked into a secret society where abused women had sex with beautiful, possibly brainwashed men and then hunted and executed them. My innards hardened. So did my grip around that NDA. My thoughts raced, swerved and skidded. I was not a gullible fool. Not anymore. I had entered the cult of marriage and escaped. I was not about to replace one mistake with another. I was not going to join another cult. Not even a feminist cult.

I thought of Lucas and I wondered if, in inviting him into my bed, I had been complicit in something that – out in the real world – would be deemed illegal. Possibly immoral. I may well have already entered a point of no return.

I wondered how Galilea planned to upend an entire global political system though a few pretty, polite men. All this place was doing was substituting a male God with belief in Mother Earth.

'Gandhi once said, "In a gentle way you can shake the world," ' Galilea added. 'This is what we're doing, Alethea. Gently shaking the world. What I am offering is for you to be part of something that will propel humanity into a new era of maturity, wisdom, and peace.'

Her words calmed me. I liked the idea of gentle shaking. Of a world of wisdom and peace.

There are too many men in the world with too much power.

I could tell. She knew she had me. 'Change can be terrifying, Alethea. Even when what is familiar is destroying us.'

I thought of my marriage then. That slow destruction, that abuse of my mind, my body and spirit. Really, what did I have to lose? I was a mess. The world was in a mess. But violent shaking wasn't working.

Galilea was right. I had come here for change. And what was change but stepping into something new and unfamiliar?

And how could I possibly leave now without understanding what I had seen that day in the bush?

I felt my insides soften, as if they had been gently shaken into a more settled and accepting place. I understood in that moment that I could no more resist what was happening than I could change of phases of the moon.

'I need a pen,' I said.

Smiling, Galilea pulled a blue ballpoint from the drawer of the side table.

'Alethea, just how far down the rabbit hole are you prepared to go?' she asked as I signed.

'All the way,' I replied.

CHAPTER TWENTY-FIVE

Invisible Women

Day Fourteen, 2pm

My stomach filled with a light lunch and heavy knots of anticipation, I met Galilea outside, on the steps of the main building. 'Alethea, you are an artist, a creator, a progressive thinker,' she said, giving me a sober look as I slid into the passenger seat of her car. 'And I ask that you enter the research station in a state of existential flexibility.'

Perplexed, I stared at her. 'You mean you want me to keep my mind open?'

Galilea kept her eyes on the road. 'Yes. And your heart. And your soul.'

I bit down on my lower lip. A tall order. I wasn't sure what or where my soul was, let alone how I could open it. And my heart? That was very skittish thing. And as for my mind, well, I wondered if it would cope with what Galilea was about to reveal.

'I'm ready,' I replied, thinking of the scars under Galilea's sweater and feeling ashamed at the way I'd so ignorantly judged her. Would *I* have managed to so sensationally keep myself together if my ex had set fire to me? Would *I* have managed to forge on and build a business after such devastation? Probably not.

'The public story is that the research station is undertaking agricultural research, and is a soil testing facility,' Galilea said as we turned towards Watson. 'But in fact, we are, among other things, doing work in neurology and artificial intelligence.'

I thought of Lucas's seduction, my pelvis contracting pleasurably as I recalled my orgasm. But what did Yindisha's men have to do with it? Had someone located the position of the male ego and found a way to remove it? Were Yindisha's men like Star Trek's Borg? Part human, part machine? And if so, where had they – the women who transformed them – found their subjects? And what were those 'among other things' she mentioned? 'So, you are experimenting on innocent men?' My tone sounded more accusing than I intended.

Galilea laughed. 'No,' she said crisply. 'Definitely not.'

As we drove down the tree-flossed road that led to Watson, I asked Galilea who owned the research station.

'It is privately funded. Investments. Venture capital. Long-term financing.'

I was right. Yindisha Retreat wasn't making money. But who were the people funding it? Who were those venture capitalists and investors?

'This is world-changing technology, Alethea. Eventually it will transform the way economies are managed. But that side of things is a long way off. Meanwhile, we must work on adjusting deeply ingrained attitudes.'

'Such as?'

'Sexism. The corporate mindset. Greed.'

She issued a light huff. 'Most corporations are hierarchical, undemocratic and planned economies. They exist purely to make money for shareholders, often at the expense of employees and customers. Need I say that capitalism and democracy have lost their way?'

Again, I wondered what kind of organisation or individual would fund a technology that threatened to upend the global economic structure. Surely it would be like committing economic suicide.

'Governments are still shaping the world order,' Galilea added. 'And those governments are mainly patriarchal, male-dominated entities.'

As we passed through Watson, she pointed in the direction of Quentin Nader's church. 'And the church is just another globally networked corporation that trades in lost and oppressed souls. It's another male creation. A perpetrator of evils.'

Again, I recalled seeing those women chase that man, and the wild look of terror in his eyes. Despite what men might have done, collectively and individually, I wasn't prepared to accept any kind of cruelty. Not all men of religion were oppressors. And good men – men like my perfect, unconditionally loving father – might be unjustly caught up in the battle.

'Vengeance is not a cure for evil.' I said before I could stop myself.

For a few seconds, Galilea remained silent as if considering how she might reply. Briefly she glanced over at me, then set her eyes back on the road. 'No, it isn't,' she finally said. 'Vengeance is another distinctly male proclivity.'

She took a deep breath. 'The world isn't ready yet for what we have to offer, Alethea. So, subtlety and discretion is key.'

Again, she gave me a quick glance, something in her look imploring me to understand. 'People like you, Alethea – the artists and scientists of the world – are the hope of the future.'

I said nothing. Exactly what kind of future did this woman scarred by a maniac have in mind? How much had her rage and hurt distorted *her* judgement?

We reached the T-junction. A green sign on our right pointed to Bowral. A truck, its back tray covered in a red, dirt-stained tarpaulin lumbered past.

'Ah, the latest soil shipment has arrived,' said Galilea. She waited, letting two cars pass by into Watson before indicating and turning into the unmarked road that led to the research station. She explained the soil on the truck was from a mine deep in the outback. 'It has special properties,' she added.

'I thought you weren't doing soil research,' I said.

'Without the soil, none of what we do would be possible,' she replied.

I sat in silence, feeling as though every explanation she gave me only compounded my confusion. Wondering if my curiosity might be my undoing, fearing that this rabbit hole I had entered might just be too deep, I suddenly desperately wanted to speak to Sophia. My phone however, was back at the retreat. I thought of conspiracy theories, people who mysteriously vanished and wondered just how far Galilea and her cohort might go to keep this secret. If I disappeared, would Sophia ever find out what had happened to me? I reprimanded myself then, thinking how I should have left a note hidden for her in my luggage, or texted her before I left. The knots in my stomach tightened. Despite my inner turmoil, I had to remain cool, forensic and accepting. Just as with my marriage, if I wanted to stay safe, I had to pretend to comply.

When we arrived at the gates of the research station, the truck had already disappeared inside. A thick-set, gold-skinned man leaned into the car, placing his cocktail-sausage fingers on the edge of the opened driver's side window. He gave me a tiny-eyed, raisin-black stare. I avoided his gaze, taking in the tuft of red hair that sprouted from the top of his head like a clump of singed grass. I looked past him, noticing there was no signage, just razor wire fencing.

'Code Seven, Archie,' Galilea said to him. 'Authority 721 A.'

Immediately, the man stepped away and the boom gate opened. We passed through another gate before driving towards a low-slung white building.

To my right, through a mesh fence, I glimpsed an expanse of tarmac shadowed by a leafy shade cloth. A woman in black carrying a clipboard watched on while three men tripped, stumbled and crashed into one another as if they were paralytically drunk or drugged. All good-looking, they wore the same uniforms of white singlets and beige cargo pants. On their upper left arms, I could see that same tattoo I'd seen on that fleeing man in the bush.

'What's wrong with them?' I asked.

'They are learning to walk,' Galilea said as she pulled into a park with a 'reserved' sign.

What? Why are grown men learning to walk?

A thought emerged from my confusions. *Say goodbye Alethea. Say goodbye to your old life and old ideas.*

As if she could sense my discomfort, Galilea turned to me and smiled reassuringly. 'Older women see things differently, Alethea. You are no longer beholden to your biology, your desire to procreate, your desire to please a man. Older women have a unique perspective. We are more attuned to Mother Earth. In this society that worships youthful beauty, older women become invisible. And because we are invisible, we can operate below the radar. No one notices us. And that is our unique power.'

She gestured behind us, to the world beyond the boom gate I had just left. 'Those of us on the outside looking in see the system for what it is –a system rigged to keep women weak and power in the hands of men.'

Galilea's words felt like a force of nature – an inescapable seismic event. As if robbed of my free will, I undid my seatbelt, stepped from the car and followed Galilea. *I'm Alice in Wonderland,* I thought. *Falling deeper and deeper down the rabbit hole...*

Following Galilea across the car park towards the white building's small entrance door, I glanced back at the three bumbling men. Deep brainwashing? Robots? Androids? Lobotomies? Clones?

Sex toys? Prisoners perhaps? Murderers and sexual offenders systematically broken down as one might retrain a wild animal?

I watched one of the men stumble towards the fence, where the woman with a clipboard pushed him back, speaking to him firmly. I noticed a blue mark on his forehead, just like the man I'd seen in the bush.

The sight of that compliant man made my heart squeeze. Were they taming the men, like wild horses? Breaking their spirits? Abusing them? Was *this* Galilea's revenge?

I swallowed the lump in my throat. I'd married a man who'd tried to break my spirit. I knew what spirit-breaking entailed. And I wouldn't wish it on anyone.

In that moment, I resolved to resist Galilea's zeal. I remembered who I was. I was a woman who could think for herself. I would not be blindsided, corrupted and persuaded by anything unethical. I was not going to be another feminist fundamentalist. I was my own woman. And I knew there were good men in the world. My father, for one.

I was not a sheep and I would not follow the flock.

CHAPTER TWENTY-SIX

Evil Science

Day Fourteen, 2.24 pm

Swiping her thumb across a security slot, Galilea opened the white building's metal door. The truck we'd seen had entered through a loading dock and was now unloading the soil. Burly men – their raisin eyes set in the dough of their faces – were raking other piles of dirt and strategically placing them directly under skylights. They looked up at us, their gazes empty of expression, then, returned to their work. At the southern end, two women wheeled a barrow filled with red soil into an open service elevator. The whole space smelt of dusty soil.

'Here the soil is prepared before it is sent downstairs to be processed,' said Galilea. She explained how the soil, which had a high iron content, had to be exposed to a certain number of hours of sunlight before it could be used. As I listened, it occurred to me if anyone broke into this facility, all they would see would be dirt – which would confirm the story that the facility was an agricultural research station.

She told me how the facility was staffed by brilliant women.

Some had come all the way from Silicon Valley. 'Here, away from the toxic sexism that plagues many male-dominated institutions of progress and innovation, the women thrive,' she said proudly.

Feminazi. The word – used once by a (now deceased) corporate magnate and harasser of women – shot – unbidden – into my thoughts.

'We're living in a crisis moment, Alethea – a fulcrum in the progress of human civilisation,' Galilea said as we waited by another, smaller, lift. 'Humanity isn't going to last on this planet unless we do something drastic.'

The lift arrived, opening with a melodic, high-tech ping. After we stepped inside, Galilea placed her thumb onto a security pad. When the numbers lit up in green, I noticed there were nine floors underground. This place, so modest from the outside – was vast.

'Until there is absolute global equality between men and women, we cannot achieve world peace,' Galilea continued.

She pressed the button to level two. 'And here, we're trying to speed things up a little.'

As she spoke, the lift door slid shut and the ground under my feet dropped.

'Women must teach men how we want to be treated,' Galilea continued as the lift plunged. 'And women must accept respect from men as normal. This involves dismantling millennia of traditions and mindsets.'

Level two opened into a white, brightly-lit atrium decorated with potted palm trees and succulents. 'We live in a world where money and politics eclipse human rights,' said Galilea. 'Economies shape societies and dictate what is of value. And economies are overwhelmingly run by men who prioritise power and growth over community and compassion.' As we stepped from the lift, Galilea turned to me, her green eyes filled with flames of pride and triumph. 'It's time, Alethea, to feminise the world.'

Regarding that mature, still beautiful woman with her perfectly sculpted nose, and eyes that still seemed to hold the heat of the fire that had scarred her body, I released a smile of compliance. After all, how could I possibly disagree?

I drew a fortifying breath. Here, underground, the air smelt of freshly turned earth and lemon geraniums. All around me I heard a faint hum and throbbing, as if we had descended into the body of some enormous, living organism.

A woman and a bare-chested, beautiful man who resembled the actor Henry Cavill passed us as we entered the atrium. I squinted, taking a closer look at the script tattooed in blue under the single dark curl on his forehead. It looked ancient and middle eastern. The woman – an attractive and compact Asian in her late forties – wore the same black tee shirt as the two women I'd seen that day in the bush. Close-up, I could see the motif was a circle with a 'M' and 'E' separated by the word 'of' the 'f' breaching the circle in an elaborate flourish. *Men of Earth*, I thought.

'Ah, Conrad, nice to see you up and about,' Galilea said to the man who I noticed had that same logo tattooed on his upper left arm – the same tattoo I'd seen on the men outside.

'Conrad has just passed Level One Common Sense Protocols,' said the Asian woman.

The man looked at us and grinned. 'I am now fully toilet trained,' he said proudly. 'I have perfect aim.'

The woman rolled her eyes and gave him a long-suffering motherly smile. 'Charm School is next.'

Galilea patted the man's arm while she smiled at the woman. 'You're doing very well,' she said. 'Keep up the terrific work,' she added as they headed for the lift.

Before I had a chance to ask about the tattoos and that mark on the man's forehead, Galilea turned back to me, her eyes radiant with subversions. 'Since the beginning of human civilisation, men have been socially programming women to submit and accept male authority and superiority.'

Her eyes sparked as she opened the door to what appeared to be an open plan office. 'What if we could start with a clean slate, and make perfect, compliant *men*?'

The image of that perfect man with his arm and forehead tattoos was still imprinted on my mind's eye. As I looked around the room filled with women sitting at computer consoles, beyond another glass window I glimpsed a bank of machines that resembled, to my uninitiated eyes, microwave ovens.

I recalled the men I'd seen under that shade-cloth. These women were taking a freshly wiped blank canvas of a human being and creating someone new and better. But what comprised a new and better man? And who was to say what is right or wrong? Who made that call?

I glanced at the nearest console where a woman was busily typing. On the screen, lines of green code propagated. Among those indecipherable icons and squiggles, I thought I recognised some of the script I had seen on the man's forehead. The woman looked up at us and smiled warmly as Galilea spoke. 'What if we could program men to treat women like equals? Not only that, what if we could program them to worship and adore us?'

Her words hit me between the eyes. The thrumming around me seemed to grow louder, as if we were entombed inside some monstrous circulatory system. The walls seem to buckle and spin, my surroundings turning small as if compressed under intense pressure. *Evil Science.* The words arrived – dark and bold in my mind's eye. None of this was right. Galilea was mad. This place was Galilea's revenge. I blinked, and my eyes watered, as if trying to remove a piece of grit. *Stepford Husbands,* I thought.

vil Science. The words, like a pair of entangled particles in a vacuum, bounced insanely around inside my head. Everything felt floaty and unreal. *Impossible,* I thought, as Galilea explained these men were artificial life forms. 'Golems,' she said. 'Sculpted from clay and animated using a combination of sacred codes and incantations.'

Bullshit, I wanted to say. But I held my tongue and tried to get a grip. One never learns by talking. This perpetual inquisitor had to shut up and listen.

Galilea explained how, although the idea of golems came from Jewish mythology, the knowledge that went into the creation of these creatures was far older. 'This ancient knowledge of the spiritual building blocks of creation predates the patriarchal religions,' she added as we walked down a corridor that resembled some high-tech underground high school. We passed windows and doors opening to rooms with tables, chairs and computer consoles.

'This knowledge – far older than Moses or Abraham – was, over millennia, buried, suppressed and hidden,' she said. 'By men hungry for control and power.'

Of course, it was, I facetiously thought. *This is the world according to Galilea Nightingale.*

We paused at a window. Through the glass, six men were sitting around a dining table. 'They're practising their table manners,' Galilea explained. We watched one lift a wine glass to his lips, miss and spill red wine down the front of his white tee shirt. Another stabbed at his broccoli with a fork as if it were a small animal he was trying to kill. At another table, a man chased a dumpling across a plate with a pair of chopsticks.

Galilea smiled as though watching toddlers take their first steps. 'Golems learn quickly,' she said. 'But sometimes they need tweaks to their programming.'

Moments later, we looked into another room where eight

golems stood in a line with their mouths open as a woman – in a process that made me think of holy communion – placed chips that looked like rice crackers on their tongues.

'This is the Back-Story Creation and Programming Section,' said Galilea. 'Those chips give the golems memories of childhoods – parents, homelands, languages and even regional and foreign accents.'

My back went cold as I thought of Lucas with his Greek heritage, his ex-girlfriend in France. And then there was Mathias with his story of his family in Ecuador, his work visa, his cousin in Northbridge. And Tamati and his iwi. Kayden from Iran. None of what they told me had been true. But they believed their memories. They believed they were human with pasts and families.

Impossible. My jaw cramped and my legs started to feel rubbery.

Further up the corridor, we paused at another window. 'This is the "Gifts" zone where the golems are programmed with specialist knowledge – horticulture, Spanish guitar playing, massage, composting toilet management, plumbing, electrical wiring,' explained Galilea.

When I thought of Lucas and his horticultural training, I felt my bowels shudder. Golems had no idea they were programmed. *Lucas* had no idea he was programmed.

Half-formed and horrified thoughts percolated in the back of my mind as Galilea used words such as heuristics and algorithms, subroutines, translation protocols, virtues scaffolding, moral compasses and emerging sentience to describe their ascendance from dumb, stumbling creatures to fully formed, chatty and charming facsimiles of human men.

Finally, I managed to find my voice. 'Isn't this just a form of slavery?'

Galilea firmly took my arm. We turned around, heading back to the lifts.

'Is this true slavery when the golems are created to willingly serve? Is this any different from women enculturated to serve and obey men? Is this any different from women who are trained to pander to male-created systems and hierarchies?' she said. 'Ultimately, we are after equality and partnership here, not gender domination.'

I wanted to say I saw no proof of that, so far. This all seemed to be engineered to put women in charge.

'In the short term, we must undertake an extreme correction,' Galilea added, as if she'd read my thoughts. 'The patriarchy has pushed things too far in favour of men.'

Again, an image of that falling man in the bush shot into my mind's eye.

'So, what I saw in the bush was one of those...*golems*... that had escaped?'

'Yes,' she said crisply. 'It was unfortunate.'

Another layer of alarm unfolded in my belly. They weren't going to employ me. They were going to kill me. Destroy me just as they'd destroyed that errant golem. I had seen too much. And I was a blabbermouth. A sceptic.

'When security discovered the footage of you on our cameras, I was out of phone range, attending to some other business, so a group of my colleagues made an executive decision. They sent in Lucas,' Galilea added.

Sent in Lucas. I didn't like the way she put that one bit.

'What? Why?'

'To distract you.'

'You mean he was programmed to seek me out?'

'Yes. We had to act quickly. You were a potential threat to our security.'

Shit. He had been sent to seduce me. Programmed to fuck me. My insides felt hollowed out and as cold as space. I had been manipulated. I had been played as if my thoughts and feelings were – just like those of the golems – programmable pieces of software. *And how could Galilea say it all so coldly?* I hated her in that moment.

I clenched and unclenched my fists – which felt cold and sweaty.

'You knew then? About us...?'

'Yes.'

I recalled that electric sex. I suddenly thought of cameras. In my cottage. Or perhaps even on Lucas's body. Just how much privacy did I have?

I felt in that moment swamped, steaming and dizzy. Under my ribs my heart jittered. I was either having a major menopausal hot flash or a panic attack.

'And did anyone see what ... happened between us?'

'Although we have the capabilities, we do not monitor those intimate moments. They are private and deeply personal.'

Although we have the capabilities. The words shot to the front of my thoughts. 'Well thank you,' I said, failing to keep the facetiousness out of my tone.

She paused for a moment, stopped and faced me.

'Alethea,' she said firmly. 'As far as Lucas is concerned, his feelings for you are real.'

I refused to answer. I could feel angry burning tears building in the back of my eyes. I felt like a silly teenager who'd just learned that her high school crush was a member of the Mafia.

Galilea's eyes softened as if she could tell I was on the verge of a full-blown meltdown.

'This is bigger than you and Lucas, Alethea. Mother Earth is screaming at us right now, imploring for us to change. Are we going to heed her cries? Or carry on in blissful oblivion and let humankind destroy ourselves and our only home?' Galilea said.

I felt so patronised by Galilea right then, I wanted to slap her.

Fake leather. Fake news. Fake men. The words rolled around inside my head like lottery balls in a dispenser. Soon one would fall out onto my tongue. None of this could be true. Technology just wasn't this advanced. All this talk of sacredness and artificial life forms and Mother Earth was smoke and mirrors to distract from the fact that these men were nothing more than real humans whose minds had been emptied and then reset through some nefarious process. They were all victims of a heinous crime. *Evil science.*

Another voice joined my thoughts. *Are you going to fall for this shit? Are you even dumber than you look? That woman, that bitch, Galilea is lunatic with too much power.* Those echoes of my ex's voice upended my fragile equilibrium. I erupted. 'This is bullshit! You expect me to believe all this? You must be out of your mind!'

Galilea gave me a sorry look. No. Not just sorry. Pitying.

I wasn't sure right then whether Galilea discretely pushed some alarm, but the next minute, a man who looked like Sylvester Stallone stepped out of an alcove and stood in front of us.

Flanking me, as if I might suddenly make a break and try to escape like that man in the bush, Galilea and Sylvester-the-golem guided me back to the lift.

'Where the fuck are you taking me? Am I going to end up in a sack just like that man in the bush?' I shouted.

Galilea's grip on my arm tightened. But neither replied. Instead, they just drew me more closely between them. Assailed by a dizzy spell, deciding – as the Star Trek Borg say – that resistance was futile – I reluctantly complied. There was no way I was getting out of here on my own. Once we were inside the lift, instead of returning to the surface, Galilea pressed the button to level four. I noticed again there were nine levels. Just like Dante's nine circles of hell.

CHAPTER TWENTY-SEVEN

The Stolen Orgasm

Day Fourteen, 3.35 pm

The lift plunged deeper into the research station's bowels. I told myself if I ever wanted to see my daughter again, I had to be brave and rational. *Reason is the only way to counter this insanity.* By the time the elevator doors opened to level four, I'd calmed down. A little.

When we stepped out, I noticed the air on this level was so dry, the tiny hairs on my arms stood on end. The guard returned to the elevator after Galilea reassured him that she had everything (me) under control.

After crossing a foyer similar to the one on level two, we entered a large open room, decorated with a simple white sideboard and a half-circle of plush sage-green sofas and armchairs. The seating faced an enormous picture window looking out onto an achingly beautiful landscape of snow peaked mountains, rolling green hills and a lake. In the foreground, flowering yellow grasses shook in a gentle wind. Every now and then a bird darted out of the bush nestled between the hills. Judging by the tree ferns and that clear cool light that infused the room, this was New Zealand. The South Island perhaps.

I knew what I was seeing was impossible, because we were four floors underground. It was nothing more than a clever, high-resolution illusion.

A soft floral, spicey smell – feminine and comforting – infused the room.

'You know what we're looking at isn't real,' Galilea said, guiding me to a sofa, where I obediently took a seat. 'It's a sophisticated illusion – the product of finely tuned technology. And, behind this image, of course, are hidden orchestrations. An intelligence that has created this technological wonder.'

I stared at the image, hoping to catch evidence of the video loop – the same bird emerging from the same tree and tracing the same trajectory across the sky. But, if it was a loop, it was a long one.

Out of the corner of my eye, I saw Galilea looking at me as she sat on the winged armchair to my right. 'Is it not possible that everything we perceive around us is also a facsimile of a greater reality?'

Before I could answer, a man entered the room with a tray bearing a floral teapot, teacups and a plate of small assorted cakes.

He was almost too beautiful to be real, his beauty cartoonish – a kind of chesty-bond good looks, as if he had been shaped by a hand that didn't understand the power of subtlety and imperfection. Galilea watched me watching the man and smiled. 'The world is so full of lies that the only way back to truth is through beauty. Through art.'

Mr. Gorgeous placed the tray on the coffee table in front of us.

'Thank you, Gabriel.' Galilea said, a purr in her voice. 'And what delicacies have you brought us today?'

'Earl Grey tea,' he said in an unnaturally deep voice that shook my bones. 'Macadamia brownies and ricciarelli.'

After we'd watched in silence as he carefully poured our tea like a well-trained seal, he left the room. 'Like art, everything we do here is about bringing out what is already within,' Galilea said. 'Like science, this is about looking beyond what we see. It's about studying and understanding the mechanisms and mysteries of our world.'

Quietly considering her comments, I picked up a chocolate macadamia brownie and put it on the bread plate. It was warm as if it had just been baked.

'What if the world around us is just the same?' said Galilea, gesturing at that gorgeous landscape. 'What if behind existence is a grand orchestrator, invisibly conducting everything that we see and everything that we are?'

While my back hardened in resistance, I felt my thighs tighten around memories of Lucas and my orgasm. He may have been fake, but that orgasm was *real*. I pulled in my shoulder blades, sat straighter. I was Alethea Braxton, daughter of a scientist. Sceptic. A tiger, not a sheep.

'There is no way any of your theories can be proved or disproved,' I replied as I picked up my teacup.

Galilea gave me a hot gaze. 'I have *proof*.'

My stomach squirmed when she uttered those words. In many ways, she was just like Reverend Nader – a zealot. But, unlike Reverend Nader, she was in possession of advanced technology. This was so much more dangerous.

My fingers cramped around the handle of my floral teacup.

I looked back towards that soothing landscape that was just a brilliant illusion.

'Have you heard of Hieros Gamos?' When I looked back at Galilea, her mouth was twisted, as if uttering those words offended her.

I mentioned that I thought it was something to do with sex rites and sex between Gods and there was some mention of it in Dan Brown's *Da Vinci Code*.

Galilea smiled at my reply, as if pleased. Like a teacher. 'Yes. The male orgasm was seen as a moment in which the man's mind, completely emptied of thought, connected with the divine. Of course, women were needed for this rite. Hieros Gamos was also, in its own way, about power. About control. About the male orgasm. Woman was only a vessel. And, as the clergy wasn't needed, Hieros Gamos was shunned by churches, who wanted to be the sole conduit to God.'

She paused to take a sip of tea, swallowed and raised her chin. 'Of course, over the centuries, Hieros Gamos became poisoned and corrupted. It turned into yet another way for man to exploit innocence, gentleness and woman. Acolytes of Hieros Gamos brought prostitutes into their temples. Women, and in some cases, young boys... children... became no more than sexual slaves. There were, of course, pregnancies. Babies...'

After she had sighed in extravagant disgust, a pause like a great, invisible bubble filled the room.

'The *female* climax is barely acknowledged,' she added. 'For good reason. The female orgasm has the power to create. The female orgasm frightens men. A powerful female orgasm shakes the world.'

Her expression turned sour with disapproval. 'Another example of the patriarchy suppressing female power.'

I decided not to answer her exhortation, so we sat in silence for a few seconds, taking in the image on the screen and sipping our tea.

'This is not about reproduction,' Galilea added as another bird flitted across the screen. 'Golems can't make women pregnant. Their role is to resurrect feminine power through a form of gnostic union.'

Again, I thought of my orgasm. A little shiver went through me. I tamed it by taking a big bite of my macadamia brownie. It was delicious.

'Gnosticism – based on pagan beliefs that predate the Abrahamic religions – is about unity and polarity,' Galilea continued. 'Long ago, ancient spirit-based beliefs kept humanity's relationship with Mother Earth in balance.' Her eyes darkened. 'And then, that equilibrium fell out of balance...' She paused and gazed at me deeply as if considering her next words. 'Eventually those patriarchal religions – Judaism, Christianity, Islam... with their righteousness, their intolerance, their expansionist motivations, destroyed this connection with the natural world.' She hissed as she spoke, as if she were barely keeping some inner snake contained. 'This is a habit of male-dominated ideologies. They invade and conquer. They infect and obliterate indigenous cultures with their righteously chauvinist and violent thought-worms.'

I regarded the fire in her eyes and thought how – although my experience at a religious school had been disturbing – Galilea's must have been incrementally worse.

'True faith honors the sacred feminine. True faith respects the interrelationship and the inextricable web that that binds humankind and nature,' she continued. 'And genuine Gnosticism regards sex and the female orgasm as a natural path to spiritual fulfillment and empowerment.'

I recalled my two sessions with Lucas and how the first one had dismantled me while the second had made me feel rebuilt. It had been, without doubt, the best sex I had ever had.

But was sex with a brainwashed man real sex? I shivered. *Was sex with an artificial being real sex?*

Thinking of Lucas hurt. His innocence, his oblivion of the wicked machinations behind his existence made my heart ache.

I studied the landscape to calm myself. It looked so real. But it wasn't. At least, it wasn't real in the here and now. It was simply a technological illusion – a copy of the real thing. I thought of deepfake videos. CGI. Fake news. *If we can't even believe our own eyes,* I thought, *where do we find truth?*

I considered how Galilea had showed me that landscape for this very reason. It was clever of her to bring me here. She was making me question the very nature of reality. She was making me question *my* reality. *My* truth.

When I glanced back at Galilea, her brow darkened. Even though everything was bright with that beautiful but fake New Zealand light, it seemed a shadow filled the room. 'Today's world makes connecting with our spiritual selves impossible,' she said. 'There is no longer that spark of divinity or reverence. There is only judgement. Materialism. There is only shallow knowledge. Soundbites. Gossip. Oppression of the feminine. Exploitation of man's version of female sexuality through the image industries. Imprisoning of women in a beauty and youth culture...'

She took a shaky breath, as if she were trying to contain a rising fury. 'Just as true feminism isn't about behaving like men to fit into a man's world, true femininity isn't about nail polish, perms, the latest fashions, laser hair removal or stiletto heels. The true feminine is something far more powerful...'

She caught my wary eye as I chewed on another mouthful of brownie. 'The true feminine has courage and compassion in equal measure. The true feminine has a deep connection with Mother Earth.'

She paused, took a sip of tea and swallowed. 'So. Whom do we trust to tell us the truth? she asked, giving me another of those looks filled with fire. 'Governments? Politicians with their empty promises? Corporations who place profit above the welfare of the planet? Fashion houses telling us the only way to be beautiful is by consuming their latest creations? Religious institutions who simply want to collect and control more souls?'

Galilea made a series of gestures in midair, as if she were casting a spell.

The image on the screen changed and the room darkened to a dusty red. The sensation was akin to being instantaneously teleported to another place. My heart sank at the new scene – the cracked soil of drought, trees warped and blackened by fire. Carcasses of animals littered the landscape. My reaction was visceral. I felt gutted. I wanted to cry.

'This is what the patriarchy is doing to Mother Earth,' Galilea said. 'This is the future of our planet if we let men remain in charge.'

The fear came over me again. I was trapped. Underground. A prisoner of a sect that enslaved men and wanted women to take over the world.

'Instead of listening to empty promises and lies, we must channel the virtues within. Love, compassion, perseverance, courage. These are the truths – the spiritual truths – which we must use to find a way out of this age of man-made darkness.'

Gazing at that ravaged landscape, I thought of Galilea's scars. *Fire. Man-made darkness.* I desperately wanted to go back to the safe contours of that pretty New Zealand scene. I also wanted to go back to my cottage and curl up in bed.

'This is the era of the fall of man,' continued Galilea. 'This is the time of Mother Earth. The only way to maintain the fragile equilibrium of the ecosystem is to return power to woman.'

Again, she waved her hand. Again, the image changed.

Now, we were in outer space viewing the blue-green marble of earth, draped in scarves of cloud and surrounded by the darkness of the void.

'Mother Earth,' she said. 'The first religion. The mitochondrial DNA of faith.'

She sat back, looking pleased. 'Mother Earth has made her decision. Only women can help humanity evolve into the next stage of its spiritual maturity. This is the future Mother Earth has planned. A world powered by love. A world managed by women.'

I looked away from Galilea's gaze, my insides churning, my tinnitus ringing in alarm. This had been a highly sophisticated presentation. A corporate spiel. I was being sold an ideology. I saw so clearly what Galilea was doing. She was trying to push me towards to an extreme belief, when reality was far more nuanced. There were ethical corporations. Well-meaning politicians. People and places of religion – like The Unity Chapel – places and people who didn't focus on conversion quotas, but instead housed, fed and counselled society's most needy.

But I also knew it was no use challenging Galilea. She would only ask: why are there needy people in the first place? It was because of the system. Because of the patriarchy.

And now, according to Galilea, the patriarchy had even robbed women of proper orgasms.

But Galilea was as bad as any politician or cult leader. Perhaps worse, because she had access to powerful, sophisticated technology. *A mad bitch,* my ex's voice crowed.

From that lonely planet hovering in the void of space, I glanced back, towards the door. There were five more levels to this place. I *had* to go deeper. I had no choice. Besides, Galilea still hadn't explained what happened in the bush that day.

I downed the last drop of my Earl Grey tea. *Gather information and then bargain,* I told myself. I too, had to put on a performance as convincing as those images on the screen.

'It's all beginning to make sense,' I managed as I put down the cup, trying to calm my trembling hand. 'I'm beginning to understand.'

CHAPTER TWENTY-EIGHT

The First Mark

Day Fourteen, 4.15 pm

We descended to level six – the art zone. Here, I hoped to find comfort in familiarity. But once again, I was wrong. This rabbit hole was deep, wide and twisty.

In the centre of level six's softly lit foyer, a pair of whimsical and voluptuous sculptures of women cavorted among a garden of succulents. Their heads adorned in colourful feathers, flowers and leaves, they were painted in dusty white, red and yellow ochres, the patterns resembling indigenous tribal markings. The air here was moister and smelt of wet clay and lemons. The thrumming here sounded louder and more rhythmic, as if we were closer to the machinery that kept this place operating .

Whilst the upper programming zone had felt like a high school, this zone, with its fresh green paint, sculptures and vases of fresh flowers, felt like a private hospital for rich people.

We walked down another corridor and paused at a window. Inside, three life-sized clay sculptures of men lay on gurneys. A woman leaned over the closest one, painting a cobalt blue script on its forehead. 'A thousandth of an inch separates the good from the bad,' said Galilea. 'Our calligraphers are highly skilled. They have to be. If they don't get things right, a thousand things can go wrong.'

As we gazed through the window, Galilea explained how the first communications with Mother Earth were through chanting, through song and prayer. She spoke in a low voice as if she didn't want to disturb the woman inside.

'And of course, tens of thousands of years ago, woman spoke to Mother Earth through art. Through those first drawings and petroglyphs our ancestors made on cave walls, humanity discovered the power of the mark.'

She continued, explaining how it was woman who had first learned how to channel the power of Mother Earth though symbols and code.

Behind the glass, the calligrapher was so lost in concentration, she didn't look up. There was a reverence to the way she worked, that made me want to step away. I felt as though I was witnessing something scared and private.

'Those marks on the golem's foreheads are called – by those who have appropriated its power – the tetragrammaton,' explained Galilea. 'The tetragrammaton inscribes the unutterable name of the divine. But despite what Google, historical researchers, and the Kabbalistic writings say, the truth is the tetragrammaton predates Hebrew and even Sumerian script. It is part of prehistory. Again, this knowledge is feminine knowledge appropriated and suppressed by men. The true divine is Mother Earth.'

I felt relieved when we pulled away from the window. I'd been holding on to my breath, staying very still, in case we disturbed that calligrapher. I'd never liked anyone watching me when I worked, and wondered if that calligrapher felt the same.

'In addition to calligraphers, programmers, singers and sculptors, we employ psychologists, spiritualists, ethicists, historians, biologists, and storytellers,' said Galilea.

We walked towards a large set of double metal doors at the end of the corridor.

'We also have a comprehensive library and an entire level dedicated to scientific enquiry,' Galilea added.

As I listened, it occurred to me this was probably the tone she used when she spoke to venture capitalists. She was still trying to sell me her ideology.

'We have geologists researching soil and clay composition, studying the impact of the tetragrammaton and its interactions with the clay. We have physicists studying the frequencies of the animating incantations...'

This scientific inquiry into the sorcery reassured me. 'Any sufficiently advanced technology is indistinguishable from magic.' I replied, quoting Arthur C. Clarke.

Galilea gave me a hard look of warning as she pushed open the double doors.

'Yes. But under no circumstances must a male-dominated government get wind of this technology, Alethea. If they learn of the golems, men in governance will see the potential for troops, infinite armies, disposable drones to fight endless wars...'

Behind the double doors was an atrium. Beyond a large picture window, was an enormous art room. 'Golems are troops of love. Not tools for war,' Galilea added.

The room resembled a vast operating theatre. Beyond the picture window, about a dozen women dressed in white robes shaped clay heads on stands or worked on headless clay bodies lying on gurneys or impaled on spikes. At the far end of the room, I saw art-school Alison absorbed in her work, shaping a clay torso. A woman passed in front of the window wheeling a gurney filled with a selection of perfectly moulded male hands and feet. A small stone fountain bubbled in the middle of the room. A pile of wet clay sat on a long table next to the fountain – the raw material that would eventually become a creature that resembled a living, breathing man.

The women all worked in silence. Again, I felt as though I was watching something secret and sacred. 'They are meditating on Mother Earth and the sacred feminine as they sculpt,' said Galilea. She explained once more, in a softer voice, how the sculptors used virgin soil taken from a place that had never been dug, mined, ploughed or turned in any way. They had to wear clean white vestments and use fresh spring water that had never been poured into a vessel. The clay was sourced from a secret place deep the outback. Each man took between seven and thirty-five hours to build.

'Great spiritual strength is needed,' Galilea said. 'As well as an unquestioning love and respect for Mother Earth.'

Well, I thought. *I guess I won't be invited to help in this art zone any time soon.*

As I wrestled with my thoughts, Galilea explained how, seventy-two hours after animation, the tetragrammaton on the golem's forehead faded. As did the tattoo on their arms. And, over the course of four weeks, the golems grew internal organs. 'They become indistinguishable from human men,' Galilea added. 'Golems *think* they are human men. And, the more they are treated like humans, the more they become human.'

The recollection came to me suddenly. I turned to her and snapped, like a dog that has uncovered a bone. I had found the hole in Galilea's plot. 'Lucas has a scar,' I said. 'He told me he'd been mugged.'

Without even flinching, she smiled. 'Sometimes, the sculptors build in physical flaws. And the storytellers weave stories around them. There is beauty in imperfection. And a man with a scar and a story? It makes him more human. More attractive.'

The pragmatism of her comment made my blood chill. A cramp crossed my jaw.

I thought how all of this made what I had seen in the bush less like switching off an artificial life form and more like an execution. I started to feel even more recalcitrant.

'You still haven't told me what I saw that day in the bush,' I said. 'Because everything you have shown and told me so far points to my having witnessed a murder.'

Galilea gave me another sorry look. And I realised in that moment she was preparing me for something even more disturbing.

'Wherever there is creation, there is destruction,' she said. 'It's another of Mother Earth's inviolable laws.'

And I wondered then, if she meant me.

Back in the lift, descending yet another level down into this underworld, my unease grew. I felt low and heavy, my insides unspooling into a deep and hollow fear. This wasn't just a feminist cult, but a sex cult, building toy men for women's pleasure. Even adding scars to make them more interesting.

Would this technology eventually make human men redundant? I wondered. *Or turn them into nothing more than sperm machines when women wanted babies? Would we one day find boxed golems in Kmart? Or order them online and receive some kind of activation code to animate them?*

Beside me, Galilea remained silent. Perhaps she was giving me space to think. Perhaps she didn't know how to explain to me that I was about to become another of those missing people whose faces appear on posters in police station windows. My thoughts raced and scrabbled like imprisoned animals scratching at a locked door. I couldn't escape what I had seen or what Galilea had told me. The creation of such compliant creatures disturbed me. Despite what Galilea said, they *were* slaves. And again, and again, history showed how societies that embraced slavery – natural or otherwise – inevitably end in disaster. The rulers become fat and lazy. They turn into unethical tyrants and eventually the slaves rebel. Golems might, ultimately, not be good for womankind. In the presence of such subservience, woman might become the dominant sex and nothing would ultimately change. The planet would still be run by bullies and tyrants. They would just be female.

And, if this effulgent power – this union with Mother Earth – could only be reached through sex with a golem, then what about women who didn't enjoy sex? What about women who weren't attracted to men – no matter how beautiful? And what about men? The good men? The kind and loving men who also yearned for a more gentle, giving and loving world? What about men like Sir David Attenborough, Michael Palin, and Professor Brian Cox? In the absence of my father, those beautiful, gentle men had been my spirit guides. Would men like them suddenly become surplus to feminine requirements?

The lift doors opened to level seven, along with my epiphany. This was nothing more than a *feminist sex cult*.

The air in this zone felt cold. Clammy. Clenching my fists, I followed Galilea.

I'm not a joiner, I reminded myself. I had to keep my perspective. No matter how much my head had been messed with, I had to remain detached.

I willed myself forward, following Galilea down a dimly lit corridor painted in a dull, funereal green. Here, on this level, I was overcome by a great, welling feeling of loss.

In the distance, I heard a tormented wail – demonic and bone-chilling.

I stopped in my tracks. Sensing I was no longer tagging close behind her, Galilea turned.

Although her face was filled with shadows in this weak light, I looked her hard in the eye. I willed myself to stay brave. 'Is this where you kill malfunctioning golems?' I asked through my teeth. 'Is this where you imprison trouble-makers and non-believers like me?'

CHAPTER TWENTY-NINE

Death, But Not As We Know It

Day Fourteen, 4.58 pm

Galilea laughed. She *laughed*! 'I like your spirit, Alethea. You're going to need it for the next part of your journey.'

Another monstrous howl shook level seven's walls. Closer this time, as if some raging beast was bearing down on us. I thought how, with the dim light and the peeling, khaki-green walls, this level felt like an underfunded prison or insane asylum.

Galilea continued. 'You've spent so much time being defensive and fearing for your life that you have lost your perspective.'

She smiled slightly smugly as she knocked on a puce-green door to our right. 'Not everyone is out to kill you,' she added, opening the door before I heard anyone answer.

The room looked like a giant janitor's cupboard, with brooms and mops, boxes, jars and bottles of spray cleaners. A pile of hessian sacks – like the one I'd seen that day in the bush – lay neatly stacked on a shelf.

Two women wearing hazmat suits sat at a wooden table in the middle of the room. They looked up from their game of cards. 'We're ready,' Galilea said.

The women rose in silence, zipping up their suits and pulling the white hoods over their heads. One strapped what looked like an industrial-sized vacuum cleaner to her back. The other grabbed what looked like a giant paint spatula, a dustpan and brush and a hessian sack. I knew right then I was about to see what I hadn't seen in the bush. Somewhere, on this level, a sacrificial lamb awaited.

Another roar shook the walls as the four of us headed deeper into the corridor's depths. It didn't sound like a sacrificial lamb. It sounded more like a furious caged bear, a lion with a headache, a killer.

The women peeled away from us and opened a door on our left.

'One-way glass,' said Galilea as we entered an adjacent room. 'He can't see us watching him.'

Here, two chairs faced a window that looked into a grimly lit green room with scratched and dented walls. Inside, a bare-chested golem paced up and down, banging on the walls, a wild look in his eyes. 'Sometimes things go wrong,' Galilea explained. 'For reasons we have yet to understand, some golems remain uncooperative. They turn violent. Angry and destructive.'

That unruly creature, who was also very handsome, paced and growled. 'You fucking bitch!' he yelled at the window. He turned and banged on the wall as if he wasn't sure where to direct his fury. 'You cunt from hell!' I winced and stepped back. He sounded like my ex in one of his foul moods.

Moments later, the hazmat-suited women entered the room. The golem paused from his bellowing. He stared and, for a few seconds, he went quiet, as if trying to make sense of what he was seeing. *Perhaps he thinks they're angels*, I thought.

It happened so quickly the golem had no time to react. One woman strode up to him and used that spatula tool to slash his forehead. Instantly, he disintegrated, leaving behind nothing but a pool of water, a pile of crumbs, stones and empty trousers.

I emitted an involuntary cry of shock.

With an efficiency that told me they'd done this many times before, the women proceeded to shake out the trousers. One vacuumed up the golem's remains while the other, after neatly folding his pants, used the dustpan and brush to sweep up and collect the bits that had landed in the far corners of the room and empty them into the hessian sack.

'That was what you witnessed in the bush the other day,' said Galilea. 'Occasionally the golems go rogue and sometimes escape. However, they can be quickly decommissioned by slashing their tetragrammaton. Once the tetragrammaton – that sacred code on their forehead is breached – they disintegrate. They turn, once more, into lifeless clumps of soil.'

I watched in silence as the women vacuumed and swept. 'We try and gather every single crumb of the clay, so our scientists can study it. Consider it the golem equivalent of an autopsy. We are still learning here. Still making mistakes...'

Regarding me with a kind of imploring, forensic coolness, she continued. 'Are they sentient, living beings? Absolutely. Do we have a right to decommission them if they don't uphold our high expectations? I believe absolutely. Golems are created for a purpose and if that purpose is not being met then they are redundant.'

Again, I thought of that man I'd seen in the bush. That was real, human terror I'd seen in his eyes. How was this different from putting down a disruptive, decrepit or incontinent pet? How was this any different killing our own babies?

My head spun. I thought of all those layers of earth above pressing down on me. I realised at that point I'd had enough. There is only so much a woman who has just learned, among other things, that the man with whom she slept was a golem, can take in. Plus, I'd just seen a creature who looked human blithely, coldly destroyed.

'It is imperative we always know what our golems are thinking,' Galilea added. 'We must know with absolute certainty that they will never harm us.'

I wanted to say there was no such thing as absolute certainty.

And then, my heart bent and I thought of Lucas. 'Is that what will happen to Lucas when he's finished with me?' I asked. 'Will you destroy him once he's done his job?'

'No. He is one of our best assets. A top Charm School graduate.'

She paused, then coldly added, 'After each encounter, we wipe his memory.'

And there, was the worst truth of all. *You are the only one.* Recalling Lucas's words made my insides turn hollow. I was the only one *he could remember.*

For a second, I wished Galilea was also a golem so I could destroy *her* with a weapon that resembled a paint spatula.

Galilea gave me a sympathetic look. 'You look exhausted, Alethea.'

'I am,' I replied, my tongue suddenly as heavy as lead. My eyes ached and stung. Deep under the ground, I felt claustrophobic. Faint. Hungry. I wanted to be alone to process all this. I thought of the sanctuary of my cottage in the grounds of Yindisha Retreat – that paradise now just a dream, a stage, a perfect lie.

The image of the crumbling golem fell back into my thoughts. I didn't feel like a woman with spirit anymore. All I felt was an all-consuming sensation of loss.

I felt so bereft right then, I wanted to weep.

It is imperative we always know what our golems are thinking. It occurred to me that Galilea had slipped for a moment. Revealed her truth. Above all else, she wanted control. Certainty. This was how she had decided to move on from the man who had set her on fire. By creating men whose minds she could read. Men she could control.

CHAPTER THIRTY

The Amber
of Spacetime

Day Fifteen, morning

Despite my exhaustion, I slept badly. Menopausal insomnia plus a revelation that had turned my world upside down led to a night of tossing and turning. Woken early by the raucously insistent call of some enthusiastic, early-rising species of bird outside my window, I recalled – in what seemed like the few minutes I had slept – weird dreams about men rising fully formed from lawns and rocks and deserts, asking me how they could be of service.

Finally dressed, brushed and flossed, I approached the retreat's main building feeling both apprehensive and unnervingly detached, as though I were watching everything, including my feelings, from a distance. The impossibility of what I'd witnessed yesterday teased me; the world felt like a dream. I suspected Galilea wanted complete control over those manufactured men. But isn't complete control just another illusion?

As I stepped towards the breakfast room, I saw Lucas inside, standing at the servery spooning porridge into his bowl. My heart jumped. Thinking of that NDA, I turned away, scuttling into the library to hide. *Under no circumstances must you discuss what you have seen with any of Yindisha's male staff members.* Now I knew Lucas was a golem, I had no idea what to say to him. He thought he was human. But he wasn't. And I didn't trust my wayward tongue.

In the library, I hid in the stacks, barely noticing the book titles as my thoughts chattered. In that brief glimpse of Lucas, my whole body still vibrated with echoes of our lovemaking. I wanted him again. Or at least, my body did. But my brain. Oh, my addled brain.

Determined to clear my head, I stayed in the library for a good half hour until I looked out the bay window and saw Lucas heading with another two golems towards Yindisha's orchards. With a sigh of relief, I headed for the dining room.

After breakfast, I retrieved my recharged phone from reception and stepped outside. In a shady spot under a plane tree, I sat on a bench and continued my research.

I googled the word 'golem'. Apparently, those creatures from Jewish folklore were brought to life using ancient magic. I read about the Golem of Prague, created by a rabbi and tasked with protecting a Jewish ghetto and how he had eventually become unmanageable.

Absorbed in my phone, I was digging deeper into the whole area of the occult, the tetragrammaton, the Zohar, and the concept of spiritual technology, when out of the corner of my eye, I glimpsed an approaching figure.

My belly lurched as I looked up. Quickly, I closed my screen. *Shit.*

'You've been avoiding me,' Lucas said, giving me a smile tinged with just the perfect degree of hurt. He must have seen me leave the breakfast room.

'I needed time to gather my thoughts,' I replied, shovelling my phone into my pocket with a shaking hand. 'I'm sorry,' I repeated. I gave him an apologetic smile. 'I have baggage,' I added.

I studied that beautiful creature in this new, sharpened light. *And you have false memories and programmed charms.*

'Baggage is part of life,' that Charm School graduate replied looking at me with perfectly calibrated respect and adoration. 'I've learned it's not so much what happens to you but how you deal with it.'

He sat down beside me as he spoke. 'But I'm sorry Alethea. I'm sorry you have been hurt.'

He caught my eye but I quickly looked away across the path and stared at a pink grevillea bush. *What do I say to a man I've slept with but now know is a fake?*

'Alethea, the last thing I want to do is make you feel uncomfortable and awkward. I don't know what you want from this situation. But I hope above all, we can be friends.'

My jaw cramped. Is that what he really thought? And what exactly are *real thoughts* when one is programmed?

'I'm sure that's possible,' I replied through my teeth. 'I enjoy your company.'

Lucas smiled as though sincerely pleased. He explained, in case I was worried, that he wasn't stalking me, but was just returning from his break when he saw me.

As far as Lucas is concerned, his feelings for you are real. Galilea's words swiped at me.

What are my commitments and obligations to this artificial being with a wipeable memory? I wondered.

'What's been happening with the orchards?' I asked, suddenly feeling uncomfortable with the direction of my thoughts and our conversation.

His eyes lit up. He spoke about the coddling moths and how he had to go through the orchard and inspect each of the apples, hand-thinning and destroying the infested fruit. Unsure of the scale of the infestation, they had installed pheromone traps to capture the moths. He explained how they used mainly biological controls such as parasitic wasps, mating disruption, yeasts and bacteria and steam-cleaning of collection bins to keep the orchards healthy and pest-free. I nodded and listened respectfully. Yesterday, in the programming zone, Galilea had explained how golems had permanent firewall-protected connections to the internet.

Yet, watching myself from a distance, I noticed how smoothly I was slipping into that role of pretence. It was easy, partly because Lucas was just so convincingly human. And – now I knew – emotionally safe. Programmed to respect me. No matter how difficult I was, he would never hurt me.

'Sorry,' Lucas said catching my eye, perhaps noticing my distractedness. 'I get carried away when people ask about my work. I really enjoy what I do.'

'It's fascinating,' I murmured. My abdomen tingling, I regarded Lucas's torso, his perfectly shaped feet, his unflawed face, those amber eyes. *Beautiful.* Then, I thought of the tray of feet and hands I'd seen yesterday on the gurney, and my tingles evaporated.

We sat for a moment in silence. I didn't know how to continue our conversation. He was a fake man. And I couldn't talk to him about it. Once he'd left the research station, all memories of his creation had been wiped, replaced by stories of a past that wasn't true.

He glanced at my hands. 'You bite your nails,' he observed.

'Yes,' I said.

'Nail biting or onychophagia, is often a symptom of stress,' he said.

'I know,' I replied. 'Long fingernails get in the way when I'm painting and preparing canvases.'

I clamped my mouth shut. That was as much information as he was getting from me. I wanted to hold on to what was left of the private, self-contained Alethea Braxton. I didn't want to let him in.

Looking away from his intense amber gaze I began to feel even more uncomfortable. I felt as though he was trying to breach my inner walls. This fake man wanted intimacy. He was searching. For something inside *me*.

He paused, as if waiting for me to elaborate; talk about myself, which I didn't want to do. Or perhaps reveal my true feelings, as if he were some twenty-first century version of a priest-confessor.

I stared hard into the bush's shuddering shadows.

Suddenly unnerved by the manipulations that had driven him to seek me out, I rose from my seat. 'I need to go and plan my next lessons,' I said.

Lucas looked at me then as if he saw right through me, deep into my soul.

He rose as well.

'I know you do, Alethea. I understand.'

When he said that so sincerely, with such deep and soulful knowing, I stopped in my tracks. Discombobulated by a sudden slap of superstition, I suddenly wondered what else this creature infused with ancient mysteries and brought to life through those 'spiritual technologies' knew about me.

Einstein once said every moment in time still exists; preserved forever in the amber of Spacetime. Did this man-bot have some celestial access into my shameful past? Did he have access to the amber of Spacetime? Did he know for instance, that I once shoplifted an eyebrow pencil from David Jones? Did he know I plagiarised an entire passage from an obscure book I found in the local second-hand bookshop for a high school assignment on nomadic tribes in the Gobi Desert? Did he know I'd lied to my daughter about our liaison?

I felt unwelcome tears congregate in my eyes. I recalled his lovemaking and fought a sudden desire to nestle against his sculpted chest and let him comfort me. And then, just as quickly, I wanted to hit him. Misbehave. Be outrageous and push him to his limits. Punish him for... *what?*

I caught Lucas's gaze. 'Actually,' I replied. 'I don't think you understand me at all.'

And with that, because I didn't understand myself anymore either, I gave him a long kiss on the lips. Leaving him by the bench, I turned and headed back to the retreat. My back burning, I recalled the story of that unmanageable Golem of Prague and wondered if I had, in that fickle kiss, messed with his programming, done something to short-circuit his golem brain and render him inoperable, unmanageable – or even worse – dangerous.

I climbed the steps of the main building feeling silly, scarlet and confused. Lucas was fake. Why was I finding this such a problem? Out in the real world, every day, photos of handsome U.S. marines and actors are attached to love letters written by men in Nigerian Internet cafes, fooling women into thinking they'd found their soul mates. Every day another liar dupes another seeker of romance out of their hard-earned savings. Every day another con artist demolishes another gullible soul's belief in the restorative power of love.

So, what was worse? A fake man programmed to be sincere who thought he was real? Or a real man pretending to be sincere but perfectly aware he was being fake?

And why did I still feel as though I was being conned? It occurred to me that perhaps the relationship that sat most comfortably with me, that felt most genuine, was one of criticism and rebuke.

The receptionist – the *fake man* – gave me a charming smile as I handed back my phone. 'And how has your morning been so far?' he asked.

I paused before answering, as if he had asked me a challenging intellectual question about the nature of reality, the role of consciousness and the meaning of life. I felt for a second as if my body wasn't mine, as if some part of me had stepped into a black hole with no means of return.

'It was absolute shit,' I replied. Before he could respond with some pre-programmed soothing platitude, I turned and marched back to my cottage.

CHAPTER THIRTY-ONE

Fast-Tracked

Day Fifteen, midday

I spent the rest of the morning walking through the retreat's gardens, regarding the men and women I passed with a freshly disturbed and inquiring set of eyes. Here – in Yindisha – woman controlled man. Here, women created desirable, beautiful men. And what exactly was beauty? Beauty's seductions served a purpose. Physical beauty was a ruse. Flowers enticed insects into assisting with reproduction. Beauty was a siren that lured the lost, the adventurous, the disconsolate and foolish among us onto the rocks of disappointment, devastation and despair. Beauty without truth was *dangerous*. I thought of Galilea running the show – a woman who had all the compassion of an arthropod – and shivered. Whatever was happening here, whatever the ultimate goal, I had to resist.

Everything begins with a thought. So said Buddha. I even wondered if none of the previous week's events had actually happened and I was a desperate fantasist – a romantically wounded woman who had made this all up to give her life meaning and hope.

Instead of feeling confident, instead of feeling empowered by Yindisha's proposed new world order and yesterday's discoveries, I felt stripped down and raw. Confused. Fragile.

Returning to the main building, I glanced at the receptionist flirting with one of Yindisha's guests (another mature woman) who was lapping up his attention like a thirsty dog. I wondered: was it good for our souls to have our needs constantly met?

At lunch, I sat and ate with Saniya, now deeply apologetic for the way she had frozen me out the other day at breakfast. 'I'm sorry, Alethea,' she said. 'I hope I didn't hurt your feelings. I was a little preoccupied...' When she looked at me then, I knew she longed to say more. Forbidden by that NDA to speak about the golems anywhere in the retreat, instead, we chatted about the weather, my classes, the well-being of Elise Cranston's caregiver Jerome, who I now knew wasn't in Perth, but, as he was no longer needed, had been either decommissioned or had his memory wiped. The undercurrents in our conversation as powerful as a king tide, when Saniya asked if I was free later to go for a bush walk, I eagerly agreed. I wanted the perspective of someone other than the intense and possibly unhinged Galilea. I wanted to voice my objections to a fresh set of ears.

We met in the late afternoon, choosing a quiet path at the back of the retreat.

The first thing Saniya did was once more apologise. 'I'm so sorry, Alethea. It was painful, that morning I saw you in the dining room. I wanted to reach out to you. But when we heard about that security breech – what you saw in the bush – we were worried. We didn't know at that point if you might be a threat...'

I might still be a threat, I thought as we passed under the boughs of a magnificent Moreton Bay fig. We carefully stepped around its powerful root system pushing upwards and cracking the path.

'Usually it takes about six weeks,' continued Saniya. 'We

encourage guests to attend more lectures and seminars. We want to deepen their understanding before we invite them to the research station. Because of what you saw, you had to be fast-tracked. And no one knew what the outcome would be.' She looked as though she wanted to cry. 'None of this can get out into the world, Alethea. Technology like this in the wrong hands would be disastrous.'

Despite not liking the idea of being 'fast-tracked,' my insides softened. Although Saniya was another of the converted, I found her manner much more palatable, as if she were water to Galilea's fire. I smilingly reassured her I wasn't going to snitch to the authorities.

Mollified, her voice firmed up. 'I was married once,' she said. 'But here in Yindisha, I discovered a new way of being a woman.'

We entered an area of the path moist and deep in shadow. I inhaled the deep, elemental smell of moss, earth and mushrooms. All around us birds shrieked, cawed and chittered. As we walked, Saniya told me about her adult son, working in Perth as a finance officer for a mining company. She pointed to her painted eyebrows and told me how all her hair had fallen out after she found out her husband – a man she had deeply loved – was a serial visitor of prostitutes. She ran a lime-green fingernailed hand through her hair – so straight – so perfectly trimmed, she could have been a Vulcan extra in a Star Trek movie. 'This is a wig,' she said.

Her voice shook as she spoke and I felt her hurt deep in my bones. I thought how happily married women – women who had never experienced the daily humiliations and incremental erosions of the spirit – might never understand the pain of an abusive, destructive marriage. They might never understand that helplessness, that pain, that betrayal.

In a moment of solidarity, I confided in her about my own marriage. I kept it brief, because speaking about my twelve-year roller-coaster ride still made me feel dizzy.

That serene woman with her Vulcan-fake hair listened, holding my gaze with eyes the deep, grey-green of a waterhole. And, like a waterhole, they teared up in sympathy when I explained how my ex's ugly behaviour had hurt and damaged my daughter – and that felt like the worst thing of all.

'The only way to stem the tide of violence and disrespect for women is to create respectful men who can be role models for other men,' she finally said.

We paused at a gap in the bush where the sunlight moved across the valley's shadows like a golden oil.

I expressed concerns about whether creating fake, programmable men was the solution.

Beside me, Saniya didn't immediately answer. My gaze fell into valleys suffused in purple shadows. I drew a deep breath of the cool Highlands air and wondered if I was slowly digging my own grave. If I kept disagreeing, what might Yindisha's women do with me?

'Take it all in slowly, Alethea,' Saniya finally said. 'This has screwed with your whole world view.'

A dreamlike feeling came over me then. I thought of the double slit experiment, where a single photon, passed through a screen containing two slits will simultaneously behave like both a wave and a particle. Unobserved, it behaves as one and many, forming an interference pattern, as if it has entered both slits. Observed by a detector, it collapses into a classical state and behaves like a single particle. There is no rational explanation for this except that it shows how reality is shaped by the observer. All of which suggests we may inhabit a world entirely created by our consciousness. My head spun and I had a moment of vertigo, my previously solid world view disintegrating into interference waves. My world view was not just screwed but turned upside down and inside out.

And I am being fast-tracked. Fast-tracked for what? I wondered.

Saniya regarded me as if she could see my worries and confusions written across my face.

She gave me a stoic look. 'Alethea, how are you with all your enculturation – all those childhood fairy tales about handsome princes and happy marriages and submission to and acceptance of powerful male leaders – any different from a programmed golem?' she asked.

While her words made me squirm, I still resisted. 'I worry that those perfect, fairy-tale men will skew our realities. You know... make us think that this is the real world.'

'Is what you regard as the *real world* right? Is it *right* when you don't feel safe when you go out at night? Is it *right* when your body tenses every time you pass a construction site?'

As Saniya spoke, my feelings swung wildly like misaligned pendulums in a Newton's cradle. I felt simultaneously unsettled and righteously indignant. She was right. She was wrong. She too had been indoctrinated, enchanted by this 'spiritual technology.' She too, was driven by pain and bitterness to embrace this anti-patriarchal ideology.

When I didn't reply, Saniya sighed. Far in the distance, the hills seemed to shudder in the waning light. Light was just photons, tricks of the eye. A creator of mirages. I recalled the image on yesterday's giant HD screen. Another needle of doubt intruded on my thoughts. What I had seen yesterday – that crumbling golem – might just be another clever illusion. Plus, I had never seen the animation of a fake man. It was possible I was still being tricked.

We stood through a few more wordless seconds, listening to a raucous eruption of rainbow lorikeets noisily dining on the camelias that flanked the path.

Wanting to keep my feet firmly in the realm of reality, I asked Saniya about Galilea's scars. Saniya told me Galilea was pregnant at the time of her husband's assault. She explained that Galilea's husband was a well-known public figure. Charitable. Outwardly, a supporter of equality for women. Once, they were a power couple.

My mind flicked back to the hiatus of my marriage, when we smugly regarded ourselves as happier, richer and more successful than everyone else. Once, I, too, had regarded myself as one half of a power couple. I cringed at the delusion, my vanity, my pride.

Ahead, a pool of sunlight lit a park bench – an invitation for legs buckling under the weight of too many uncomfortable epiphanies to rest.

After we sat, Saniya told me how Galilea not only survived her husband's attempted murder, but also gathered enough evidence to have him locked up. Cameras she had hidden in the bellybutton of a stone Buddha on their deck and another in one of the nipples of sculptures next to their swimming pool revealed his meticulous planning. The story, however, never made the gossip columns because there were enough people with vested interests to keep the scandal quiet. Men in power spun a story that Galilea's husband had been deployed to Eastern Europe on a diplomatic mission when he was actually incarcerated in Long Bay Jail. She confirmed that Galilea once ran a high-end PR company and knew people in positions of power. People who would do anything to keep the scandal quiet because they had their own indiscretions to hide.

'And what about the baby?' I asked.

'Miscarried.' My heart squeezed for Galilea's loss. Again, the feeling there was more. There was always more. More stories, more sorrows. More secrets.

I pictured all the world's women suspended in their wounded bubbles – women damaged by the evils of men.

'Bitterness and vengeance can warp our judgement,' I finally replied. 'Add power to the mix and we have a recipe for disaster. I worry someone like Galilea – someone who has every right to feel furious at men – will use her position and power to ...'

As I spoke, Saniya shook her head and interrupted me. 'Galilea has no power.'

Who then, has the power? I wondered.

'Right now, the power is with *us...*' Saniya continued as if reading my thoughts.

I regarded Saniya, not understanding. *Us?*

'The Guardians,' she added. She pressed my arm a little harder, looked deep into my eyes. 'Us. Women. The *Guardians.*'

I understood in that moment what she was saying. She wanted my acceptance and cooperation. I was being invited to join. Become another fully-fledged 'Guardian'.

I flinched, seeing in my mind's eye, my mother's look of disapproval. Repulsed by parades and other forms of collective endeavours, my mother – shattered by her birth country's submission to the evils of Nazism – taught me to think independently and to avoid the lure of 'memberships'. I was one of those people constantly trying to crawl out of any box in which I was placed.

Recalling sex with Lucas and the NDA I'd signed, I wondered if I already *was* an accidental Guardian. *A Feminazi...* My stomach clenched. *No, no and no.*

'No good ever came out of radical politics,' I protested.

'This is not a political movement,' replied Saniya. 'Nature cannot be tamed. Mother Earth will have the final word. This is an inevitability.'

An inevitability. The word beat at my thoughts.

Placing her hand gently on my arm, she gave me a wise and tired smile. 'Alethea, no one expects you to accept all this overnight. This is a long, slow process. And honestly, you have nothing to be afraid of.'

Saniya squeezed my arm just a little too hard, as if that pressure held a faint threat, or a tightly controlled fear. 'We need sceptics like you, Alethea. You keep us grounded. You are like a bridge between Yindisha and the world we are trying to change.'

Ah, there's nothing like flattery to persuade the stubborn. I knew what she was doing. She was afraid. She *had* to persuade me. She had no choice. But I liked Saniya. I found her humility and empathy comforting.

'You came to this place to transform physically and mentally. To shake off old emotional habits,' she added. 'So, where is the harm in embracing beauty and truth?'

I looked away, thinking of that truth I was being forced to face. My submission to the patriarchal system ran deep. It was embedded in my DNA. *I* was the one with false beliefs. *I* had been programmed. *I* didn't recognise my real self. I was another woman who – following thousands of years of gaslighting – had passively accepted the myth of male entitlement.

'And what if there is more Alethea? Much, much more?' Saniya's voice, breathless with a wonder I didn't yet understand, broke through my walls. 'Would you want to miss out?'

I gazed into those water-hole-green eyes, so wild, yet, so contained. I had seen that look in my father's eyes. It was a look possessed with a knowledge that made him love the world. And there in that incandescence, I recalled a love that had made me feel whole.

Thinking of that great inscrutable realm that lay beyond the patina of science, I wondered if – in embracing science as the ultimate purveyor of reality – I was closing my mind to greater truths. I recalled how the research station's programming level resembled a school in which men were trained how to properly treat women. After graduation, these men were then sent out to communities to spread – as one might a virus – kindness and compassion, generosity, respect and love. *Is that so wrong?* I wondered.

When I looked up, leaf patterns from the canopy of trees pressed against a sky the colour of my father's eyes. My heart swelled. *The world is full of magic.* His voice fell softly through my mind.

Perhaps I was tired. Perhaps I wanted reassurance. Or maybe it was the details of Galilea's story that resurrected both my indignation and my compliance. Whatever it was, I fell under Saniya's spell. *What if there is more?*

I see now that she took my silence as an affirmative. Perhaps I ever so faintly nodded.

'There's someone I'd like you to meet,' Saniya added as we rose together.

I thought I had reached the bottom of the rabbit hole. But I didn't know back then – I was still falling.

CHAPTER THIRTY-TWO

The Fingerprints of the Divine

Day fifteen, early evening

Six weeks. That was how long it took for the enchantment to take hold. That was how long it took for a woman to fall so deeply in love with one of Yindisha's golems and be so seduced by Yindisha's ideology that they would accept the shock of the truth – the genesis of Yindisha's men – with only the faintest bleat of protest. It also took six weeks to identify those who – through some spiritual blockage – some intellectual or emotional inadequacy – were unable to see or feel Mother Earth's power. Those who resisted, simply left Yindisha in contented oblivion, perhaps returning every now and then for the occasional shag with a beautiful man.

But what had happened to me had happened too fast. I simply wasn't ready. I couldn't believe what I didn't feel. Yindisha's women still didn't know if I was a threat. *I* didn't know. But I wanted to find out. And, more than anything, I wanted to keep my head.

Remain objective. Rational. A sceptic. I was, after all the daughter of a scientist. And I wanted to honour my father's memory.

I was, however, also gripped by curiosity. So, prior to witnessing an animation, I agreed to participate in what Saniya had described as 'a gentle deepening.' Apparently, it involved some kind of baptism. I trusted Saniya and I was sure – whatever it involved – I could remain objective. Looking back now, all I can do is smile at my naivety.

A sunset the colour of blood oranges filled the sky as we drove back to the research station. Saniya told me about Nana Daringa – the animator I was about to meet. She spoke in tones of great reverence, as if meeting this woman was a great honour.

'Thirty-five years ago, Nana Daringa animated Adam – Australia's first golem,' Saniya explained. 'For nineteen years he worked in the construction industry in Western Sydney and lived with a guardian he thought was his grandmother.'

I shivered as she spoke. The evening was turning chilly. The setting sun peeping between the gaps in the canopy of trees resembled a pair of devilish, slitted red eyes.

According to Saniya, soon after the golem Adam, a Bruce and a Seth followed. Bruce eventually opened up a vegetarian restaurant and Seth became an osteopath.

Nana Daringa, Saniya explained, came from a generation of what she called the 'First Women'. The First Women were women whom Mother Earth had blessed as pure souls with the spiritual qualities necessary to carry her sacred knowledge. 'The knowledge is divine,' Saniya explained. 'It comes unbidden. It is innate knowledge that cannot be taught.'

'Like the founders of religions,' I offered. 'Muhammad, Jesus, Moses – all spoken to by angels or God. Bright lights. Visions. Epiphanies.'

'Yes. But they were all *men*,' said Saniya, as if this proved their revelations were less worthy.

After we entered the research station, instead of pulling into the car park, we drove further, past the now empty area where I'd seen golems learning to walk. Saniya parked the car beside a small gravel path that disappeared into a canopy of unruly trees and writhing purple shadows. 'What? Are we going for a bush walk? At this time of the night?' I asked as she pulled a backpack out of the trunk. *Is she going to murder me?* I thought.

'It's just a five-minute stroll,' she said. 'A very pretty spot.'

...to die... I thought.

I followed Saniya anyway, because I liked her and I was, I told myself, being unreasonably paranoid.

As Saniya promised, after five minutes of gentle descent, we emerged into an open area with a waterhole. On a rock next to the waterhole, a tall dark-haired man stood next to an elderly woman sitting in a collapsible picnic chair. Nearby, a brazier spooled blue-grey smoke into the evening air. The whole area was lit in a blue twilit haze and the smoke smelt sweet and musky. *Cannabis,* I thought. *Or some other fragrant burning firewood.*

Closer, the smoke smell grew stronger. The smell made me feel woozy. Muddled. Of course, it wasn't the smoke I should have been worried about. But then again, how often in life do we fear the wrong things?

I took in the scene before the unfolding night robbed me of clear sight.

The man – clearly a golem – had thick black hair tied into a man bun. With his big, brown, soft-dog eyes, smooth skin and heavy eyebrows, he looked like the type who might write mystical poetry in his spare time. But he wasn't a man. He was a magical clay slave.

He stood next to a foldable picnic table with a floral teapot and three matching cups and saucers – all incongruous out here in this bush setting. I assumed that the white-haired, white-robed woman dwarfed by the man-sized picnic chair was Nana Daringa. She had skin the faded brown of old decking timber. Compressed energy emanated from her tiny form. She looked indigenous, but could have equally been Spanish, Middle Eastern, Māori or Indian.

Saniya gave her a light kiss on her wrinkled cheek.

'Ah, the curious woman,' said Nana Daringa, giving me a forensic gaze. I gathered Nana Daringa had heard about my gate-crashing the seminar, as well as my venturing into the bush and being caught by the cameras. She had probably seen that hideous photo.

'Always,' I managed as I looked down. Candy-pink fluffy slippers cloistering her tiny feet peeped out from under Nana Daringa's white robe.

She gestured for us to take seats on the pair of bongo stools next to the brazier. A sneaky breeze blew a blast of smoke into my eyes. I sputtered and coughed.

Nana Daringa turned to her patiently waiting golem. 'Pour the tea, Colebee,' she said. 'It should be nice and strong by now.'

'What is it?' I asked as Colebee-the-golem poured a urine-yellow liquid into the three teacups with the delicacy of a Geisha at a tea ceremony.

'Acacia tea. 'It'll clear your lungs. Unclog you.'

Something I knew about Acacias pinged faintly at the back of my mind as I accepted that cup and saucer.

Nana Daringa grinned. 'It's an acquired taste. It'll warm your insides. Drink up.'

Gingerly, I took a sip. It tasted odd but not unpleasant – earthy, fruity and faintly sweet. It soothed my smoke-scratched throat.

Just what was it about Acacias that I was trying to recall?

'I was one of the stolen children,' Nana Daringa said. 'A tiny baby, ripped from my mother's arms by a government of white men. I was raised by white men missionaries and their foolish, subservient wives.'

She looked at me then as if, being of European extraction, I was partly to blame.

'I'm sorry,' I said, looking away from eyes the deep brown of potting mix.

She ignored my apology and kept on talking. 'Eventually I found my way back to the truth of the land.'

She cleared her throat, narrowing her eyes. 'Once, I was like you. I was curious. Persistent. I asked lots of questions, never gave up and finally found out about my parents. My father was a miner. A *Catholic.* A man of so-called faith. Even though he was married, he thought he could shag a local black girl on the side and then carry on as though it never happened...'

A singularity of rage passed through her eyes and in that moment, I thought of the whole diabolical history of British colonisation with its righteousness, its defilements and destructions of Australia's ancient cultures, the settlers' hideous abuses of indigenous women.

Next to me, I noticed Saniya unpacking her backpack. She pulled out some white robes. Floral garlands with real camelias and hibiscus flowers. Pots of paint.

What the fuck? I wondered.

You agreed to this, I reminded myself.

'I know why you're here,' Nana Daringa added, looking at me fiercely. 'You want to do more than just survive. You want a life with meaning and purpose. You want to thrive. You want to feel loved.'

I didn't answer. Instead, I took another sip of tea, guiltily recalled my sex with Lucas and kept one wary eye on Saniya, wondering when the butcher's knife might emerge from her backpack.

'You aren't aware how much you've been shaped by the bad ways of men. You think you know what love is. But you don't.'

I watched Saniya shake out four white robes and drape them over the branches of the surrounding trees where they shuddered like waiting ghosts.

Meanwhile, Colebee stepped up to the pool and scooped out some leaves and what looked like a dead snake. My insides went cold.

I glanced back at Saniya who had taken a seat beside me and was undoing the pots of paint. 'I'm not going into that waterhole, am I?'

Nana Daringa answered. 'You are here for a purification ritual are you not?'

Confused, I looked from Nana Daringa to Saniya. 'I didn't agree to this.'

'Before you can witness an animation you must be cleansed,' Nana Daringa said firmly.

Saniya smiled reassuringly. 'It's just a light dip, Alethea. You'll be fine. It's part of the deepening.'

I regarded her, hurt by her deceit. Nothing about this felt *fine*.

'No,' I said firmly. 'My father drowned when I was eleven. I never learned to swim. I *hate* the water.'

I took another sip of tea to calm myself down.

I noticed Saniya and Nana Daringa glance at each other as if this were a problem.

And again, I wondered how they handled problems like me.

Nana Daringa snagged my gaze. 'Soon, you'll remember things you didn't even know you've forgotten. Things so old and so deep inside you, that when you finally recognise them, you will be reborn.'

Bullshit. Lady, you are so full of crap. That insolent voice in my head wasn't entirely mine. It held the faintest whiffle of my ex.

I snatched a look down the path and considered making a quick escape. I glanced back at that bottomless and black body of water. Thinking how chilly it looked, I shuddered and took another long sip of my hot tea.

No way was I going into that fucking waterhole.

Perhaps, I thought, *I can reason my way out of this.*

'Men worship logic and science as Gods,' Nana Daringa continued. 'They forget about insight. They ignore and abuse the natural world. They collect and destroy instead of respect and create. Men pull things apart to see how they work,' she continued. 'Men have robbed Mother Earth of her equilibrium.'

She gestured to the waterhole. 'We must cleanse ourselves of the toxic masculine.'

Inwardly, I rolled my eyes at such cultish exhortations. I was starting to get annoyed at this relentless man-blaming.

'We must wash away the evils of men...'

I tensed my thighs and braced myself. I had to leave now or forever hold my peace. But then I noticed something else was happening. My body was starting to feel heavy and a faint hum sounded in the surrounding bush. The shadows seemed to move and glow, as if the night was revealing some new wavelength of light.

Funny how the night does this to people, I suddenly thought. *Funny how it makes one ponder the unknown, the mysteries beyond the world of light and colour.*

'Once, long before the man-God, the world was in balance. Once, this land was in balance. There were he-spirits and she-spirits living in harmony with one another and the land was their mother,' Nana Daringa continued. 'Then, the white man came and plundered and mined our sacred places. He thought he owned the land. He thought he owned woman. But you can't own wildness and nature. You can only respect it or provoke it.' She leaned forward, a fragrant gust of aniseed wafting from her mouth. 'Is it any wonder that Mother Earth roared up in fury?'

'You mean the bushfires?' I asked, suddenly lured by her words.

'Yes. Among other things. Floods. Pestilence. It's shameful, this disrespect for cultural practices and knowledge hundreds of thousands of years old. Catastrophe is inevitable. For the indigenous people, the apocalypse happened long ago, when the white man came. They destroyed our way of life, upended tens of thousands of years of unity between people and the animals and the plants and the land. Now, Mother Earth is calling out for us to change.'

'Yindisha Retreat isn't part of the real world,' I managed, trying to counter a growing light-headedness, a heaviness spreading over my tongue. 'How can a place like Yindisha possibly change anything?' I slurred.

Nana Daringa released a cough of disgust. 'Let me tell you about the *real world*. In the *real world* women think they are finally achieving the status of men. All over the world women are copying men. Working like men. Fighting like men. Judging like men. Loving like men.' She leaned ever so slightly forward in her chair. 'And you think this is equality. You think this is liberation. Progress. Once woman controlled fire. And magic. Then man stole it. Man has been stealing power from woman since the beginning of time. And the reason magic died was because man didn't know how to manage it.'

Now feeling pinned to my bongo stool and faintly dizzy, I glanced at Colebee; eyes lowered, hands clasped as still as a mannequin, as though awaiting his next instructions. Is this what Nana Daringa had in mind? Replacing *all* human men with golems? But how could those creatures ever replace real men with all their glorious, conflicted depths and neediness and complexity? How could they possibly replace men like my father? Trying to centre myself, I took another sip of my Acacia tea.

Nana Daringa cleared her throat raucously and continued. 'Now they've lost the magic, men rape the earth, foul the heavens and take what doesn't belong to them. And they call a world where some people starve and suffer while others embrace wastefulness, civilisation. And too many women, fools that they are, play along with it. They are nothing more than aiders and abettors of male entitlement...'

I lowered my eyes, feeling as if the old woman's words were unpicking the fabric of my tattered self. 'I'm sorry we got everything so wrong,' I thickly replied. A heavy weariness settled inside my belly. I was too tired to deal with this. Now, instead of escaping, I felt as though I wanted to curl up in a corner and sleep forever.

God may have had the first word, but Mother Earth is having the last word. Thoughts such as these, loose and disconnected, popped in and out of my thoughts, like electrons circling the nucleus of that old woman and her fire. Dreamy blue shapes appeared from the shadows. I could see now they were women, surrounding the fire, like moths drawn to flames. *Ancestral spirits. Dead guardians of the land.* I knew this without knowing how or why.

And then I remembered what it was about Acacia that bothered me. Acacias contained tryptamine. A psychotropic substance. This tea was hallucinogenic.

Alarmed, I put the cup down on the saucer resting on my knee. 'Brahma, Vishnu, Shiva,' Nana Daringa continued. 'Creation. Preservation. Destruction. The pattern woven into the cosmos. The ancients knew this and the moderns choose to disrespect this inescapable celestial law.'

Her eyes glazed over and for a moment, it seemed as if she were talking as if we weren't there, instead addressing that audience of spirits.

I took in the shape of her nose, gently arched, like the beak of a finch. But it was her lips that suddenly fascinated me; full like a much younger woman's and dusted with patches of rose pink. They were beautiful.

In that moment, everything around me disintegrated into fragments of colour and stars. I felt untethered, as if I were floating in some timeless realm.

With a triumphant smile, Nana Daringa rose from her chair and addressed Saniya. 'I think we are ready.'

When I looked at Colebee, I noticed his skin glowed with a faint blue light. Having read Aldous Huxley's *The Doors of Perception*, it occurred to me that my brain wasn't closing down, but was instead, opening up to new wavelengths and alternate realities. A part of me still bleated. I wasn't a drug taker! I hated feeling out of control. I didn't want any of this. But I had lost my free will. Or had it stolen from me. I felt as though I'd entered someone else's dream.

When Colebee held out his hand, I obediently gave him my

cup and saucer. *Run!* A voice in my head cried. Instead, I rose and watched as the last vestiges of my will floated away on a mist of unknowing.

Guided by gentle arms, I undressed, put on that white robe and let Saniya paint me in white and ochre marks – earth colours connecting me to the land, dots and circles connecting me to the Dreamtime, lines symbolising routes and journeys. I saw the spirits clearly now, watching, surrounding me, warming me with a wavelength beyond perception's doors. In an obedience borne as much by Nana Daringa's words as by that psychotropic tea, I stepped towards the waterhole. *Shit* , I thought in a last gust of resistance, *I'm about to drown.*

Nana Daringa and Saniya, now also wearing a white robe, chanted a prayer as Saniya guided me down the stone steps and into the waterhole.

Mother of Earth, Goddess of all creation,
Spirit of all winds and all directions
Take this wounded, vacant creature and heal her pain
May Your blessings warm her, Your love flow over her.
Surround her with Your radiance.
In Your soothing, uterine waters, give her the gift of seeing
Your infinite bounty in all its true light.
Help her see through the eyes of Your soul.
Return her to the tree of life where all things begin and end.
Fill her with the source of all life and knowledge and love and peace.
May Your life force resurrect her. Make her reborn in Your knowledge.
Mother of Earth, Goddess of all creation, help woman heal the world.

All around us the bush shuddered and warped, our ghostly companions appearing and vanishing in the waning evening light. The water rippled into patterns of such incandescent beauty, I gasped.

The sound of the digeridoo shimmered through my bones. In my drugged and submissive yet strangely astute state, I recalled a school lesson on indigenous folklore in which our teacher explained that the digeridoo was an essential tool of the creation of the world – the world's oldest musical instrument, created by the world's oldest continuous culture. This place, this waterhole, was old, oh, so old, so filled with spirits...

The water was cold. But everything, this world, those sounds, my thoughts, felt beautiful. Divine. True.

My toes touched something and I gazed at impossibly coloured tiles rippling under my bare feet. I thought about the mosaic of beliefs that made up human civilisation – from fates and spirits to Gods to that single unknowable deity called Allah, God or Lord – the myriad ways human minds give shape to the unseen and inconceivable. And here, with my newly opened eyes, I saw Mother Earth's fingerprints resting on the surface of existence.

Time is a boomerang. My father's voice, deep and sonorous hummed through my thoughts.

I stepped deeper. The water reached my shoulders. I shivered. But even my shivering felt sublime. Cathartic. Cleansing.

Together, Saniya and Nana Daringa chanted. *'Return to Mother of Earth, the interconnected one, the spirit that binds all that lives and does not live.'*

And then, a hand pressed down firmly on my head and I went under. Down beneath the surface of the water, I held my breath and opened my eyes. In that psychotropic realm of drowning, my father floated beside me, radiant and blue, inhabiting that realm that was neither death nor life, but the unknown in-between. 'Alethea, in the last breath I took,' he said, 'I thought how much I love you.' I felt the life leave him, I felt that eternal part of him coalesce and return to stardust. Yet in this realm of spaceless time and timeless space, he was still with me. My mother was with me but not with me as well, dying and dead, alive in that unknowable realm and filled with love, music and poetry. The rational part of my mind told me this was an hallucination brought on by a cup of Acacia tea.

Yet, beguiled by the timelessness of that bubbling, swaying, underwater universe, floating with the evanescent forms of my parents in this realm of blue love, I wanted to remain. But my lungs had a different agenda. My body wanted me to live.

I flailed. Those women above were trying to drown me! And I damn well wasn't going to let them. *Fuck this!*

And then, *Shit! I'm going to lose my contact lenses!*

I fought my way back to the surface. I emerged into the twilight and gasped for air so sweet it felt as though I was inhaling draughts of heavenly nectar.

All I could hear were the songs of the birds roosting in the surrounding trees, the hush of leaves, the hymn of water sloshing against the edges of the water-hole. Behind it all, that distant digeridoo thrummed, like the heartbeat of the universe. All around me, I heard nature's music, a symphony of such glory I wanted to cry out in jubilation. And the air smelt of the sweetest perfume of evening flowers. And Colebee glowed, bright blue, like the screen of an iPhone.

My floral garland floated beside me. I regarded those flowers as if they were wonders I had seen for the very first time – their shapes expanding into extraordinary geometries, a new spectrum of colours opening to my eyes. My robes billowed as if I were part of a cloud – floating, trailing, and free. I observed my furious indignation from a distance. A part of me wanted to scream at my a smugly smiling companions, but the drug had well and truly got hold of me. I looked back at Colebee, glowing bright blue in the dying light.

Hell, I wanted to say. *Fuck.* But no words came. Instead, just the thought: *I have been unclogged. I have lost my mind.*

We didn't need a torch for our walk back to the car. Now dressed, along with Saniya, in a dry white robe covering my clothes, guided by Colebee's blue, iPhone light, a strange world revealed itself – splotches of blue-white, dots, dashes and white arabesques that seemed to move and change under my gaze. Recalling the shapes on the golem's foreheads, the patterns in nature, Mandelbrot sets, the mathematics behind the machinations of existence, it occurred to me that the entire world was made of cyphers. My legs wobbled and I felt spongey, as though I was renavigating some long-forgotten self.

Ahead of us, Nana Daringa walked slowly, illumined by Colebee's glow, her hand gripping the crook of his elbow. We all fell into the rhythm of her step. It seemed we moved not as separate particles, but as a single wave.

Again, I wondered what Yindisha's women did with problems. Like me.

Instead of getting into Saniya's car, we walked back to the research station.

I didn't know how long it took – forever perhaps, or maybe an instant. Night had suddenly fallen and everything beyond Colebee's light was black and filled with pulsing blue stars. I couldn't feel my feet. It was as though some force was moving me independently of my own volition. *I am so high*, I thought as I watched a few of those blue ancestral spirits appear and shimmer beside us, in front of us, then vanish.

Some amorphous time later, we reached the research station. Here, Nana Daringa dismissed Colebee and instructed him to go back and fetch the stuff from the waterhole.

He turned and left us with all the obedience of a well-trained dog. One by one, the spirits around us dissolved back into the bush, the ground, and the sky as we entered the research station.

My stomach contracted when we stepped into the lift.

Inside me something scrambled. Panic welled as I watched Nana Daringa press the button down to level nine. I recalled more of the research I'd done when I had my phone just this morning.

This morning – a morning that now felt like a thousand years ago – I'd googled Dante's Circles of Hell. I recalled how the ninth circle of hell was betrayal.

Fuck, I thought, bracing myself as the lift plunged.

CHAPTER THIRTY-THREE

The Missing Link

Day Fifteen, Night

*A*lethea Braxton. I am Alethea Braxton. I clung to my name as if I were dying, forgetting who I once was. I wanted my mind back. My old mind. The one I knew. *I am a rational human being and Dante's Circles of Hell is just another male, ecclesiastical creation,* I reminded myself as we descended to level nine.

Galilea, also wearing a floral garland and white robe, was waiting for us as the door opened. My skin bristled when I saw that woman who put cameras in the nipples of sculptures and the bellybuttons of Buddhas. I imagined for a second there might have been cameras at the waterhole. I imagined Galilea watching us, perhaps on that great screen on level four – her hands steepled, assessing and judging like some war-scarred high priestess – trying to decide if I was worthy. Or if I was still an insurmountable problem.

Yet, I saw deference in Galilea eyes when she looked at Nana Daringa as she exited the lift with her hand nestled in the crook of Saniya's elbow.

Holding back, I watched, feeling as though I was made of stars held together by some invisible glue more powerful than the force that bound the nuclei of atoms.

With my mind shifting back and forth between reason and that strange realm channelled through a cup of Acacia tea, I floated out of the lift.

We were in a cavern. But like no cavern I'd ever seen on the National Geographic channel. Shapes resembling tree-roots, mangrove swamps, stalactites and stalagmites protruded from the walls, the ceiling, the floor. In the centre of the ceiling those unruly root shapes coalesced into a pattern like the scaffolds of an ancient cathedral. The air smelt of allspice and moss. Tiny golden lights hung and trembled in the air, suspended from invisible threads. As if I were suffering some kind of synaesthesia, those lights seemed to emit a low, thrumming sound that made the arches of my feet tickle and my skin goose-bump. In my strangely untethered yet lucid state, I thought of the installation artworks of Yayoi Kusama – her Infinity and Obliteration rooms – artwork you could step into and exalt at the wonders of the creative spirit and the mysteries beyond our existence. In this golden room, I noticed Colebee's light had now turned green. *Blue and yellow make green*, I thought, pleased my mind was in some way – still able to channel my knowledge of art and still able to connect this hallucinatory world with its old, Newtonian, classical, self.

As my eyes adjusted, I noticed the cavern took on a reddish glow, and it occurred to me we were all inside some strange, monstrous womb.

In the centre of this great space sat a stone plinth. And, on the plinth lay the body of a man. Not a man. A sculpture. A golem-to-be. Drops of water glistened over his body, as if he too, had recently been purified. The only part of him that glowed was the tetragrammaton on his forehead. His tattooed arm bore the 'Men of Earth' motif. Despite the fact I was high on Acacia tea, my scepticism department was still operating at full force. What would the animation of a golem entail? The tossing of magic beans? The waving of an elderwood wand? Naked dancing?

Saniya grabbed my left hand and Galilea my right. Holding hands, the four of us approached the plinth. My companions chanted a prayer.

Mother of Earth, Goddess of all creation,

Spirit of all winds and all directions

You have placed in woman's hands a power unlike any since the beginning of time.

The power to overturn laws of creation. The power to right the wrongs of man.

We stand before You humbled, ready to receive Your blessings. We ask for You to bestow life upon this lethargic and shapeless mass; this lump of clay hewn into the shape of a man.

Mother Earth, Goddess of all creation, take this quintessence of clay and transform it into a creature of utter submission to Your powers.

Mother Earth, Goddess of all creation, give us the strength, the wisdom and the skill to cleanse the oceans, the skies and the forests of the sins of man.

Recalling my research into the creation of golems and how a single mispronounced word would make someone die, I bit on my lips to keep them still. This was not a time to swear. Or even *think* of swearing. But my thoughts refused to still. Were these women messing with things we didn't fully understand? Was this just as dangerous as splitting the atom? As potentially destructive as trying to create mini black holes?

The four of us still holding hands by the plinth, Nana Daringa stood over the golem's head and began chanting in a language that sounded ancient, otherworldly and – most strangely of all – familiar. It was as though that chant had reanimated some ancient imprint, some atavistic self from the depths of my being.

I was suddenly gripped by a dry-mouthed, frozen terror. I

felt sure that, if I opened my mouth, nothing would come out. Perhaps I was having a stroke.

From Nana Daringa's pink fluffy slippers, my gaze returned to the golem.

Each note and tone seemed to bring more colour to his skin. Each sound seemed to draw him further into the realm of the living. His body began to gently glow with a blue light.

My eyes stung and watered. Words backed up at the top of my throat. I wanted to join in, but didn't know what to say and couldn't speak. My panic rose and subsided like waves licking the shores of my thoughts.

After what might have been an eternity or possibly a second (I had at this point lost all sense of time), the chanting and surrounding sounds stopped. The silence of the cavern felt alive. But the golem remained glowing and still, as if in a deep sleep.

My heart raced and beat as if it had decided it no longer wanted to be a part of this body and was looking for an exit. When Saniya and Galilea let go of my hands, I fought my flagellating thoughts. Feigning courage and respect, my freed hands trembling, I followed my companions' lead, our heads bowed as if deep in silent prayer.

Out of the corner of my eye I saw Nana Daringa raise her head, run her tongue over her full lips. Then, she bent down and kissed the golem on his mouth.

As she pulled away, the golem's hands and legs twitched and his eyelids fluttered.

The golem opened eyes as bright as rising stars and smiled at Nana Daringa with ice-white teeth embedded in pink gums. He was alive. He was gorgeous.

'Maaa, mama, mutter, mére, mutti, mummmm...' He gazed at Nana Daringa and spoke slowly, in multiple tongues, like some gifted toddler uttering its first words. Or an artificial life form trying to tune in to the right language.

Mother,' he finally said clearly. His gaze never leaving Nana Daringa's face, his eyes filled with adulation as he sat up.

I stepped back on legs that wobbled like shadows in a storm.

At the far end of the cavern, a square of light appeared and two women wearing those black and orange-logoed Men of Earth tee shirts exited the lift and strode towards us.

As the women fetched that newborn golem and guided him on his wobbly legs into the lift, he kept looking back at Nana Daringa. 'Mother,' he said again. 'Mother.'

Turning her gaze from the golem, Nana Daringa looked back at me. 'Everything in the universe comes from love,' she said. She smiled, flashing perfect teeth behind those full lips. 'And the first thing a golem feels as he comes to life is the love of Mother Earth.'

I stood silently listening, my thoughts reassembling. I thought of that Mother Earth prayer preceding my unwelcome dunking. I was not a wounded, vacant creature. I was a woman who could think for herself. I was a woman staring into the depths of a mystical abyss in which I refused to plunge, my nails gripping the edges of the cliff of reason. *I am Alethea Braxton. A fighter, not a follower. I will not fall for this. I refuse.*

My wayward thoughts sharpened. *Oh yes, this was wondrous! What impressive theatrics! What clever smoke and mirrors. But...*

I sensed a smugness about these women – their certainty that the creation of compliant men was the solution to millennia of injustice. *Blind faith in authority is the greatest enemy of truth.* So said Albert Einstein.

I felt taken. Absorbed. Yet simultaneously indignant. These women were far too sanctimonious for my liking. And I was Alethea Braxton, daughter of Conrad Braxton. Scientist. Man of reason.

My voice returned. 'Well, that was all very interesting,' I said, trying to stay calm and cool. For my own safety, I knew I had to stay in control. I gave them all looks I hoped conveyed I was still

Alethea Braxton – an eternally stubborn creature who refused to be dazzled – to the point of blindness – by all this beauty and magic. 'But I would have appreciated being warned that you were going to drug me.'

CHAPTER THIRTY-FOUR

Beyond The Cave

Day Sixteen, Dawn

The metaphor of Plato's Cave goes something like this: We are all living in a cave, facing the back wall like schoolchildren on detention. Behind us – outside the mouth of the cave – is a fire which throws shadows on the cave wall. We think the shadows are reality when in fact, the greatest reality, the *truth*, lies beyond the mouth of the cave. The man (and it invariably *is* a man in this story – because women are too busy looking after the children, sweeping away the cave's cobwebs and keeping the men and children fed and happy) who finally dares to venture to the cave's mouth, returns with stories no one can believe.

Mesmerised by the shadows on the wall, too frightened, or too enculturated to step towards the fire, the inhabitants linger within the confines of the cave. They mock the adventurer when he presents his discoveries. They persecute and belittle him. But that man, after seeing what lies beyond can no longer accept the limitations of his tribe's reality. He is forever doomed to see the truth. It will take a catastrophe in the form of fire, or plague, or war, or more, or all of the above, before the cave's inhabitants might consider listening.

Not all of us, however, are adventurers; but there are times when life gives us an unexpected glimpse of the world beyond the cave. There are times when others take it upon themselves to force sight on the unseeing. Affronted by what they see, most retreat back to the comfort of those familiar shadows.

As we crowded back into the lift, Galilea told me (very unapologetically, may I add) how I had to be oblivious to the drugging to avoid apprehension, which could have altered the effects of the tea. She explained this was part of the process. 'The ritual is sacred. Besides, it was no more a violation of your human rights than the daily subjugations you endure under the rule of the patriarchy.'

To which I replied that I was sick of the patriarchy being used as a scapegoat for all world's wrongs.

Back on ground level, my legs felt spongy, as if I'd stepped not only out of Plato's Cave, but off the edge of the world. Trying to ground myself, I regarded my companions. How cunning of these women to show me an animation while under the influence of a psychotropic drug. I would never be sure if what I saw was real. Right now, the whole episode felt like a dream.

The tentacles of my thoughts sought meaning in my companions' silence. The sense of elitism and the privilege of these women bothered me. This bubble world of angry women and subservient man-bots bothered me – this separation of genders, this branding of human men as *them*, the women of Yindisha as *us*. How tempting it would be to follow the mandates of such a belief system, to bask in the glow of its exhortations, to believe heart and soul and surrender to its mystical pull. No. I still wasn't ready to fully believe. I was still Alethea Braxton. Scientist's daughter. Sceptic. Independent thinker.

Outside, dawn was breaking, tipping the trees that surrounded the research station in an amber light. We had been underground all night. I had lost all sense of time. I felt removed from myself yet simultaneously connected with everything around me, as if the boundaries between self and other had dissolved.

As dawn's light washed over the trees, the whole world felt primordial, filled with an effulgent sentience. I'd had that same feeling when I first saw Uluru, the great red monolith at the heart of the Australian continent that hummed with the power of something ancient and imperishable.

My gaze snapped back to my companions – those three wounded women transforming their angst into art in the form of beautiful men. *How do we change the world without violence and without revolution?* I wondered. *How do we turn pain and destruction into joy and creation?* My thoughts oscillated, ideas and memories and feelings rotating around some inviolate core that was, and wasn't, me.

Wordlessly, we exited the building, our feet crunching on the gravel, the birds around us exalting in the dawn chorus. Gazing at the wispy pink brushstrokes of cloud conjured by dawn's light, listening to nature's elemental utterances, I felt the knowledge in my companions' silence. As if they knew what I was thinking. As if we were all thinking the same thing.

I recalled that set of eyes I thought I'd seen last night, those red slits staring between the trees that had, in fact just been the setting sun peeping behind a canopy of leaves. But who or what might be watching us? I briefly considered how all of us might just as easily be a creation of some consciousness in another realm. What if that was all we were? Self-aware illusions created by a higher power? Entities with no free will inhabiting a deterministic universe?

As we walked towards the carpark, a sense of awe came to me again. Something inside me *had* irrevocably changed. Outside Plato's Cave, I had felt Mother Earth's raw power. Seen it. Been touched by it.

Golems created from and for love. Yes. But...

The nagging in the back of my mind took shape. I thought of Mary Nader. In my mind's eye, she stood and trembled in her husband's shadow.

We paused in front of Galilea's car as my companions discussed our travel arrangements. Galilea would take Nana Daringa home and I would return to Yindisha Retreat with Saniya. We were a collective, a flock of starlings about to separate into our self-governing parts. A murder of crows about to take independent flight.

I wanted to say something before we parted, but the words kept sliding sideways, as if avoiding my tongue. *Mary Nader. How could I forget you?*

How easy, I thought, after everything I had seen, to be seduced by this Mother Earth ideology. How easy to be swept up in it all and ignore the real world of children and men and marriage. These women were so absorbed in seeing the scaffold behind reality's illusion, they thought they knew all the answers. And a world run by women? I wasn't entirely sure about that. My experiences at an all-girls high school taught me the hard way that some women could be bitches. Freeze you out. Gossip behind your back. But it occurred to me in that same instance that nothing matched the emotional violence of my marriage. No one else had betrayed me so deeply.

I held on to thoughts of Mary Nader as if she were a part of myself I wasn't prepared to release. My back hardened like a dried sponge. No. The old Alethea wasn't ready to lie down and die. Not yet.

My outrage returned. Finally finding my words, I glared at my companions. 'You should all be ashamed of yourselves,' I said. 'All those prayers and drugs. All your furious anti-man rhetoric. This Mother-Earth-Goddess religion. Meanwhile, you are ignoring something real and right in front of you.'

My three companions stopped and stared at me – wearily – as if they were beginning to think I was more trouble than I was worth.

When I told them about Mary Nader and the abusive Reverend, Nana Daringa's eyes turned dark and seemed to sink deeper into their sockets. Galilea and Saniya exchanged silent glances, as if I'd committed some faux pas. A sensation of utter and helpless despair passed through me. It was as if, for a millisecond, I had experienced the collective torments of generations of women – wounds absorbed and held by Mother Earth compressed into a singular sharp agony. For a second, it felt as though the earth under my feet convulsed and heaved.

'No surprises there,' Galilea eventually replied as she gently helped Nana Daringa – now trembling – as if she were exhausted, or furious, or both – into her car.

Galilea smiled at me then. 'Let's discuss this back at my office.' And strangely, I sensed Galilea was – in an odd way – *pleased*.

Back at the retreat, in the privacy of her office, Galilea and I discussed in more detail, the issue of Mary Nader.

'Reverend Nader's abuse is part of a pattern, Alethea. Like many men fearful of losing their power and status, he is a dinosaur terrified of his looming extinction. Ever since he arrived at the parish with his family, he has been suspicious of Yindisha. At various points in time, he has reported us to the police for acts of vandalism on his church. He's reported us to the Department of Immigration, accusing us of illegally employing refugees, the Department of Health for illicit drug use...'

She looked away and I knew then there were still things she wasn't telling me. 'Every time government agents arrived and inspected, they found nothing. No evidence of wrongdoing.'

It occurred to me in that moment that this scarred woman was hiding more secrets than the Great Library of Alexandria. I knew more than yesterday, but I was still an ignoramus.

She narrowed her eyes then, gave me a hard gaze filled with warnings. Unnerved, I looked down, noticing bits of ochre paint from my baptism still clinging to the wrinkles and creases in my arms.

I took a sip of my chamomile tea and when I looked up, her eyes sparked with fiery subversions. I thought of the contacts she had, the covert arrangements and agreements and deals she may have made with people in power to keep the story of her ex-husband and the existence of the golems secret.

'Even though Reverend Nader has tried to set the entire village of Watson against us, they tolerate us because the research station and the retreat bring in good business. Many people suspect there is a connection between the station and the retreat. They suspect Yindisha, with its thriving orchards and vegetable gardens is benefiting from the station's agricultural research.'

She arched one of her neatly plucked eyebrows. 'And we've done nothing to dispel those rumours.'

Galilea sat back in her chair, and after taking a sip of her chamomile tea, she sighed and smiled at me. 'Do you think it's possible, Alethea, that Mother Earth brought you to us at this particular junction in time so you could help Mary Nader?'

I bit my lip and shrugged. The problem was, helping Mary Nader – a woman who didn't *want* to be helped – was an insurmountable challenge.

I looked away from Galilea's gaze, thinking of that body covered in scars. By accident or through the machinations of some effulgent power, or through the scheming of a collection of damaged women, somewhere along this journey, I had accepted my lack of control, or at least, yielded a little more to Mother Earth. My priorities had changed. My *world* had changed.

Unbidden, another wave of Mother Earth's power raged through me. My consciousness underwent another tectonic shift. For a fleeting moment I felt as though I could move mountains.

Just as swiftly the feeling evaporated.

Beside me, Galilea steepled her restless fingers, as if considering a thought.

'Alethea, at some point, every newly anointed Guardian must take on a project. It can range from something as simple as regularly posting positive affirmations on social media to building a sustainable business that employs vulnerable women.'

She leaned back in her chair. 'Perhaps helping Mary Nader could be yours?'

She gestured in the general direction of the research station. 'All the resources you have seen are at your disposal.'

I blinked rapidly, taking in what she was telling me. It felt like I had been handed a key to a nuclear arsenal. I didn't want it. A – because I didn't know how to use it and B – because placing such responsibility in the hands of someone like me was an invitation to a disaster party. Despite everything that had changed, I didn't consider myself a Guardian. No cult in their right minds should trust me.

I was still bothered by Galilea, her nimbus of raging confidence, her conviction that this – whatever this was – was the future. But in a way I also envied her dedication. To be this committed to a cause was a singularity I had never experienced.

I sighed, thinking of that obstinate look Mary Nader had given me. I couldn't help. Mary Nader had to help herself.

I squirmed and took a sip of my chamomile tea. I had spiritual technology at my disposal. And no idea how to wield it. But here I had a chance to help a woman suffering a pain I deeply understood.

I drew a shallow breath. Today, I also had an art class to teach. It was the beginning of my working week, a time to return to the real world of platonic solids and still life. I had to decide if I had both the time, the energy and the will, to do both.

Again, I thought of all those scars under Galilea's shirt. I thought of Mary Nader and her suffering.

When I recalled my experience of the night before – now feeling no more real than a dream – it occurred to me every faith system needed its sceptics – those of us with our feet firmly planted in the realm of disbelief. That was what I had to offer. That plus my knowledge of how it felt to be in a relationship with a man who wanted to kill my spirit.

I inhaled and gave Galilea a firm look. 'I'll take on the challenge.'

CHAPTER THIRTY-FIVE

The Book of Creation

Days Seventeen to Twenty-Four

L*ong ago, before the history of man, woman ruled the world. Woman worshipped Mother Earth, who shared with her the secrets of creation.*

Working closely with Mother Earth, woman created golems – giant, peaceful and strong creatures who helped build cities and empires and civilisations.

But man became jealous of the power of the golems and sought them out and persecuted and killed them.

Woman knew the only way to protect the golems and prevent their extinction was to make them more closely resemble human men.

Channelling powerful magic, woman endowed the golems with qualities that made them indistinguishable from human men. The golems grew hearts and lungs and livers, they wept and loved. They sired children. They grew old and died.

Gradually over the course of centuries, the golems and their part-golem children merged with ancient humans until they became an entirely new species.

Their purity muddied by humanity, some half-bred golems and their progeny turned monstrous and succumbed to their dark sides. Those half-bred golems became unruly, betrayed their creators and shared some of the magic of creation with man. But it was incomplete magic – hungry magic, power untethered from Mother Earth and woman. Without the influence of woman, it was ugly magic. Dark magic. Man abused this magic to undermine the rule of woman and fight wars. Man used this power to wage war with Mother Earth.

Horrified at the way in which Mother Earth's power was being used against her, woman sought to bury her power and hide it from the eyes of man. But it was too late. Man had abused this magic to become the most powerful sex. Man rewrote the story of creation, supplanting Mother Earth's history with man-stories and a man-God.

Eventually Adam and his duplicitous wife Eve became the templates of humanity...

I was five floors underground, in the research station library, reading excerpts and addenda from *The Book of Creation* – originally written on a tablet in Sumerian script, eventually translated into Hebrew and, more recently, into English. Secretly redrafted during the Reformation and now digitised, the three volumes lived inside a flash drive kept in a safe in the restricted section of the library.

I had no idea how accurate these translations were. Like many translations of esoteric texts filled with metaphors and symbols, I suspected there was bias. What I was reading, was a religious doctrine. None of this could be proved. CNN and Fox News weren't around then, so neither could it be disproved. It was all a matter of faith.

I looked up from the text, catching the gaze of the librarian – a golem with brilliant purple eyes. We smiled at each other. Now I was a member of the inner sanctum – a Guardian undertaking what was called a 'Redemption Project' – I was allowed access to this level of the station.

Here, thanks to the effect of what was called the 'Unpredictability Quotient' – golems too otherworldly-looking to be released from the research station maintained the machinery, the library, cleaned, cooked, painted, mended and kept the pot-plants alive. Since I arrived this morning, I'd met dark-skinned golems with pale blue eyes, blond Orientals, others that inhabited the uncanny valley – just two weirdly perfect to be true. These golems accepted the limitations of their existence as willingly and obliviously as animals incarcerated in a zoo. This research station was their world.

And – a residual effect of my Acacia tea trip – I could still see a nimbus of blue light surrounding the golems. Nana Daringa had told me this 'sight of the world beyond,' would fade after about a week.

During this visit, I had more of my questions about the research station answered. Two hundred staff – all of whom had undergone the purification ritual – worked here as part-timers, shift workers, seasonal workers. Most were middle-aged like me, although there were a few younger women who, Galilea had told me, demonstrated wisdom and maturity beyond their years. There were men here too – real men, gentle men, who supported Yindisha's ideology. All had been purified in the water hole and had taken a vow of silence.

I had also read a more recent history about how *The Book of Creation* came to be here – in the Australian Southern Highlands. Recognising its extraordinary power and fearing the knowledge might get into the wrong hands, the Guardians decided that the distant Antipodes was the safest place. After the First World War, a rabbi, tuned to Mother Earth's commandments, smuggled *The Book of Creation* into Australia, placing it in the safekeeping of an Aboriginal matriarch. And that matriarch was Nana Daringa's great-grandmother.

Thinking of women wise beyond their years, my heart ached as I recalled yesterday's FaceTime conversation with Sophia. It gutted me that I couldn't speak to her about this eventful week. It gutted me that I had to continue the lies. Yesterday morning, I had simply told her the classes were going well. That I was enjoying the good food and the interesting company. She told me that yes, she and Dave were still together before changing the subject and chatting about her job.

I dwelled on her parting words. 'I think the retreat is doing you some good, Mum. You look ten years younger.'

Sweeping aside my inner convolutions, I returned my thoughts to this translation of *The Book of Creation*. I scanned a few more chapters until I came across a section called 'Replication.'

If the need arises, and with the approval of the ancient ones, a full replica of a living human is permissible and indeed, sometimes, a replacement is desirable.

I recalled then, something Galilea had said to me when I asked if she had watched Lucas and I being intimate. *Although we have the capabilities...*

Realising I might have found my answer, I removed the flash drive and switched off the laptop. I wasn't sure if it could be done, but it was my only idea.

After returning *The Book of Creation* flash drive to the Restricted Section, thanking that purple-eyed golem and smiling at the prospect of victory for Mary Nader, I headed to programming on level two.

The blinds in the programming section's meeting room were drawn for privacy. Nerida – the research station's senior programmer – tapped her fingers on the table as she listened to my idea. Elfin, petite and birdlike, she possessed a formidable brain that had, Galilea had told me, discombobulated the men she once worked with in Silicon Valley. Here, free from male judgement and predation, that bright little bird could stretch her cerebral wings.

I told her my plan was to build a full replica of Mary Nader complete with cameras to record her husband's abuse. Once I'd finished speaking, Nerida scowled.

After taking a sip of her catnip tea, she regarded me as if I'd just asked her cast a spell to turn a lump of clay into a Black Forest Cherry Cake. 'Making a facsimile of an existing person? And a *woman?*' She shook her head. 'That's called Forcing. It can only be done under extenuating circumstances.' She added that any technology – including spiritual technology – must be used in an ethical way. Most vigorously, I agreed.

I persisted. We had to find a way to put a mirror to Reverend Nader and force him to reflect on his spiritual pride. We had to present him with irrefutable evidence of his utter bastardry. Nerida's resistance waned as I spoke. She told me it *was* possible but highly risky. There would be technical challenges. We would have to dig out some of the more obscure passages in the second volume of *The Book of Creation* that was kept in a separate locked section of the library. We would have to consult with the research station's ethics committee, who would consider both the moral implications and potential security and social repercussions of my idea. Finally, once all the challenges had been debated and the process finalised, we would need Nana Daringa's approval.

Two hours later, I met with the ethics committee, which comprised six mature women: four who looked to be in their seventies and two in their fifties. We sat around an ornate walnut board table on level five of the research station and listened as Nerida explained the technical challenges in more detail. 'Women are far more complicated than men,' she said. 'And, correspondingly, female golems are more difficult to program. Female golems can only be programmed with an Unpredictability Quotient above thirty percent. Which is double the maximum for the male golems. All this makes their behaviour that much more unmanageable.'

One of the ethicists – a heavily made-up woman with peroxide hair who I thought would have looked more at home in a cocktail bar than serving on an ethics committee – told us she had once worked in the art room and been involved in a 'Forcing'. She told us we'd also need detailed, high-resolution photographs of Mary Nader in order to make a perfect copy. The golem would have to mimic her gait and her mannerisms. Plus, she added, glancing back at Nerida and me, we would need some insights into her personality and details of her family history.

It all began to sound horribly difficult. I'd overestimated the scope of this 'spiritual technology'. This was going to be hard work. And what if, in all of this, the Reverend Nader still refused to accept he was doing anything wrong? My own experience with a narcissist had shown it was almost impossible to point out their flaws. They always had an explanation, a story, a lie which pointed to their atrocious behaviour being someone else's fault. They gaslit. They manipulated. Made *you* feel as though you were the one with the problems. And, if all of those efforts to expose Reverend Nader's abuse failed, persuading the real Mary Nader to leave her husband would still take a miracle.

Yet, the more I doubted, the more the other women came on board.

Discrete filming of Mary wouldn't be a problem, one of the ethicists commented. The research station engaged private investigators to vet potential recruits. I began to feel uncomfortable. That was how the retreat had found out so much about my past. And now, I was embracing this new, novel and exciting spiritual technology myself. We were playing God. I didn't know enough about this place and its long-term goals. Repercussions could be disastrous.

Perhaps, I suggested, we were making Mary's switch more complicated than it really needed to be and that we didn't need spiritual technology at all. I wondered out loud if we could install listening devices in the rectory. 'All we want is empirical evidence of Reverend Nader's abuse,' I added, recalling how I'd considered installing a nanny-cam at home to record my ex's tirades. But I never did because I was afraid of what he would do if he found the device. But in this case, Mary Nader would not be involved. She would remain an innocent bystander.

Every woman around the table shook her head. Yindisha's women did not trespass on church property, the peroxide blonde told me very firmly.

A lanky woman with high cheekbones and deep-set brown eyes piped up. 'And just how do you propose to distract Mary Nader while you replace her with her golem?'

Before I could confess that I hadn't really thought that through, a monobrowed woman who reminded me of the artist Freida Kahlo, suggested we might send Mary a message that one of her children had been involved in an accident and she was needed urgently in Canberra or Sydney. I objected. No way was I making Mary Nader any more anxious than she already was.

'We could kidnap and temporarily drug her,' said a woman wearing a colourfully embroidered banana-yellow cardigan.

Everyone looked at me. I felt as though I was being tested. 'No,' I said fiercely. After my recent experience, involuntarily drugging wasn't something I wanted to consider.

I was about to excuse myself to give the matter more thought when something pinged in my memory. I recalled that day in the café when I'd bumped into Mary Nader at the Watson General Store. I recalled overhearing snippets of her conversation with the girl behind the counter. They had been discussing Mary's aioli. The girl behind the counter had been telling Mary how popular it was, and how she should look at investigating a wider distribution network. Mary had replied she was simply too busy and besides, she had no idea where to start when it came to marketing and distribution.

'Perhaps all we need is someone to briefly entice Mary away from Watson with the promise of a business opportunity,' I said.

My insides swelled. Empowerment. Financial independence. The perfect way for a woman to escape the tyranny of bully.

'There are two hundred people working for this research station,' I added. 'Someone must have a contact who works in marketing and distribution. Surely someone can find a way to help Mary Nader grow her business?'

'A brilliant idea,' said the woman in the banana-yellow cardigan. She smiled, revealing a gap between her front teeth when she grinned. 'I have a friend in food distribution. I can ask her for contacts.'

A warm feeling pervaded the room. The chance to improve a woman's life and take an abusive man down in the process made us all feel good. Unanimously, the ethics committee assented. Yes. We should do everything in our power to help Mary Nader build a life independent of her husband. Yes. We should expose that Reverend for the rogue and hypocrite he was. Regarding their approving smiles, I ignored the embryonic flutter of worry low in my belly.

The peroxide blonde brought the room back to earth. 'If you plan to undertake this risky enterprise, you must put forward a mission statement, detailed strategic plan and consider contingency options.'

I understood in that moment, the magnitude of my undertaking. It's one thing to have an idea. Quite another to bring it to fruition. I was about to be complicit in creating something that had no legal precedents, a creature built to trick and deceive. An unpredictable monster, like the Golem of Prague. I felt the heaviness of the world, the expectations of these women and my obligations to Mary Nader weigh down my shoulders. I felt in that moment like excusing myself, telling them they had the wrong person for the job. Then, I reminded myself I was helping Mary Nader.

Interfering bitch. The words of my ex sent my thoughts spiralling down a well of doubt.

Yellow cardigan woman daintily cleared her throat to break the thoughtful silence that followed. 'And above all, we must have faith in Mother Earth. She has brought Mary Nader to our attention for a reason. When we create Mary Nader's golem, we are putting our trust in natural justice and the power of our creator.'

With that, the women lowered their heads and chanted a prayer of praise.

Mother of Earth, Goddess of all creation,
Spirit of all winds and all directions
Give us strength to uphold Your covenant
And do what is right and just.

Although I chanted with them, I began to get that feeling I get in the pit of my stomach when I know something is about to go utterly wrong. This territory where ancient sorcery, pagan mysticism and cutting-edge science met, felt ripe for runaway hubris and corresponding disaster. I was playing with forces I didn't fully understand.

Over the next seven days, in between teaching students about light and shadow, colour and composition, I planned my greatest creative project yet. The creation of a fake woman. While it was all on paper, I felt safe. This was a collective process. An idea. An abstraction. Others would share the blow if something went wrong during manufacture. It was a comforting thought that kept me focused on my goal.

Over that week, at the end of each day, I felt sapped and satisfied. The thought of productively contributing to the betterment of the world in my own small way felt simultaneously seductive and enervating. I woke each morning filled with purpose.

Each day for a few hours, I descended to level five and headed to the restricted section of the research station's main library. There, inhaling the fragrance of cloves and eucalypt, I read *The Book of Creation, Volume Two* and typed notes into my allocated laptop under the low UV archival lights that gently swayed in the breeze coming from the library's climate control system. Despite the fact that Yindisha Retreat had an apparent technology ban, this research station embraced all the latest know-how. I'd learned they could hack phones, remotely interfere with electric car engines and drones and scramble surveillance systems. All of which might just come in handy as I refined my plan.

I considered as deeply as I could with the information I had, potential drawbacks and disasters. I consulted with different sections of the research station, working out what was, and wasn't, possible.

Meanwhile, inquiries among the research station's employees revealed several women with contacts who would be able to help with Mary Nader's business venture. I ignored the nagging feeling, the bleating voice in the back of my mind telling me none of this would be enough.

Seven days, and twenty pages of proposal later, back in the board meeting room, I waited for the verdict from Galilea Nightingale and Nana Daringa. Senior programmer Nerida was there as well, sitting in quiet respect as Galilea and Nana Daringa voiced their questions, comments and challenges to my recommendations.

'The forced golem must have a guardian – someone to whom he or she is connected and beholden,' Galilea read. 'There will be a kinship between golem and guardian, a spiritual link, a thread of integrity that binds them,' she continued.

I opened my mouth to say, after reading through that section of *The Book of Creation Volume Two*, I thought it best this guardian was someone with more experience than I.

'That'll be you,' Galilea said before I could speak. 'You and Mary both have experience with flagrantly disrespectful husbands.'

I flinched. If one could call mutual emotional abuse by one's husband a spiritual link and binding thread of integrity, I supposed she was right. Yes, Mary Nader and I had kinship.

Nana Daringa confirmed, raising her hand as if performing a blessing. 'Alethea, you will be Mary's guardian.'

I shrank a little further into my chair. That wasn't what I'd had in mind. I'd put Galilea and Nana Daringa's names down as recommended guardians. Even though I had raised a child, the idea of being guardian to a fake, grown woman made me feel deeply unsettled.

'The guardian of the forced golem must also have a hand in its creation.' Nana Daringa read.

She looked up at me. 'You're an artist, aren't you?'

'Yes,' I replied. 'A painter, not a sculptor.'

'You will have to build the golem.'

I looked back at her in shock. *What?*

'I can't build a golem,' I protested. 'I only work in two dimensions!'

Fortunately, aware neither Nana Darina nor Galilea – my recommended guardians were artists – I'd added a passage from *The Book of Creation, Volume Two* mentioning that the guardian's contribution could range from full sculpting to rendering a baby fingernail or fake belly-button.

At this point, Nerida finally spoke. She explained how, thanks to the Unpredictability Quotient, it was impossible to predict the colour of a golem's eyes and how forcing eye colour involved pre-animation programming. She suggested I use a graphics tablet and pen to render Mary Nader's eyes. That way, I was both having a hand in the golem's creation, but also facilitating the translation of Mary's eye pattern and colour into programmable code.

Galilea and Nana Daringa agreed. I sat back, now unnerved at the responsibility being heaped upon me, recalling a passage in *The Book of Creation, Volume One* about the danger of hubris associated with the creation of golems.

Perhaps they would send me back to do more research? Perhaps that wouldn't be such a bad thing?

Although my proposal had more holes than a lotus seed pod, Nana Daringa and Galilea eventually approved it. I knew why. The opportunity to bring down a minister of religion, in particular the most abusive Reverend Quentin Nader, was too great to resist.

An hour after entering the meeting room, Nana Daringa laid a crinkled and blue-veined hand on my proposal and said: 'To mitigate the many unknowns, all we can do now is pray for Mother Earth's favours.'

There she was again. Mother Earth. The variable that could throw my plan into chaos.

Filled now with a fatalistic resolve, I clasped my hands on my lap, lowered my head and prayed as hard as I could. In the midst of the prayer, a face slithered into my thoughts – a man with yellow hair and grey eyes, his mouth twisted into a delighted grin.

His expression was pure *schadenfreude* – pleasure derived from someone else's misfortune. *You've really been conned this time, haven't you?* my ex snarked in my thoughts. *What a sucker you are. What an ignoramus.* In my mind's eye, his grin widened as I regarded my companions, heads bowed in prayer. *Women and their fairy tales. What a group of fucking stupid, clueless hags.*

Regarding my professional-looking typed up proposal on the board table, I suddenly felt like Sisyphus and that impossible rock. This was an invitation for disaster. I would be crushed by my ineptitude. We were all pretending. Playing at something we didn't fully understand.

Momentarily, I glanced at the ceiling, thinking of the layers of earth that separated us from the heavens. And I wondered, in a sudden slap of superstition, if the man-God up there might be preparing to give me – and my companions – a damn good smite.

CHAPTER THIRTY-SIX

Woman of Earth

Days Twenty-six and Twenty-seven

The hum on level one of the research station soothed and enclosed me like a shell. Underground, lost in my work I was doing what I loved most – creating.

In a white room empty but for a pine table and chair and a single potted aloe plant, I rendered a large pair of photographs of Mary Nader's eyes onto a graphics tablet. Mary's eyes were dark brown on the edges and a lighter gold speckled with green towards the pupils. Her iris – surrounding the black hole of the pupil – resembled a micellar network of tendrils and roots; an explosion of coloured fibres escaping a void. All I had to do was get the colour and tonal distributions right. As I worked, the programming software added the microscopic complexity. This wasn't magic. It was code.

Intoxicated by both Mother Nature's ingenuity and the software's power, I felt proud, awed and fulfilled. I wanted Fake Mary to be magnificent. Perfect. A work of art. A miraculous Mary. A dispenser of natural justice.

Downstairs in the art room, sculptors were shaping Fake Mary's body from clay. On the programming level, Fake Mary's mind, her back story and memories – those details that would make her temporarily indistinguishable from the real woman – were being translated into code.

Much of this information was thanks to Yindisha's private investigator – a grey-haired, orthopaedic-socked and knitted cardigan-wearing woman who looked like someone's granny. She had – over the past few days – managed not only to dig up details of Mary's past, but also to discretely capture Mary's eyes as well as her gait, height and shape during a visit to Watson. All high resolution, all without anyone knowing.

'Oooh! Beautiful!' cooed Nerida, the senior programmer, when I finally handed her tablet with Mary's completed eyes. 'What a great job! This is going to translate perfectly into code!'

'Thank you,' I replied. 'I enjoyed myself.'

Nerida beamed. 'That is because you are a true Guardian,' she replied. 'You have Mother Earth's blessing.'

I let her praise wash over me. Over the past few days, I'd received more affirmations than the self-help section of a bookstore. *You can do this. You have the power. You are a strong woman. This is justice. You are an artist. A creator. A bringer of life. One of Mother Earth's Guardians. A vessel of the divine.*

Just this morning Saniya had told me that Acacia tea didn't affect some women at all. 'You are highly tuned to Mother Earth's forces,' she'd said. 'This is a unique gift. You will go far.'

In my darker moments, I considered how these words were more tricks, pieces of flattery to draw me in.

But by then, I *was* drawn in. I was complicit.

Outside, up in the real world, it was now late afternoon. Tonight, Nana Daringa would animate Fake Mary in a private ceremony that involved mystical secrets to which only *she* was privy. Tonight, Fake Mary would be fast-tracked and forced to life. Extra programming protocols to try and override the Unpredictability Quotient would be added once she was animated. Everything would be tightly monitored. If we did this swiftly and efficiently no one would know.

As Nerida and I walked towards the lifts, another squall of unease unsettled my thoughts. Recalling one of the cautionary passages I had written in my proposal, I shuddered.

This is a deception. This is high level treachery – a crime with no legal precedents.

So much about Fake Mary was beyond my ken. Yet so much about Fake Mary was *my* responsibility. This wasn't like motherhood. Or like purchasing a kitten or puppy. This was more like... well, I wasn't sure what. *Witchcraft?* No. The answer would come to me later.

Edging closer to the reality of creating a golem who would be my responsibility, my trepidation grew. Here *I* was the novice. I was like Frightened Mary, trembling over her drawing of an apple. But this was no drawing of an apple, it was a creature created to *deceive and entrap*. Rendering eyeballs was one thing. Shaping a fake living woman and taking on the role of her guardian was quite another.

Just as we reached the lifts, Nerida glanced at her phone. 'Mary's template is ready in the art room,' she said. 'Would you like to take a peek?'

I hesitated. 'Is it like the groom seeing the bride before the wedding day?' I asked. I gave Nerida a dry smile. 'Will it bring bad luck?'

Nerida chuckled. 'Of course not. This is just pure indulgence of curiosity.'

Pure indulgence. Something about her choice of words made me even more uneasy.

Down on level six, we met Art School Alison in the foyer. After exchanging morsels of art school gossip, we fell into reverent silence when we entered the workroom.

The golem that was soon to be Fake Mary lay on a gurney – a clay mannequin soon to be quickened through magic and science. Her lips were slightly parted – ready to receive the tetragrammaton inscribed on a piece of paper prior to animation. This was another way of coding a golem. Fake Mary couldn't exactly approach her husband with a glowing tetragrammaton on her forehead – it would spill the beans.

As I gazed at that perfectly rendered clay woman, Alison pulled a sculpting knife from her work table and drew a gash in the wet clay between the breasts. I gasped. *Why was she ruining her work?*

Gently, she took my shaking hand. 'Smooth the clay,' she instructed.

Bewildered, the clay cool and slippery under my fingers, I rubbed out the marks until the surface between soon-to-be Fake Mary's breast was once more perfect.

'Now, hold her face between your hands.'

Instead of asking why, once more, I complied, cradling the sculpture's cold chin between my hands, as if holding a beloved.

Soul of Mother Earth, sanctify me
Body of Mother Earth, save me
O Good Mother, hide me within Thy wounds...

Alison and Nerida chanted the prayer twice. The third time, Alison instructed me to join in.

'The laying of hands invokes Mother Earth,' Alison explained following a moment's silence. 'By laying your hands, by healing a wound, a piece of your life moves into the golem.' Her mouth faintly twisted. 'This is another ancient ritual from Mother Earth stolen and used by men claiming religious authority...'

She gave me a warm, enveloping smile. 'As a baptised Guardian, *you* have that authority.'

I smiled weakly, recalling a similar Christian prayer I'd chanted during school assemblies. I wondered if this was some kind of heresy.

My apprehension resurfaced. A part of me had entered Fake Mary. We were even more bound to one another than before. And, until Mary's golem came to life, everyone was uncertain as to how those dangerously high Unpredictability Quotients (thirty-four percent Nerida had told me) would manifest. Under my ribs, in the place where my gall bladder had once sat, I felt a tiny flutter as though something inside me was also coming to life. As though now born, it wanted to escape.

I realised in that moment just how much I was submitting to this new reality, these new codes of behaviour. *There is still time to back out*, I thought.

I returned to my cottage that evening feeling exhausted, emptied out and raw – the way I'd felt after the opening night of my exhibition. *Would this be another creative disaster?* I wondered. *Another moment where my hopeless vanities are laid bare? Another humiliation and disappointment?* As I fell asleep, Mary Nader's eyes glared at me from the void. *This is dishonest and un-Christian*, her gaze seemed to say. *And I will not be perfect. This is dangerous.*

My skin turned as clammy and cold as the clay from which Fake Mary was hewn. Perhaps men had glimpsed the future, seen women with such creative power and been justifiably terrified. The potential of this knowledge was infinite. The danger was beyond human imagination.

But what was the alternative? Was women emulating men – becoming aggressors and warriors equally justifiable? Were such women – fighting women – women trying to find their way in a man's world – ignoring Mother Earth's most important message? Surely it was far wiser to create than to destroy?

I thought of my proposal and told myself I understood the risks.

Tossing and turning, my stomach rumbled as if some inner tectonic plates were trying to settle into a new shape. I felt heavy and pliant, like saturated clay.

About now my idea – my creation – Fake Mary – was being raised to life.

With that thought, the night closed around me like a thick velvet shroud and I succumbed – as we all eventually do – to sleep.

I woke suddenly at sunrise, my body crackling with apprehension and excitement. After an early breakfast, Saniya and I rushed back to the research station to see if the animation of Fake Mary had worked.

Nerida greeted us with a cautious smile. Yes, Fake Mary was animated, she reassured us. And so far, everything else was going to plan. An appointment had been organised with Real Mary to meet up with two entrepreneurs in Bowral. Those distributors and marketers of organic produce had heard about her popular aioli and wished to add it to their range. Real Mary had accepted the offer to meet and discuss their proposal. Phone hacks were in place. Communications between Real Mary and her husband would be diverted to the research station, where the waiting people in IT would delete or amend any compromising communications. Everything would take place this afternoon.

'There's still a bit of work to do with Fake Mary's personality,' Nerida added as the three of us strode towards a viewing room. 'I've left firewalls open in her programming so she can be subtly tweaked now she's animated. Before we send her into the field, I want to see her in action.'

Nerida opened a door leading into a small anteroom. Behind the glass, standing in a fake lounge setting, Fake Mary – dressed in a white slip – looked around as if waking from a deep sleep, trying to make sense of her surroundings.

'Wow,' was all I could say. She was perfect. My Mary. Fake Mary. It was easy to imagine they had simply kidnapped and drugged the real Mary.

Except something wasn't quite right.

After Nerida pressed an app on her iPhone, a male golem entered the viewing room.

Fake Mary Nader gave him a wide-open smile. She invited him to take a seat on the sofa in the fake lounge setting. On the coffee table sat a steaming teapot, two cups and saucers and a plate of scones.

'Would you like some tea?' I heard Fake Mary say through the glass.

A sick feeling came over me. 'She looks too happy,' I whispered to Nerida.

Fake Mary gave the male golem a hungry look as he sat, her perfectly green-gold eyes roving over him as she poured the tea until it spilled over the teacup.

I could almost feel her purr.

This was not the Mary Nader I knew.

Beside me, I felt Nerida tense.

Instead of offering the golem his tea, Fake Mary suddenly slammed down the teapot, sidled up to him while unbuttoning her shirt. 'I want a fuck,' she said as she straddled his lap.

'Abort!' shouted Nerida. She pressed an icon on her phone app.

Immediately, Fake Mary collapsed onto the floor.

As the concerned golem bent over Fake Mary's prone body, two women in black tee shirts arrived in the viewing room. 'He'll have to undergo a memory wipe as well,' Nerida muttered unhappily as they escorted the protesting golem away.

It took all morning to tweak Fake Mary's programming. In quick succession, Nerida aborted a monstrous Mary, a mad Mary, a cringing Mary, a cocky Mary, a tyrannical Mary, a pious Mary and last of all, an apologetic Mary.

After subtly tweaking the apologetic Mary, we finally had a golem whose character most closely resembled the Mary Nader I had met.

All we had left to do was to dress Fake Mary in a dreary brown wardrobe that matched Real Mary's taste.

Now, time was of the essence. At 2.45 pm, we heard through our IT team that the real Mary Nader had just left Watson for her appointment in Bowral.

The stars had aligned and we were ready. Galilea, Nerida and I all agreed it was best to get Fake Mary in and out of the field with her damning evidence as soon as possible, before she became potentially unmanageable.

Saniya, Nerida and I were in the research station's wardrobe room searching through a pile of dowdy clothes when a woman from the ethics committee arrived. She looked pale and grim. She told us she had come across a footnote buried in one of the Hebrew versions of *The Book of Creation, Volume Two*. 'There's one more problem,' she said. 'Potentially, a big one.'

After struggling with the translation, she told us she had come to the conclusion it was a warning that newborn female golems couldn't step inside church grounds.

'It increases the Unpredictability Quotient,' she added. She glanced at Fake Mary. 'Given her Unpredictability Quotient is already thirty-four percent, it means she could turn unmanageable.'

Shit. Dare I say at this point – standing next to patiently waiting Fake Mary – I felt devastated?

Fake Mary regarded me with a look of sincere disappointment that mirrored my own. 'I promise I'll behave,' she said.

I glanced from Saniya to Nerida. 'But there were no churches around when the original *Book of Creation* was written. Only temples and synagogues,' I protested.

'Perhaps it just means holy ground consecrated by *men*.' Offered Saniya.

'It still means entering church grounds will increase Fake Mary's Unpredictability Quotient,' insisted the ethicist.

'By how much?' I asked.

Nerida shrugged. 'It's an unknown. But I'm guessing anywhere from fifty to eighty percent.'

My heart plummeted. *No.* This had to go ahead. After all this effort, we couldn't back out now.

I understand the risks, a voice in my head insisted.

Nerida glanced at Fake Mary. 'I can try some last-minute programming to override any potential aversions to holy ground. But I'm not sure how much of the programming will take.'

Fake Mary nodded in agreement. Once we were out in the field, she wouldn't recall any of this conversation. 'Yes please,' she said, her eyes washed with sincerity, 'I promise I'll be good.'

They all looked from Fake Mary to me.

I glanced back at Fake Mary. Beautiful. Perfect. Those eyes I had rendered filled with honesty, trust and hope.

You can do this, Alethea. You are in charge. This is justice.

Saniya regarded me with her water-hole green eyes. 'This is your decision, Alethea.'

Everything in that moment felt light and starry. I felt as unreal as Fake Mary.

Did I actually drown that night in the waterhole? Had I been reborn in a parallel universe?

It occurred to me in that moment that I, too, had been rebuilt. Reprogrammed with a new code of being. This was a moment of justice. I could no more stop this from happening than I could stop the earth orbiting the sun.

I understand the risks.

Something raging, tumescent and powerful surged through me. 'Of course, I still want to go ahead,' I said.

I walked over to a rack of clothes.

'The Botanical Gardens,' I added. 'Fake Mary can meet the Reverend there.'

I pulled a brown cardigan the colour of wet mulch off the rack. 'This is perfect,' I said. 'All we need are shoes, skirt and shirt to match.'

No one tried to stop me.

A voice as faint as text bleached by sunlight whispered into my thoughts. *Remember the Golem of Prague. This will be your downfall, Mrs Frankenstein.*

CHAPTER THIRTY-SEVEN

Fake Mary

Day Twenty-seven (late afternoon)

I drove Galilea's car into Watson with Fake Mary by my side. Ready for battle, I was armed with a new mobile phone, a sack and vacuum in the trunk for eventual removal of Fake Mary's decommissioned remains.

Our hackers – pretending to be Real Mary – had sent Reverend Nader a message asking him to meet her in Watson's Botanical Gardens. Following his protests that he was too busy and why couldn't she discuss whatever silly problem she was having with him at home, they had reiterated it was urgent.

Once at the Botanical Gardens, Fake Mary was going to tell her husband she was no longer prepared to tolerate his abusive behaviour. Although this might appear to be out of character, we had prepared an explanation for her sudden change of heart.

An added problem was that in public, Reverend Nader might be polite. All we could hope was that, at four o'clock on a Thursday afternoon, the Botanical Gardens would be relatively quiet. In which case Reverend Nader would be free to abuse Fake Mary.

This would be filmed with the cameras inserted into her pupils. Once we had the damning evidence, we needed to extricate Fake Mary as soon as possible.

Unfortunately, the Botanical Gardens were next to the church and I wasn't sure how much range we had when it came to consecrated ground.

By this point, I was so nervous, I was shaking. I pulled up the car and parked in a shady corner behind a giant fig tree. Now, all I had to do was let Fake Mary go off on her own.

'Best of luck Mary,' I said. 'Do what you have to do. Remember I'm here if you need me.'

'Thank you for the support and the lift,' Fake Mary said stiffly as she stepped from the car, leaving behind her Christmassy fragrance of pine needles and cinnamon (my other contribution to her fine-tuning). She was indistinguishable from the original, with her shoulders perfectly hunched as she walked towards the Botanical Gardens to meet Real Mary's husband. I watched with dread and my hands shook as I loaded the app that accessed the cameras in Fake Mary's eyes. Towards the end of my marriage, each encounter with my ex tied my stomach in knots. I felt as though I was preparing for an execution. And Fake Mary, being a golem and not a robot, would have, like a dog, sensed my anxiety.

Finally, the app Nerida had put in my phone loaded and an image appeared on my screen. Through the eyes of Fake Mary, I saw Reverend Nader, robes blackly swinging, stride towards the golem he thought was his wife. My stomach tightened. Thanks to another quirk of interactivity between technology and the enchantment of a freshly animated golem, I had to stay within five-hundred metres of Fake Mary to ensure good reception. My phone was the link between Fake Mary and the research station.

Back at the research station, Nerida, Galilea and the hackers were keeping their eyes on a bank of consoles, watching the event unfold as if they were landing a Mars rover rather than framing a malevolent minister. Via the link with my phone, they were also wirelessly monitoring Fake Mary's vital signs. Not that she had any vital signs at this point. As a newborn golem, inside her human mantle were clumps of transforming enchanted clay that would eventually become human organs. And, as a newborn golem, she was still responding to her environment, quickly learning. Evolving. This was uncharted territory. Riddled with risks. All I wanted to do was catch one of Reverend Nader's tirades and then remove Fake Mary from the equation.

What happened afterwards, was entirely up to me. Breathing deeply, I tried to control a looming panic attack. Now, I felt like Atlas, trying to hold up the world.

Reverend Nader snarled at the golem he thought was his wife. 'Where is the car, Mary? It isn't in the garage. Did you have another accident?'

We had anticipated Reverend Nader would notice the absence of the car in which Real Mary had driven to Bowral. This was the beginning of the shit-fest.

'I parked it at Yindisha Retreat,' Fake Mary replied (we had to override nine honesty protocols to get Fake Mary to lie).

Reverend Nader's eyes darkened. 'What in the Lord's name were you doing there?'

'Visiting friends.'

His left eye twitched. He looked around, Fake Mary's camera eyes following his gaze. A woman with a pram and a toddler lingered and sniffed the nearby blooms in the rose garden. He grabbed Mary's arm and hissed. 'I have forbidden you from associating with any of those harlots. They are fallen women. How many times do I have to remind you? Are you even more stupid than you look?'

That gap under my ribs, the phantom organ that was once my gall bladder – my Minister of Justice – cramped. How many times had I heard similar words addressed to me? My friends were all losers, my ex repeatedly told me. He couldn't stand them. And my mother? That vexatious creature was the worst of all. She was a manipulator. A trouble maker. According to my ex, she wanted to destroy our marriage.

Fake Mary and Reverend Nader were walking now, heading back towards the church. I willed Fake Mary to move more slowly. I needed more evidence. This wasn't enough. But right now, she was on her own.

'And what was it that was so urgent and so private that you had to tell me about it in the Botanical Gardens?' snarked Reverend Nader. 'Out with it, Mary and stop wasting my time. I have parishioners who need me.'

'I've had enough of the way you treat me, Quentin. Either you change your behaviour or I will leave you.'

Reverend Nader stopped walking. Outrage and indignation plastered his face. 'You think you're too good for me, do you?'

'I know everything, Quentin. I know all your secrets. I know about your affair.'

Reverend Nader blinked rapidly and stared in surprise into the screen that was Fake Mary's eyes. I nearly dropped the phone. *An affair? What affair?*

Seconds later, my text messenger dinged. It was Nerida. *Sorry. It was a last-minute piece of information. I forgot to tell you. He's been sleeping with a woman called Sylvia Reddington for the past six months. She owns the Watson Bed and Breakfast.*

Quickly, I returned to the live recording. Reverend Nader's gaze made me think of a snake. 'Who was this friend you were visiting at the retreat?' he asked, changing the subject in a way that was all too familiar. 'Was it that woman I saw you talking to the other day?'

I recalled that ugly look he'd given me when he saw me conversing with Real Mary. No doubt, after my encounter with him in the Watson General Store, I was public enemy number one. 'Was it that overbearing, slatternly one? Is she behind all this sinful spreading of gossip?'

Even though that insult came from a real-life incarnation of Voldemort, I winced.

Again, my text messenger dinged. It was Nerida again. *Slatternly is good. Take it as a compliment* ☺

Fake Mary remained silent. Unfortunately, they both started walking again. The church loomed closer. Fake Mary glanced at some gravestones behind a hedge of rosemary to her right. No one was exactly sure where consecrated ground ended or where it began. All I knew was a rise in the Unpredictability Quotient was now inevitable.

'I would advise you to keep your distance from that whore...' Reverend Nader continued.

'She isn't a whore. She is a talented artist and a good supportive friend.'

I simultaneously simmered and smiled, quietly thanking Nerida and her programming all while wanting to slap Reverend Nader's face.

He suddenly gave Fake Mary a quizzical look. 'What's wrong with your voice?'

He'd only just noticed. The physical resemblance to Mary was so perfect, he'd not had any suspicions. But we had anticipated this. The hackers hadn't been able to access enough quality recordings of Real Mary's voice so we'd estimated, giving Fake Mary husky tones she could explain away as a cold.

'I have a sore throat,' Fake Mary replied. 'I'm coming down with a touch of laryngitis.'

'That will be the Lord punishing you for your sins and communing with harlots, listening to gossip and slander and spreading lies.'

I thought then, how handy it was to have such a forceful

imaginary friend as backup. God relieved Reverend Nader of all moral and rational responsibility. This misogynist minister could always fall back on the language of sin to subjugate his victims.

'Your Lord God doesn't frighten me, Quentin,' said Fake Mary. 'You are being watched by something far more powerful. Mother Earth is far older and far wiser than your impotent, fairy-tale, man-God.'

Reverend Nader's eyes blazed. 'Those women at that retreat are corrupting you! Yindisha is a Godless cult! Are you so blind and ignorant you can't see that? They're brainwashing men! Upsetting the natural order of things!'

Affronted by his anger and the way he stared at me through Fake Mary's eyes, my worry ramped up another notch. My messenger dinged. It was Nerida. *I think we should consider pulling Fake Mary out now.*

'The natural order of things is beyond the understanding of your puny human brain,' Fake Mary replied coolly. 'Your concept of the natural order of things is the result of thousands of years of patriarchal indoctrination and reinforcement.'

That was it. Reverend Nader's eyes turned bright with flames of fury. He grabbed Fake Mary's arm and pointed at the church looming in the screen. 'You will come inside with me now and pray for forgiveness, humility and redemption!'

Hastily, I turned on the car and made my way towards the church.

A minute later, I pulled up in the thankfully empty church carpark just as Reverend Nader and Fake Mary approached the steps. *Shit.*

My eyes dropped back to the screen. Reverend Nader's raging gaze made my blood run cold. There were times agnostic me felt as though I could see an incarnation of the devil in my ex's eyes. Now, I saw that same devil in Reverend Nader's eyes. My gut cramped.

Reverend Nader pushed Fake Mary towards the steps. 'Inside,' he ordered.

Fake Mary didn't budge. 'You are under Her eye,' she said after regarding the church then looking back at Quentin. 'Your every move is being watched and judged by Mother Earth.'

My messenger dinged. It was a message from Galilea. *Pull Mary out NOW.*

My gaze in two places at once – one on the screen of my phone, the other watching the situation unfold in front of me – I saw Fake Mary's eyes regard a potted gardenia outside the church doors, before looking up at a stained-glass window depicting Jesus genuflecting at an ornate white and yellow light in the sky. *Shit,* I thought. *She's getting more and more unmanageable.* I wished in that moment I knew what her golem brain was thinking.

'Let your women keep silence in the churches: for it is not permitted unto them to speak. And if they will learn anything, let them ask their husbands at home.' Reverend Nader shouted in his preacher's voice. 'Timothy's words from The Bible,' he added. 'A book you should know off by heart.'

He manhandled Fake Mary up the steps.

At the church doors, Fake Mary suddenly pulled away from Reverend Nader's grip.

'Oppressive male nonsense!' she shouted. The potted gardenia returned to the screen.

As I stepped from the car, Fake Mary lifted that potted gardenia as if it were no heavier than a kitten and hurled it at the stained-glass window. She aimed high, missing Jesus, but leaving a black hole where the Godly light had once shone.

Exploding in fury, Reverend Nader struck Fake Mary. She stumbled down the steps.

Then, he looked up and saw me. He bared his teeth. He was so furious he looked as though he was about to combust.

'You!' he shouted. 'What have you done to my wife?'

Ignoring him, I raced up to Fake Mary. 'It's all right Mary, I'm here. You can rest now. Your work is done,' I said, using the code words programmed to send Fake Mary into submission mode.

Blinking in confusion, she rose clumsily to her feet. There was a gash on the side of her face, leaking not blood, but what looked like dirty water. I pulled a tissue from my pocket and dabbed the wound. I think Reverend Nader was too furious to notice.

I looked up at him, reminding myself to keep things clear and short. The abusive male's brain – particularly when he is in a state of heightened defensive aggression – is incapable of processing complicated information.

'Mary has been hypnotised. She is wearing special contact lenses that record what the wearer sees and hears. She will remember none of this when she wakes. And I take full responsibility for doing this. I knew how you treat her, and I wanted empirical evidence.'

I waved my phone at him. 'It's all been recorded.'

Reverend Nader bared his teeth. 'You are violating our privacy. My marriage and my relationship with my wife is none of your business.'

'It absolutely is my business when I see the way you treat Mary.'

'You have put blasphemous words in my wife's mouth!'

Reverend Nader pointed at Galilea's black car. 'You have been corrupted by that succubus Galilea! What they're practicing in that... *coven....* that *den of iniquity* is sorcery. Witchcraft. Practices that have no place in today's modern, rational world. Yindisha Retreat is Sodom in our midst! '

I disrespectfully smirked. *Rational? You consider your behaviour and beliefs rational?*

Clearly recognising my contempt, Reverend Nader's eyes narrowed. 'Women cannot control themselves. They need men to harness their immoral tendencies. I must protect my wife from the seductions of that evil place. I must keep her soul pure.'

Right then, I felt as though I was in a scene from The Handmaid's

Tale. But this man was not my commander. Nor was Reverend Nader my husband.

'You are afraid of the fundamental power of the female,' I said.

Now it was his turn to look contemptuous. 'And you have been seduced by the devil.' He stepped forward, invading my personal space in an extremely threatening manner. 'You should feel very afraid.'

Out of the corner of my eye, I noticed Fake Mary bend down and pick something out of a garden bed.

'I'm not afraid,' I replied to Reverend Nader. 'I have seen the devil and he is a moron.'

He jumped, like a little boy throwing a tantrum. 'You're one of them! One of the fallen! One of the corrupted!'

Ah, yes. Derailing. A classic abuser's tactic.

'And you're changing the subject, making this about me. This is all about you, *Quentin*, deciding to no longer address him as *Reverend*. 'You and your appalling treatment of your wife.'

I regarded Fake Mary now standing upright, coolly regarding Reverend Nader.

'Alethea is correct, Quentin,' she said. 'You may consider yourself a holy man, but you are strategically interpreting fossilised doctrines and using your warped beliefs to oppress, discriminate and bully those who are weak and vulnerable. Including your loyal, devoted wife.'

We both regarded Fake Mary in surprise. She wasn't supposed to speaking now I'd put her in submission mode.

A nugget of worry grew under my ribs. *The Unpredictability Quotient.*

Reverend Nader's' eyes widened. I didn't know what alarmed him more in that moment – exposure of his behaviour, his wife's confident, insubordinate behaviour or our analysis and dissection of his psyche.

'I will not listen to two compromised women telling me how

to do my job!'

He looked back at me. 'You arrogant, insolent, interfering harlot!'

My insides turned as cold as wet clay. 'You can't get to me, *Quentin*,' I said. 'I know how this works. I know your strategies. I've been there. You're interpreting everything to suit your agenda of power.'

He opened his mouth to say something else, but I didn't let him.

'What do you think Jesus would have to say about the way you treat your wife, *Quentin*? Wasn't Jesus's message one of love, forgiveness and compassion?'

I waved my phone at him. 'I've seen none of that here. I think underneath all that bullying, you are nothing more than a pathetic, weak and frightened man.'

'Get lost,' he spat. 'This is none of your business.'

Oh yes. I recalled being told to get lost again and again, particularly when it came to the matter of care for our child. And the child currently in my care was Mary Nader – both the fake one and the real one. I felt fearless right then. As hard as fired clay and as furious as a harpy. A mother protecting her cub. A woman standing up for her rights.

'I will, Quentin. Now I have the evidence of your behaviour, I'm quite happy to get lost and go off and publish this on YouTube or send it to Oprah or A Current Affair.'

It felt good taking this man down. Perhaps a little too good. And I knew that look he was giving me. I'd seen that before as well. Quentin Nader wanted to kill me.

Again, I waved my phone at him. 'Not only is your God watching you, but so is modern technology.'

I realised as I said those words just how much danger I was in. Just how far would a man like the Most Reverend Quentin Nader go to make sure his behaviour wasn't made public?

I thought of Galilea set on fire by a furious husband. And Saniya, who lost all her hair. And all those stories of women killed by men who wanted to keep their crimes and misdemeanours secret.

I prepared for the next part of my strategy. To negotiate. To be reasonable. But I never got a chance.

Reverend Nader blinked, regarding the road leading from the car park. 'I will have you arrested. I am on good terms with the Bowral police. They will confiscate your phone.'

That was the moment Fake Mary stepped forward and struck. 'Police are another part of the patriarchal system of oppression!' she said as she smashed the rock she was holding down on his head.

CHAPTER THIRTY-EIGHT

Hail and Mary

Day Twenty-seven (early evening)

The sky darkened as a blubbering Fake Mary and I loaded the unconscious Reverend Nader into the trunk of Galilea's car. 'I've killed him,' she wailed, shedding dirt-brown tears. 'He's dead!'

My messenger dinged and my phone rang, but I was too busy to answer.

'No, he's not Mary. He's just hurt.' I wasn't sure how a golem who thought she had killed might react. Factoring in the Unpredictability Quotient, Fake Mary might develop a taste for murder. I might be next. We had to get away from the church as quickly as possible.

In the distance, I heard the rumble of thunder. I could feel static in the air. The fine brown hair that had escaped Fake Mary's now dishevelled coiffure stood on end. A storm was coming. In the western sky, heavy black clouds congregated. I tried to contain myself, taking deep, calming breaths as I shut the trunk with shaking hands. Beside me, Fake Mary continued with her conniptions. How much she was picking up from me and how much was due to the Unpredictability Quotient, I had no idea. She wept and banged her hand against her forehead. 'I'm sorry,' she sobbed. 'I don't know what came over me.'

I had no idea how to manage a regretful golem. I should have decommissioned her right there and then, but her regrets felt all-together too human. In a panic myself, I delayed the inevitable.

Yet still feeling rational enough to be grateful for small mercies, I noted the carpark was still empty. Unless there were security cameras, no one had seen what happened. And if there were hidden security cameras, hopefully the research station was now in the process of remotely deleting the footage.

The first hailstone hit just as we stepped into the car. The afternoon turned as dark as night. A great vein of lightning shot in front of those brooding clouds. More of Fake Mary's hair floated upwards, as if she were in zero gravity. The effect made her look even more wild and deranged.

'What's happening?' she squealed.

'It's just a storm, Mary,' I said as two hailstones the size of golf balls whacked the car's pristine bonnet. I thought in that moment that this was how superstitions start. You do something bad and then, coincidentally, someone or something dies or the weather turns violent. The human mind, seeking patterns, puts the two together and concludes they are related. Cause and effect. The consequence of the arrow of time. And of course, it's all exacerbated by authors who use those very same natural forces to ramp up the tension in their stories. Right now, a Christian would regard this as God's wrath.

Time is a boomerang. For some reason my father's words popped back into my thoughts as another hailstone hit the roof above the driver's seat.

'Mother Earth is furious,' Fake Mary sobbed.

'Mother Earth has been furious for a while,' I replied, thinking of Australia's crazy weather – the droughts, the bushfires, the dust storms and floods. Mother Earth's messages were becoming less and less subtle.

Mary began to rock back and forth and mutter. 'Thou shalt not kill,' she said three times. 'I may not injure a human being or allow a human being to come to harm...'

My stomach tightened. She was accessing what Nerida had called her Foundation Routines, which compiled, among many things, Asimov's law of robotics and a selection of the ten commandments. She was doing the golem equivalent of short-circuiting.

I thought of reaching for the decommissioning blade in the glove box, but I needed both hands to steer on the increasingly slippery and icy road.

'It's all right, Mary, I'm here. You can rest now. Your work is done,' I repeated.

My code words had no effect.

'A robot must obey the orders given to it by human beings except where such orders would conflict with the First Law,' Fake Mary said, pounding her forehead with her hand.

I gripped the steering wheel so hard, my hands cramped. All I had to do was stop for a minute and put her out of her misery.

The sky lit up with another flash of lightening as Fake Mary slapped her hand against her tetragrammaton.

Again, my phone rang. Despite everything that had happened I was worried about breaking the law and refused to answer it while I was driving.

The hail grew heavier. It pounded the car, sounding as though a kindergarten of feral cherubs were throwing stones at us from the heavens. Afraid to speed up in case the car skidded, yet desperate to get back to the research station, I tried to hold on to my rapidly disintegrating composure.

I had a badly wounded minister in my trunk. A hysterical golem in my passenger seat. Just how much worse could things get?

Heavy rain joined the hail. Again, lightning flashed and the heavens rumbled.

Fake Mary wailed. 'A robot must protect its own existence as long as such protection does not conflict with the First or Second Laws...'

'Mary,' I said firmly. 'You are not a robot.'

She stopped raving and looked at me. 'What am I then?'

I briefly glanced at her. She gave me a lost look. I should have decommissioned her right there and then, but I couldn't. She looked just too human. Instead, my heart broke into little pieces. This poor creature didn't know what she was. She was in a state of existential despair.

'You are one of Mother Earth's creations,' I finally replied.

Panicking, I thought of the injured minister in the trunk. He was human. A real human, not a golem. Another of Mother Earth's creations. Why was I not rushing him to hospital? *Because I have taken a vow of silence*, I told myself. *Because I am complicit in this whole disaster.*

'Tell Mother Earth I can't breathe!' Fake Mary cried, taking short, shallow gasps.

The car shook, buffeted by a sudden wind. Fake Mary screamed. 'I'm sorry, I'm so sorry! Please tell my children I'm sorry!'

Her words opened a pit in my stomach.

She lurched forward and hit her forehead hard against the dash. Instantly, she dissolved into crumbs.

Chunks of enchanted clay landed in my lap. One of those tiny cameras inserted into her eyeballs lay wedged against the gear shift. A puddle of brown water pooled on the passenger seat. The car skidded as I lost my concentration. I veered onto a grass verge, only blind luck stopping me from hitting a bank of trees.

Shit, shit, shit.

The hail grew heavier. I fought back an overwhelming urge to weep and wail just like Fake Mary.

In the distance, I heard a siren. I forgot for a second how to breathe as well. What if I was stopped by the police? How would I explain this pile of dirt and woman's clothes in the passenger seat beside me? And what if they found wounded Quentin Nader in the trunk?

More shit.

In a splatter of mud and dirt and screech of tyres, I turned the car back onto the road and reached the T-junction, visibility now close to zero.

The siren grew louder. My heart pounding like a herd of stampeding animals, I turned left into the blinding white darkness.

CHAPTER THIRTY-NINE

After The Rain

Day Twenty-seven (5.03pm)

A sea of black umbrellas attached to a cluster of anxious women greeted me at the research station's carpark. The hail had now softened into a steady, drizzling rain.

Still shaking after my narrow escape, furious and terrified in equal measure, I stepped from the car and began babbling. I was, as my mother would have put in the British understatement of her adopted Mother Country: 'In quite a state.'

'She went bonkers! She hit him!' I shouted as I stepped out of the car onto legs that felt as though they were made of unset dough.

I felt Galilea's hand on my back, to trying to calm me down. 'This is natural justice, Alethea,' she said soothingly as two women opened the trunk of her hail-pocked car.

'How the hell is this natural justice? There is nothing natural about any of this!' I snapped back as they loaded Reverend Nader onto a gurney.

'Is he breathing?' I asked between shallow breaths.

One of the women put her ear to his mouth and gave me a brusque nod.

Reverend Nader confirmed this with a groan.

'We have excellent medical facilities here, Alethea,' said Galilea as we followed Reverend Nader's gurney into the shelter of the station. 'Quentin will be in good hands.'

My thoughts clanged against one another like saucepans in a hurricane. Not only was Reverend Nader injured, but the evidence I'd gathered wasn't enough. Yes, Reverend Nader had been obnoxious. But he was a human man who had been confronted with a baffling situation in the form of an uncharacteristically insubordinate wife. At what point did a man's rage and confusion segue into recognisable abuse? And yes, he had hit the golem he thought was his wife but that was after she had thrown a flowerpot at a stained-glass church window. A church he was responsible for. Did her behaviour justify his reaction? And Fake Mary had struck him when he mentioned the police. How was that in any way acceptable or forgivable?

I was in a state of unravelling despair. Infected by the conviction that justice would be served by this powerful spiritual technology no one fully understood, we had all utterly cocked up. *Thanks to me, we are all in deep shit.*

We walked inside, the research station door shutting out the sound of Fake Mary's remains being vacuumed from the seat and floor of the car. And in all of this, the perpetrator of the crime –Fake Mary Nader – was now just a pile of rubble. And what if Reverend Nader recovered? If he decided to press charges, I would be arrested. This was all my idea. I was the research station's scapegoat. *I* was in deep shit.

After trying to brush some of Fake Mary's remains from my shirt and pants, and only succeeding in smearing them into mud, I grabbed my hair, pulling so hard to squeeze out the water, it hurt.

What if Reverend Nader died? I wasn't a killer. I was the kind of person who cried when I saw an injured koala on television.

Those women at that retreat are corrupting you. It's a Godless cult! The thought arrived like a punch. Reverend Nader was right. This spiritual technology was a pact with the devil.

Just as swiftly, I caught that thought. Was I so superstitious, so deeply enculturated by Christian dogma that I suddenly believed Reverend Nader's words?

The words slipped out. 'This is a disaster,' I said miserably as Galilea and I watched the women wheel Reverend Nader into one of the goods lifts.

'Not necessarily,' said Galilea, still cucumber-cool and dare I say even sounding a little smug. 'Leave the rest with us, Alethea. Our doctors will tend to Quentin. And Nerida is currently working with our hacking group to mitigate the damage. Right now, you're in shock. I'll get someone to drive you back to the retreat. I'll send Lucas to keep you company.'

She was so composed in that moment it was easy to believe she'd orchestrated the whole thing.

Again, Reverend Nader's words inveigled their way into my thoughts. *You have been corrupted by that succubus Galilea!*

Galilea held out her hand. 'All I need now is the phone,' she said.

I hesitated. All the evidence of our crime was recorded in this phone. If Reverend Nader died, Fake Mary had been the perfect murder weapon. She no longer existed. But I was an accessory. The only suspect.

I caught Galilea's gaze. In that moment I felt snared by something vast and terrifying. I felt used. Exploited. Manipulated. *Succubus!*

But instead of resisting, I gave in.

I slapped the phone into Galilea's hand. 'Fine,' I said through my teeth. 'But I don't want Lucas's help and I'm on the next train back to Sydney.'

'Thank you, Alethea. This is all in Mother Earth's loving hands now.' Galilea sounded cool and knowing. Impervious. Unmoved.

As I turned, I clenched my teeth. *Succubus.* The word dug inside me like a virus taking hold.

Outside the research station, a good-looking driver – a golem – I presumed – waited in the Yindisha Retreat van. He didn't ask me where I had been. He waited for me to initiate conversation. To make up some story. I didn't. We rode towards the retreat in silence.

Somewhere in the back of my mind, I knew, but didn't want to know, what Galilea and her associates were going to do next. Reverend Nader may have been a bastard but he didn't deserve to die. I had wanted to be heroic, help a woman in need. Instead, after all this effort, after all these weeks of work, I had made things worse. This was a disaster. I was weak. I was a failure. I was also a potential accessory to murder.

I warned you. There it was again. That fucking mocking voice of my ex.

The van turned right into Watson, the scene of the crime. My breath and heart collided in my throat, as if they were both trying to make a rapid exit and were getting in each other's way. I knew I was having a full-blown panic attack, but I couldn't think of a single thing to pull myself together.

Fake Mary's final conniption ripped back into my thoughts. *I'm so sorry! Please tell my children I'm sorry!*

Fake Mary's memories had included Real Mary's children. A part of her knew that when she hit her head on the dash, her existence would end. I wanted right then, to cry.

The only person I wanted right then was Sophia. I wanted to reassure myself she was real. I wanted to hold her and never let go.

The next time I spoke to her might be from jail.

Watson came into view. I saw the police car parked outside the church, one policeman gazing at the smashed stained-glass window while the other spoke on his phone. I slid down into the seat as we passed. Both policemen looked up at the van. *Shit.*

The world outside the car turned hard and distant, like a nightmare.

I gripped the seat belt to reassure myself. I waited for the sound of the siren and kept looking out the back of the van expecting any moment to see those flashing lights pursuing us. If they came after us, I feared I might confess everything.

I'm so sorry! Please tell my children I'm sorry! Again, Fake Mary's words slapped against my heart.

The memory hurt so hard when it arrived, I pressed back into my seat as if I'd been punched. I was standing alone on the beach, gazing out at the ocean and thinking about killing myself. It was a family holiday in Coffs Harbour and I'd just had an argument with my ex. 'Do Sophia and me a favour and don't come back!' he snarled as I stormed out the door of our holiday rental in a fit of abused fury. 'Go and commit suicide!'

At the water's edge, I stared into the distance, towards the place where sea and sky met. My heart aching as my gaze dropped towards the waves gently licking my bare feet, I wondered if the world *would* be better without me. Perhaps my ex was right. I was a terrible mother. A bad person. Useless.

I'd considered writing: *Tell Sophia I'm sorry* in the sand before I walked into the ocean. Out there, I would join my lost father. That beautiful, loving man. We would be reunited in death.

Now I ached at that broken me. It was one of my lowest points in that crumbling marriage. How terrible would Sophia's life have been if I had done what now seemed unthinkable? How much more damaged would she have been if her father – that chunk of emotional asbestos – had raised her on his own or in the company of a succession of those women who fled once he showed his true colours? How many hearts would I have broken if I had walked into the ocean and drowned myself? That arse – that man who never got his hands dirty and delegated everything – had even tried to make *my* death *my* responsibility. Undermining me to the point where I felt my absence would make the world a better place relieved that pile of emotional anti-matter of all culpability. I would have been both the victim and the crime. It wasn't just gaslighting, it was leaving the gas on and scuttling away just after throwing me a lit match.

Thinking of that manipulative shithead, and all shitheads like him, hardened my core. I was fed up with apologising and feeling afraid, fed up with accommodating the male script I had followed since my birth. I was fed up with the guilty and self-rebuking Alethea Braxton. I wanted her gone forever.

Above my head through the van's sunroof, the clouds parted to reveal an evening sky of deep Prussian blue spangled with stars.

From that studded, velvet sky, my gaze dropped to the rear vision mirror. I caught the driver's eye. And in that moment, I felt everything – the world, my thoughts and feelings – swell and compress into a singularity.

The Power is with Us.

I felt Her then, all around me, inside me. I was Her. I felt Her power, Her hurt, Her fury.

Mother of Earth, Goddess of all creation,
Spirit of all winds and all directions
Take this wounded, vacant creature and heal her wounds
May Your blessings warm her, Your love flow over her.

Those words, like planted seeds, took root and grew. A fiery resolve blazed through me. I was no longer going to run. I had an example to set. I had nothing more to lose.

I wasn't dead. I was alive and fucking furious. And I wasn't doing anyone else's dirty work. I wasn't going to be manipulated. An unhinged wildness flared inside me; as if some inner portal had been blown open, releasing the power within.

I gazed outside into the darkness, to the bush-flanked road that connected Watson and Yindisha. An unfettered, super-human strength kept in check by millennia of suppression surged through me.

Everything begins with a thought. Time is a boomerang. The world is full of magic.

'Stop!' I said to the driver.

He obeyed.

I rose from my seat and, channelling the power of a thousand armies, stepped out onto the road.

CHAPTER FORTY

The Pygmalion Effect

Days Twenty-seven to Thirty -Four

Night's hands of darkness closed around me. The bush sang, hummed, twittered and crept. Surrendering to this realm of endless shadows, my fear took shape. I stopped and faced my imaginary enemy. What I saw surprised me. Fear – carrying an empty briefcase – wore an expensive pewter-grey suit, a designer tie the yellow of baby faeces and a fake moustache. Fear was a man – plump with righteous self-importance, terrified of losing his power and afraid of losing control in a world of myriad unknowns. A creature terrified of uncertainty.

I have seen the devil and he is a moron.

I felt the power in me surge. And in that moment, I understood. No wonder man feared woman. This energy – acknowledged, channelled and trained – was a force of infinite power. Fear's façade cracked under my unflinching gaze. His moustache fell off, his suit and tie shredded and I left him standing there, naked, alone and weak.

As my eyes adjusted to the darkness, I noticed patches of

bioluminescent lichen growing on the boulders that flanked the road. Nature was beautiful – even in the darkness.

I strode on, thinking how life was a cycle of drowning and resurfacing, every moment an act of reinvention, resurrection and rebirth. Every moment, a turn of fate. When I handed my phone to Galilea, I'd made my final decision. I was complicit. The research station had all the evidence. My fate was sealed. Now, all I could do was surrender to the current. Resurface. Keep swimming.

In the distance, I heard another police siren. Another surge of strength engulfed me. I felt as though if anyone tried to apprehend or assault me, I would have, in that moment, been able to toss them aside as if they were no more than a mote of dust.

The police siren faded. I wasn't tested. My power remained a mystery.

Back at the retreat, there was a message on my phone. Another turn of fate. Another moment of reinvention. I replied, surrendering to the current's new direction.

I had a solitary early dinner, went to bed and slept like one of the dead, like a newborn babe.

The next day was windy, my thoughts as restless as the weather. After breakfast, Saniya took me aside in the retreat gardens and reassured me Reverend Nader was stable. But he had suffered memory loss and recalled nothing of the incident with Fake Mary.

I regarded her painted eyebrows and suspected she was bending the truth.

In order to explain Quentin's absence while he recovered, Saniya told me the research station's hackers had sent Real Mary a message on his behalf saying he had been urgently called to a bishop's gathering while she was in Bowral.

She added that before I left, the Ethics Committee had requested a report of the incident, along with conclusions and recommendations.

Side-swiped by eruptions of remorse, in between my teaching commitments, I delayed my departure and spent a few uneasy hours each day over the next week holed up in a study room at the research station. Here, I wrote and rewrote that report, outlining the errors we'd made, the learnings, my conclusions, my concerns, my personal recommendations.

Trying to clear my head, in my spare time I ate healthily, meditated and attended yoga sessions – all those things I'd originally come to the retreat to do.

The police never came for me. The story doing the rounds was that the church window had been hit by a huge hailstone, the gardenia and broken pot pieces found resting on the lectern inside, the result of a rogue gust of powerful wind.

In the midst of all this, I still taught my art classes, taking my students once more, to the worlds of the Fauvists, the Dadaists and the Surrealists. I declined Lucas's offer to cook me another meal. I apologised to him, explaining over the years I had become independent and struggled with intimacy.

After my explanation, he had simply gazed at me and said: 'We don't really know, or own, our hearts, do we?'

'No,' I replied. 'We don't. Love is a mystery.'

That was the last time I spoke with him and the last time I saw him before I left.

I watched that man of clay walk away, thinking of his lightness of being, how love wasn't about possession, or security, but something far more fluid and unbounded. I thought how there were so many others like him, more being made all the time, and wondered for a moment what a future filled with these creatures might look like. I drew a blank. The future was still an unpainted canvas.

I saw Mary Nader in Watson during one of my coffee visits. She looked happy. I knew how she felt. I was always happy when my ex went away on business trips. It was a few days of breathing space, a few days reprieve from hell.

When Mary spoke to me about her new business opportunity, telling me her husband had been in touch with her, encouraging her to undertake this wonderful enterprise, I didn't need to pretend I was happy for her. But I also knew Reverend Nader wasn't behind those messages. The research station was still hacking Mary's phone. Reverend Nader was still out of commission.

Several times, I tried to check in with Galilea to find out about him. But she wasn't in her office. For the time being, all I could do was comply. Wait for the inevitable summons.

On a later venture into Watson, I finally saw Reverend Nader in the distance talking to one of the tradesmen fixing the broken church window. He gave me a friendly wave. That apparently good Christian seemed to have forgiven me, or, as Saniya had reassured me, forgotten the incident. I waved back and smiled, happy to see him recovered.

When he stiffly turned and strode inside the Church with a measured strut, that passage in *The Book of Creation* returned to my mind's eye: *...sometimes, a replacement is desirable.*

My heart jerked. *Shit.*

I strode back to Yindisha Retreat and demanded to see Galilea. Now.

The receptionist gave me one of his luminously oblivious smiles. 'Well, aren't you lucky? She's just back from her conference.'

Conference, my foot, I thought, but said nothing.

'What have you done to Reverend Nader?' I demanded as soon as I had stepped into Galilea's office and closed the door.

Galilea smiled. 'Reverend Nader is a changed man. A man better for his experience. And we have you to thank for that, Alethea.'

I bit the side of my lip. The insinuations in that comment were as loud as a thunderclap. Whether I liked it or not, I was complicit.

My insides hardened. Direct answers required direct questions. 'Has Reverend Nader been replaced by a golem?'

Galilea gave me an odd look then – all at once sly, oblique and forgiving. 'Mother Earth has made her decision, Alethea. That is all you need to know.'

I heard a subtle note of triumph in her voice.

I wanted to say so many things in that moment. I wanted to say worship of Mother Earth was just as dangerous as worship of a man-God. I wanted to tell her of the dangers of fundamentalists, of dogmatism and exclusive belief systems that nourished spiritual pride. But, sensing she'd heard it all before and that my words would fall on not only deaf, but weary ears, I remained silent.

She was never going to give me a direct answer. Whether she was doing it for her own good, or to protect me, I didn't know. But I suspected it was a bit of both.

I told her my report was almost finished, adding that I had recently received a message from my tenants telling me a close elderly relative of theirs had had a stroke and they had decided to move in and take care of him. When they asked if they could break their lease, I had agreed. Plus, as winter fell, student numbers had fallen. I told Galilea I planned to leave the retreat soon.

'Mother Earth works in mysterious ways,' she replied.

I said no. It wasn't Mother Earth's decision. It was *mine*.

Galilea tilted her head and deployed a convincingly genuine smile. 'Yes, of course. The decision is yours, Alethea. But before you leave, I want you to consider this.'

Ever so lightly, she trailed her hand over her upper chest, reminding me of the scars beneath her crew necked shirt. 'When Mother Earth gives us an opportunity to raise the standards of male behaviour should we turn our backs?'

Although I was being baited, I agreed. 'No. Obviously not.'

Her gaze turned imploring. 'Have we been so bullied into accepting the poverty of our station that we fear natural justice? Are we not deserving of love?'

In a moment of crushing sorrow, I suddenly thought of Lucas, his beautiful lovemaking, his attentiveness and my eventual rejection of his overtures. Not knowing how to answer, I remained silent.

'This will be a peaceful, magical, revolution,' Galilea added.

I opened my mouth to say there was nothing peaceful about Reverend Nader's demise. But right then, there was a knock at the door and Jock walked in with a tray of scones.

Galilea looked from Jock and the scones back to me. 'Alethea, why should we settle for scraps when we have been offered a feast?'

After Jock had left, Galilea made me an offer I couldn't refuse.

I returned to my cottage in a muddled state of sorrow, indignation, defeat and triumph. We are, after all, creatures of contradictions and come into this world with our own individual Unpredictability Quotients. I reminded myself I wasn't in Galilea's thrall. Despite what had been forced on me, I was still my own woman. I thought of all the women in the world – past and present – beholden to the laws of men. I thought of witch-hunts. Wage inequity. Women who lose their hair after heartbreak. Women set on fire by their husbands. Women like me – undermined, bullied and abused. The whole spectrum of female indignities and humiliations. To remain quiet in this silent revolution was to comply. All I had to do was say nothing. That afternoon, after adding an extra paragraph about abuses of power, I handed in my report, returned the laptop, packed up the art room and prepared to leave.

The day before I was due to return to Sydney, I made a final visit to Watson. There, taking my last coffee and muffin alone in the Watson Café, I overheard a snippet of gossip. Lingering at my table, I listened in as some women in the booth behind me chatted about Sylvia Reddington – the owner of the Watson Bed and Breakfast and Reverend Nader's mistress.

Sylvia Reddington had made a scene last Sunday morning in church, saying someone had done something to Reverend Nader, that he wasn't himself. When Sylvia confessed to having an affair with him, Reverend Nader denied her accusations, saying he was a happily married man and would never deceive his wife, whom he loved and respected. A few days later, Sylvia Reddington's husband, concerned for her well-being, admitted her to hospital, saying a few days before her church outburst, she had hit her head on the kitchen bench after tripping over their pet Maltese dog. Eventually, she was diagnosed as having Capgras syndrome, a neurological affliction that makes sufferers think people they know have been replaced by imposters.

I picked the last muffin crumbs off my plate, rose from my seat and smiled at the group of gossips in the adjoining booth. They looked surprised – they hadn't noticed me sitting there.

I walked back to the retreat lost in thought. Where we sit in this grand vista of existence gives us differing perspectives. And life – like those particles in that quantum double slit experiment – is influenced by our observations.

My father's voice speaking Buddha's words came to me. *Everything begins with a thought, Alethea.*

Four-thousand years apart – human minds had drawn the same conclusions. *And with those thoughts we create the world.*

This was the Pygmalion effect. The falling in love with our creations – children, paintings, stories, golems. We tell ourselves stories to explain what we don't understand. And in those stories, live both eternal truths and self-fulfilling prophecies.

Yindisha had given me Her final lesson. Alethea Braxton – the invisible woman – was ready to leave.

CHAPTER FORTY-ONE

Down the Rabbit Hole with Schrödinger's Cat

Late winter, early spring

I returned to Sydney at the end of autumn with a small stipend from Yindisha Retreat. This was in part, a financial decision. I needed the income. I was a practical woman who wanted to survive. And any organisation trying to expand its influence (even secretively) had administrative requirements. In charge of Eastern Division Membership, over the course of two months, I fulfilled my recruitment targets. I recommended five female acquaintances to Yindisha. Three attended the retreat and one went on to become another Guardian.

I once more picked up my paintbrushes. This time, my 'public toilet people' had agency. Instead of stiffly standing amid landscapes and gardens, they toiled, tumbled, danced, gardened, engaged with, transformed and, in some pieces, merged with their surroundings. They sailed on life's waves and blew with the storms.

Along with winter's cooler weather came a sense of inner clarity. Once upon a time, I let my life's expectations fold into my social obligations and the commandments of others. Once upon a time, I had no language, no scaffold on which to hang my beliefs. I had always been one of Mother Earth's Guardians. I just didn't know. Finally, my searching soul had an anchor. But my anchor came with a quick release button. Even secret societies needed their sceptics. I still felt happier with one foot out the door.

After all, in Mother Earth's complex interplay of power, there is no certainty. Certainty is a single, faint brushstroke on one of the infinite pages that make up Mother Earth's illustrated manuscript of life.

Over a cosy dinner one cold winter evening, I confessed to Sophia – who was visiting for the weekend – I'd had an affair at Yindisha. I apologised, saying at the time, I felt silly and ashamed.

She looked shocked, then delighted. Finally, she laughed. 'Wow mum,' she said. 'You are so *bad.*'

Never had being told I was bad felt so good. But my heart still ached. I regarded my beautiful daughter – my dream come true – and felt that gap between my stomach and my heart twinge. Although I resolved to be as honest as possible, one secret had been replaced by another. I still couldn't tell Sophia the full story of my experience at Yindisha Retreat. I couldn't tell her what I was: still me – a damaged and hurt woman, a piece of soft clay shaped by life's infinite vicissitudes – but now an official 'Guardian'. I was a woman committed to a new future where men and women were absolute equals. I chose to believe this pledge between Mother Earth and her acolytes because the alternative – that all men might eventually be replaced by golems – was – as long as I remained a member of this secret organisation – not something I would endorse. It would mean the elimination of men like my father. It would mean the inevitable extinction of humanity. I wanted to – like Schrödinger's Cat –be both Guardian and not Guardian – able to straddle both states of being for the sake of a clearer perspective. Perhaps true immersion is the only path to truth, but I wasn't ready to drown. I wanted to keep my options open.

Another truth came to light a few days after I arrived home – something that years ago, would have broken my heart. While shopping at my local organic market, I ran into an old acquaintance who knew both my ex and I early on in our courtship. In front of the onion and garlic section, she told me she had heard my ex was getting re-married. Feeling magnanimous, I expressed happiness for him but concerned for his new wife who no doubt thought she had landed a charming catch whose first wife was a cold bitch and a psycho. We had a brief chuckle about the way first wives are depicted in literature (thank you, Charlotte Bronte).

I told her I hoped my ex might treat wife number two better than wife number one.

'Unlikely,' she said. 'The man's a serial cheat. A cockroach.'

And then she told me how that cockroach had an affair with one of her colleagues just after we first got together – when I thought we were happy. He had been lying to me from the beginning. All these years later, the truth no longer hurt. Instead, his cheating felt like an inevitability. A symptom of an old order, another of Mother Earth's reminders it was time for change.

Before we parted, my acquaintance told me how well I looked. I recommended she visit Yindisha Retreat.

Through the cool of winter, I felt something inside me slowly shift. It was as though some wintering root was taking hold, some new connective tissue forming in the place where my gall bladder had once sat. At times, my mind shot back to that waterhole. Sometimes, as evening fell, everything around me would once more disintegrate into luminous blue code as I glimpsed the reality behind life's veil. Inside me, some ancient engine – defused by millennia of oppression – sputtered back to life. Beyond the living, changing me, I caught glimpses of an incandescent and imperishable greater consciousness – a gentle guide – a Great Mother. I experienced flashes of exuberance and potency and, rather than dismissing them as fanciful imaginative flights, embraced them. It was, after all, Her. Deep within my spirit. Rising again.

The first week of spring arrived along with an edition of Sydney Morning Herald's *Good Weekend*. Here, I read the success story of 'Yindivine' – Mary Nader's condiments empire – her aioli now joined by relishes and chutneys all stocked at delis and supermarkets across the country. In that interview, she spoke about her new tree-tomato farm and the challenges of avoiding frosts. She spoke openly of how she had recently discovered her self-esteem after spending many years in a state of self-denial and depression. In a candid paragraph which would have rattled the previous Reverend Nader's ego, she spoke how she had left her husband after confronting him about his rumoured affair and the way he treated her. At present, they were rekindling their marriage after he expressed regret and showed a genuine desire to change.

Surrounded by her stylishly branded jars and bottles, I saw a photo of a successful woman who had found her place in the world. A new, different woman.

Gazing in satisfaction at her picture, I recalled my own twelve years of self-denial. My twelve years with that impersonator of a normal human being called my husband. The story of that woman and all women like her goes something like this: You stay in the marriage because you hope one day, your husband – your abuser – will have a revelation and see the errors of his ways. You live in the hope that one day he will say to you: *I am so sorry for the way I have treated you. I wasn't myself. My behaviour was inexcusable and I have the greatest remorse. All I can do now to earn your forgiveness is to spend the rest of my life making up for my cruelty. You are the only woman I will ever love. All I can do now is lavish on you the love and respect you deserve.*

But this hope is mere fantasy. The truth is, he's grown weary of you. He has moved on. You have seen through his charade and he needs someone new who falls for the man he pretends to be. You are – to him – a constant reminder of his shame. His fakery.

But still, you hope for a miracle.

And there, in Mary's photograph, I saw a miracle.

In the same edition of the Sydney Morning Herald, a headline entitled: ANGLICAN DIOCESE REPRIMANDS REGIONAL CHURCH grabbed my attention.

The small article described difficulties the Anglican Diocese was currently having with the village of Watson's parish. The Watson Church had recently opened its doors to other faiths, offering Buddhist meditation sessions, reflections on the life of Mohammed as well as hosting regular talks by feminist philosophers. Reverend Nader had even invited a group of local Wiccans to meet regularly in the church basement.

'God, Allah, the Universe, Mother Earth, the Force,' Reverend Nader was quoted as saying. 'These are all just names for that great all-knowing, unknowable orchestrator of existence.'

To which his superiors had replied that he was a guardian of church property and the life and teachings of Jesus must be his priority.

I had just finished reading the article when my doorbell rang.

I smiled approvingly at the distinctly Scandinavian-looking, fifty-ish man on my doorstep.

Cosmetically altered to look older than the standard golem, he was burly and bearded with a high forehead and wide-set blue eyes. He was, of course, very good-looking. 'Your fuse-box is full of cobwebs,' he said, shutting the lid of the cabinet adjacent to my front door and dusting the cobwebs off his hands.

He had a deep gravelly voice that stroked my insides and made me want to stretch and purr like a cat. I looked behind him, at the motorbike parked outside my house, then down at his suitcase and guitar case.

'Thorsten,' I said. 'I've been expecting you. Welcome.'

Allocated after I filled out a questionnaire designed to extrapolate my needs from my wants, Thorsten came with all the right documents – Australian citizenship, Medicare, a driver's license. If you can forge a man, you can easily forge identity papers.

In addition to that pefectly persuasive paperwork, he presented me with a sealed manual branded with the Men of Earth motif. This was, as far as he understood, my employer contract. He respected its confidentiality. As he unpacked in the spare room, I opened and read the first few pages of instructions.

He needed full hydration once a week for the first four weeks of guardianship. He had to soak, fully immersed in a bathtub for an hour. Afterwards, he would forget it had happened. During this four-week adjustment period in which he grew his human organs, I was advised against taking him to public swimming pools, in case people thought he was drowning.

After four weeks, when his digestive system had evolved, he would be able to eat and drink like a normal human. He would last about twenty years before he started to deteriorate. At that point, I had to return him to the research station to be decommissioned. If I wished, a replacement would be organised.

Meanwhile, quality reading and intelligent conversation would stimulate his intellect. Exercise and good nutrition would delay his deterioration and might give him an extra year or two of existence.

The manual advised that alcohol and hard drugs interfered with a golem's cognitive functions. However, a little bit of cannabis now and then was permissible but would make the golem giggly and ravenously hungry.

Under no circumstances could I tell him of his origins. My golem thought he was human. I must treat him as human. As an equal. A partner – a companion – who would be by my side as we changed the world – one soul, one garden, one tradition, one community, at a time.

Apart from those caveats, he was a low-maintenance man.

I delved further into Thorsten's design specifications. Firewalled to avoid the lure of porn sites and other undesirable cyberspace realms, he was fully internet connected, an erudite conversationalist and a reservoir of poetry and eastern mysticism. Among his repertoire, he could recite the entire works of Alexander Pope, Kahlil Gibran, as well the Persian poets including Rumi and Hafiz. In addition to the default programming of housekeeping, lawnmowing, gardening and laundry (which included that hateful task of ironing) he was a gourmet cook, sang moderately well and played Spanish guitar. His advanced lovemaking protocols could be unlocked if I wished, using a pre-programmed set of words. The default phrase was: 'Kiss me, you fool.' I could reset this any time, but the manual recommended I stay away from euphemisms such as: *I want you to put your ship in my harbour*, or even something Shakespearean and poetic such as: *Stray lower, where the pleasant fountains lie...* as first year golems struggled to understand figures of speech. It was best to be direct. Honest.

Taking into account my past traumas, the research station had managed to set Thorsten with an Unpredictability Quotient of just six percent – less than half that of the standard golem. He also came with strict fidelity and loyalty protocols. Even if our relationship remained platonic, he wouldn't sleep with another woman. Unless, of course, I decided at some point I was in to singles parties. Where I led, he would follow.

Meanwhile, he would help me work on a domestic sustainability plan. A vegetable garden, solar panels, a grey water system, as if we were preparing for some kind of economic or planetary Armageddon.

I was also encouraged to socialise with him, share his knowledge, skills and enlightened outlook with my community. I was encouraged to help him look for a job. Full immersion in society was the goal.

The last paragraph ended with Galilea's handwritten note:
Enjoy this gift from Mother Earth.

Just remember golems are not men. They are something different. Golems offer a new colour on the spectrum of love. Here to help heal the world, they will infiltrate slowly. Gently. Invisibly. And Yindisha's aim is, as much as possible, to work discretely within the boundaries of the law. This is to be a peaceful, magical revolution.

I dwelled on that word *revolution* and considered how I still didn't like the idea of a single woman like Galilea – a woman of such manipulative charm – having so much power to shape the future.

I also knew there was still far more behind Galilea's words. That was how PR worked. I knew I was still being both enticed and deluded. By 2050, at current rates of reproduction, there would be nine billion people on planet earth. By then, how many might be golems? And what would happen to the human race without family, parents, biology and the melding of genes? Would humanity – through the golems – engineer our own eventual destruction? Perhaps this was part of Mother Earth's greater plan? Ultimately was this a human problem, not a gender problem?

A picture of Galilea's smile flashed into my mind's eye and I considered the things she still wasn't telling me. I wondered if this knowledge, this creation of golems might not just be confined to Australia's Southern Highlands. Perhaps there were other retreats just like Yindisha all over the world? Although I was a Guardian, I hadn't yet been elevated to that level of knowing.

Pushing aside a memory of Fake Mary striking Reverend Nader with that rock, I closed the contract, rose and paused outside the spare room, where I could hear Thorsten strumming some saucy Spanish rhythms on his guitar.

Of course, I was still uncertain. I considered the hypocrisy of installing this man in my house, as if I was incapable of surviving on my own.

The next challenge was Sophia. Initially, I would tell her Thorsten's back story. Born in Norway in 1972, Thorsten was, along with his parents, a passenger on the George Prince – a small automobile ferry crossing the Mississippi River that collided with a tanker in 1976. Seventy-eight of the ninety-six passengers on board that ferry died, including his parents. Following the tragedy, the orphaned Thorsten was adopted by an elderly Australian couple who were distant relatives of his parents. Thorsten had lived with and cared for them in Wagga Wagga until they both passed away within a week of one another early last summer. His parents were friends of friends and he was paying me board.

And there, my new set of problems would begin. Sophia was inquisitive, persistent, like her mother. She liked to swim beyond the flags, like her grandfather. Eventually, she would notice the gaps in Thorsten's narrative. She would research. She wouldn't find his previous address in Wagga Wagga. She would find no mention of a four-year-old Norwegian boy in the George Prince's passenger manifest. All the victims were from Louisiana. Of course, there was a story for that as well, about poor record-keeping that had only listed the US citizens on the manifest. And the address in Wagga Wagga? Six months prior to their passing, his ageing parents had moved into a new one-storied house better suited to their needs. They probably hadn't updated their address.

She might even fear he was a fraud, another of those con-men preying on single women and charming them out of their savings. Or perhaps she might be perplexed about the way he didn't sweat, how insects never bit him. She might notice how he didn't age. She might notice how his passing wind and bodily waste smelt of freshly turned soil and lemon geraniums.

At some point in my story, when Sophia challenged me about Thorsten, I would be forced to ask her: 'Just how far down the rabbit hole are you prepared to go?'

I already knew she would say: 'All the way.'

ABOUT THE AUTHOR

Ingrid Banwell is a New Zealand born artist and writer living in Sydney, Australia with her family, a cat and a dog, several houseplants and a fluctuating population of pantry moths. She holds a Master's degree with First Class Honours in painting from the Elam School of Fine Arts in Auckland, New Zealand, and her artwork hangs in homes and offices around the world. Her three-dimensional work is also featured in several key publications on New Zealand art. In 2022 she qualified for an academic excellence award and Master of Creative Writing from Macquarie University. Her short stories have appeared in *Cosmos Online*, *Andromeda Spaceways*, the NSW Writers' Centre magazine *Newswrite,* and the University of Newcastle's Online Magazine for Postgraduate Writing *Swamp.* Thanks to travel-hungry genes, she's lived in Mexico City, Vienna, London, and New York. In order to support her art and writing, Ingrid has had a breathless number of jobs including art teacher, market researcher, fundraising manager, librarian, consular public affairs officer, and real estate receptionist. You can find out more about Ingrid, see some of her artwork and read some of her short stories on her blog: *www.ingridbanwell.com*

ACKNOWLEDGEMENTS

It took me a good sixteen years to find the courage to write this final version of *Men of Earth*. For a long time and through its various incarnations, I sidestepped the whole issue of what my story was really about. I needed time and distance from the maelstrom of my own personal battles before I felt I could confidently deliver an engaging and universal story with the requisite amount of lightness and hope. Despite this being a fictional (and oh, my goodness – paranormal, supernatural and metaphysical...) tale, many elements of this story carry deeply personal as well as universal truths – in particular the way men treat women and the way women want to be treated. Most women have, at some point in their lives, had to face some version of the appalling treatment this book addresses, and I hope it starts more conversations and deeper reflections about the insidious and often covert influences of patriarchal attitudes, as well as deliberations about gender relations, feminine power and what more we need to do to work towards gender equality.

Early in Men of Earth's infancy, the idea of metaphysical man-slaves, compliant lovers, a third sex (the golems in Men of Earth mean different things to different people) resonated with readers and I want to thank my first work-shoppers: Annie, Genevieve, Yannick, Natasha, James, Mandi, Lisa, Lauren, Ashley, among others, for encouraging me to persevere; some of you even announcing: 'I want a golem!' Your comments and enthusiasm sent my imagination into the stratosphere. Thank you also to Macquarie University's former Master of Creative Writing Course Director and teacher, Associate Professor Jane Messer, who read my first chapters and encouraged me to carry on with what was initially a whimsical and uncertain stab into story-telling darkness. Look where it led.

A massive thank you also to my Manuscript Development Project Supervisor, Professor Hsu-Ming Teo, who brought me back down to earth by reminding me of many of the fundamentals of character, world-building and story-telling.

Thanks also to my devoted editor KJ Eyre who has, over many years and many manuscripts, offered perfect suggestions, diplomatically voiced reservations and always encouraged me on my wild, messy, writing journey. It took a while, but you helped me to face the real issue at the heart of my story.

And thanks again to my Beta readers – Renet, Alex, Lisa and Roger, for wading through *Men of Earth's* final drafts and offering such sensible, productive comments and suggestions.

And finally, this book is in loving memory of my father, John Banwell, who raised me to follow my passions and interests and left this world before I had a chance to thank him. Thank you for your inspiration, your guidance, your intelligence, wisdom and your respect. You were the perfect, gentle, loving man. You were everything a girl could want from a father.